I0653917

BEACHY HEAD

An absolutely gripping crime mystery with a massive twist

ADAM LYNDON

Detective Rutherford Barnes Mysteries Book 2

JOFFE
BOOKS

Joffe Books, London
www.joffebooks.com

First published in Great Britain in 2022

Cover art by The Brewster Project

ISBN: 978-1-80405-515-1

AUTHOR'S NOTE

This book is set in 2005–7, but black operational police uniform was not widely introduced until around 2010, while bodycams were not a standard-issue fixture until about 2015. I beg the reader's indulgence with the minor liberties I have taken with the chronology of modernising the police service.

PROLOGUE

September, 2005

"Mandy! Open the door!"

The baying voice punctured her sleep like a rusty knife.

"Open the fucking door!"

BAM-BAM-BAM.

The loud, dull thud of the front door being shoulder-barged, or kicked, or whatever. A terrifying sound, in any case. The sound of violation, of normality shattered, of every moral code she had been raised to honour being carelessly ignored and flagrantly disrespected at eleven o'clock at night. Late, but not that late. Not so late that people wouldn't be up. Early enough to suggest he did not give a flying fig as to whether he was seen or heard.

"Amandaaaaah!"

Guttural, poisonous.

She sat upright in bed and the nausea hit her like a freight train. Her stomach tensed and bile rose in her throat. These episodes of midnight harassment were, she thought pointlessly to herself, just like vomiting. There was the feeling of low dread, escalating into that rush of inevitability, the horrendous climax of outpouring, then the temporary relief as the wave subsided.

Then, just when you thought it was all over, it came again.

"Mandy! Let me in!"

She slid off the bed into the small patch of floor next to the window, and pressed herself back into the corner, fumbling above her for the phone on the bedside table.

She did not think he would be able to get in, but somehow that didn't matter. She felt like an addict, intoxicated by a fix of fear, knowing that when this was all over, she would, like all the other times, feel stupid and cross with herself for how scared she was, as if she were coming down from a horrific high.

"Open this door, you dirty skank!"

And James was not here.

He had not been here for every instance of her ex-husband's unsolicited visits, but he'd seen enough of them.

She checked her phone's display: 11.22. He would be home from work soon, surely. She thought briefly about 999 ahead of calling James, but experience had taught her that the latter tended to prove the most reliable. In any case, one of the neighbours would have called the cops by now, surely.

Or maybe not. Maybe they were used to it.

"Mandy! I just want to talk!"

Oh, sure. Well, in that case, come on in.

"Fuck off!" she screamed in frustration.

She fumbled with the phone. Swipe, swipe, *swipe*. The screen of the bloody phone refused to obey her clammy touch. It was a new one that James had bought her, insisting she have it near the bed, but it had no buttons, just a screen that you pressed in order to see *pictures* of buttons. Who in the hell thought *that* was a good idea?

She pawed her nightdress to dry her hands off a bit and tried again.

Swipe, enter PIN, unlock, go to contacts, type: J-A-M . . .

Jesus Christ, there had to be a quicker way! She knew there was some kind of speed dial or voice activation function within this damnable gadget, but she was buggered if she could remember how to use it. Even the panic alarm, with its direct line to the police control room, was downstairs.

She remembered the exchange with the cop from the domestic abuse unit. An older guy, nearing retirement. She'd had the option of an activation switch in the bedroom or the front room, and, through some arbitrary and now inexplicable logic, she had opted for the front room. She hadn't even asked why she couldn't have both — that had been James's question, much further down the line. When it was asked, the answer had to do with budgets — hence the appearance of a mobile phone that she had come to loathe.

It had gone quiet outside. She counted — ten seconds, twenty seconds, forty seconds, one minute.

Nothing.

She dared to poke her head up over the bed.

Had he gone? It was possible. Sometimes the cops took him, sometimes James threatening to come out did the trick, sometimes he just got bored and left.

She could but hope.

BAM-BAM-BAM-BAM-BAM!

"Mandy! Amanda! Open the door! Open the fucking door now!"

The noise startled her, and she dropped the phone, babbling and cursing through her tears as she tried to find it in the dark. He was coming in this time, of this there was no doubt. He was going to get in, with no one here to save her, and . . .

A car.

Headlights sweeping across the front of the house.

James!

The sound of a car door slamming, and James's voice, strong and steady, telling Tommy to leave now. Conciliatory — if slightly condescending — tones from Tommy, trying for comradeship: *these bloody women, eh?* Amanda imagined him rolling his eyes and grinning.

But James wasn't having it.

That's all very nice and blah-blah-blah, but you can leave now.

They'd never been face to face, she thought.

How would it play out?

Maybe Tommy fancied his chances. Maybe, with his drink-addled brain, he didn't care one way or another.

James was big enough, but Tommy was a proper villain.

She was suddenly scared for her boyfriend, and she raced to the empty bedroom at the front of the house, the one she and James had already talked about turning into a nursery.

The tableau played out below her on the driveway, perfectly lit by the car headlamps, like some avant-garde attempt at contemporary theatre.

There he was, a fat, disgusting sight in his England top, can of Special Brew in hand, the chunky bracelet clanking against it as he swigged. Mandy felt revulsion that she'd ever been married to this beast.

James was impassive, attempting to manoeuvre himself between Tommy and the house while trying to keep Tommy reasonably calm. Even big men get scared, don't they?

Just kill him! Amanda wanted to yell. *Just take him from our lives once and for all!*

Tommy's tone was changing, moving through the range from appeasing to goading to threatening. And he wasn't backing off. If anything, he was closing the distance between him and James. Maybe it had suddenly occurred to him that this might be a golden opportunity to rid himself of the competition.

Then Mandy surely would be dead.

She clapped a hand over her mouth. Instinctively, she took a step back from the window, her blurry, double-glazed reflection appearing between her and the outside world, the crescent scar on her cheek visible. It looked like a second mouth in her double-vision mirror image.

She moved back to the window, and her reflection vanished. Tommy was squaring up to James, threatening to put all those skills learned in basement pubs and backstreet alleys into practice, all those dirty tricks that didn't really rely on size or stamina, only will. Tricks James didn't know.

The shirt came off.

The can was flung down. It clinked on the paving and rolled down the driveway.

The blade came out.

Amanda screamed.

They tussled, moving as one like a huge land crab down the driveway — Tommy trying to thrust forwards with the knife, James pinning the weapon.

They moved around the corner and out of sight, into an adjacent narrow alley festooned with weeds and rubbish that seemed to serve no purpose other than a spot for the local oiks to go and score weed.

Only sounds now — panting, grunting, shouting, the scuffle of feet — all amplified through the removal of sight, forcing Mandy to imagine the worst.

She barrelled down the stairs and flung open the front door. Lights flicked on in the houses opposite, people standing in their front doorways, arms folded, unsure of what to do.

A dull, flat, smacking sound, followed by an unbelievable, sickening *crunch* that sounded to Mandy like it could only be bone on concrete.

Then silence.

Then sirens.

Mandy screamed.

ACT ONE

March, 2006

Four hundred and seventy-eight days.

Barnes toed the carpet. They'd replaced it since he was here last. It was still some horrible public sector–standard synthetic pile, but the new roll was royal blue, rather than dishwater grey, and smelled relatively new.

Barnes had only been made to sit outside the divisional commander's office twice. There was a circular coffee table the size of a dustbin lid with two unreadable glossy magazines lying on its glass surface, and two blue bucket seats that forced the doubtless already uncomfortable occupier into an upright position.

Twice.

Now, and when he'd been suspended.

Four hundred and seventy-eight days ago.

The window behind Barnes featured a view of the solid brick wall of the side of the Town Hall five metres away, but all the action was happening in front of him, where support staff rushed about the open-plan office to keep the senior management team organised and studiously avoided eye contact along the way.

In a way, it was justice catching up with him — just not for the reason he'd been expecting. Plant evidence on a suspect and the coalition of the prevailing circumstances meant that he'd somehow swerved the fate he had been expecting — and arguably deserved — despite the fact that said suspect was murdered under his nose. Take a detour with a prisoner who arrived at custody with a broken jaw and an open fracture of the hand, however, and they circled like vultures.

Put another way, get away with something you shouldn't have, and it will come around one way or another.

Barnes folded his arms as the reflection took hold. A prisoner who'd been arrested for locking his toddler in a cupboard for two days, no less. Barnes may have been guilty, but that didn't mean he felt it.

A year and a third was not an especially long time to be away from one location. Not much else had changed. A policing career was a long service, in the scheme of things. You might get posted off Division and not return till two, five, ten years later, if at all. The office was still there, the case files were still there, the people — by and large — were still there.

It had only felt like a lifetime in the last forty minutes, when, without a warrant card, he was just a visitor, and subject to the same niceties as any other. The cheap plastic wallet and lanyard around his neck advertising the fact felt like a leper's bell.

There was a small traffic light panel outside the office door that looked older than Barnes. It worked, however: a few minutes later the red 'DO NOT ENTER' light went out and the green 'ENTER NOW' light came on with an angry buzz. The amber light read 'WAIT', which Barnes didn't really understand.

"You can go in," said the secretary. He barely looked up, but Barnes thought he could detect an insincere smile.

Barnes stood, shot his cuffs and tapped lightly on the door.

"Welcome back," added the secretary.

Barnes pushed the door open. Maybe not so insincere after all.

* * *

Gabriel 'Gabby' Glover was built like a garden composter, with arms like Canadian lumber and a head that had been Bic-razored that very morning to offset the toilet-seat hairline that remained. He wore a long-sleeve uniform dress shirt, but always rolled the sleeves up to the elbows. Barnes himself had only done this once before deciding it wasn't worth the effort, and had simply opted for short sleeves from there on. He could only guess at the intended effect on Glover's part.

What the office lacked in square metres it made up for in height — cramming in an L-shaped desk and a conference table had been a squeeze, but the ten-foot wraparound Georgian sash windows with the March sun streaming through them offered more light than a greenhouse.

Glover stayed behind his desk, leaving Barnes with the conference table, which suited him fine. On a display unit behind Glover was the standard array of framed certificates and carefully selected photographs — wife and son on a skiing trip, Force rugby team grinning post-match, the man himself showing the home secretary around some new station or other.

With his Tudor pomposity, weak chin and the telltale signs of overloaded arteries, Barnes was unable to decide whether Glover was a scrum half gone to pot or a prop forward on a health kick, but then decided the contents of the display unit told him more than he cared to know about Chief Superintendent Glover.

"Mr Barnes."

"Sir."

"I'll get right to it. And, let me be clear: your suspension is not being revoked for anything other than the natural conclusion of due process."

Barnes remained silent.

"That is to say, proceedings have concluded, the allegations against you were found proven, and the sanction recommended by the panel is that of a final written warning."

Still Barnes did not speak.

"Barnes, you've had access to the Fed and an advocate throughout, so I am assuming you understand me?"

"I do, sir."

"Suffice to say, you couldn't slip much more than a gnat's pube in the gap between a final warning and the sack. It'll hang off your P-file like a lead weight for a year or so, and if you fuck up in that time, you'll be fast-tracked to dismissal. Understand?"

"Yes, sir."

"In fact, the excess-force complaint is the only reason you *weren't* sacked. Anything else — dishonesty, data leaks, sexual malfeasance — and you'd have been out the door."

Barnes stared.

"The fact that the bastard probably deserved it is irrelevant — as is the fact that neither the red tops nor the moral majority are losing any particular sleep over it."

Glover reached down into a drawer and pulled something out. Barnes swallowed, wanting to hurl himself through the Georgian windows rather than accept the poison pen letter that was coming his way. As if sensing this, Glover's face suddenly broke into a smile that stretched his face like a seismic event.

"But your DCI will actually issue the damned thing and go through all the minutiae with you. My job is to welcome you back. Give you this."

He produced a small leather rectangle and slid it across the desktop with a chunky finger. Barnes stood up and went to take it. Glover's index digit remained on the warrant card.

Their eyes met.

"One fuck-up, Barnes."

"I won't let you down, sir," Barnes said, just about able to part his teeth.

Glover released the tin.

"Welcome back, officer."

Barnes looked down at the warrant card. He opened it out, ran his fingers over the Braille under the metal crest. The grim-faced photograph had never been updated — it was still the same one he'd had taken the day he joined. He remembered the picture being taken — it was one of very few he hadn't smiled for; remembered thinking, *It's time to grow up now.* Like his picture knew something about his future that he didn't.

The sound of Glover's chair creaking made him look up. The divisional commander was leaning back, fingers steepled in front of him.

"You're Part One qualified, am I right?"

"Part Two as well."

Glover's eyebrows went up.

"Really?" he said, elongating his vowels.

"I just got it in under the wire."

"So, you could, in theory, be promoted tomorrow."

"That would be a matter for the Chief Constable, I guess."

Glover grinned again. A gold incisor gleamed.

"You leave that to me."

"Come again?"

"I said . . ."

"You're going to promote me?"

"Don't sound so surprised, Barnes. As of tomorrow, all bets are off. Sure, if you drop a bollock you'll be heading for the exit, but the inverse isn't true. No reason you shouldn't pick up your career where you left it. Besides, the change would do you good. You've notched up a few decent results over the years, but you've been buried under case files for too long. Punching your way out of it could be considered a little extreme, however."

Barnes tried to process this. His eyes roamed over the carpet, and he noted, absently, that the blue squares were an alternating two-tone.

"Detective Sergeant?" he croaked.

Glover sat forward again. "The *reason* you weren't sacked is because all your transgressions were for the right reasons. Your ambition and arrogance just got too far ahead of you, that's all. Your mistakes were solely down to the ingredients that make up Barnes. It's a new day, Barnes. Take those ingredients and ice that fucking cake."

Barnes kept his surprise buried, and his delight buried further still. Barnes circa 2001 would have backflipped out of the office, but even after five short years — spent, as Glover had mentioned, in a CID no man's land decorated with case files — Barnes knew there was some small print coming.

"We don't promote on a whim, Barnes. We have too many sergeant vacancies, so we have to promote. It's a simple equation. So don't look at it too personally. Organisational need has no emotion."

He paused, to allow the town hall bells next door to cease their hourly toll.

"It's timely, actually."

Here it comes, thought Barnes.

"I have a case. A one-punch homicide. Due for trial in a few months. It needs strong leadership, a keen eye, an analytical mind. There aren't many I would consider giving it to."

There aren't many that want it, you mean.

"I'll be honest — I think you deserve that — there isn't exactly a boatload of public sympathy for the victim. There's even less for a prosecution. It needs an objective view, Barnes. Someone who won't be swayed by headlines and soundbites and placard-wielding bleeding hearts. Someone who will do the right thing."

"What, if not prosecuting, is the right thing to do?"

Glover's grin disappeared. The temperature in the room dropped a degree or two, despite the sunshine.

"DS Barnes, it'll be a cold day in hell before I allow a murder to go undetected on my watch."

He picked up his notebook and began writing, placing his palm across his brow.

"Sir, I simply meant . . ."

"That'll be all, Barnes. Close the door on your way out."

* * *

"You're back, then?"

Barnes had been sloping out of the station in something of a daze when DJ had caught his eye from behind his window and raised a mug in front of him. Barnes — halfway out the door — capitulated and went back behind the counter to join his colleague.

Barnes took the white WE LOVE GRANDAD! mug of dirty instant coffee gratefully. He passed the plastic visitor badge back.

"Won't need this anymore," he said. "Swap you."

The office was quiet, it being too early for the general gaggle of parking complaints, lost property, driving document producers and miscreants signing on for bail that tended to haunt the front counter at the police station in Grove Road.

Dominic Davenport-Jones's nickname — DJ — was practically as old as the man himself. He had retired as a sergeant some six years previously, and had been a cadet prior to his thirty, which meant his cumulative policing experience was almost forty years. He had thick white hair, a kind face and his bespectacled eyes tended to disappear behind round rosy cheeks whenever he smiled. He'd been working behind the front counter for as long as anyone could remember.

"It went well, then?"

Barnes nodded emphatically. "You could say that. He even promoted me."

DJ's thick eyebrows went up. "Did he now? That calls for something more than nasty coffee. Well done you."

"Thanks. The trade-off is a case that's got 'poisoned chalice' written all over it, but I think I can hold it."

"Let's hope so," DJ said. "That's not bad going. You're back in the fold, promoted on day one with — what? Twenty years to go?"

"Twenty-three."

"The seven-year itch."

Barnes shrugged. "It feels like a hundred and seven."

"Well, no career is linear, although I imagine it does age you rather prematurely."

"Suspension?"

"In almost forty years I managed to dodge that particular bullet."

"It's incarceration by drip feed. It wouldn't be so bad if you knew up front that the thing was going to take a year plus. You could get on with things. Go to night school or something."

"They kept moving the goalposts, eh?"

"Somebody definitely wanted me out. The odd supervisor popped by to make sure I hadn't killed myself, but other than that I pretty much just moped about and waited for phone calls. My brooding irritated my wife to the point of exhaustion. It's taken its toll."

Their eyes met for a moment.

"Well, tomorrow is the first day of the rest of your life, or something," DJ said, setting down his mug. He swivelled on his chair to address his first customer of the day, turning back to Barnes before he did so.

"In any case, welcome back, sarge. It's good to have you back."

It rained. It had rained for a long time — through, it seemed, autumn, winter and now the first glimpses of spring. Enough rain, Barnes thought, and everything turns to mud.

He looked up from the file as his next-door neighbour, Eleanor Parkes, pulled up onto her driveway. She was a tall, regally attractive, sixty-two-year-old widow who had moved in next door almost a year previously. Not long enough to be overly familiar with the intimate affairs of her neighbours, but long enough to know that Eve had been living there one moment and not the next.

Despite his misgivings at the mild overtones of Miss Havisham that Eleanor seemed to project, Barnes had eventually got over his natural wariness to the extent that they were now almost friends. Certainly, if she still thought it odd that Barnes did most of his paperwork while sitting on the driveway in his Orion, she no longer showed it. Eccentricity breeds kindred spirits.

He gave a little wave as she emerged, but she was too preoccupied by wedging her brolly over the car door to notice. She removed her eight-year-old grandson, Aidan, from the back seat, and looked over at Barnes long enough to return the wave. Barnes gave Aidan a thumbs up as Eleanor hustled the boy out of the rain and into the house.

Barnes returned to his papers. He craned his neck over the file resting on his knees, the rain drumming on the car roof like muted applause.

He shook his head. No wonder nobody wanted the case. 'Poisoned chalice' didn't actually do it justice, and any detective who wasn't repaying nineteen different implicit favours would have kept it at arm's length. In fact, that was exactly what had happened — the file had gone from pillar to post like a mangy stray cat before finally finding a home with Barnes.

One punch. The suspect, a retained firefighter, arrived home to find his partner's scumbag ex-husband bellowing at the upstairs window — and not for the first time. The ex turned on the incumbent, they scuffled, the partner — younger and fitter — threw a punch. It connected, the ex went down, cracked his head on the kerb.

The cops were already en route at that point — the suspect, James Reeve, had waited patiently indoors. The ex was carted off to hospital — he was laughing and joking for the most part, then something went wrong in his brain and he pitched forwards on the trolley in minors and goodnight Vienna. They went back for the suspect, but some hours had passed and he'd already gone to work early, fed up of waiting. When word reached him that things weren't quite as straightforward any longer, he presented himself at a police station.

No jury in the world would entertain it.

But the boss wouldn't entertain an unsolved homicide.

* * *

The waves of emotion that swept over Barnes as he walked up the driveway were so intense that they physically slowed him down. Nostalgia and regret, most certainly, a twinge of excitement, but also a curious sense of incarceration — as if the wasted seconds they'd spent apart had marched inexorably forward that much faster than if they had been together.

Eve's mother answered the door. It must have been five years since Barnes had physically laid eyes on her — with her shock of frizzy hair and patchwork knitted jumper, she seemed to have become five times crazier in the intervening period. She eyed Barnes suspiciously, her lips clamped together, a cigarette between her fingers. She was tall, almost five-eleven, and the curves — later inherited by Eve — that had kept her fighting them off until well into her fifties had disappeared under a new build resembling a tank. *Sometimes*, Barnes thought, *it all just goes to shit*.

She let him in, called up the stairs and returned to the kitchen. She knew better than to interfere, but he also thought he detected a glimmer in the woman's eyes — as if the prospect of his ending Eve's brief return to her maternal bosom might help the gas bill resume more tolerable levels.

His stomach leapt with butterflies when he heard Eve coming down the stairs. It had only been a couple of weeks or so since they had last seen each other, but the encounters had been sporadic, suspension and separation having occurred at more or less the same time. Whether you put this down to coincidence or not was something Barnes didn't particularly want to dwell on. She'd popped in fairly regularly at the start — probably to make sure he wasn't swinging from the banister — but the visits thinned out as his suspension drifted onwards, with precious little in the way of news.

Drifted. Just like he and Eve had done. Drifted, like ghosts in the mist.

She was dressed simply, in a white T-shirt, jeans and boots, but seeing her made him recall the thunderbolt of when he'd first clapped eyes on her. That time, of course, there had been no shared history — but at least there had been a future. This time, he wasn't so sure.

He wanted to run to her and snatch her away before the world kept her from him forever.

"I feel like I'm collecting you for the prom," he said.

"No corsage?" his wife said, adjusting her earrings.

He smiled, spreading his hands apologetically.

"Snapdragons. I gave them to your mother. She's probably already fed them to her army of cats."

She smiled, and he held the front door open for her as they walked to the car. Eve moved the Reeve file onto the back seat.

"We've got time," he said, peering out of the window as the sun took a chance and broke through the clouds. "How about a little walk?"

She looked at her watch.

"I don't know . . ."

"Come on. Once round the park. It's on the way."

She shrugged, and that was good enough for Barnes. There was so much riding on this meeting that the word *reconciliation* seemed far too simplistic, and now Barnes wasn't sure he was ready for it at all. Something with at least some semblance of normality would do them both good, on a number of levels.

He drove to Hampden Park. The clouds were rolling away, and the sun was suddenly warm as they walked slowly around the lake, surrounded by daffodils, as swans skimmed across the water.

"Feels like spring," Barnes said.

"I know. That sun is glorious."

"Want an ice cream?" he said, pointing at the colourful bunting outside the tea chalet in the distance.

"Maybe later."

They passed another couple walking the opposite way. He wanted to reach out for her hand, but something stopped him. He pictured her gently wrestling it away, and he wasn't ready for that.

They walked on past the lake into the woods, where squirrels scampered along the branches of a huge monkey puzzle tree and the sprawling path cutting through the thick foliage brought J. M. Barrie to mind.

They walked past a small clearing, where a bright blue one-man tent had been erected, with a stove and folding chair outside it. A faint snore drifted from within, and somewhere a duck found it riotously funny.

"How was your first day back?" she asked.

"Strange."

"It was always going to be, I guess."

"Still, got a promotion out of it," he said, turning to her.

She frowned. "In exchange for what?"

Irritation flickered somewhere in his brain. "And I thought I was cynical."

She shrugged. A sarcastic reply about her lack of congratulations formed on his tongue, but he managed to push it down. Lord knew they'd both been burned enough for her to hold her views without judgment.

They walked on in silence, eventually pausing to sit down on a log.

"Are you ready for this?" he asked, puncturing the quiet with an unintentionally sharp tone. A tiny voice shouted *shut up shut up* in his head, but he couldn't help it.

Her smile faltered. She looked like she wanted to hide behind the bunch of flowers he hadn't brought her.

"Ready as I'll ever be, I suppose."

He eyed her for a moment.

"You remember this was your idea, right?"

"I don't remember having to handcuff you to go along with it."

"Do you actually think we're going to get away with it?"

"We agreed . . ." She was wide-eyed.

Barnes felt righteous anger bubble in his chest, but he pushed it down. The peaceful setting seemed suddenly to be far away, and he led her back to the car.

* * *

The social worker demolished every stereotype and preconception that Barnes had stockpiled over the years. She was some kind of cast-off rock chick in her mid-fifties, with snow-white hair that hung carelessly about her shoulders.

She wore denim jeans, knee-high patent leather boots and an off-the-shoulder pink jumper that looked like it was about to jump right off her and start playing the drums.

Surrounded on the sofa by a bed of scattered papers, she wore a perpetually baffled-looking half-smile. Her voice was as light as icing sugar, and she had a trick, Barnes noticed, of not writing down their answers immediately, only picking up the pen when some other topic came along some minutes later.

She made Barnes exceedingly nervous.

He couldn't exactly imagine her storming in somewhere and raucously seizing the children off some substandard, ill-equipped parent, but he *could* imagine her using her rainbow-light fairy dust tones on some such unsuspecting wretch until they were hypnotised into surrendering said children with a skip in their step and a *thank you for coming*.

Barnes tried to relax.

"I noted the age gap with interest," the social worker said. "Quite unusual, wouldn't you say? Even in this day and age?"

They were perched together on the edge of the opposite sofa — Eve with her hands in a ball in her lap with one of Barnes's wrapped around it. Barnes's thigh pressed against his wife's — despite the situation, the flutter deep in his loins was impossible to ignore.

"I don't think so," Eve said, without, Barnes noticed, a hint of defensiveness. "We're both young and fit. We're very focused on healthy living."

"Mr Barnes, you're . . ." the social worker said, checking her papers, ". . . thirty-four, yes? Mrs Barnes, you're forty-three."

Barnes wondered if she was verbalising to make sure she got the ages the right way round — he felt sure that at first glance she would have been forgiven for believing the inverse to be true.

"Yes," Eve said.

"That means a five-year-old placed with you would have an adoptive mother of fifty-six when they turn eighteen."

"I don't think that's unusual at all," Eve said. "Besides, as I said, if you're both healthy and fit and enjoy each other's company . . ."

"And how *would* you describe your relationship?" she said.

"Well, we have the same stresses as many other adults. We're only human, after all," Eve said. "But there's a deep bond there. One built to last."

Inwardly, Barnes was both impressed and repulsed by how easy his wife seemed to find lying. Even he was convinced.

"That much is obvious, dear," the social worker said. "Especially after the difficulties with the IVF. That can place *such* a strain."

Barnes felt Eve tense beside him.

"You . . . you know about the IVF?" she said.

"Oh . . . yes?" The social worker made a play of rifling through a bundle of papers. "It's in your screening form."

Eve fired a quick sideways look at Barnes, who tried to avoid her eyes.

"Look, I'll be honest with you . . ." the rock chick said, with an expression halfway between a smile and a grimace, ". . . a big part of my job is dealing with illusions. We're not looking to place bright pink newborns with kiss curls. The kids that need homes could be anything up to ten years old, with troubled, sometimes disturbing, backgrounds. English might not be their first language. Physically, you might look very different. There might be a lot of tough times before the joy. But they are the ones that really need help."

Silence. Barnes didn't know where to look.

The rock chick gathered her things and stood.

"I'll leave you to reflect on what I've said. Depending on why you are doing it, it might be a lot to process, or a little."

Barnes stood. Eve didn't. The rock chick stopped in the doorway and turned back.

"When you've talked, call me. You are a lovely couple, and I'd like to come back."

Eve raised her head.

"I'll see you out," Barnes said.

He followed her to the hallway and held the door open. She pressed past him without meeting his eyes.

Barnes shuffled back to the living room; Eve was down his throat before he could draw breath.

"You *told* them about the IVF?" she said.

"Why wouldn't I?"

"Why? Because it's a heat-seeking missile they will package up and launch back at us."

"It also happens to be the truth, Eve."

"Truth doesn't have to mean fucking confession!"

Barnes sat heavily on the sofa the social worker had just vacated. The seat was still warm. He rested his elbows on his knees and loosened his tie. He exhaled like a punctured tyre. The clouds had started to roll darkly in again over the Downs.

"What are we going to do if they actually see fit to place a child with us?" he said quietly, looking over at the fireplace, where their wedding photograph still occupied the mantelpiece.

Eve said nothing.

"Are you going to come home? At what point do we start using the front room as a front room again, rather than a bunch of stage props we just trot out when the vicar comes to tea?"

She opened her mouth.

"The proverbial vicar."

She closed it again.

"Was your plan really no more than to take delivery of a baby, and then just sort of iron out the kinks from there?"

"That's not fair, Barnes . . ."

"Or am I no more than the adoptive equivalent of a sperm donor?"

He eyed her, and sat forward.

"Was I even part of this plan going forward?"

"Of course you were . . ."

"Adoption fraud is a thing, you know."

"Barnes, for Christ's sake! I don't know, I just thought . . . maybe things would work out once we finally filled the enormous gaping hole between us."

He laced his hands on top of his head and sat heavily back again.

"They'll see straight through us," he said to the ceiling. "And it'll be worse the longer it goes on."

He stood up. An elbow joint cracked.

"At least if we try to make another go of it, we wouldn't be lying to anyone. I haven't touched anything. You can move straight back in where you left off." He tried to keep the urgency from his voice.

She didn't say anything.

"Come on, then," he said. "I'll drive you home."

* * *

The drive back to Eve's mother's was interminably slow. It would have been quicker on a bike, but Barnes had the choice of either traversing the Levels or going back via Hampden Park. Neither held much appeal, and the steady shimmer of resurgent spring rain made everything five times slower.

According to the file Glover had given him, the address where the fatal punch had landed was off Willingdon Trees, so Barnes figured he could drop Eve back at her mother's in Langney and then come back via the crime scene. That way he would only have to suffer the level crossing once.

"Two p.m. on a Wednesday, and it's like this," Barnes said, rubbing his brow. They were motionless on Kings Drive.

"You have to be somewhere?"

"Only the office."

"Drop me, if you want. I can get the bus."

"Don't be silly."

"I really don't mind. You'll only have to come back this way."

He turned to look at her.

"What are you saying to me?"

"What do you mean?"

The traffic started to move, just as a curtain of sunlight broke through the clouds again and lit up the wet road like a camera flash. Barnes edged too close to the car in front and toed the brake pedal sharply.

The Reeve case file slid forward off the back seat, scattering papers all over the footwell.

"For Christ's . . ." he said, grabbing behind him to carelessly gather up the pages. "Can you really not stand to be in my company? Or is giving you a lift what real married couples do? As opposed to complete fakers."

"I'm just trying to save you a journey. I'm sure you're busy at work, and—"

"Busy at work? Since when do you make concessions to my job?"

"Why are you being so petulant?"

The traffic started to move again. Barnes didn't answer, mainly because he'd started to wonder if maybe this really was it. He knew he was given to petulance on occasion — and was aware it was his least attractive feature — but ordinarily he would backpedal, concede, trying to put the genie back in the bottle so as not to lose the whole day to a sulk.

But he wasn't feeling it now. The fatalist in him was feeling a curious sense of inevitability, like a train derailing at seventy. Five years ago, one of Barnes's maiden cases had overspilled into his home life, nearly killing Eve.

He should have left then. He should have quit and gone to work in a bank. But he hadn't, and — to a lesser extent, admittedly — his CID cases had been a constant incursion into his marriage ever since, punctuated by three failed IVF cycles along the way. It was a wonder they had got this far at all.

None of it was her fault. But weaponising his guilt was an almost irresistible means of dealing with it.

The flow of traffic started to pick up as they passed the hospital, and Barnes signalled to head off down Cross Levels Way. A siren echoed faintly in the distance.

"Second gear. Nice one," Eve remarked.

Another anomaly. Eve making the first conciliatory attempt when the atmosphere was brittle was unheard of.

The glare on the road was suddenly blinding, and it all came to Barnes at once. That strange, somehow exhilarating realisation that waiting, waiting, waiting . . . needn't have been the case.

The siren got a little louder. Two of them, this time. Maybe more.

"I . . . I don't think I can do this anymore."

"What?" Her voice was thin and hoarse.

"This . . . pretending to reconcile. This *limbo*."

"Are you giving me an ultimatum? That's not fair. You can't just force me to make a decision . . ."

"I just don't know what we're waiting for. I don't know what you need from me. I haven't seen the terms and conditions of whatever goddamn endless probation I seem to be on!"

He pressed the pedal down, sweeping into the left-hand bend off the roundabout. He took the bend too fast, pushing the car out towards the double-whites. The case file shot off the back seat again and onto the floor.

"*Barnes!*"

The sirens were upon them. The blue lights were lost in the glare of the sunshine on the sodden tarmac, but the alternating headlight flash a hundred feet away shone out like a search beacon, drawing Barnes's eye when it really needed to be on the road right in front of him, on the flatbed lurching towards him on the wrong side of the road, suddenly filling his vision in an explosion of white metal.

* * *

Four months later, Barnes was pretty sure he didn't really remember it. He stood on the street outside the recovery yard, where the mangled skeleton of the Orion still lay under a dirty tarp, title having passed slowly and silently from Barnes to the police to the coroner to the insurance company.

The gates of the yard were bolted shut. Midges buzzed around the weak sodium lamp overhanging a sign displaying the yard's opening hours.

The traffic sergeant had visited him at home afterwards and, sitting in Barnes's deathly silent front room, gave him the gospel — or as near as dammit — version of what had happened. Barnes's brain had recreated the events around it, giving him a kind of patchwork memory that was part-real, part-imagined.

The one part he did remember was the sound. Her scream, the colossal deafening bang of the two vehicles meeting in anger.

And then the silence.

It was a 1992 Mercedes — older even than Barnes's pickled Orion, but built like a Panzer — and there had only been one winner. According to the sergeant, the forensic collision report said that the oncoming truck had pulled almost all the way across the road, which meant that Eve's side ('the nearside,' the sergeant called it, which Barnes liked; the sparse, technical language was somehow comforting) took the brunt of the impact. It had crunched into Barnes's car and carried on going, mounted the steep grass verge on the opposite side of the road that separated the hospital grounds and the cycle path from the road, rejoined it and then offsided the roundabout.

The pursuing police vehicles had stopped at the scene to help the casualties: Eve, Barnes — who had sustained a fractured tibia and collarbone — and the lady in the car behind who had rear-ended Barnes's car after the initial impact.

Barnes wasn't quite sure he would ever forgive them for this. It was unquestionably the right thing to have done — and in any case the control room inspector had directed that the pursuit be aborted at that point — but the break in continuity gave the truck enough time to force its way through the traffic at the DGH roundabout and then disappear into the estate off Rodmill Hill.

They found it abandoned a mere eleven minutes later, but it was long enough. The registered keeper was from Orpington, but initial enquiries suggested the vehicle had passed through multiple cash-in-hand sales since. The pursuit had come about as the result of some local intel — fly-tipping, suspicious activity and reconnaissance in burglary hotspots, possibly some cannabis dealing — but no single identified individual had yet been linked to it. There were descriptions from house-to-house of two or three men leaving on foot near where it was abandoned, but no one identified. Scenes-of-Crime would turn the interior inside out, but a fingerprint would only tell you that the owner of said print had once been in the van, not that they were driving at the time.

The official cause of death would later be given as catastrophic head trauma and multiple organ failure due to massive blood loss. Barnes thought that felt like a nice catch-all. The traffic sergeant — because Barnes had asked — said it was probably a combination of Eve striking her head on the side window and the slightly elevated position of the van putting downward pressure on the front end of the Orion. Several hundredweight of jagged metal spearing down on her lower body in an instant, biting into every soft, fragile, essential piece of the jigsaw puzzle that made her.

Barnes stared through the chain link fence at the dark forms of twisted metal hulks piled high in the yard. In the dim moonlight, he wondered which one was the Orion.

Immediately after the crash, Barnes had wanted to go and see his car. The traffic sergeant advised against it, but Barnes had wanted to get what scattered property he could out of it. Eventually the sergeant talked him out of it, on the understanding that he would try to remove the Reeve case file from the rear footwell for Barnes.

Bring it as it is, Barnes had instructed. Don't dry or remove pages.

If the pages have her blood on them, don't leave them out. Just bring it.

3

July, 2006

"That one?"

"Nope."

"How about this one?"

"Uh-uh."

"This?"

"No."

"Come on, Airplane, look at the state of it. It's practically held together with filler. I can see at least twelve con-and-use offences from here." PC Peter Lamb pointed at the Transit as it passed in front of them.

PC Jefferson Riaz stared at the van for a moment from their vantage point on Memorial Roundabout, and then shook his head.

"Nah," he said, gazing out of the window. "Ty Godden, born 6 June 1985. Two outstanding fail-to-appear warrants, one for assault, one for burglary. Disqualified from driving and believed to be bimbling around in a black Ford Capri, index X492 PCM."

"Very nice," Lamb said. "What's that got to do with us?"

"He's over there," Riaz said.

"Now you're talking," Lamb said. He put the marked Focus in gear and swung around in a graceful arc onto Devonshire Place.

They caught up with the Capri on Royal Parade. Both officers tensed up as Lamb hit the 360-degree STROBE button on the dash, his radio to his lips.

The blue lights on the roof of the car flared. The Capri touched the brakes and signalled left. It cruised slowly forwards for a moment or two. Lamb flashed the headlights, and the Capri pulled into a bus stop and stopped, indicator blinking, the brake lights indicating that the driver's foot was still on the brake pedal.

"Easy," Lamb said as Riaz opened the door. "He's not put the handbrake on."

Riaz had one foot on the road when the Capri's engine suddenly shrieked and fishtailed out into the flow of traffic, causing a Vauxhall Zafira to stamp on the anchors and swerve out of the way.

"Get back in the car!" Lamb yelled, pulling back onto the road with Riaz still half out of the vehicle.

Riaz righted himself, attached his seatbelt and activated the 999 button on the dash, which fired up every light, siren, bell and whistle on the vehicle. The Capri was four or five cars ahead of them, but Lamb quickly caught up as the line of traffic in front of him began to part like the Red Sea for Moses.

The same could not be said of the Capri. It thumped a left down Beamsley Road and then a right onto Seaside — where, as usual, traffic was heavy in both directions and moving at little more than twenty miles per hour. The Capri was showing blind disregard for this fact, however, carving up the line as it sped up the middle of the road, forcing angry drivers out of the way. There was a shrill screech from up ahead as the Capri braked heavily to avoid a Corsa that hadn't seen it, then a low thump and a tinkle of glass as it clipped the Corsa's offside wing. The impact knocked the Capri's centre of gravity slightly, but it stayed roughly on course.

It swerved around the keep-left bollard at the zebra crossing outside the Arlington Arms, and just about got out of the oncoming traffic before it collected the front end of a Ford minibus.

"Jesus, he's really going for it," Lamb yelled as he swerved to avoid a bus and tried to keep the Capri in sight.

"I'm going to call it, Pete."

Lamb was reluctant. "FCC won't allow this to continue."

The Capri crashed through the barriers at the closed-off slip road at the Tesco roundabout, narrowly missing a parked van decorated with advertising boards.

"If he kills someone, we'll roll," Riaz countered, grabbing the dash handset. "Echo-Echo-two-zero-one, Sierra-Oscar."

"Two-zero-one, go ahead, over." The controller caught the urgency in Riaz's voice.

"Two-zero-one, have a fail-to-stop just heading north on Lottbridge Drive. Pursuit initiated."

"Reason for stop, two-zero-one?"

"Driver wanted. Two warrants, and he's disqualified from driving to boot."

"Conditions?"

"Traffic heavy. He's driving dangerously, cutting up traffic, and . . . it's starting to rain." Riaz peered out of the window at the heavy, rolling clouds.

"Roger that, two-zero-one. Stand by for safety broadcast. Keep the commentary coming."

"Christ, don't sugar-coat the pill," Lamb remarked, hurtling past an ambling Nissan Micra with a geriatric driver who had registered neither the Capri nor the police patrol vehicle.

"Ops-One, Sierra-Oscar," chirped a silky female voice on the radio.

"Ops-One, go ahead," the controller replied.

"Ops-One, abort pursuit. Abort pursuit. Too dangerous — poor weather, heavy traffic, known offender — we can pick him up another time. Preferably when he's on foot."

"Roger that. Two-zero-one, pursuit cancelled. Deactivate blue lights and other warning devices, pull over to the side of the road and stop. Advise when stationary."

"I fucking *knew* it," Lamb said. He took a breath and then acknowledged the direction. He eased off the throttle — just not quite as quickly as he could have done.

As he did so, the Capri aquaplaned through some standing water on the road surface and lost the rear end. It spun once and came to rest on the grass verge by the turn-off to the Eastbourne Golfing Park.

Lamb pulled around a people carrier, narrowly missing its front bumper. The horn sounded angrily. He touched the throttle to get alongside the Capri, just as the driver's door was flung open and the driver made to run.

Riaz was out of the door before the patrol car had stopped, and he took off after a rapidly departing Ty Godden.

Lamb wasn't far behind. He yelled, "Decampers!" into his radio and then followed Riaz along the verge in a way that suggested he was unlikely to make up ground.

The traffic was stationary now — all drivers and passengers fixed on the foot chase. From the quarry's point of view, it was the worst place to make a run for it, with no hiding places or rat runs, just the open expanse of the Levels on all sides.

Riaz caught up with Godden just as the burglar started to lose his wind, and pounced on him with a try-saving tackle.

Godden didn't resist. He lay passively while Riaz handcuffed him.

"Fuckin' pigs! Leave him alone!" shouted a voice from the road as a car cruised past.

Lamb shook his head as he arrived to assist. "Believe these people?" he wheezed.

"Don't worry," Riaz said. "Fortunately the kind of people that appreciate us actually catching criminals aren't the kind of people that rubberneck while yelling out of their car windows. Pete, you want to get our car?"

Lamb looked back. The car was fifty yards or so behind them, blocking an entire lane. Cars were carefully weaving around it.

He took the keys and returned a few moments later with the patrol car.

"Got more abuse for blocking the highway," he said, dismayed.

"That's the least of your worries," Riaz said.

"What do you mean?" Lamb looked worried. "Oh, you're talking about the pursuit that we kind of didn't quite abort? Shit, good point. They'll have our hides."

"I won't tell them if you don't. We'd already pulled back when he legged it from the car."

Lamb looked down at Godden with a worried look on his face. "Airplane . . ."

"What?"

Lamb nodded down towards the still-prone Godden.

"Ixnay on the . . . you know."

"Look, pal. Can I get some stuff out of my car?" asked the burglar called Ty Godden between mouthfuls of grass.

"Fine. I'm going to search it anyway," Riaz said, and frogmarched his charge back along the road.

Lamb whistled as he looked over the car from the other side.

"Don't see many of these any more. This thing's a death trap."

Their eyes met over the roof.

"How do you do it, Airplane?"

Riaz shrugged and carefully placed Godden in the rear of the patrol car. He tossed the keys to Lamb, who went to lock the Capri but thought better of it.

"What's the point?"

"Oi," was the only retort from the sullen-looking Godden.

"Sorry, pal. There isn't even nostalgia value in a Capri. Now, if you had an Audi Quattro . . ."

Riaz read out the arrests to Godden. Driving while disqualified, failing to stop for police, dangerous driving and the two warrants. They moved off down the road, leaving the Capri wedged up on the verge, its hazard lights blinking feebly as what was left of the battery began to evaporate.

Lamb shook his head all the way to the cell block. After they had booked Godden in, they sat in the reports room. Lamb made coffee while Riaz started on the file build.

"Come on, Airplane, what's your secret?" Lamb whispered, putting a styrofoam cup in front of him.

"What do you mean?" Riaz asked.

"You know what I mean. You know how long ago it was since we had the briefing that Godden *might* be out and about and he *might* be using this car?"

Riaz just shrugged.

"Seventeen days. I checked my notebook. I sat there in the briefing with you, I put Godden's details in my notebook along with the Capri's registration number like a good Christian copper, I got called out to a job and I haven't thought about it since. So how the hell did you remember it?"

Lamb nodded towards an array of charts and league tables on the wall above the computer monitors.

"You make me look bad. You notched more arrests this year than anyone else on the district. Not only that, but most of them were self-gen."

"Lucky, I guess."

Lamb was not the only one to have noticed Riaz's prowess for thief-taking. His arrests were not just the result of routine calls like domestics and shoplifters; they were mostly self-generated — suspicious cars found to contain drugs, disqualified and drunk drivers spotted with mathematical precision, offenders wanted on warrant scooped up on a daily basis. Nice little tickles, as the saying went.

The patrol officers were subjected to a daily briefing where they were bombarded with a host of information — the previous day's crimes, disorder hotspots, wanted offenders, suspected disqualified and drunk drivers and the vehicles they and other criminals were using — all this information was crammed into a fifteen-minute briefing.

The officers took notes, and wrote down CRO numbers and vehicle registrations — the idea being they would go out and look for these villains. In reality, however, once the briefing ended and the calls started coming in, those diligent notes were usually consigned to history. Moreover, conventional wisdom suggested that officers could only usefully assimilate up to seven items of information in the briefing — any more and you might as well be speaking Russian once the 'retention ceiling' was reached.

Not so for Riaz. He took mental snapshots of the registration numbers and the faces in the rogues' gallery on the briefing projection slides, and if one of these crossed his path while on patrol, it was like an alarm going off inside him. The Force had recently invested in automatic number plate recognition software for its CCTV cameras — if a criminal in a car drove past one of these cameras, a host of alerts would go off for patrols to hunt them down. With Riaz out on patrol, ANPR was virtually redundant.

"You want to watch out," Lamb said. "Rein it in a bit. People who do too well attract a lot of attention. The bosses don't like it. Makes them twitchy."

"Why?"

"Come on, Airplane, don't act so innocent. They'll think you're cutting a few corners. Keeping dubious company. Using *improper practices*. Get what I'm saying?"

"You're saying I should do my job less well in case someone thinks I'm cheating?"

"You're a man of principles, Airplane, I'll give you that. Just be smart, that's all. Once you're in their sights, it'll be like the Cold War in your living room. You want a quiet life, don't you?"

"Pete . . . are you jealous?"

"Am I what?"

"Jealous. You know, are you telling me this so I can be mediocre like you? Make you feel better?"

Lamb flushed, and then got to his feet.

"Is . . . is that what you think? Well, fuck you, Jefferson. It was a bit of friendly advice from someone that's been around the block, that's all, and you go getting on your high horse."

Riaz said nothing. Lamb threw his hands up.

"Fuck it. Don't come crying to me when they put your door in."

4

"Only two people *really* know what happened in the alley-way that night." Hamilton Tate ran a hand through his thick sandy hair. "And one of them is dead."

Beside him, Barnes squinted at the case papers on the table for the millionth time and pulled at his collar. The small conference room was stuffy in the July heat, and a fan whirring quietly on top of a filing cabinet did little to assuage their discomfort.

"It isn't the first time I've said this," Barnes said, "but I think they're going to acquit him."

Tate sighed and sat back in his chair, arranging his robes as he did so.

"I know that. But it isn't down to us to decide his fate. That's down to the jury. Give your evidence. You're the last prosecution witness. A good performance by the police witnesses will give our case a boost."

"I checked our figures, you know. This would be the first case we will have lost as a double act."

"You can't win 'em all," Tate shrugged.

"Not only that, but the vast majority of your contemporaries would have long ago suggested we quietly chalk this one up to experience and move onto something with better odds."

"Everyone loves an underdog, though, am I right? Anyway, I'd have done the same thing if it had been someone else running the investigation."

"I was at the back end of a reluctant queue. What have the other side said about the defendant giving evidence?"

"He's desperate to. He's maintained his innocence throughout and he wants his chance to have his say. The jury will love him."

Barnes looked over at the lawyer. They'd only become friends *after* Tate had traded his burgeoning police career for one in criminal law some years previously; the friendship outside the courtroom had begun after their collaboration on the rape trial of an angelic-looking defendant that had started with long odds but ended with a fourteen-year sentence. The partnership had gone on to yield a fair run of successful trials — Barnes put the formula down to the mutual complement of Tate's optimism and his own pessimistic attention to detail.

Barnes's phone trilled in his pocket. Caller ID — DCI Shaw. He held the phone up to show Tate — *excuse me a minute* — and stepped out into the corridor.

"DS Barnes."

"Rolls off the tongue, doesn't it?"

"Boss?"

"Just a quick call — I know you're at court. You know Col Brennan?"

Rhetorical question. The tubby little DI had a 1940s RAF moustache and was one of only a handful of CID who regularly got into battle gear and went out on late shifts.

"What about him?"

"Poor bastard had a stroke doing a section eighteen."

"Shit. Is he okay?"

"He's with us, but it doesn't look very good."

"Well, I . . ."

"We need to backfill him."

"He . . . what?"

"Main office has enough green files to line a football pitch. It's terribly sad, but I need to be thinking about maintaining the business. You've got the exam, right?"

"I . . . yes."

"Great. You're an acting DI, Barnes, effective immediately. Review in three months, but I don't think the poor bastard is coming back to work."

The line went dead in his ear. Barnes held the phone lightly in his fingers, staring at nothing.

He stepped back into the office and sat back down at the table.

"Everything okay?" Tate asked.

"Not for Col Brennan," Barnes muttered.

"Come again?"

"I'm temporarily promoted, it seems. Acting DI, effective immediately."

Tate winked.

"Beautiful."

The speaker over the doorframe clicked on and a tinny voice crackled into the room.

"DS Barnes to Court Two, please. Officer Barnes to Court Two."

Both men stood up. Tate pulled on his wig.

"Good luck. Give 'em hell," he said. "And drop the 'Acting'."

* * *

"Detective Inspector Barnes, could you state your role in this investigation, please?" Tate's baritone voice reverberated around the wood-panelled courtroom.

"I was deputy senior investigating officer."

Barnes stood in the witness box, his hands clasped in front of him. The butterflies in his stomach had been rife during the walk from the CPS conference room to the courtroom, but as he began to speak, he relaxed a little.

"All practical matters and lines of enquiry pertaining to the investigation were run through me. I reported directly to the senior investigating officer, Detective Chief Inspector Edward Shaw."

It wasn't an untrue statement, but Barnes and Tate had agreed that additional context along the lines of an orphan case that had exchanged numerous supervisory hands — none of whom wanted any part of it — before it was bestowed upon Barnes didn't exactly have *prima facie* wow factor in a courtroom. Nor would, *If I HAD been involved from the off, it would have been less of a shitshow.*

"And, I think, at the time of your appointment as deputy S . . . I . . . O . . ." Tate said, crisply enunciating each letter as if he were sucking a sweet, ". . . you were a detective sergeant, correct?"

"That's correct."

"So, you have been promoted to the rank of inspector since then."

It wasn't a question. Tate was looking down at his notes. Barnes got butterflies again, relishing the use of his new rank. "In your opinion, all pertinent lines of enquiry were followed?"

"Yes. The investigation was thorough and painstaking. I believe all reasonable efforts were made to ensure a fair and impartial investigation."

"It's thus fair to say you have a reasonable grip of the investigation. For the benefit of the jury, could you please summarise what you believe to be the essential facts of the case?"

"Gladly. The defendant is in a relationship with defence witness Amanda Luis. Thomas Gayle — Ms Luis's ex-husband and the victim in this case — was an alcoholic criminal known to the police. At 2317 hours, Tuesday the sixth of September 2005, the victim approached the home of the defendant and Ms Luis — the former marital home that Ms Luis used to share with the victim. The victim was drunk and banged on the front door shouting abuse. The defendant returned home during this and an argument ensued. The argument continued out onto the street and ended up in an alleyway adjacent to the house, where the defendant punched the victim, who fell backwards, striking his head on the pavement. He later died from his injuries. The defendant was charged with manslaughter."

"Let's be clear. The charge is manslaughter, not murder."

"That's correct."

"How many times did the defendant punch the victim?"

"Once."

"And his account in police interview?"

"Essentially he claimed a pre-emptive strike as self-defence."

"I see." Tate turned to face the jury, thrusting a thumb through a loop in his robes and leaning on the other hand. "And had the victim ever behaved like this before?"

"Yes. Usually when he was drunk. He did not accept the end of the relationship terribly well, and often went to his old house to remonstrate with his ex-wife."

"And how did these previous occasions usually resolve themselves?"

"Sometimes a police patrol was called and he was escorted away, usually willingly. Sometimes Ms Luis told him to go away and he did, eventually. More often than not the front door was not opened to him."

"I see," Tate said again. "Presumably there are police records of these previous instances?"

"The ones that were reported, yes."

"And these have all been disclosed to the court?"

"Every one."

"Let us just return to your previous comment about the front door not being opened to the victim when he embarked on these — how shall I put it? — *hostile* visits. What method did Ms Luis usually employ to direct the victim to leave?"

"According to her statement she usually yelled at him from an upstairs window."

"And did the defendant ever speak to the victim himself?"

"Not usually."

"And did the victim ever threaten violence or, in fact, commit any criminal act while misbehaving on the front doorstep of a house he used to own?"

"Not according to our records." Out of the corner of his eye, Barnes became aware of Mandy Luis standing up at the back of the court. The artificial light created a shadow underneath the scar on her cheek, making it look worse than it was and causing her face to look sunken. She quickly sat down again. Barnes flicked his eyes over to the dock, idly noting that Reeve was in a dark blue suit, and appeared to have made quite the effort, dress-wise.

"So, is it fair to say, do you think, that when the defendant returned home and found the deceased on the driveway, he had a fairly good idea that, based on previous form, the victim was unlikely to pose much of a threat or indeed threaten the safety of himself or Ms Luis?"

"Yes."

"One could, in fact, argue that no risk existed to any of the parties involved — until, that is, the defendant arrived home?"

"Yes."

"Your Honour, I must protest." The other barrister, a rotund individual by the name of Browning, rose to his feet to address the trial judge. "My learned friend is leading the witness and inviting him to pass non-expert opinion."

The trial judge lifted his chin from his laptop and peered at Tate.

"I'm afraid I agree with counsel for the defence on this one. Mr Tate, you will please refrain from editorials until your closing statement. Thank you."

"Obliged, Your Honour." Tate bowed slightly and turned back to Barnes. "DI Barnes, was the victim ever arrested for his behaviour at the home of the defendant and Ms Luis?"

"Twice. On both occasions to prevent a breach of the peace — each time he was taken straight home and released. No charges were ever brought."

"Were any other suspects ever identified?"

"No. There were no other suspects."

Barnes then remained in the box while the video of the interview was played to the jury. Barnes noted that this edited version, agreed by counsel on both sides, came in at a little under fifty minutes. The original interview had lasted almost seven hours. When the video had finished, Tate confirmed a couple of minor points with Barnes about the interview and then sat down.

"Thank you, DI Barnes. No further questions, but I imagine my learned friend will have some for you."

Browning rose to his feet and peered at Barnes.

"Detective Inspector Barnes, have you ever encountered my client before?"

"No."

"Never? You've never met this man before?"

"No."

"Then it would come as no surprise to you that my client has no previous convictions?"

"No."

"It would come as no surprise to you that my client — a retained firefighter — has never been charged, summonsed, arrested, reported or even investigated by the police? In fact, other than the four occasions when he dialled 999 because the deceased in this case was harassing him on his own doorstep, the only time my client has ever had dealings with the police was six years ago when he bore witness to a robbery. Were you aware of that, DI Barnes?"

"Yes, I am aware of that."

"Then you are aware that, on this occasion, my client attended the police station, provided a statement, participated in identification procedures and attended court to give evidence, and for no reward other than discharging his civic duty."

"I am aware of that, yes."

"My client gave evidence and the culprit was duly convicted — and now my client finds himself in the same dock as occupied by the criminal he testified against. A position which my client finds difficult to reconcile — as do I, it must be said."

Barnes said nothing, knowing to keep the answers short and simple, and Browning had not actually asked him a question with this last delivery. He couldn't suppress an inward grimace, however — sliding in the line about Reeve being a retained firefighter had been a slick move.

"Officer, I must ask you. What are we all doing here?" Browning spread his arms and looked from the jury to the public gallery and back again.

Barnes frowned. "What do you mean?"

"I mean, officer, what are we doing in this courtroom? Why has my client been brought here to answer a charge before a jury of his peers? It seems quite clear to me that there is not a *prima facie* case to answer. My client's defence is quite valid. I must tell you, officer, that counter-charges of unlawful arrest, false imprisonment and degrading treatment under Article 3 of the European Convention on Human Rights are not beyond my consideration."

Barnes thought for a minute before speaking.

"It is not for the police to decide the guilt or innocence of an individual. My role as deputy SIO was to ensure all reasonable lines of enquiry were pursued, and that all available evidence was collected to present before a court. The CPS decided on the charge. It is for the jury to determine the guilt of Mr Reeve, or otherwise."

Browning smiled — a thin, snake-like action that looked more like a grimace.

"Yes, officer, it is." He made as if to sit down, but then rose again as if he had just remembered something.

"Officer . . ." he said, his thick grey eyebrows knitting into an exaggerated frown, ". . . can you please tell us why this investigation was handled . . . locally?"

"What?" The question had caught Barnes genuinely off guard. He understood it, but it was not one he was expecting.

"This investigation . . . was not handled by officers from the Major Crime Branch, correct?"

Barnes thought for a moment, if only to eliminate the possible alternative answers. But there were none.

"That's correct."

"And why was that?"

"I'm afraid I don't know."

"Officer, please don't be disingenuous. Surely you, as deputy SIO, would have more than a fair handle on the governance of a homicide investigation. Did you not influence the allocation of resources to this particular case?"

"I . . ."

"Let me put it plainly, officer. Homicide investigations are generally the remit of the Major Crime Branch, yes?"

"Well . . ."

"What was so different about this case? You and I both know that besides yourself and the SIO, you begged, stole and borrowed detectives from their other core duties. The policies were written on the back of a cigarette packet, and the whole thing was a sticking-plaster operation for one reason only: there was never enough evidence to suggest a crime had even been committed, much less that my client was guilty of it. Certainly not the kind of case that the professionals in the MCB would want to associate themselves with."

Barnes could feel himself starting to bristle, but he held it in check as Browning continued.

"This is not about justice. I put it to you, officer, that your pursuit of my client was nothing other than personal, that it was cooked up solely by you. You cut a host of corners and turned in a slipshod investigation purely to maximise the disruption to my client — an honest and upstanding citizen."

Barnes ran his tongue over his teeth.

"One might even consider that you had a personal vendetta against my client. Why would that be, I wonder?"

Browning turned slowly around, looked Mandy Luis dead in the eye, and then looked back to Barnes, eyebrows raised.

"That's nonsense," Barnes said, but it came out as a croak.

"You took this case on around the same time that your wife died, correct?"

Barnes blinked in disbelief.

"What?" His voice was barely a whisper.

Some of the jury shifted uncomfortably in their seats.

"Your wife. She tragically died some months back, I believe. I am exploring the likelihood of this being a factor in your bloody-minded pursuit of my client."

Tate rose, his hands spread, but the trial judge was ahead of him, and raised a finger.

"Mr Browning. That is enough."

Browning informed the trial judge that he had no further questions, and then immediately requested a short recess, which the judge granted. This was another tactically skilful move by Browning — allowing his closing remarks to linger in the minds of the jury before Tate could piece Barnes together again through re-examination.

After the courtroom had emptied, Barnes took a moment in the box to compose himself, trying to get the anger and disbelief under control. He scanned the courtroom — it seemed so unobtrusive when empty. He eyed the royal crest above where the trial judge had been sitting, and then turned his gaze to the now-empty jury box. He remembered the first day of the trial — it had been delayed by two hours because one of the jurors had been arrested the night before for being drunk and disorderly in a pub in the Lanes. She had accepted a fixed penalty notice for the offence, and had made all haste to the court, hangover and all — only to find the door shut and her place taken by a replacement juror, sourced at the last minute at the direction of an impatient trial judge. Tate had later remarked that, prior to becoming indisposed, the female in question had slept through most of the first day in any case.

The silence became too much. He replayed the exchange with Browning over and over in his head, and the empty courtroom was not helping.

Outside, on the public landing, Barnes stood some distance from where Tate stood with two other police witnesses.

Midway through his evidence, he was forbidden from conversing with anyone at all, but that didn't stop Tate marching over.

"Sorry about that," Tate said. "There's below the belt and below the belt, and I'm afraid Mr Browning has the monopoly on both."

"Thanks. Don't worry about it."

"I'm not worried, particularly, but His Honour is. He's called stumps."

"He has?"

"Yep. Go home, get a couple of brandies down you, and we'll put you back together again tomorrow."

5

"Aha, now we're talking." Lamb hit the light bar and went after the BMW that had just rolled past them with its thumping woofer shaking the tarmac.

They followed it for a few hundred metres, past Memorial Roundabout and along Devonshire Place towards the seafront. Lamb gave a quick blast of the siren, and the BMW finally rolled to a stop across three vacant parking bays.

"No interest, Pete."

"Run it anyway," Lamb said, getting out of the car and pulling his hat on.

Riaz ran a check on the patrol car's data terminal and proved himself correct. Taxed, insured and nothing of any note, intelligence-wise. It was, however, a low-slung M3 with a huge spoiler and blacked-out rear windows, which was presumably enough for Pete.

Lamb was summoning the driver out onto the kerb, followed by the passenger. They were both about eighteen, both wearing sports gear, and both looked nervous. Riaz got out of the car and his mood darkened.

"Pete, there's nothing on the car."

"I smelled weed as it went past us."

Bullshit, Riaz wanted to say. But he didn't.

"Why have you stopped me?" the driver said. Despite the question, his tone was polite.

"Weed."

"Weed?"

"Are you deaf? I just said I smelled weed from your car."

"I don't think that's possible, officer."

Riaz looked at the driver. Polite, and quietly spoken. Nothing belligerent about him. The passenger stood obediently, saying nothing.

"Whose is the car?" Riaz said, just as Lamb stuck his chest out to argue.

"My dad's."

"Licence, please?"

The boy produced his licence and Riaz checked the details. They matched what he'd just found on the computer.

Lamb walked around, stuck his head inside the BMW with his torch between his teeth and started rummaging around with gloved hands.

"It'll just be a minute, okay?" Riaz said to the driver, writing out a section 23 stop-and-search form. "Eastbourne's a landing pad for drugs during the summer. We wouldn't be doing our jobs if we didn't deal with it. If he says he smelled weed, that's grounds to search."

The boy looked at Riaz.

"Meaning you didn't smell anything?"

Riaz stared at him and tore the stop form off the pad.

"How we doing, Pete?" he called, not taking his eyes from the driver.

"Car's nearly done," Lamb said. "Thinking about bringing them in for strip-search, though."

The two boys went from nervous to scared.

"Did . . . did he say . . . ?"

"Hang on a second," Riaz said.

He left them both on the kerb and walked around to the driver's side of the BMW where Lamb was still rummaging.

"What are you doing, Pete?" Riaz said, addressing Lamb's backside.

49

"What do you mean?" said Lamb in a mumble, his torch still between his teeth.

"You know as well as I do there's no grounds to bring them in. All we'll do is end up with a complaint and sucking the rest of the team into a punch-up. There's enough jobs to cover without making our own."

"Making our own is what I'm about, Airplane," Lamb said, emerging from the car with a small notebook, which he held up to show Riaz like he'd found the Holy Grail. "Could be a deal ledger."

Riaz flicked through the notebook, which seemed to contain a bunch of algebraic equations.

"Might be a code," Lamb said.

Riaz peered at the backseat, where science books and ring binders were spilling out of a holdall.

"Find any actual drugs?"

"Slowly, slowly . . ."

"Pete . . . please don't finish that sentence."

Lamb eyeballed him.

"Did you actually smell weed from their car, Pete?" Riaz said. "Or was it some other reason? Because I am standing here in front of the car and I can't smell anything."

Lamb's face lost its usual good humour.

"What are you trying to say, Airplane?"

"They're students, Pete."

"Doesn't mean they aren't making some pocket money." Lamb spoke into his radio. "Comms, Echo-Echo two-zero-one."

"Go ahead, two-zero-one," came the tinny response.

"Any sus-act calls this morning in the town centre? Doing a stop on a BMW in Devonshire Place. Index reads Bravo-Seven-Papa-Lima-Hotel. Two male IC3 occupants aged about eighteen. One wearing a red Chicago Bulls top, the other in a blue Adidas hoody."

"Stand by, two-zero-one," the controller said, and then, after a short pause: "That's a negative."

"Roger that."

"We've done this to death, Pete," Riaz said.

"That mean you're free from your stop, two-zero-one?" the controller continued. Her voice was clipped and businesslike.

Lamb's shoulders slumped.

"Showed my hand, didn't I?" he said. "What you got, Comms?"

"Uncovered immediate response call. Disturbance, 41A Bailey Drive."

"Oh, great."

Riaz and Lamb ran back to the car, leaving the two boys bemused on the roadside. Lamb hit the blue lights and two-tones and headed down towards the seafront.

Riaz knew the address — most officers on Eastbourne District knew it. It was a relatively new build of largely social housing in Hide Hollow, next to the crematorium, and it had gained notoriety in a matter of weeks.

Riaz brought the incident log up on the screen.

"What is it?" Lamb asked as he raced around an idling ice cream van. "Domestic?"

"Doesn't look like it. Short version seems to be: Ty Godden's mother has been assaulted by her next-door neighbour."

"She's the complainant?"

"Neighbour is the suspect."

"Unusual, to say the least."

The journey took eight minutes through the traffic, and as they entered the estate and pulled up outside the address Riaz wished Lamb hadn't been quite so sharp with the driving.

Lamb got out and looked at his watch.

"If we don't lock anyone up, then we might still be off on time. Want to speak with Jean and I'll have a word with the neighbour?"

"You're all heart, Pete."

"Hey, she called us. I'm doing the hard yards by manfully approaching the suspect single-handed. Anyway, at least we know the old man isn't around."

Even from the pavement Riaz could hear the screams of abuse from the back of the two council houses. These were the worst kinds of incident, and even with three years' service he was never quite sure how to deal with them. People screaming obscenities at police officers had to be pretty bad to justify an arrest, and yet standing there with broad shoulders trying to pacify someone spitting swear words in your face did not engender public confidence in the average onlooker. It made them look weak, scared, unsure.

As he walked up the path Riaz heard cries of 'Old Bill!' from inside the house. This was followed by 'Fuckin' Paki!' A young voice, impossible to tell if it was male or female. Riaz knew from previous experience that there were at least four juvenile delinquents in the house, and no way to prove who shouted the insult, so that was already one he'd have to let go — and he hadn't even knocked on the door yet.

The warning of his approach had done little to neutralise the screams and yells coming from the house. Riaz rapped on the door with the handle of his baton, and got nowhere.

Exasperated, he wedged the letterbox open with the thin end of his baton.

"Police!" he barked through the gap. "Open the door or I'll kick it in!"

The screaming from inside stopped briefly, and Riaz saw the outline of four figures move to the door through the frosted glass.

Then the screaming began again. The door flew open, and Riaz was confronted by four screaming females of various ages.

"You fuckin' pig bastard!"

"Who's gonna kick my door in?"

"You try and come in here and I'll fuckin' knock you out!"

"I'm going for a piss."

With the emphasis on the 'p' of this last, apparently irrelevant utterance, a tiny droplet of spit flew from the mouth of its maker and landed on Riaz's lower lip.

Innumerable possible outcomes to this apparently hopeless situation raced through Riaz's mind, but the only one he could latch onto was that his training had never prepared him for situations like this. He briefly considered trying to arrest all of them for disorder, but he gave up on this — it would never hold up because they were all still in their house, but also because in their current state of excitement it would take at least another eight officers to bring them all in, something for which he did not think he would be popular.

If Riaz had any misgivings about how incidents like this did little to endear the police to the average passer-by, they were not helped by the fact that while his brain tried to identify a way out of this mess, his face simply stared agape at the four creatures howling at him from the front door.

Eventually, after a minute or so of breathless yelling, Riaz simply reached in and pulled the door shut on them. He made his way down the front path and looked up at the cracked and yellowing plastic cladding that fronted the house, composed himself and tried again.

He went back to the front door and knocked. The occupants returned and opened the door — the screaming having continued unabated. Riaz held his hands up in an exaggerated display of surrender, and eventually the sound died down.

"Now you've finished yelling at me, are you going to let me talk to you?"

"Talk to you? Talk to you? Youse the fuckin' pig threatening to kick my door in!"

"Yes, I apologise for that."

"I got fuckin' cancer and I got to put up with this shit."

Riaz stared at her. She was indeed a wizened, emaciated creature with blackened teeth and shiny bald head. The mention of the illness was nothing new — Ty Godden's mother, Jean Tully, used the issue of her apparent condition like a weapon, although it had apparently done little to blunt her bilious capacity for rage and violence.

"A misunderstanding," he continued. "You see, from all the noise I was concerned someone inside was being assaulted."

"Someone has been fuckin' assaulted. Me!"

"Okay, now we're getting somewhere. Jean, may I come in and speak to you about this assault?"

There was a pause, then with a flick of the head Riaz was ushered in and the door shut behind him.

Ten minutes later he emerged, dazed and not really any the wiser. His repeated instructions for the women to keep quiet until their turn to speak had gone unheeded — he had been bombarded relentlessly in quadraphonic sound, and his notebook contained only a vaguely coherent allegation of assault levelled against the next-door neighbour — although Jean Tully had no injury to speak of — and four different kinds of spittle.

He walked down the path, the voices still audibly raised, and he wondered how people like this survived from day to day, in between one police incident report and the next. He looked at his watch and thought about taking some holiday time.

Lamb met him on the path.

"How you getting on?" he said.

"Not well," Riaz said.

"Hardly surprising. You've only just locked up her offspring for a bunch of warrants."

"That is not maternal rage," Riaz said, pointing at Jean Tully's house.

"No, but it is the rage of someone who has to go and get her own fags for a day or two. She make a statement?"

"Not interested, unsurprisingly."

"And even if she had, she'd hardly be Witness of the Year."

"Let's swap," Riaz said. "You might have more luck."

Lamb looked momentarily perturbed, but Riaz pushed past him.

The neighbour's house was quiet and dark. After knocking three times to no avail, Riaz pushed the door gently. It swayed open an inch, and a voice called from inside.

"It's open. Come in."

Riaz stepped into the hallway. "Police," he called.

"Yeah, yeah. In the front room."

Riaz walked through the hallway and into the front room — the layout was exactly the same as 41A but as if in a mirror. He stopped in the doorway of the front room and saw the owner of the voice.

"PC Riaz, sir. I've come about next door."

"I know, I heard. Thee did well to get out in one piece." The man was shaven-headed and bare-chested. He was crammed into an old armchair, and was rolling a cigarette between thick fingers.

"Sir, one of the occupants has made an allegation of assault against you."

"I bet she has."

"She has decided not to press charges, however, so if I can have ten minutes to take your side of the story, I'll be out of your hair."

"By all means," the man said. "Take as long as thee needs. Sit down. The name's Jimmy Januarie." He gestured to a couch with a heavy arm.

"Mr Januarie . . . like I said, she doesn't want to press charges."

"I guess once she'd had her fifteen minutes with a copper she sort of lost interest."

"I don't know you, do I?"

"No, PC Riaz, tha don't."

Riaz made no comment on the strange inflections in Jimmy Januarie's speech, and after only a few minutes he stopped noticing.

"Just moved here?"

"Few weeks. Down from the smoke. Bit of sea air, away from the hustle-bustle of the city." There was a hint of sarcasm in his voice.

"I guess you haven't met her fella, then? Anjou?" Riaz said.

"Haven't had the pleasure. I tell you what, though, I wish I'd stayed up town. Tha family next door . . . does thee know the whole street's scared to death of 'em?"

"I know that, yes."

Januarie sat forward in his chair.

"And either the pleece ain't interested, or the neighbours are too shit-scared to make a statement about it. 'Cause it don't matter what protection is on the table or what sentence they get, it ain't cops that got to live next door to 'em. So they do what they like, and today they tried to put the frighteners on me. But I ain't having it."

"So what did you do?" Riaz was now writing in his book.

Januarie sat back and lit his cigarette.

"I clocked her one. Not hard. Just hard enough to let her know I ain't going to put up with it."

"Which one?"

"The little shrivelly one. Looks like a goblin."

"Goblin . . ." Riaz didn't finish the sentence out of a sense of professionalism, but Januarie guessed at it.

"Good word for her, ain't it? She tell thee she's got cancer?"

"Yeah."

"She tell everybody she meets, at least four times a day. Like it gives her a licence to act like a banshee. Like she knows it's too late for her and she got nothing to lose. Like her place in hell is already booked."

"So what happened then?"

"Well, she got a shock. This street knew about thirty seconds of peace and quiet straight after I slapped her. She just stared at me over the garden fence, lost for words. Then the cursing started for real."

"I presume you already told my colleague this." Riaz glanced towards the front door.

"Sort of. He didn't seem too interested, in truth. Kept looking at his watch."

"Thank you, Mr Januarie." Riaz got up to go.

"Let me tell thee of something, PC Riaz," Januarie said, stubbing out his roll-up. "This estate is a shithole. People think London slums are worse, but this one holds its own. The council's forgotten it, the pleece don't give a monkey's, and everyone here is living in mortal fear."

"That's a lot of observation for someone who's only been here a matter of weeks."

"I've talked to everyone in this street, and I'm no fool, PC Riaz. And after today my neighbours will think better of me than they do the pleece. What I did today was a little pointer to them next door that I won't take their shit."

"I think they got the message."

"I doubt it. But I'm prepared to do more, PC Riaz. I'll do what it takes to protect myself and my other neighbours. And I tell thee, I'm prepared to go to prison for it."

Riaz couldn't think of anything to say. Giving a stock warning against vigilante action seemed weak as a counter to Januarie's earnest words, so he changed tack.

"How do local police compare with the Met?"

Januarie grinned. "Thee does okay. Tha seems to be less riddled with the corruption, or is that a daft thing to say?"

"I can't say I've noticed."

"How much service?"

"Me? Three years."

"Long enough. If thy Force was bent, you'd know it." Januarie thought about this for a moment. "Although, these days, it's easier for criminals to become pleece than it is for pleece to become criminals."

"You may be right," Riaz said.

Januarie didn't answer, but instead scribbled something on a yellow pad with a stub of pencil that he took from his ashtray. He handed the paper to Riaz and nodded.

Riaz thanked him and, without looking at it, stuffed the piece of paper into the wedge of other forms and pads that formed his notebook.

He compared notes with Lamb and they rattled through the day's events. Between them, they decided that there was nothing that couldn't wait until tomorrow to be written up, and so they drove back to the station, Januarie's closing shot still running around Riaz's brain.

6

Barnes arrived early at court the following day, and then wished he hadn't. He drifted up to Hove nick to make some tentative enquiries as to what the life of a newly acting DI entailed, but, after seeing the state of his inbox, abandoned the idea and instead walked pointless circuits of the county ground, chewing the case over in his mind.

Homicide, once the excitement was stripped away, was straightforward enough to investigate — insofar as the allocation of resources was generally bountiful. Once the victim died, a dedicated team of detectives from the Major Crime Branch were dispatched and took over from Division. An SIO was appointed, SOCOs flocked to the scene, key witnesses were interviewed, Home Office pathologists attended, house-to-house enquiries and searches were conducted thoroughly within carefully determined parameters, intelligence was harvested, motive and victim profiles were considered, reconstructions were made, telephones and computers were analysed, witness appeals were launched — the list was long but finite, and as Barnes had earlier surmised, it was just a matter of casting the net wide enough. Theoretically, all crimes ought to be investigated in the same way as homicide, but, of course, cost prevented that from being realistic.

This case — as Browning had gleefully pointed out — had been slightly different. Tommy Gayle had been punched once and banged his head on the kerb. A local patrol had attended — they were well used to the address. The initial report had been one of ABH — nothing more.

Gayle had been taken to hospital and was laughing and joking with the officers, who took his statement and then left. It stayed as a ten-a-penny divisional assault investigation — until Gayle suddenly keeled over and passed out while sitting up in bed talking to a nurse. He suffered a brain haemorrhage caused by the bang on the head, which was quickly followed by a cardiac arrest, and he did not wake up.

It was then a case of going back to square one and trying to reconcile everything that had happened in the investigation during those first two hours. This tail-chasing — and the fact that the charge was manslaughter, not murder — meant that Division retained the job, rather than Major Crime. But these things weren't written in blood, and after the file had bounced around like a hot potato, Barnes had somehow found himself as deputy SIO, a role that should technically have been assigned to someone from MCB. Barnes was already several months late to the party and found himself scrabbling around for resources to work a homicide with a 'day job' workload to contend with as well — for a case he didn't really believe in. If James Reeve's answer after caution had been the oft-heard, "Shouldn't you be arresting bad guys?", Barnes's answer would likely have been, "Probably." But then, that wasn't really the point.

For the most part, everything was sound — at least Reeve had been arrested and a signed statement produced by Gayle before he died. However, this didn't alter the fact that the level of attention had been commensurate with the Division's response to this level of injury — which meant that for two hours, the scene was unguarded, the house-to-house enquiries remained on the morning's to-do list, and the same officers had dealt with both victim and suspect — anathema, according to the Murder Handbook, in which cross-contamination is the original sin.

Maybe that was why it had been an orphan case, until it fell to Barnes — it was a homicide that needed investigating, but nobody wanted to be the one to put James Reeve before a jury. The red tops loved it — have-a-go-hero persecuted by bean-counting cops — and until Hamilton Tate got on board, Barnes had wondered — more than once, thanks to a career spent cultivating razor-sharp paranoia — whether the clear-up with the least public sympathy for a decade had fallen to him for a reason.

The court building eventually opened for the day's business of delivering justice. Barnes checked in with security and drifted up to a vinyl couch in the witness waiting room with only an assortment of very old gossip magazines for company. He made a mental note to bring in some of his old paperbacks next time he was here.

After about ten minutes a black-robed usher drifted past the open door like an apparition. Barnes grabbed her and asked her for a sitrep.

"Reeve . . . Reeve," she said, checking her clipboard. "Ah yes, here we are. Oh, the case with the missing juror."

"Pardon?"

"One of the jurors failed to show. Again," she tutted. "His Honour is most unhappy. Second time during the trial. We're just trying to find a replacement."

She scuttled off. Barnes sat heavily for a moment on the couch, then left the waiting room and headed down the stairs to the tiny cafe recessed under the stairwell, directly below the mezzanine level. He bought a coffee and a small pack of custard creams that looked like they had been on display since about the same time that custard creams had been invented, and sat down at the back of the building.

The news about yet another juror failing to show seemed so ludicrous that Barnes wondered if their case actually had half a chance. Certainly, it shortened the odds of a conviction — the system seemed so weak as to render anything possible until the final verdict was delivered.

Barnes wondered what direction Browning would take after his double-barrelled onslaught the previous day — the politics of investigation management and the fact of Barnes's bereavement.

What he couldn't quite get his head around was how Browning knew about the finer — and frankly rather mundane — points of exactly who should be investigating. The advocate seemed exceptionally well-informed — more so even than Barnes, who as a DS had not been privy to the conversations between Major Crime and Divisional Command which had essentially ended up with Division being told, "You keep it."

Barnes could only guess at the specific reasons — like every other detective who'd got wind of the case, MCB had, in all likelihood, smelled the acquittal from the off and wanted no part of it. Politics notwithstanding, Browning had latched onto the point and had used it to make this look like a half-baked investigation. The fact that the lion's share of this was nothing whatsoever to do with Barnes was irrelevant: there was a cop in the box to take the hits, and that was all that mattered. Barnes had been around long enough to know that defaulting to lazy investigation was an old favourite of many defence advocates, and it was something that juries really did not like.

The anger started to rise again — he figured he would find out soon enough what Browning had in store for him. He shut his eyes and willed himself to banish Browning's smug face from his mind, and instead focused on the small but steady stream of people coming and going.

The morning rush for first hearing had been and gone; now, the two security guards on the door looked half asleep. A woman with a pram tried to manoeuvre her way through the search arch. Two besuited lawyers exchanged urgent whispers at the foot of the stairwell — even from twenty feet away, their diction was like cut glass.

The tannoy clicked on and a muffled voice echoed around the building.

"All parties in the case of Reeve to Court Two please. Parties in the case of Reeve . . ."

Barnes sighed and stood up. He hesitated for a moment, wondering how he was going to refrain from laying Browning out cold, then picked up his coffee cup, eyeballing the entrance foyer once again as he tipped it to his lips.

One of the lawyers had stepped backwards and crouched to help the woman manoeuvre her pram, without taking his eyes from his colleague or pausing the conversation. A short, hunched man with unwashed hair and his hands shoved into the pockets of his hoody hurried to the exit, overtaking a tall, well-dressed, slim man as he too approached the doors from the stairs. The tall man didn't break stride; in fact, he seemed to *glide* . . .

There was a shout and a thump from above Barnes's head.

He froze as the tepid coffee touched his lips.

"Stop him! Stop that man! He's escaped!"

The cup shattered on the hard floor, a casualty of Barnes's response to the alarm as he pelted for the doors, arriving at the bottom of the stairwell a moment before the court jailer barrelling down the stairs.

The two lawyers were closest — they stared first at the source of the yelling, then turned to stare at the main doors, but were otherwise rooted to the spot.

Barnes reached the doors first, dimly aware that he had been joined by the two guards manning the entrance as well.

He burst through the doors onto Lansdowne Road, pulling up short for any telltale signs that might give him an idea which direction to take.

Nothing.

No flashing heels, no prone pedestrians, no carjacked motorists.

Nothing out of the ordinary.

"Shit!" Barnes cried.

He turned to the court jailer.

"Who was it? Reeve?"

"Yeah! I brought him up and . . ."

"Tell me later," Barnes said, interrupting. "Head down towards the sea. You two—" he pointed at the two door guards — "work back up the road either side of the court. One takes Holland, the other Palmeira. If you don't see anything obvious inside five minutes, head back to the court building and start searching the grounds. If you do see anything, call 999 before you make any kind of approach. I'll get some backup."

The court security split in a nonplussed trident and shuffled off to discharge their hastily assigned responsibilities.

"Don't be afraid to run!" Barnes called after them.

He stood for a moment, watching his instant deputies fan out while he pulled out his phone.

His thumb hovered over the keypad as he debated whether to call the office, call a friend or call the control room. In the end he figured the safest bet was 999, and he put the phone to his ear.

"Police, what's your emergency?"

It was faint, and almost lost in the ambient street noise, but as Barnes was about to speak he heard a screech of tyres and a long, angry jab on a car horn.

The sound ricocheted off the street towards him, and he spun on the spot, trying to work out the direction it had come from.

Figuring the court guards had everywhere else covered and would stumble across anything noteworthy, Barnes started to run east down Lansdowne Road, in the eventual direction of Brighton.

"Hello? Caller? Are you there? What's your emergency, please?"

Barnes knew from experience that expelling half his wind trying to give a commentary would eat into his progress, and so he pocketed the phone and ran towards the junction with Furze Hill. A bolt of lightning shot up his not-quite-healed leg, and the run became a brisk hobble. He ignored the pain.

Scanning. Scanning. Scanning.

There.

Two cars, by the junction with Furze Hill. Hunched by the kerb, hazards on, practically on top of each other, traffic snaking around them.

Two men stood on the kerb, engaged in animated-if-restrained conversation. The car in front, a gold Honda, had signs of an eye-watering crunch on the rear end.

Barnes approached the men, warrant card held out in front of him.

"Morning, gents," he said. "Everything all right here?"

One of the men — sixty, florid, trembling white moustache — snapped round to Barnes, taking a second or two to process the warrant card. When he did, he vomited out his version of events like the worst kind of righteous queue-jumper.

"Officer, this young idiot needs his eyes testing! I was just heading to my bridge game, doing the speed limit — no more, no less — when he rear-ends me . . ."

"Wouldn't have happened if you'd indicated," muttered the other driver, a sallow, ginger youth who looked thoroughly miserable.

"I DID BLOODY INDICATE!" cried the other man.

"All right, all right, why don't we just take it easy," Barnes said. "I just wondered if you'd seen—"

"I tell you, my neck is absolutely killing me — I've got whiplash and twenty-two years' unblemished no-claims gone in a flash. Gone!"

"Never mind your no-claims, my premiums are gonna go through the roof. I'm a young driver, and . . ."

"You should have stayed on your bloody bike . . . Officer, why aren't you writing anything down?"

"You just need to swap your details, and the insurance companies will do the rest," Barnes said. "What I wanted to know was—"

"Oh, that's just bloody fantastic," the older man said. "Bloody police today. Why are you even here, then?"

Barnes shrugged. "I'm busy looking for rapists and murderers. I can see I've wasted your time, however, so . . ."

He turned and started to head back towards the court.

"You still shouldn't have stamped on your anchors like that, mate," the younger man said.

"I was reacting to the idiot that pulled out in front of me. If my reactions hadn't been quite so sharp, *I* would have hit *him*."

Barnes paused, and spun slowly back around.

"What did you say?"

"Someone pulled out," said the older man, pointing at the mouth of Brunswick Place. "Going like a right imbecile. Didn't stop, or look, or anything. Just cut me up and headed off into town . . . oh, *now* you've got your notebook out."

Barnes was indeed scribbling.

"What kind of car was this?"

The man pouted. "I'm not good with cars. Small thing. Hatchback."

"Colour?"

"Maybe silver . . . or grey. Possibly dark blue."

"Old car? New?"

"Neither, really."

"Did you get a look at the driver?"

"Male. That's all I can tell you."

"Any sort of description?"

"That's all I can tell you." The man folded his arms.

"Would you recognise him again?"

The man made a noise like a horse snorting.

"Was he alone in the car?"

"Don't know."

"I suppose it would be overly optimistic to ask if you saw the number plate."

"No, I didn't."

Barnes pocketed the notebook and spun on his heel, heading back to Hove Crown Court.

"Hey," the older man called. "Does this mean you're going to look for this clown?"

"Oh yes," Barnes called back. "I most certainly am."

7

Barnes eventually reconnected with the 999 operator, triggering the activation of resources that would allow him to lock down Hove Crown Court in its entirety.

Hove Police Station was spitting distance from the court building, which, while fortuitous, required some extra elbow grease to maximise the benefits of its proximity.

A marked Focus with the full light show going screamed to a halt on the corner of Lansdowne and Holland.

Barnes, warrant card aloft, walked over to the two cops as they emerged. They were strapping lads with jarhead haircuts and biceps thicker than Barnes's thigh. In other circumstances Barnes might have been tempted to chuck some condescending macho terms their way, but they were first on scene, which meant they were all right by him.

"DI Barnes," he said as he approached, never failing to marvel at the shift from gum-chewing attitude to instant deference. "Need to get a cordon on. Get some scene tape around the building. Close Lansdowne here and down at Palmeira Ave. Can't do anything more until we get more people."

"Yes, guv," said the driver.

Barnes turned to go, and then a thought occurred to him.

He walked back to the Focus, where the driver was rummaging around in the boot for scene tape. His oppo was standing beside him, collecting the items that had been discarded during the search.

"You're early turn response, yes? Tipped out from Central?"

"Yes, guv," said the oppo, a shovel and stack of traffic cones in his arms.

"Who's in there?" Barnes said, pointing at the police station with his mobile phone.

The cops shrugged.

"Community, traffic wardens, maybe some schools officers . . ." said the one holding the cones.

"Anyone operational?" Barnes said.

The cop with the cones shrugged again. Barnes stared at him for a moment, then made another call to the control room.

"It's ADI Barnes again. Can you patch me through to the tannoy at Hove nick?"

The cop holding the cones stared at Barnes. The other one stopped searching to do the same.

"Attention. This is Detective Inspector Rutherford Barnes, East Downs CID. Any officer in Hove police station who is not currently at death's door, *tending* to somebody currently at death's door or dealing with some other life-or-death situation is to report *immediately* to Hove Crown Court. It's all hands to the pump, ladies and gentlemen. This is a lawful order. There are no exceptions."

Barnes ended the call. The two cops smirked to themselves and resumed their activity.

Barnes walked back to the front of the court, where more cars from the early turn patrol strength were arriving. It was a fine sight.

With the steady influx of further resources, Barnes closed Lansdowne Road to traffic at the junctions with Holland Road and Palmeira Avenue, and started dotting officers in pairs at all the exits.

It took twenty minutes. This wasn't bad — especially given the reluctant exodus of manpower trickling bemusedly down from the police station like *Day of the Dead* — but it was still too long.

When the court building was sealed, Barnes called his team of four DCs to a makeshift rendezvous point he had fashioned by parking his pool car at an angle across the intersection.

It was sheer luck that there were five of them there on the day — Barnes had covered most of it alone up until this point. The interview team — Sofia Johnson and Craig Furness — had been warned for their evidence from today onwards, while two of the (admittedly de facto) outside enquiry team comprising Yashid Hinton and Monty Beck had also been summoned. It wasn't quite clear why only these two had been called, but then Crown Court warned lists were often something of a lottery. Monty had also had the dubious pleasure of arresting their defendant, which made him good sport for the jury.

They gathered round Barnes at the open driver door of the Focus.

"Okay. Early turn have got the building sealed," Barnes announced. "Now we have to clear it. Sofia and Craig — you two are my liaison with the court staff. I want all the staff outside on the pavement — that means cleaners, cafe staff, ushers and advocates."

Johnson stopped chewing. Her eyebrows went up behind her enormous Jacqueline Bisset sunglasses.

"Yeah, I know. This is their patch, not ours. In all likelihood they won't take kindly to being organised. One or two might even try to compare salaries."

"They'll be in trouble if they go down that road," Sofia said. The gum in her mouth popped loudly.

"Why do you think I'm asking you to do it?" Barnes said with a smile. "Be polite, but firm. And just bear in mind that any one of them could be complicit in this mess.

"Yashid, Monty — get down the cells. Security are going to be our allies in this. Find the senior person and give them my mobile number. Defendants on bail: we want to get them out and send them home, but we don't — for Christ's sake — do that without reference to the court clerks. Defendants in custody: we brief G4S on what's happened, but I don't want any of them going back to prison until we've documented and photographed every one.

"You've got twenty minutes. Once we control the site, I'm going to put the dogs through. Search team too if I can cobble one together. We're off-division here, so no doubt someone's going to take umbrage with me closing half of Hove."

He shut the car door.

"Go do it."

To Barnes's relief, local support from Brighton and Hove command was not the parochial wrangle over toe-treading he had feared it might be. In fact, having emptied Hove nick of everyone except the cleaner, resources began to flood in from Central until Barnes wondered if someone above a lowly inspector would be needed to shepherd the embarrassment of riches.

Still, he got his search team. He put them through the building with two dog handlers until they were satisfied that Reeve was definitely not in it.

Once Force Gold had got wind of the minor excitement just north of Hove seafront, the responsibilities became a bit more evenly spread.

The duty uniformed inspector assumed command of the search and containment effort, while Barnes's counterpart in the Divisional Intelligence Unit back cast dedicated a pair of DCs to start researching a definitive list of Reeve's known associates, and patrols were systematically deployed to the address of each one.

Lucky the prick didn't escape at 5 a.m. on a Sunday, Barnes thought. *I'd have been doing it all myself.*

Information markers were put on Reeve's vehicle and the vehicles of his associates, and patrol cars from Roads Policing were set up at intersections of all the major routes within a two-mile radius of the building. A third DIU officer was assigned to check all taxi firms and ambulance control, while the British Transport Police were put on alert at major railway stations in the area. An all-ports bulletin of Reeve's description was circulated shortly afterwards. When the intel DI called to update him, Barnes asked for covert observations to be set up on the addresses of Reeve's partner, Mandy Luis, and his mother — who were pretty much all he had in the way of nearest and dearest.

Barnes was told that might take a little longer to set up, but that it would be "explored". He asked for telephone monitoring as well, but that caused air to be sucked in through the teeth, and Barnes decided not to push it. For now, at least.

He ended the call; the phone rang again almost immediately.

"DI Barnes."

"Guv, it's Monty. Reckon you might want to come down to the cells. Might have something."

"I'll be right there."

Barnes pocketed the phone and surveyed the small island of ordered chaos he had managed to cultivate. The court building had been cleared, and the search teams had splintered off to start working their way through the residences in the immediate area.

All in all, it was fairly tidily done. Deciding that he felt as confident as he could be that the various arms of this operation could function temporarily without him, he entered the court building and walked down to the cells.

* * *

Barnes stood at the doorway of Reeve's now-sealed court cell, clicking his pen against his teeth. The sound echoed around the airless, yellow-lit vault.

DCI Ed Shaw was en route from the station, having received the news of Reeve's escape with restrained good humour.

"Well," he'd said on the phone. "At least now he can be convicted of something."

Despite its flippancy, the DCI had made a valid point which had prompted another question right at the forefront of Barnes's thinking. The "how" of Reeve's escape was being overshadowed by the "why".

Unless some sort of skulduggery was involved, no trial outcome could be guaranteed, but Reeve must have had one of the better chances of acquittal than almost any other defendant in history. If not for Tate's determination to ensure a jury decided Reeve's guilt — or lack thereof — the CPS would have dropped the case long ago. Even Barnes himself remained ambivalent about Reeve's criminal liability.

But until a verdict was reached, he remained a defendant, obliged to stand trial until the question of his guilt or innocence was answered. So why this act of monumental stupidity?

Monty Beck, a powerfully built Ulsterman with icy grey eyes and a boisterous accent, approached Barnes from the small office that the court jailers used as a rec room. His brogues clacked loudly on the concrete corridor floor.

"Guv," he said in a half-whisper. Barnes whirled to face him immediately. The tension in Monty's voice was immediate and unmistakable — it meant they had something.

"Talk to me, Monty," Barnes said.

"Five court jailers on duty today, including a supervisor," Monty said, consulting his notebook. "The one who got chinned by Reeve is very uncomfortable. Young lad. He's in there, with the supervisor." Monty indicated towards the office with his head.

"What's his story?"

Monty looked at his notebook again.

"Says he took Reeve up to the dock when they got the call. Reeve blindsided him when the bracelets came off, clambered up the sides and was on his toes."

The men stared at each other.

"Bullshit," Barnes said. "Give me that."

Monty handed Barnes his notebook.

"Let's go have a chat," the DI said.

The jailers' office made the average police station interview room look positively festive. It was about sixteen feet square and painted in a dubious shade of mud. There was a row of military-green lockers on the far wall, with a matching filing cabinet on the adjacent wall with a dartboard above it. On the opposite wall was a roll-cot and a small fridge with a kettle on top of it. To the right of the door was clearly the workstation — a chipboard desk scattered with papers and a pinboard bearing various notices and timetables. Being underground, the room was windowless, and the single strip light made the beige colour scheme seem sickly and rotten.

Sitting at the desk in an ancient office chair was a jailer with an eyebrow piercing and blond crewcut — and an impressive-looking black eye. Next to him was an older man with SUPERVISOR emblazoned on his epaulettes. He was overweight, with a florid face and burst capillaries in his nose, and looked like his health was only robust enough to withstand a finite amount of stress.

Barnes stood in the doorway, with Monty behind him, and made a point of craning his head forward to read the scrawled interview record in the notebook.

"Stuart . . . McKinnon, yes?" Barnes said.

"That's right," said McKinnon.

He straightened up and handed the notebook back to Monty, keeping his eyes on McKinnon. The boy was extremely nervous.

He perched on the edge of the desk.

"How old are you, Stuart?"

"Um . . . twenty-two."

"So, tell me what happened."

"Um . . . I told . . . I told him," McKinnon said, nodding towards Monty.

Barnes smiled broadly. "I know. And now I need you to tell me." He erased the smile abruptly. "But I need you to think carefully before answering. If you made a mistake, you must tell me now. You must tell me the absolute truth. If you don't, you risk falling under suspicion for aiding and abetting the escape from lawful custody of a defendant in a homicide trial."

Barnes's delivery was comparatively gentle, but it had the desired effect. McKinnon's eyes brimmed with tears. His supervisor pursed his lips in a manner that suggested his patience had evaporated some time ago.

Barnes folded one leg over the other and laced his fingers around his knee. "So, take me through it again. You say you brought him up to the dock this morning. Was that for the first time?"

McKinnon spent a good ten seconds clearing his throat. "Yeah. I'd not met him personally before today, but I'd heard about him. You know, you tend to get word of the cases that are making the news. Murder and the like."

"How long have you been doing this?"

"Almost a year. I applied for the cops, but I didn't pass the interview. I thought this would give me some experience."

"So, the clerk calls down to say they're ready for him, and you went to the cell to get him?"

"That's right."

"Then what?"

"Well, I took him up to the dock . . ."

"We secure the defendants. Handcuffed to one wrist, and each door is locked in turn before the next one is opened," interjected Bill the supervisor.

Without expression or acknowledgement, Barnes slowly flicked his eyes towards Bill, and then back towards McKinnon. "Who else was in the courtroom when you brought him up?"

"No one. A few in the public gallery maybe, but they sit overhead and are out of our view. Defendant always appears before the judge and jury sit."

"I know," Barnes smiled. "Why did you bring him up if we were still one juror down?"

McKinnon shrugged. "First I've heard of it. I just got the call to bring him up. We get that call fifteen, maybe twenty times a day. I didn't ask questions, but everybody works to a schedule. If pieces weren't lined up like they were meant to be, doesn't mean that everybody would be told in time, necessarily."

Barnes eyed him. "When you brought him up, was there any conversation between you?"

"No. I used to try to make conversation with the prisoners but gave it up last year when one threatened to stab me in the eye."

"What happened once you got to the dock?"

McKinnon shrugged. "Well, I led him in, and took the cuffs off as we sat down."

"That normal?"

"Yes. He's been good as gold, but we do it for all of them regardless."

"And then?"

"Soon as they were off, he smacked me in the head and scrambled up the sides and over the top. Like a sodding Royal Marine. He was already out the courtroom before I realised what was going on."

Barnes smiled, and gestured towards Monty for his notebook again. Monty obliged, and Barnes peered at the notes again, loosening his tie as he did so.

"Did you bang your head or anything?"

"Yeah, I did. On his fist."

"He just hit you the once?"

"Sucker-punch, more like. I went down, hit my head on the bench."

"Ironic, really."

"Think I have a concussion."

"Did you land on your back?"

"Yeah."

"So you watched him climb up the sides of the dock?"

McKinnon rubbed his eyes and took a deep breath.

"Do I have to answer these questions?"

"Of course you bloody well do," Bill said. Were it not for the police presence, Bill looked ready to go a couple of rounds with his apprentice.

"What I mean is: I'm not under arrest or anything, am I?" Some cogs appeared to be turning behind McKinnon's eyes.

Barnes leaned forward. "No, you're not under arrest. But any refusal to cooperate on your part is only going to add to my suspicions. Which, it has to be said, are doing a little jig at the moment. And besides . . ."

Barnes's gaze fixed on a spot on the far wall over the heads of both Stuart McKinnon and Bill the supervisor. The DI slowly slid off the edge of the desk and walked over to the bank of lockers on the far wall.

There were five of them in a row. They were too narrow to hold much; each was only about a foot wide. Surnames were stencilled on the front of each one. The one with McKINNON on the door was unlocked, the door ajar.

Barnes, out of habit rather than any kind of real need to preserve the surface of the door, used his pen to gently push it open.

Nondescript items were scattered on the shelf inside: a rucksack, a comb, a can of deodorant. But conspicuously resting in the centre of the shelf was a thick roll of cash.

Barnes looked from McKinnon to the cash and back again. The young jailer was by now visibly pale and taking deep, panicky breaths. Barnes pulled on a latex glove from his pocket and fingered the roll. All fifties, and he estimated the total amount as being in the region of a thousand pounds.

"If this is the money you're earning as a jailer, I wouldn't bother joining the cops," he said, thrusting the roll under McKinnon's nose. "Care to explain this?"

"It . . . It . . . I don't know . . ." McKinnon stuttered. Barnes was already reaching for his handcuffs. "I don't know how it got there. It isn't mine."

Barnes gently pulled the jailer's wrists behind his back and slipped the cuffs on. Bill watched in stunned silence. The sound of the cuff arms ratcheting home was almost offensive in the quiet.

Barnes and Monty guided McKinnon out of the custody block, covering his uniform with Barnes's jacket. Once they got outside, Barnes beckoned a couple of uniformed cops over from the cordon, who took over the escort and walked a trembling McKinnon to a waiting police van.

As the rear door slammed shut, Barnes noticed his boss, DCI Ed Shaw, standing by a blue Mondeo, hands in pockets. He — along with everyone else on the cordon, including a gaggle of press photographers — had clearly been watching the prisoner being escorted from the building.

Despite himself, Barnes's stomach did a little leap. No one else would have known, but he still castigated himself inwardly for such a juvenile feeling at having pleased a superior.

Barnes spoke briefly with the two patrol constables taking over the escort — mainly to ensure their charge was taken to Eastbourne rather than Brighton custody — and then sent the van on its way. He made a call to the office for two DCs from the enquiry team to meet McKinnon at the cell block.

He walked over to his boss, trying to ignore the irritation that rose in his throat whenever he saw the man. Shaw was far too young to be a DCI, in Barnes's humble opinion. He hadn't quite worked out whether he was *actually* younger than Barnes himself, but if he wasn't, he looked it. He was built like a distance runner, and his suit was two sizes too big, which, with the shock of thick sandy hair that would have looked at home on the head of any thirteen-year-old, didn't help counter the overall effect of a youthful Kevin Bacon thrust headlong into a DCI's job — though Barnes would have described his boss as neither footloose nor fancy-free.

"So, you've made an arrest," Shaw said, blinking in the sunshine. "Where does that take us?"

"Not very far, I'm afraid, sir," Barnes said. "Bribing an impressionable jailer into helping him escape was always going to be a likely scenario, but I doubt very much if McKinnon has any information on where he might have gone. Once he admits to taking the bribe, I think we'll hit a brick wall."

"What do we know about him?"

"Not much, as yet. He only became a suspect five minutes ago. Missed out on the police recruitment interview, thought some security work might bump up his CV. But I wouldn't get too excited about him. It all feels rather staged to me."

"Staged? What do you mean?"

"A roll of cash left on the shelf of an open locker? He'd have tried to hide it, wouldn't he? And his reaction when I found it — well, if it wasn't genuine, it was quite an act. I rather feel someone's trying to fit him up."

"Who? The other jailers?"

"Maybe. They'd have the easiest access to the lockers. Monty and Yashid are interviewing each one as we speak. We'll have a little look into their backgrounds as well."

"CCTV down there?"

"Been out of action for months, apparently. We won't take their word for it, though — we'll excavate the whole system shortly. Anyway, there's enough to arrest McKinnon. If they wanted to scapegoat him for something, then as far as they're concerned they've had a result. Especially if they've got someone watching us."

"They might let their guard down," Shaw said, his eyes locked on Barnes — resisting, he thought, the urge to look all around him after Barnes's last comment.

"Precisely. The wheels will turn where McKinnon is concerned, but I'm still more interested in the 'why'."

"You and me both."

"He must have had better odds of acquittal than anybody else who's set foot inside the place in the last century." Barnes put his hands on his hips and shifted his weight from foot to foot. Fidgeting was a common reaction to questions he didn't know the answer to.

"Got your bloody friend Tate to thank for that," Shaw muttered. "So why risk it?"

"I don't know, sir."

"The DIU turn up anything?"

"Not yet. Nothing recent has leapt out at them."

"What about his woman? Luis?"

"She's being questioned now in the court, but the last update was that she's as in the dark as everyone else."

"Is it an act?"

"We'll know soon enough if it is."

"What else?"

"The net's been cast as wide as possible based on what we know so far."

"What about foul play?" Shaw chewed his lip.

"You mean kidnap? It's possible, I suppose, but that's another 'why' I can't see. We might know more once we've dug a little deeper into the other jailers."

"Excuse me! Officers! Might we have a word?"

The female voice came from outside the cordon. Both Barnes and Shaw turned to see a young woman holding a microphone, flanked on either side by a boom operator and a cameraman who looked like they had been camping in the wild for six months.

Barnes frowned. Neither he nor Shaw were wearing ID — as far as anyone else was concerned, they were just two guys in suits. Then he realised that journalists were second only to criminals in being able to spot plain-clothes cops.

"Reckon that's on you, sir," Barnes said, trying not to grin. Ten minutes earlier and he would have copped it himself.

"Oh, great," Shaw said, a flicker of panic flashing across his face. "Thought I wouldn't be speaking to the press until after the prick had been convicted. Call me later, okay?"

Shaw turned on his heel and approached the trio, placating hands held aloft. Their number increased rapidly when word got round that the SIO was holding court.

Barnes watched him begin his statement — and grudgingly conceded that it was impressive, as far as ad-libbing went — then turned his attention back to the building. He stood, arms folded, praying for a development of some kind. It was early days — if there was going to be news, it would surely come soon.

8

Barnes surveyed the activity, trying to pick up on any detail that might seem out of place.

He found one without too much difficulty.

The man was facing the front of the court, with his back to Barnes. His hands were buried in his pockets, the panels of his linen jacket hooked behind the wrists so his enormous stomach could be seen straining against the maroon shirt that barely contained it. Small clouds of smoke puffed rhythmically from his mouth, like a chugging train.

He was standing in Lansdowne Road, about twenty feet inside the cordon. Not posing any obvious risk to crime scene integrity, but reason enough to go and have a chat.

Barnes ducked under the scene tape. The man turned as he approached.

"Morning," Barnes said brightly. "Mind stepping out of my cordon? I . . ."

As the man turned, Barnes saw the tin. The leather holder was hooked over his protesting belt. It was the local Sussex crest, same as Barnes's own.

"Rather sobering when such a hallowed place of justice becomes just another crime scene, wouldn't you say?"

"Sorry, I didn't realise . . ." Barnes said, and then regained some of his composure. Cop or not, this was Barnes's command, and *everyone* had to have a reason to be here.

Barnes stepped in front of the man so he was now between him and the court building. The man was Indian-looking, at least sixty, and huge — around six-five with feet that could have doubled up as skis. His head was like a shiny brown bowling ball, with two or three strands of white hair combed back tight against the pate. His bone-yellow teeth had a clay-coloured churchwarden's pipe clamped between them, and his solid belly would have resisted even a modest challenge from a Saracens flanker.

He turned his back on Barnes to regard the crowd of people outside the cordon. Uniformed cops were stationed in pairs at the various pinch points, and the sight of a roll of blue tape and yellow jackets, especially outside a court building, always attracted attention.

The man removed his pipe from his mouth and waved the end of the stem towards the cluster.

"*The apparition of these faces in the crowd . . .*" he said.

"I'm sorry?" Barnes said, thinking, *Great. A CID thespian.*

The man turned again to face Barnes and stuck out a massive hand. Barnes stared at it briefly before returning the shake.

"Detective Inspector Marlon Choudhury, Professional Standards," he said with a grin. He pointed the mouthpiece of the pipe towards Barnes. "And you?"

Barnes stared for a moment at the end of the pipe. He half-expected it to have been chewed, but it wasn't. It was, however, black and shiny with saliva.

Choudhury saw where he was looking.

"*Petals on a wet black bough,*" Barnes said, meeting his gaze. The lines around Choudhury's eyes were deep. There was a sprinkling of liver spots at his jowl, and Barnes realised that sixty might have been a generous estimate.

"You're quoting Ezra Pound, I believe," Barnes added.

The man called Choudhury beamed at him with what seemed like genuine delight.

"DS . . . I mean, ADI Barnes, East CID."

Choudhury raised an eyebrow.

"You aren't sure?"

"It's a recent thing," Barnes muttered. "I'm afraid I'm the reason for all this." He waved a hand at the array of marked vehicles and crime scene tape. "Defendant from my case escaped the cells. Manslaughter trial," he added in a transparent and instantly regrettable attempt at self-inflation.

"Pity. I'm here for a cop who likes to gaslight his wife. Turn the oven up and then beat her when she's burned the dinner, that kind of thing."

"Anyone I know?"

"One soon-to-be-former Sergeant Anthony Shillingford. A straightforward case, insofar as there is little sympathy for the man. From anyone," Choudhury added.

"My experience, domestics against cops are tough to prove."

"On the contrary," Choudhury said, winking. "You just have to be a little, ah, creative. Especially when he has thirty years' unblemished service and she's been knocking on the door trying to get someone to listen for at least seven of those."

"And you finally opened that door?"

"Maybe it was a fresh pair of very old eyes. The service has been dismissive of what goes on behind closed doors for almost two hundred years, but, actually, it's the one strain of brutality that will reliably win out when all the drugs and fire-arms charges collapse at the finish line. Provided you think about it a little."

"He's just about to retire," Barnes said.

"Indeed. Unfortunately, one cannot resign one's way out of actual crimes," Choudhury said. "There are some supplementary charges also — not content with domestic abuse, he had a growing tendency to defraud elderly burglary victims also."

Barnes shook his head.

"Sounds like a real charmer. He's probably set public confidence back ten years, single-handedly."

"A veritable house of cards, but yes. We've had to impose a media embargo for his own safety."

Choudhury's accent did not sound like it had ever been beyond the grounds of Trinity College.

"I suppose I'm lucky," he said. "Police officers aren't generally flight risks, so unlike yours, my man was on bail. All I've had to do is send him home. A pity," he said again as he tamped more tobacco into the pipe.

Barnes glanced at him. What was a pity? The unexpected adjournment, or the fact that Choudhury's defendant — a police officer who was innocent until proven guilty — was at liberty?

"I don't think I've heard of you," Barnes said.

Choudhury grinned again. "I transferred to Sussex last year. Metropolitan before that. Wanted to see out the autumn of my career with some sea air in my lungs. So, DI Barnes, are your bases covered?"

Barnes prickled. Respect for rank was a virtual absolute; in turn, attaining rank was often such a hard-fought battle that being called to account by a supposed equal was often as uncomfortable as deference for the next rung on the ladder was unquestioning.

He took a breath. This was just two CID middle managers comparing notes. He needn't get defensive. Besides, the old duffer had at least twenty-five years on him. It was probably a generational thing.

"He thumped the jailer and vaulted the dock. Jailer might be on the take — he's in the bin. We've got DIU setting up covert and overt monitoring of friends and family addresses, telephones and bank accounts. Uniform are doing house-to-house, the dogs are out and the helicopter's up. We've got a media appeal, an all-ports alert and he's been circulated on PNC. That about cover it?" he said, instantly regretting this last sentence, which just sounded petulant.

Choudhury raised a thick white eyebrow.

"Indeed it does. Have you—?"

"There's a net over the city. He isn't going anywhere." Barnes folded his arms.

"I sense you don't like the jailer as a suspect."

Barnes screwed up his face.

"When did I say that?"

"You didn't. Hence, 'I sense it.' Am I wrong?"

Barnes eyed him for a second, and then exhaled.

"Bit too easy. The lad's only been doing the job a few months. We're looking into his home life and vetting clearance before we interview him, but I have a sneaking suspicion he's a smokescreen."

"Provided by and for whom?"

"I'll let you know."

Choudhury sucked thoughtfully on his pipe, then gazed at the sky.

"What is the *point* of putting the helicopter up in a built-up area such as this?" he asked, more, it seemed, to himself than to Barnes.

Barnes smiled without parting his lips.

"Flush him out. Chopper's up, people come out to look, they know something's going down. Makes them more likely to report stuff that they otherwise wouldn't."

"Someone's hiding in my Wendy house."

"Exactly."

"Well, DI Barnes, sounds like you've got it all covered. I assume you do have a first name?"

"Rutherford."

"Rutherford, if, in the course of your investigation, you uncover anything that requires my involvement, I would consider it a privilege to assist you." Choudhury produced a white business card and slipped it into Barnes's hand. He didn't let go of it immediately. "One would assume that if your man did have the presence of mind to buy his way out, he would have engineered an escape plan also. And such ventures are often difficult to accomplish without, ah, a little help from the inside?"

Choudhury released the card, and walked off to the edge of the cordon.

"The 'whys' are often infinite," he called back over his shoulder.

He ducked under the tape — a surprisingly deft move for one so large — and ambled off towards the seafront.

Barnes looked down at the card, then slipped it into the breast pocket of his shirt. When he looked up, Choudhury had already disappeared.

The sun was warm over Hove, and the ambient sounds of traffic faintly comforting, but Barnes felt as though the temperature had dropped a couple of degrees.

The whys are infinite.

* * *

After sixty more minutes of silence and inertia, Barnes stood down the search teams, dog handlers and the officers forming the cordon. He kept four back and asked them to patrol in unmarked vehicles, in case Reeve was still in the area and the sight of all the uniform leaving coaxed him out. Barnes walked away from the court building and stopped on a strip of green turf a couple of blocks back from the sea. He sat on a bench and tried to shut out the noise of the traffic flow that circumvented the green.

"Cheer up. At least we've got something on him now." Barnes looked up and saw Hamilton Tate standing in front of him. He had disrobed, and in his three-piece pinstripe he just looked like a slightly mischievous law student.

He sat down next to Barnes with two styrofoam cups of coffee. He held one out to Barnes.

"That's exactly what Shaw said. Thanks." Barnes took the coffee and examined it. "What, no Costa?"

"Shit coffee until the verdict's in. That's the rule. Any news?"

"Nothing yet. I stood everyone down."

"So I saw."

"There's four unmarked cars staying in the area in case he's still here and thinks the coast is clear."

"Good thinking, but I'll bet he's long gone."

"I think you're probably right."

"What else did Mr Shaw have to say?"

"Not a lot. To consider kidnap."

"Because his escaping just doesn't make sense?"

"Yes."

"Difficult to pull off, but I think I agree with him — it doesn't make sense."

"He also took your name in vain — blamed you for bringing a case to trial that didn't have a hope in hell of a conviction."

"Ah well, maybe he's right. I can hear the told-you-sos in chambers from here."

"Don't let it worry you — he's just vexed that you earn more than he does now."

"You're quite sure Reeve's not still in the building? The cell, even? The place is sealed on every possible level — there's no way to escape undetected."

"What are you, my boss? I know you were a cop once, Hamilton, but trust me — I've got the reins on this," Barnes said. He broke his gaze and looked out at the traffic. A sliver of sea was barely visible in the distance between two Victorian buildings.

"Sorry, just vocalising my amateur detective skills." Tate paused. "You're thinking about it now, though, aren't you?"

Barnes sipped at the coffee. "What do you think about Browning?"

"Browning?" Tate mulled the question over. "I've had worse opposing me, I suppose. I don't think he's bent, if that's what you're asking."

"All defence lawyers are bent, as far as I'm concerned."

"Don't be so dogmatic. It makes you sound naïve." Tate rubbed his chin. "He only practises defence, of course."

"That makes him even worse."

"Interesting that you think so. I would actually be more wary of a lawyer that bats for both sides. At least Browning has the courage of his convictions. Or should that be acquittals?"

"Unlike you, our very own champion of democracy and justice."

"And due process. If I had my way I'd set up camp in your office the minute you got the 999 call."

"And I'd welcome you. Not sure about anyone else, though." Barnes grimaced as he sipped at the coffee. "What exactly does happen when the eager young barrister's trial is cut unexpectedly short? Rest of the week on the driving range?"

"You know me better than that," Tate said. "And anyway, I thought this thing was going to wrap up yesterday. For a supposedly straightforward trial, it's certainly been eventful."

"The missing juror thing suddenly became rather old news, I expect."

"Well, indeed. His Honour was most unimpressed until his defendant was on his toes, then he suddenly had rather more on his mind. Ah well, I'm just grateful for the opportunity to catch up a bit."

"One man's downtime is another man's active investigation. My workload has just tripled thanks to this idiot doing a runner," Barnes said.

Tate flushed slightly. "Yes, sorry. Forgot about that, momentarily. And I am. Sorry, I mean."

"You are?"

"Yes, you know. For what you had to put up with in the box."

Barnes tilted his head. Tate only had a few settings, and getting into the emotional minutiae of his friends' deepest demons was not something he majored on.

"I told you: don't worry about it."

"Well, I'm still sorry. How are you . . . you know. How are you doing?"

Barnes stood up, just as his mobile phone started to ring. "I'd better go," he said, flipping the phone open. "Yes? What have you got for me?" The remainder of the conversation was brief, and Barnes didn't take his eyes from Tate as he listened.

"That was Johnson. One of my DCs," he added as he closed the phone. "There's been a burglary this afternoon. A stone's throw from the court building. Only thing missing is the car."

"You'd best be going. I'll call you when I get back to town. You can buy me a drink."

"Done. I've a feeling I may still be on duty, though." Barnes began to walk away.

"I'm glad I gave up that shit," Tate muttered. He flung the remainder of the coffee on the ground and tossed the cup into a bin.

* * *

Barnes returned to the court. Sofia Johnson was waiting for him outside, her face impassive behind sunglasses while she sucked on a cigarette.

"Thanks for the best task in the world. At least three shitbags asked me if I'm a solicitor," she remarked before Barnes had a chance to speak.

"Did you set them straight?" he asked.

"Yeah. Told them to plead guilty. Still, they had more manners than certain barristers I could name."

Barnes laughed through his teeth. "What's the news?" he asked as the pair of them entered the building.

"Burglary in Wilbury Grove, reported direct to one of the cordon officers as they were standing down. It's about quarter of a mile west of the court building."

They slipped through the metal detector archway and flashed their warrant cards at the security guards.

"Happened about forty minutes ago," Johnson continued. "Single female occupant was unloading shopping from the boot of her car. Left car keys on the hall table as she went back and forth. She was in the kitchen when she heard the car start. She didn't see which way it went."

"Petrol?"

"Full tank. Victim filled up after she'd finished at Tesco."

"Any witnesses?" Barnes asked as they ascended the stairs to the mezzanine level.

"None, but the victim's handbag containing cash and credit cards was next to the keys on the table. It was left behind. Seems the burglar was only interested in the car . . ." Johnson left the sentence hanging.

"Sounds like our man. You say it happened forty minutes ago?"

"Yeah, and I called you the second it reached me," Johnson answered, anticipating Barnes's insinuation as they stopped outside a consultation room.

"So why the delay?"

"She's not what you call a strong character. She dithered for a good ten minutes — called her sister and went round to all her neighbours before she contacted us." Johnson slipped her sunglasses into her handbag. "And even then she didn't use 999 — according to the call taker she was on hold for a good fifteen minutes waiting to be connected."

"Jesus." Barnes rubbed a palm across his forehead. "Okay, what have we done so far?"

"The cordon officer is still with the victim, taking the crime report. The vehicle's been circulated and attached to Reeve's APB. It's on the ANPR hotlist too. No tracker fitted. SOCO have been called to the scene but they're reluctant to attend — they said he was in and out so quick there won't be anything there for them."

"I don't care. I want them there."

"Leave it with me. Craig's in here with Mandy Luis."

"Okay, thanks, Sofia. Get yourself down to the scene. I'll sit in with Craig. What has she said, by the way?" Barnes asked, jerking his head towards the consultation room door.

"Not a lot. She's claiming to be in the dark about the whole thing."

"What a surprise."

"You know she's been anti since day one, and this hasn't done a lot to improve that. Plus, Browning's holding her hand and getting his oar in wherever he can."

"Okay, thanks. I'll see you later, Sofia." Barnes entered the consultation room without knocking. Browning and Amanda Luis sat together on the far side of the melamine desk, facing DC Craig Furness. Furness spun round as the door opened, and a mix of relief and tension spread across his face when he saw his inspector.

"Guv," he said. "You okay?"

"Yeah, just come to check on you. I've sent Sofia down to the burglary scene."

"Burglary?" Mandy Luis asked, her stare bright and hard. In the natural light the scar was less pronounced, a light brown crescent hooking the corner of her mouth and her cheek.

"That's right, Mandy," Barnes said, meeting her eyes and sitting down. "Not far from here. Happened half an hour ago. Car stolen while the owner was unloading her shopping, ignored the cash and credit cards that were right next to the car keys. That sound like James Reeve to you?"

Mandy Luis snorted. "How should I know? In any event I'm sure you'll find some poor innocent moron to charge with it."

Barnes placed both palms flat on the tabletop. "Innocent? Today's actions are hardly those of an innocent man. Look at what he's risked — he's bribed a jailer barely out of nappies to let him out and taken to his heels. He is now a fugitive from justice — which I can't understand, as all the clever money was on his being acquitted this week."

"Officer, may I remind you that we are still part way through a trial," Browning interjected.

"Yes, we are, but if I don't start getting some leads the trial is going to remain a work-in-progress — indefinitely." Barnes turned back to Mandy Luis. "So why would an innocent man do something like that?"

"You'd better find him and ask him," she said.

"I intend to," Barnes replied, edging slightly closer. "So, did you visit him today while he was in the cell?"

"I'm not allowed to until we've both given evidence." Her voice hitched. "I haven't spoken to him since this bloody trial started. I don't know how he's feeling, I don't know what must be running through his head. He must be out of his mind, I just don't know . . ." She started to cry.

"How would he get his hands on over a thousand pounds in cash? Could he have smuggled it from the prison? Or was it given to him today? Or did someone else pay off the jailer?"

She didn't answer. Browning cleared his throat. "Officer, Miss Luis has been through an awful lot this week, and today really caps it off. Might I suggest we take a break for today, and then we can reconvene some other time. Miss Luis can be given her full rights, and access to my instructing solicitor—" Browning checked his watch — "as I'm running a little overdue, and—"

"Rights? Miss Luis isn't a suspect, Mr Browning. This is a witness interview, same as the countless others we've conducted this afternoon. If you're late for your golf game, maybe you'll feel better if I tell you that you're superfluous here. Unless, of course, you feel we *should* be treating her as a suspect?"

Browning cleared his throat again. Barnes refocused on Mandy Luis.

"Look, Mandy, James needs to end this quickly and quietly. Let's say he isn't guilty of manslaughter — this is only making things worse for him. Is there any other reason he would run like this?"

Mandy just shook her head, the tears flowing freely now.

"You have to promise me that if he tries to contact you, you will try to convince him to turn himself in. And you must tell me straightaway, you must—"

"Why?" Mandy cried. "You're the only reason he's here at all! You're the reason he's spent two months on remand, like a common criminal. He's innocent. He punched Tom once, that's all, defending himself. Manslaughter? You make me sick. You, and that lawyer. You cooked it up between the pair of you — he didn't do anything. Now he's gone, and, oh Jesus . . ."

She began to sob freely into her hands. Browning offered her a handkerchief. Barnes stood up, and Furness followed.

"I've heard that all before from you, Mandy. It doesn't alter the fact that we're all cogs in the machinery now, and there's a process to be followed. We'll be speaking to you again — best you stay home tonight, okay?"

Browning stood up. "That will do, officer. This is now in the realms of the irregular. Please leave."

Barnes stared at him for a moment, then he and Furness left the room.

9

When Barnes was satisfied the net had been dropped as effectively as it could be, he left Hove Crown Court and zeroed in on the only tangible thing he had resembling a lead — the young jailer named McKinnon.

For reasons that eluded Barnes, McKinnon had been taken to Hastings custody, rather than Eastbourne. Brighton was closer, but the wranglings over taking a prisoner to a cell block off your patch verged on the parochial. One could argue that the original index offence had taken place in Eastbourne, but the latest crime — escaping — had happened in Brighton and Hove, and although Barnes knew he should be afforded the same treatment as a result, he knew he wouldn't be. Bottom of the list, last in the queue — the local customs for what amounted to a non-home prisoner were patently ridiculous, but fascinating at the same time. It was Brighton, not Beirut.

Monty and Sofia already had McKinnon in an interview room by the time Barnes made the torturously slow journey along the coast and reached the cell block. The dim lighting, low ceilings, narrow corridor, ancient, grubby walls and lack of windows had earned the place the nickname "the dungeons". The smell of booze, sweat, blood and sick from ten thousand prisoners had seeped into the walls, and the echoes of ten thousand more howling at the moon from their cells could almost be heard. The decor stretched to a dark glossy blue, recently repainted thickly on doors, walls and woodwork. Barnes almost shuddered. Anyone coming here with mental health problems was going to have a whole lot more when they left.

He went to the small kitchen behind the bridge, pulled a styrofoam cup of powdered hot chocolate from a stack labelled DETAINEES ONLY! in cardboard handwriting and filled it with water. He grimaced when he tasted it, and topped it up with the contents of a second cup.

He went to sit with Stu Nippers, the late-turn custody sergeant, who had his feet on the desk and his nose in a Peter James novel.

"They're supposed to be for the guests," he said in a thick Tyneside accent, not looking up.

"You want one?" Barnes said.

"I meant we have our own makings if you want a semi-decent brew," he said, nodding at a small cafetière on the counter.

"That's okay," Barnes said, pulling up a chair. "But thanks. Any good?" he added, nodding at the book.

"Not bad," Nippers said. "Bit heavy on the namedropping." He put down the paperback and looked at Barnes. He had a youthful face, pocked with tiny craters, which should have made him look younger than his forty-eight years, but somehow didn't. His skin and eyes were pale, and his mop of thick curls and eyebrows were already more white than brown. This, Barnes surmised, came of working night shifts in the windowless subterranean vault that was Hastings custody. Barnes reckoned you got institutionalised here pretty quickly. "How can I help you, Inspector?" Nippers asked.

"What's the story with my man? McKinnon?" Barnes said.

"I guessed you meant the young lad. There's only two others here and they need to come back to planet earth before anyone can speak to them."

He nodded at the whiteboard, where the prisoners' names were scribbled in marker pen, alongside their gender, age and a comments box that detailed their schedule of checks, ailments, warnings and any other information that might be relevant to the safety of all involved.

The two other prisoners Nippers was referring to had "BITES! HEP C! NO BAIL! VEGETARIAN" scrawled alongside their names. The 'Offence' boxes were filled with multiple charges: warrants, shoplifting, resist, assault.

"He's probably one of the more interesting cases I've had in here for a while," Nippers said. "Not often I get to write 'aid and abet escape lawful custody' up there."

"He's in interview already, I take it?"

"He wouldn't shut up. He didn't even want a lawyer, until I managed to persuade him it might be a good idea."

He eyed Barnes. Barnes just nodded.

"I can think of more than a couple of DIs that would have locked me in one of my own cells if I'd told them that."

Barnes shrugged. "Must be the 'acting' in me. Did he say anything interesting?"

"Nothing significant. He just wanted to spill his guts."

"Who's the brief?" Barnes nodded towards the interview room door. "Just duty?"

"Aye. Webster's."

"Great."

Barnes looked at his watch, then over at the interview room door. It too was thickly painted in navy-blue gloss, and an illuminated red sign sat over it: "INTERVIEW LIVE — DO NOT ENTER."

"You know what, I might have one of those coffees after all . . ."

Nippers stood up and disappeared off to the kitchen with the cafetière. He hadn't been gone two minutes when the red light to the interview room clicked off and Stuart McKinnon emerged, flanked by Sofia and Monty. The duty brief, a short, squat man from the Force's least favourite defence firm who looked like he'd seen even less daylight than Nippers slunk out without a word.

McKinnon was wide-eyed and looked exhausted. He looked even more wide-eyed when Sofia told him he would have to go to a cell. The fact they had proceeded straight to interview meant McKinnon hadn't yet had the pleasure of one of the en-suite chambers, but Sofia's clipped tones made it ill-advised to argue. Nippers set down the steaming cafetière on the counter and led McKinnon away down the corridor, giving him the guided tour voiceover. McKinnon just trudged away like he was en route to the guillotine.

The three detectives hustled back into the interview room. The airless, soundproofed cube smelled of coffee, sweat and Sofia's perfume.

"So," Barnes said.

"Didn't want a brief, wanted to cough his guts up. And denied having anything to do with it," Sofia said.

"As you might expect," Monty said. "He swears blind he took Reeve up to the dock, got sucker-punched, and that was that."

"We believe him?"

Sofia shrugged. "It's a pretty impressive shiner for twelve hundred quid. Could have fractured his orbit, banged his head on the way down, anything."

"And the money?"

"Planted," said Sofia, as Nippers appeared in the doorway.

Barnes said nothing for a moment.

"What does your gut tell you?" he asked eventually.

"I follow the evidence, boss, as you know," Monty said, deadpan, "but personally, I believe him. It's not enough cash to risk losing everything, and he doesn't have the connections to make a career out of being bent."

"I agree, but he might just be an inside man. As a young, impressionable and rather naïve person he might be exactly the opportunity the main organiser of this operation was looking for."

"If it was an operation," Monty said. "Still looks opportunistic to me. Apart from the cash, of course."

"Well, if it was an integrity test, he fucking failed it," Sofia said.

Monty eyed her and grinned. "Also reckons we should look at some of his longer-serving colleagues," he said. "Says they probably are persuadable to a bung."

"If he has been fitted up then we owe him that much," Barnes said. "And it might explain how a roll of cash got into an otherwise secure subterranean basement."

"Someone could have snuck it down after Reeve legged it," Monty suggested. "The place was bedlam. Not hard to get in unnoticed."

Barnes thought about this for a minute.

"Okay. Let's search his place. I want all his devices. Then we bail him out."

Sofia and Monty looked relieved, as this meant they'd swerve an overnight file, but nowhere near as relieved as Nippers.

"I'm glad you said that," he said from the doorway. "That boy's a suicide risk. I don't want him here any longer than necessary. He'll still be a suicide risk at home, I'd wager, but being with your own curtains rather than this nuthouse might just take the edge off it. In any case, that's your problem, not mine."

"Did you find us any coffee, Stu?" said Barnes, not looking up. Nippers sloped off.

"Got his phone already," Monty said.

"Just his house and car, then," Barnes said. "Where does he live?"

"Shoreham," called Nippers cheerfully from the kitchen.

Sofia groaned. "Remind me why we didn't take him to Brighton custard?" she said.

Barnes pulled his phone out and started dialling a number. "Don't sweat it. I'll find someone to do it. You'll need to supervise, though. But at least they can make a start."

"You good for the overtime, then, boss?" Monty said. "I need to get my bathroom finished."

96

"Get going," Barnes said as the call was answered.

The two DCs sloped off, and Barnes, not waiting for coffee, headed upstairs to the CID office.

It was nearly dark by the time he'd finished making calls and satisfying himself that everything was boxed off. Finding Reeve now relied on intelligence or a public sighting. They were finally setting up an OP at Mandy Luis's house, but they simply didn't have the resources to staff it twenty-four-seven, much less monitor all his nearest and dearest, much less covertly. Barnes didn't think there would be an outpouring of public support for his recapture, either.

His phone buzzed in his pocket. It was a text from Sofia: *HOUSE AND CAR DONE. GOT XBOX AND LAPTOP. STANDING DOWN.*

"He's going to be well happy," Barnes muttered, and called Nippers to get McKinnon out.

Barnes gathered up his stuff, fired off a couple of emails, tidied his inbox and walked to his car.

He left the station, passing a pool of blood two metres wide in the custody garage that hadn't been there when he'd arrived. It had been cordoned off with scene tape, and under the dull strip light it looked black.

One of the late-turn PCs was smoking nearby.

"What's that?" Barnes said.

"Kev Millins," said the cop. "Brought him in for shoplifting, but he's got about eight warrants, so he ripped open an abscess in his groin so he could spend the weekend in hospital rather than here. Silly berk is lucky he didn't bleed to death."

Barnes shook his head and walked off. The first time he'd ever been to Hastings custody he'd opened the car door to see a rat with its head bashed in at his feet. It was the kind of thing you didn't see anywhere else.

These days, the station car park only had space for marked cars, so Barnes had parked further down Bohemia Road. It wasn't until he passed the fleet of marked cars silently lined up, waiting for the next call, that he saw the figure at the car park entrance.

It took a moment in the half light, but he recognised him as McKinnon. He wasn't waiting for a lift, either. He was clearly waiting for Barnes.

"You waiting for a cab?" Barnes said, hopefully.

McKinnon shook his head. His eyes gleamed in the darkness, and Barnes took an almost imperceptible step back.

"I didn't do it," McKinnon said. "You have to believe me."

Barnes put his hands up.

"This isn't a conversation you want to be having outside a police station," he said. "For your protection as much as mine. You've had your interview, and I don't—"

"Can't a bloke just talk to a cop?" McKinnon's voice was wavering, and Barnes quickly, almost subconsciously, weighed up the odds of a cracked trial as a result of inadmissible conversations under a streetlight against the likelihood of him leaving McKinnon where he stood, only for the jailer to throw himself off the East Hill lift station as soon as Barnes's back was turned. He also noted, somewhat shamefully, that his motivation for each option was borne largely from an instinct for self-preservation.

"Come on," Barnes said. "You want a lift?"

"Fuck, yes please. I'm skint," McKinnon said. "And I haven't a clue where I am."

They walked down Magdalen Road, and Barnes tried to stop worrying about the myriad possible insinuations that might surface from this encounter — *he tried to make me confess, he bribed me, he touched my leg* — as he thought about calling up the control room to let them know what he was up to. In the end, he did nothing.

"This a company car?" McKinnon said as he got in the passenger side.

"Very funny," Barnes said. He had replaced the Orion with a large Rover 75 saloon with cream leather seats and an inviting bank of lights on the walnut-panelled dashboard. It was, by Barnes's own — almost proud — admission, an old man's car. When he'd bought it, he'd permitted himself a quiet moment imagining Eve needling him, but there was just something about well-preserved relics.

McKinnon seemed to relax as they headed down to Warrior Square and pulled out onto the seafront. The evening was warm and still, the horizon a pink line wrapped in a thick swathe of indigo cloud as nightfall saw off the remnants of the daylight.

"Lawyer was a dick," McKinnon said, looking out at the promenade, where a cluster of gulls was attacking the remnants of a carelessly discarded kebab. "Told me not to say anything."

Barnes didn't speak.

"That detective of yours, the girl. She told me it was only advice and I didn't have to take it. Cor, he didn't like that."

"So what are you wanting to tell me?" Barnes said. "That you weren't part of a breakout gang?"

"No, I wasn't," McKinnon said. "But I was approached."

Barnes looked sideways at the young man, taking in the piercings, bleached blond hair and soft jowls.

"What do you mean, 'approached'?"

"Two guys. About two months ago. They were waiting near my car."

"What happened?"

"They were pretty casual about it. Ballsy, too." McKinnon stared straight ahead as he recalled the details. They had left the slow crawl of the westbound traffic at Little Common behind now, and were hurtling along towards Wallsend as the road opened out. "Just said, did I want to make any extra money by giving them some information on a prisoner."

"What did you do?"

"Ignored them. Didn't even speak. Just carried on walking. I had earphones in, which made it a bit easier. I went round the corner, hid, then went back for the car when I was sure they'd gone. Bit pathetic, really."

"Clever. So they didn't get your phone number, email, nothing like that?"

"Nothing. I had a jacket on over my uniform too. The only thing they could have got was the number of my car, maybe."

"You able to describe them?"

"Big men. Thirties, forties. Ugly. Tracksuits and donkey jackets. London accents, maybe. One had a gold tooth, I think, but I didn't get a really good look at them. I was trying not to make eye contact."

"Fair enough. And nothing else? They never tried again?"

"Nothing."

"What do you think that means?"

McKinnon snorted.

"Seem pretty obvious to me. I don't think they went for me particularly — they were just working their way through the numbers, trying their luck. I'm sure they moved onto the next one until they found someone willing to play. The money in the locker was probably just a little 'fuck you' for saying no."

"You willing to help with a statement, photographs, things like that?"

"I guess. I never heard them tell me not to talk to the cops, but I expect they did. Don't think they cared much."

"We can get extra patrols, cameras, that kind of thing."

"Que sera, sera."

"Do you remember when it was? We can put out a witness appeal, look for CCTV, all that kind of stuff."

"I don't remember the date, but I do remember it was the day of the Shillingford prelim. What a bunfight that was. Family in court practically tried to kill him."

"Why didn't you report it at the time?"

"I knew you were going to ask me that. I was going to, but I slept on it and then decided it was no big deal. And, if I'm honest, because I couldn't be bothered. It isn't the first time some idiots have tried their luck. We don't earn much — they probably see us as an easy target. The weak link in the chain."

Barnes belted down the bypass that cut through the Pevensey Levels. Cattle and sheep were grazing on the marshes among the head-high river reeds, with a flock of lapwing and other waders circling overhead against the last crimson strips of daylight on the horizon.

They were held at the Pevensey Bay level crossing for a lifetime, and then McKinnon directed Barnes down towards Beachlands.

"Stop here for us?" McKinnon said.

Barnes pulled up outside a circular pod of a house that couldn't seem to decide if it was a holiday home or a beach hut.

"I thought you lived in Shoreham," Barnes said.

"Nan's house," McKinnon replied. "She'll feed me."

Barnes said nothing, thinking furiously about searching this place too.

"You're welcome to come in and sniff around. Even if I was hoarding hot gear, Nan would have my hide if I kept it here."

"Never mind," Barnes said.

McKinnon got out. Barnes offered him a hastily scrawled carbon from the property register.

"I'm afraid we've got your phone and laptop. Here's a receipt." Barnes winced inwardly. Seizing people's phones was often like amputating a limb without consent. It never tended to go down well.

But McKinnon just shrugged.

"I'm probably due an upgrade. Might get one of those new flashy phones with the little cameras on. Or it might be quite nice to be disconnected for a while, anyway. But you do believe me, right? You're gonna be in touch?"

"We'll do everything we can," Barnes said. "I'm duty bound to at least look into it, in any case."

He started the engine.

"You tried for the cops, right?"

"Yeah."

"What happened?"

"They never tell you, do they? They offer you feedback, but it doesn't help you much. They just say 'failed to demonstrate competence in the area of communicating effectively,' or whatever. It's all guesswork."

"Worth trying again," Barnes said.

"I'll get that in writing when you have five minutes."

Barnes gave him a half-smile and headed off.

* * *

The close was quiet when Barnes pulled in. He sat for a moment on the driveway, the engine idling. The ground floor of Eleanor's house was all in darkness, but her bedroom reading light glowed warmly through the curtains. The window next to it was framed in a faint blue tinge from Aidan's nightlight.

Barnes peered out at the silent, dark frontage of his own house, then reversed back out onto the street and drove to the office.

10

Riaz reached into the bag for another crisp, not once blinking or taking his gaze from the building sandwiched between the Polish convenience store and the second-hand mobile phone outlet.

He chewed vigorously while he watched. Beside him, on the passenger seat, lay the scrap of paper given to him by Jimmy Januarie.

It didn't say much. Enough for a recce. Time, day, date, address, estimated delivery weight in kilos. He'd consigned it all to memory in any case, but somehow wasn't quite ready to dispose of it just yet.

It didn't say much. But maybe it said everything.

He peered up at the building itself. The Old Fire Station. It was certainly old. And probably prone to fire, as it happened. It was a narrow, red-brick building surrounded by chipboard hoarding, with "NO PARKING" sprayed on it in dripping horror-film red. It was little more than a carcass on three floors, with windowless frames and a section of the roof missing. Even calling it a squat would have been generous.

He carefully folded the bag into a square, slid it into his pocket, then pulled up the hood of his grey sweat top and sank a little lower in his seat.

A car pulled up outside. It was new, silver, not cheap. At first Riaz thought it was a taxi, then saw a small logo on the boot and realised it was a hire car.

A slim white man in a blue velour tracksuit and huge, ridiculous sunglasses that looked like ski goggles emerged from the driver's seat. Riaz recognised him instantly — Ty Godden.

Riaz shook his head. Whatever due process had taken place since he and Lamb had brought Godden into custody on a fistful of charges and outstanding warrants, it clearly hadn't been enough for the court to deprive him of daylight and fresh air.

Godden went to the back of the car and looked around nervously before opening the boot.

Riaz shook his head for a second time. *What an amateur*, he thought, and not for the first time. Nothing attracts attention like looking around nervously. There was even a word for it in the code of practice for police officers using their power of stop-and-search — *furtive*. As in: *Would you say the defendant was acting furtively, officer? Oh, without a doubt, Your Honour.*

Godden pulled out a holdall from the boot. Riaz tensed up, suddenly paralysed by indecision. He looked to be either dropping off or picking up — from the apparent weight and shape of the holdall, Riaz surmised the latter.

There were only a few feet between Godden and the doorway he was likely to be heading to. If Riaz intercepted him now, he could probably control him — assuming he wasn't armed — until backup arrived. On the other hand, if he didn't let him make his collection, he might only get grazed knees and a complaint. No sense in showing out for nothing.

But if he allowed him to go into the house, he'd need a warrant — which meant a planned operation, a cavalry of officers, a command structure, and rather more exposure than Riaz was comfortable with. And if, having summoned the world and his wife to the party, the holdall turned out to contain Tupperware, then Riaz didn't think he wanted the grief that would bring.

No, better to just do it alone, quickly and quietly, test the cut of Januarie's information, and then take it from there.

There was a loud thump on the driver's window.

"Give me all your money!"

Riaz leapt four feet out of his seat and his heart bolted like a startled gazelle. He turned to the source of the noise and saw Pete Lamb's grinning face.

"What the hell are you doing?" Riaz hissed.

He looked across the street just in time to see Godden slipping inside a chipboard door built into the hoarding that surrounded the building. The door swung shut behind him.

He shut his eyes momentarily, swallowed down the frustration he felt bubbling up inside him, and wound down the window.

"Get in the car," he said.

Lamb walked around to the passenger side and got in, clutching a grease-stained paper bag.

"What are you doing here, Pete?"

"Morning to you too. Just out for my morning constitutional. Via the Cav, of course," he said, holding up the bag. "Saw your car parked up, so the better question might be: what are *you* doing here?"

Lamb's eyes bored deep into Riaz, and Riaz knew a bluff was pointless.

"It's nothing. Just testing some information."

"You mean you're waiting to see if Ty Godden comes back out with a bag full of drugs?" Lamb said. "Doesn't sound like nothing. Sounds to me like some unsanctioned surveillance. Off duty, no less."

Riaz stared at him: *So what are you going to do?*

Lamb pulled a donut out of the bag and offered one to Riaz.

"Hey," he said, raspberry jam oozing from the edges of his mouth. "I'm just worried about your safety. You might need an extra pair of hands."

Riaz opened his mouth, but then Godden reappeared in the doorway of the Old Fire Station, his holdall clearly no longer empty.

Riaz was already out of the car and running across the street before some other interruption changed his mind.

He didn't look as he crossed Cavendish Place. There was a screech of brakes and the sound of a horn. This caught Godden's attention, who turned just as his hand was going to the handle of the car door.

Riaz ran straight for him. He saw the fear in Ty's face, realised it had frozen him to the spot — *amateur, told you* — dropped his shoulder and, without further pleasantries, tackled Ty Godden for the second time in almost a fortnight.

There was a *whoof!* as Godden took the hit like he'd been nailed by an All Blacks flanker and collapsed onto his back.

Riaz had stayed more or less on his feet, and managed to flip Godden onto his front and pin him prone by wedging his knee into his shoulder socket and pushing down with all his weight.

Godden made babbling protests and pleas for salvation — that is, until Riaz shoved his warrant card under his nose and said, "Police. Mind if I take a look in your bag?"

Thereafter, Godden changed his tone and began to struggle and kick furiously, letting rip with a hail of expletives.

Riaz heard a noise above him. Movement in the carcass of the Old Fire Station. At least two, barrelling for exits that wouldn't take them past the incriminating scene out front.

Lamb appeared next to Riaz.

"There's more in there," Riaz yelled. "Get after them."

Lamb looked at him sideways, then moved tentatively to the door in the hoarding and disappeared. He yelled "Police!" but without much conviction.

Riaz dug his knuckle into the notch behind Godden's earlobe, and told him to be still while he dug his mobile phone out of his pocket.

"Police, please." The 999 call was connected. "Yeah, this is PC Jefferson Riaz, off duty. I've detained someone for a street deal."

He wedged the phone between his ear and shoulder and used his now-free hands to peer inside the holdall, while his prisoner rocked and swore beneath him.

"Bloody hell," he said. Difficult to be sure, but there were about ten — possibly fifteen — square brown lumps in cellophane, about the size of postcards. "Cavendish Place, outside the Old Fire Station, by the Polska store. I'm on my own and he's kicking off a bit, so don't spare the whip, okay?"

He ended the call and pocketed the phone. Beneath him, Godden, having heard the words "off duty", was now furiously kicking and struggling, making one final desperate attempt at escape before the real police arrived and he was stuffed forever.

He nearly succeeded. With an almighty jolt he arched his back, almost toppling Riaz from his position.

Mercifully, a town centre patrol had heard the call and arrived just as Riaz was about to realign his priorities. *One to remember for the future,* he thought. *Prisoners can hear your phone calls. Now who's the amateur?*

The patrol car pulled up onto the kerb and cut the siren. Two patrol officers got out and ran over. Riaz didn't recognise them, and, given that they were the closest to a town centre call, figured they had come straight from the Tutor Unit at Grove Road. The fact that one was grey-haired and seemed to be at death's door, the other wide-eyed and not yet shaving, seemed to bear this out.

"Nice little tickle," said the grey-haired one as the handcuffs went onto the now-crying Ty Godden. "What, were you doing your shopping?"

"Something like that," Riaz said. "I was just passing, and there he was, trying desperately to look normal, and it kind of had the opposite effect. I went to have a chat, and there it was."

They patted Godden down and shoved him into the car, and then had a quick rummage through the holdall. Riaz followed them as Lamb reappeared.

"Nothing," he said. "Starburst. Couldn't catch them."

He didn't look out of breath.

"Gave it a good go, though, right?" Riaz said.

"Don't be sarky, Airplane. It doesn't suit you."

Riaz turned to the two real cops.

"I've already said the words," he said, eyeballing Lamb. "It's my arrest, okay? My name on the whiteboard."

"Whatever you say," the grey-haired cop said. "This is quite a seizure. You should have called before you stopped him, though. Might have been armed."

"Well, wanted to make sure it was worth your time, really. It could have been Tupperware."

ACT TWO

11

"What the hell . . . ?"

Barnes didn't like surprises. He preferred a 0300-hours call getting him involved from the off over walking into the office at 0730 hours to find a stack of overnight green files and CAD printouts on his desk. He'd never enjoyed being late to the party.

On this particular warm July morning, however, he'd have gladly opted out. He was rapidly discovering that the joy of an acting promotion was only a joy if someone was brought in to backfill you in turn. Otherwise, for "acting" read "two full-time jobs for the price of one".

The CAD printouts had been arranged in a neatly staggered pattern on the desktop like a game of solitaire. Four bodies, all found at the foot of Beachy Head. They seemed to be unrelated — responding to a report of one poor soul washed up on the rocks often yielded the discovery of another.

All had had some form of CID involvement the previous day — DSs had been to the scene and had ticked off the contingency plan responses one by one — instantly losing interest once they'd satisfied themselves the deaths were not suspicious — and had escalated the initial response accordingly: duty inspector, control room inspector, district command, divisional command, Force Gold. That Barnes hadn't had a call on any of them was unusual, but not out of the ordinary. The cases themselves were all sitting with the Coroner's Office, but all necessitated some kind of over-sight by the duty DI — one of the bodies was a missing person, one had recently been released from police custody, one couldn't be identified but appeared to be a teenager, and one had some questionable injuries.

This last one had a Post-it note stuck to the printout: *BARNES — CALL ME RE THIS ONE! — TONY.*

Tony Sarwan was a retired sergeant who had jumped — via a six-week cruise in the Caribbean — straight into the Coroner's Office after retirement. He was a minor legend among cops for giving thirty-four years' unblemished service to the police, during which time he had, among other things, rescued a baby from a burning house, been slashed across the face trying to stop an armed robbery off duty and adopted a dog whom he had found alongside his long-dead master after a neighbour concern report. Tony had kept the beast in the station for almost three months before the inspector made him take it home.

Barnes read the printout before he called, and he had an inkling that he knew what Tony was going to say. It wouldn't be the first time a coroner's officer had uncovered a homicide that had been overlooked by the cops.

"Coroner's office, Tony Sarwan," he said, answering on the first ring. He had the same cheerful, laconic greeting he'd always had, even when the world around him was going to shit.

"Tony, it's Barnes."

"Aha, just the man!"

"I was afraid you'd say that. Is my workload about to be tripled?"

"Well, maybe the opposite," Tony said. "If this turns out to be a stone bonker homicide then you can hand it over to Major Crime lock, stock and barrel before you get your fingerprints on it, no?"

"I wish it were as straightforward as that."

"Okay, well . . . anyway. Response took a call from the chaplains about one over the Head . . . nothing much they could do in the darkness, so they waited for morning. Then, as you know, we got four for the price of one."

"Yes, got all that," Barnes said, not meaning to sound irritable.

"So sorry, dear boy. Let me get to the point."

Barnes pinched his nose and shut his eyes. "Sorry, Tony. I just—"

"Already forgotten, old chap. The one you're interested in is our bloater. Looks to have been out in the drink for at least a couple of days before he washed up. I'm going to send you some photos, but I don't like his hands. The PM will confirm, but my strictly lay opinion is that all his injuries are consistent with someone falling six hundred feet and then being submerged for a few days. With the exception of his fingers."

"Oh?"

"You'll see what I mean when you see the pictures. Have you got them yet?"

Barnes saw an email from "SARWAN, Anthony" appear in his inbox. He clicked on the attachments.

There were six photographs, all taken in situ, and they all told the story as they zoomed in sequentially. Whole body, torso, arms, hands, fingers. The fingers were little more than mangled bloody stumps, the injuries black like volcanic rock after a few days or so at sea.

"Jesus," he said quietly.

"I know, right?" Tony said, and Barnes wondered how a veteran cop of Tony's legacy picked up millennial vernacular. Maybe it was social media. "Here's my theory: he went over, landed on a ledge, and then spent all night trying to climb back up. Why would somebody suicidal do that? Wouldn't you just continue your journey straight down?"

"He might have had a touch of the seconds at the eleventh hour," Barnes said.

"That's true," Tony admitted.

"It's not unheard of, once the survival instinct kicks in. But in many cases it's too late to do anything about it."

112

"But it can't be ruled out, though, right?"

"Nothing can be ruled out on the basis of a five-minute phone call. I can get a DC looking into his background on the quiet. See if there's a motive."

"You taking it on, then?" Tony sounded hopeful.

"Not unless we find something. You may be right, Tony, but it's pretty hard to throw someone off a cliff who doesn't want to go."

"Yeah, I get that," Tony said. "Thanks for looking into it, Barnes."

"Do we have an ID for him yet?"

"Not yet. No tattoos or anything obvious to run through PNC. DNA and fingerprints were taken in the mortuary. If there's nothing on the books it'll be dental."

A thought occurred to Barnes.

"Tony, listen. It's a long shot, but take a look at serial 284 of the . . . sixth."

"What is it?" Barnes could hear him tapping on the keyboard.

"Missing person. One of my jurors didn't show for trial. Judge asked for a unit to wake him up and they found an empty house."

"The judge 'asked'?" Tony snickered.

"The kind of question there's only one right answer to, but in fairness, the fact that the defendant escaped an hour later made it a moot point."

"You think it might be our bloater?"

"Well, it might be nothing, but they took his toothbrush anyway. It'll take a day or two, but we can get the sample compared with your man."

"Does it look like him?"

"He's been in the water for two days. He doesn't look like anything," Barnes said, and hung up.

His hand stayed on the receiver while he thought, his index finger tapping. He had another call to make.

* * *

"You should know that I'm pretty pissed off."

Barnes was standing in front of Shaw on the other side of the desk, his hands clasped behind him. He had not been invited to sit down. The DCI's face was slightly flushed, and, despite the choice of words, he looked a little hangdog. Barnes wondered if the impending message was one that Shaw had himself already caught full in the face — most likely from Glover — and now it was sliding on down the hill.

He'd been ranting for a little while, and Barnes was only really half-listening in any case. He was scanning the office shelves fervently, searching for a certificate, a family photo, a diploma — anything that would tell him exactly how old the DCI was. He wondered if he was becoming obsessed. And what would he do if it did actually turn out Shaw was ten — even *five* — years younger than he was, as opposed to just looking it? If Shaw were ten pounds heavier, had a sensible haircut and a better-fitting suit, they'd be more or less on par and Barnes would stop worrying about it.

"I'm aware of that, sir, but it's nobody's fault."

That, or some evidence of privilege — public school education, landed gentry or some other pedigree stock. Anything that might indicate Shaw had been dealt a better hand, that the playing field wasn't entirely level, might take the sting out of the tail.

"Oh really? And just how have you arrived at that conclusion?"

Shaw scratched his brow and then straightened up, placing his palms flat on the desktop, fingers splayed. Barnes couldn't help wondering if this was a lift from some leadership body language instruction manual.

"Well, first of all, we are not responsible for the security of defendants in court. That's the MoJ's job. Secondly, there's a chance he had a bit of help. The jailer he supposedly thumped to make good his escape may well have been in on it. Thirdly, well . . . court escapes are not that uncommon. Almost an occupational hazard."

"Barnes, are you telling me 'shit happens'? The only thing I am interested in is that the defendant in a murder trial escaped court on my watch, which makes it common enough for me."

"Manslaughter trial," Barnes corrected him.

"*Homicide* trial, then," Shaw said. "Either way, the public is going to shit."

"Sir, this man is not the Yorkshire Ripper. The red tops called him a have-a-go hero and have been crucifying us for taking it to trial in the first place. Now he's escaped they'll whip it up into an escaped-killer fear-of-crime feeding frenzy. You'll never win."

Shaw scowled and exhaled heavily. "Tell me more about this jailer."

"Stuart McKinnon. Young lad. Ended the day twelve hundred pounds richer than when he started, hence the inside-job theory. Roll of cash found in his locker, which—"

"I take it he's not claiming to know where Reeve went?"

"He says he doesn't know, and I believe him. McKinnon says the money was planted, and what concerns me is that I think he might be telling the truth. He says he was approached outside court a few weeks ago, which he thought was an intimidation attempt. We've only his word for it at the moment, but—"

"How would Reeve come to be in possession of that much cash?" Shaw asked.

Barnes tilted his head. Was the man not listening?

"Not that difficult to smuggle in, to be honest. He was low-risk, and my personal view is that if he'd faced different judges along the way he'd have been granted bail instead of being remanded in custody. He was allowed visitors to the cell — his partner, his lawyer. But, like I say, if the money was planted, then there's at least one other unknown person in the equation. Two, if his intimidation story checks out. Which will leave us with a fitted-up court jailer and people on the outside who may be Reeve's friends, but who could also be his enemies."

"What's the advocate's name — Browning? Have we questioned him?"

"I've an appointment with him at his chambers this afternoon."

"Good. Get me an update by the end of the day."

"Understood, sir."

"And Barnes?"

"Sir?"

"You're an acting DI now. Clue's in the title."

Barnes chewed the inside of his cheek and stepped out.

He paused outside the office for a moment, pulling at his collar. He'd made it sound like all the bases were covered, made it sound like the investigation was tighter than it really was. He checked his watch, wondering how much of his trade was simply talking a good job.

He hurried down the stairs, hoping to eat something before his meeting with Browning. He headed into the foyer, chancing a look over at DJ's counter for a quick hello, but his queue was four-deep. The man himself looked to be concentrating fiercely on completing a form, and all Barnes saw was the brilliant thick white of the top of his head.

Arthur Browning's chambers were based in Hyde Gardens, in the middle of a cluster of buildings housing similar law practices. Barnes sat on a green leather chaise longue in the bay window of the waiting area and admired the surroundings. The secretary worked behind an oak desk and a Schubert symphony played softly from unseen speakers.

"Officer? Come through." Browning emerged from a panelled door and beckoned Barnes towards him. "Sheila? Tea for two, please." The secretary nodded, and Browning shut the door behind himself and Barnes.

"Do sit," he said, gesturing to a chair and resuming his own position behind his desk. Barnes inspected his features. Browning did not make eye contact until he sat down, and when he did, recognition appeared on his face, causing his brow to furrow.

"Ah, are you DI Barnes?" Browning asked.

"Yes. We spoke on the telephone, sir."

"Aren't you the officer in the case of my client? Mr Reeve?"

"I am." Barnes smiled without parting his lips. *You know exactly who I am.*

"Strictly speaking, at the time this drama unfolded I was part way through my cross-examination of you. It's not exactly ethical for me to be speaking to you now. Are you the officer in charge of investigating my client's disappearance?"

Barnes just shrugged, and continued smiling.

"Strictly speaking," Browning said again, "that's a conflict of interests. There should be another officer appointed to oversee this investigation."

Barnes shrugged again. "In an ideal world, Mr Browning, that would happen. Unfortunately, unlike private advocacy, policing has suffered a bit of late. You may have noticed. Shoestring budgets, not enough people and cut-corner practices. In this case, I'd not long left the witness box when I got the news, I was first to take the report and I was the first policeman to Reeve's cell. That kind of makes it my case."

"I see."

"Besides, my chief concern is finding Reeve alive and well. I'll worry about the legal minutiae if he ever ends up back in court."

Browning frowned.

"Is there some concern for my client's safety, officer?"

Barnes got his notebook out. "Mr Browning, I wonder if you could describe to me the mood of your client on the day he disappeared."

"His mood? He was . . . normal. Well, as normal as one can be when one is being tried for a homicide." Browning paused. "I'm afraid I can't say too much about my client's behaviour, officer. It is subject to legal privilege."

Barnes looked up. "How did you arrive at that conclusion?"

A thin smile crossed Browning's lips. "You really need me to answer that question?"

"Okay, let's move on. We've established that one of the court jailers received an amount of cash prior to being overpowered by Reeve."

"I trust you've arrested this individual?"

Barnes ignored the remark.

"We're trying to identify how Reeve came to be in possession of that amount of cash. It's unlikely he had it on him when he left the prison yesterday morning, which means someone got it to him while he was in the court cell."

He was interrupted by the sound of the door opening. Sheila entered the office, set down the tray of tea, and then left without a word. Browning busied himself with pouring.

"As I was saying," Barnes said, "someone may have handed him the cash while he was in the court cells. Did you visit him in the cell, Mr Browning?"

"Well, of course I did."

"Anybody else? Miss Luis, for instance?"

Browning eyed Barnes narrowly. "You'd have to ask her."

"Did she pass him any money? Or anything else?"

"I have no idea. Highly unlikely, in my view."

"Did he have any other visitors?"

"I have no idea," Browning repeated.

"Did Reeve say anything that seemed . . . unusual?"

"I'm afraid I can't answer that."

"Legal privilege?"

"Mmm-hmm."

"Was Reeve optimistic about his chances of acquittal?"

"No comment — although, I daresay, considerably more so than the police."

"I tell you what, I'll just write 'LP' in my notebook." Barnes set down his notebook and reached for his tea. "Mr Browning," he went on, yo-yoing his teabag into the tiny china cup, "do you have any idea where Reeve is now?"

"None whatsoever."

"Has he tried to contact you?"

"No."

"Is he likely to?"

"Officer, my client's disappearance is as difficult for me to comprehend as it is for you. My principal concern, like yours, is that he turns up alive."

"Or you don't get paid?"

Browning's face darkened. Barnes closed his notebook and stood up, drawing the virtually pointless interview to a close.

"Thank you for your time, sir, and for the tea. I may need to ask you some more questions — at a mutually convenient time, of course."

Barnes turned on his heel and left the office, shooting Sheila a winning smile before he trotted down the steps into the tiny car park at the rear of the building.

He did a double-take as he made to go. Six spaces, two cars. One was rather nondescript — maybe Sheila's? — which meant the white convertible Mercedes with the number plate AB BAR 1 had to be Browning's.

Barnes stared at the car for rather too long and then, thinking that looking around would just draw attention to himself, he squatted down and carefully began unscrewing the valve caps of the convertible's chunky tyres.

When he had let the air out of all four, he slowly hauled himself up, brushed the grit from his knees, and carried on down the street, back to the station.

12

The patrol centre was at its busiest midweek, during the early-to-late shift changeover. Riaz didn't start until 1500 hours, but arrived an hour early, almost fifteen minutes of which were spent driving around the Hammonds Drive industrial estate looking for a parking space.

He finally found one down by the Peugeot showroom, and as he walked back up to the station he wondered how much significance there was in the fact that you couldn't get a parking space on a weekday afternoon, but on a Friday night, when the radio was busiest, it was all too easy.

End-to-end, the open-plan office was about forty metres long, and about half that widthways. At the far end there was a row of cubicle-size offices for the inspectors; besides that, the only other separate room was the briefing room, which was annexed in the far corner.

Riaz joined his patrol team in the briefing room. The others talked and laughed raucously, delivering punchlines and ripostes as the sergeant, Tam Bates, delivered the briefing. They were like hecklers at a stand-up routine — with Pete Lamb, Riaz noticed, leading the charge.

Bates, standing by the projection screen at the front of the room, looked flustered, as he often did. He had twenty years' service under his belt, mostly as a community beat officer, but he had only been recently promoted and hadn't quite got used to the pace of uniformed response.

Riaz eyed his colleagues. Extrovert behaviour seemed to come so easily to most patrol cops — it went with the turf — but, even though Riaz was considered senior patrol material with just three years' service, he'd never morphed into a boisterous buffoon the way he'd seen some of his younger colleagues do.

He scanned the rest of the team — ten other constables in total. No, eleven. His eyes came to rest on a new addition to the team, who, like him, was also sitting quietly, notebook in lap.

"Okay, listen up, everyone," Bates said, bringing up a colour image on the screen. "Lots to talk about. This is the number-one item. You all remember Op Biscay, the manslaughter investigation?"

There were murmurs of assent. The team had been on duty and had taken the initial call. Everyone, that is, except Riaz, who had taken the day off. When he'd found out what he'd missed, he hadn't quite forgiven his mother for having a hospital appointment on that particular day.

"James Reeve escaped from Crown Court four days ago, prior to the defence beginning its case. He is still at large today. We've had a number of possible sightings, but no reliable intel on where he might be. CID have a list of individual checks to be made throughout the shift by double-crewed cars."

"How the hell did he escape?" a voice piped up.

"Don't know. CID are flummoxed. They're theorising either an inside job, a kidnap or just sheer bloody-minded opportunity. The photograph's pretty good, but I gather he shaved his head inside. He's six-two and was last seen wearing a blue suit with navy shirt and yellow club tie. I'll dish out the tasks afterwards."

Riaz thought of Jimmy Januarie. The sergeant rattled through the Persons of Interest and the night's incidents of note, before turning to the new addition.

"I'd like to introduce you all to PC Claudia Knight. Claudia is a transferee from the Met and is joining us full-time as of today. She has seven years' service, all in uniform, and . . . and . . ."

". . . and I'm very pleased to meet you all," Knight smiled, rescuing the faltering Bates.

The team murmured greetings, then contributed to the briefing one by one. Lamb flipped open his notebook.

"41A Bailey Drive," Lamb began, when it was his turn. A few groans were heard. "Yeah, we all know it. Call there last set, seems the new neighbour at 43A has imposed the title of village vigilante upon himself. Jean Tully had a go at him, and he floored her."

There were whoops of glee.

"That's not a crime," someone muttered.

"His name's Januarie," Lamb continued. "Jimmy Januarie. Moved onto the patch a few weeks ago from London. Tully didn't want to go ahead with the assault, but this guy Januarie told us in no uncertain terms that he'll put up with no nonsense from 41A, and is prepared to do time to protect himself and the other residents. Sounds like good news, but we're not popular down there at the moment, and it could get nasty."

"Won't be breaking our necks getting there, then," someone else said. "Let them sort it out between themselves."

"Jean Tully spawns for the sole purpose of getting someone else to thieve for her," another voice chipped in, ostensibly for Knight's benefit.

"Where's the old man these days?"

"Anjou? Still inside for using her as a pincushion."

"Okay, okay, let's get to it," Bates said, shouting above them. "Any other business?"

The laughter died down.

"Okay, thanks everyone. Don't hang about getting mobile — the queue's already at twenty and climbing. Claudia, you work with Jefferson tonight. He can tell you about how busy he was on his days off, bringing down drug dealers and the like. Good job, Airplane," Bates said, eyeballing Riaz.

Riaz and Knight exchanged brief glances; Knight nodded slightly.

The team filed out. Riaz's musings continued in the locker room, but once he headed back over to the main building, they ended abruptly.

As he lugged his kit bag down the corridor to load up the patrol car, his pace slowed, as if a deep freeze were descending on him. There were two unfamiliar men in the corridor.

Two men who were clearly waiting for him.

One was huge and Indian-looking, with a brilliant-white comb-over on his otherwise hairless brown head. He was wearing a linen suit and looked to be heading rapidly towards seventy — or possibly beyond. The other man was white, with a designer beard, bad teeth and a dark grey flannel suit. He was smaller, younger and generally more forgettable. They both wore their warrant cards hanging over their breast pockets.

The older man smiled broadly when Riaz approached.

"Constable Riaz?" he said, extending a hand. "Marlon Choudhury, Professional Standards. This is DS Phil Fountain."

Riaz offered his hand limply in return, a cold blast of fear coursing through him like air conditioning. PSD only turned up unannounced and in person if there was some deep trouble circling. Finding them waiting to ambush you after briefing was like waking up to find a vulture on your bedpost.

Riaz looked past Choudhury's shoulder to the small foyer at the end of the corridor. A couple of the team were huddled there, pretending not to watch.

"Can we have a word?" Choudhury asked.

"I've got to load up," Riaz said, stupidly, and took a step forward.

The big man dropped a heavy hand on his shoulder. The fingers were like tensile springs, and Riaz could feel their weight settling on his skin.

"The Great British public will manage without you for ten minutes," he said, still smiling. "This won't take long."

* * *

They congregated at the small conference table in the DI's office, although the DI himself was conspicuously absent. Riaz had no way of knowing if this was deliberate or not.

"Do I . . . should I have someone with me?" he asked.

"You can have whatever you like," Choudhury said. "You don't have to say anything at all, if you don't want to. But you should know that this meeting is going to happen, one way or another."

Riaz swallowed.

"Okay."

"Okay," the Indian man said with a smile, and sat back in his chair. He rested his hands on his barrel of a belly and exhaled heavily. As if on cue, the DS called Fountain took up the slack.

"I'll be upfront with you, Mr Riaz," Fountain said. "You know the rogues' gallery you run through every day at briefing? Well, we have something similar, only ours is full of cops. Just lately, your name has been pushed nearer to the front."

"What . . . what have I done?" Riaz said in a croak, dimly aware that his career was flashing before his eyes. It took the form of polished dress shoes and glinting silver buttons on parade, jinked into adrenaline-pumped weekends that smelled of alcohol and blood and vomit, then twisted into a coiled serpent of paperwork, complaints, penny-pinching and shifts so long that you could look up and find three years had passed in the blink of an eye.

This all happened in less than ten seconds, during which time DS Fountain had methodically arranged a series of thin files in front of him. He folded his arms on the edge of the desk and fixed Riaz with his gaze. Riaz noticed that there were dry patches of what looked like psoriasis behind his ears and reaching up into his hairline, and that the man had made the mistake of wearing a dark suit.

"Tell us about Ty Godden," Fountain said.

Riaz opened his mouth to answer but was distracted by the sight of Choudhury tamping tobacco into his church-warden's pipe. Riaz's mouth stayed open as the DI produced a box of matches and lit the pipe.

"There's no . . . I don't know if there's smoking in the nick, guv," Riaz said.

Choudhury said nothing, but widened his eyes and nodded emphatically, grinning with the pipe between his teeth. He shook the match out.

"Ty Godden," Fountain said, apparently having missed the whole thing.

"He's the guy I arrested last week. The drug dealer. Born 6 June 1985, Eastbourne. White British, five-ten. Last known address 41A Bailey Drive. Last conviction, shoplifting on 12 June — conditional discharge at Sussex Eastern Magistrates. Again. Last period of imprisonment . . ."

"We've heard about your superhuman memory, Mr Riaz," Fountain interrupted. "But there's really no need to show off."

Riaz was silenced. Fountain pulled a series of A4 glossy photographs from the folders and presented them on the tabletop in a storyboard.

Riaz leaned forward and peered at them. Ty Godden walking down Ashford Road, looking decidedly shifty. Ty Godden disappearing into an alley leading down past Leaf Hall Road towards the railway tracks behind the abandoned Junction Road multistorey. Ty Godden appearing again and heading up Cavendish Place. Disappearing into the Old Fire Station.

More pictures — Riaz parked in his car further up Cavendish Place on the forecourt of the car rental place, sucking down an extra-thick banana milkshake. Riaz was mildly embarrassed to note that he stuck out like a sore thumb in the picture. Even a half-blind geriatric badger could tell he was a cop on a recce. Then Ty Godden reappearing from the Old Fire Station — with his full holdall — looking even more shifty than before.

Riaz shut his eyes. He knew the story before he'd finished looking at the remainder of the pictures.

"You stumbled across Operation Liphook — a proactive drugs operation that was ten months in the making," Fountain said, in a curiously detached way. "Five more minutes and they'd have called strike, and you'd have been scooped up with the rest of them. Instead, they called abort, because you just happened, off duty, to find Ty Godden in possession of two kilos of pure cut heroin . . ."

"Mr Fountain apologises," Choudhury said suddenly, leaning forward, his pipe still between his teeth. "He did not mean to use the word 'stumble'. You did anything but 'stumble', Mr Riaz. Am I correct?"

Fountain looked from Riaz to Choudhury and back again. Choudhury let the silence hang in the air.

"There was an undercover police officer in that building, Mr Riaz," Fountain said. "You very nearly put them in extreme danger."

Riaz swallowed.

"We commissioned a bit of data analysis," Fountain said. "Your arrest rate is higher than anyone else on your division by a clear twelve per cent. Good jobs too, self-made. Jobs you can build cases on, not two-bit shoplifters and handbag scuffles outside King's. Not only that, but seven per cent of all the arrests made on this division last year happened as a direct result of a call from you. Off duty."

Riaz said nothing. In a way, he was enthralled by the story.

"So, some might say that you coming across the hapless Mr Godden when you did is in keeping with your MO."

Fountain let the silence build for a moment.

"I . . . I remember details."

"Look, we get it. You're young, not long out of probation, you live alone, you're single."

"I don't actually live alone."

Fountain waved a disinterested hand.

"I don't imagine an infirm grandmother gives you much pull to finish early."

"How did you . . . She's not my grandmother. And I have to . . ."

"Whatever," Fountain interrupted. "My point is: the job becomes everything. On duty, off duty, who cares, right?"

"Enough," Choudhury said. "Let us arrive at the point, before poor Mr Riaz electrocutes us with his nervous energy."

Fountain said nothing but snorted through his nose like an exasperated bull.

"Mr Riaz, we want your source."

"My what?" These two were like a bloody Swiss clock.

"Source. Your source," Fountain said. "If you're getting actionable Level Two intelligence, you don't keep it to yourself. You stick it on a five-by-five, and then you forget about it. You do not, with three years' service, run informants."

"I'm not . . ."

Both PSD men stared at him.

"Look, it was just a call, okay? Stupid neighbour dispute."

"Anjou there?"

"What?"

"Anjou Acosta. Was he there?"

Riaz eyed Fountain. *That's a question you don't need* me *to answer.*

"He's in prison."

"I see."

"Anyway, I turn up, the so-called offending party gives me his philosophy on life, then passes me a slip of paper with the time and location of the drop on it. I turned up out of curiosity, saw the subject looking shifty, and stopped him."

"His name."

"It was a strange name . . . hold on." Riaz pulled out his pocket notebook and flipped through the pages. "Here we are. Januarie. With an I-E. Jimmy Januarie."

Fountain wrote it down, exchanged glances with Choudhury, then took the address and date of birth.

"You know this guy?" Fountain asked.

"Never met him before he biffed Jean Tully on the nose."

"Was the intel relevant to the call?"

"Not in the slightest."

"So why do you think he gave it to you?"

"You'd have to ask him," Riaz said, folding his arms and feeling, for the first time, like he might have wrestled back a tiny piece of the equation.

"Where's that paper now?"

Riaz unfolded his arms. His airways purged as an adrenaline shot did a quick-fire circuit of his body.

"What's this about?"

"Was Mr Januarie given to passing you regular intelligence?"

"Was?" Riaz croaked.

Fountain placed another photograph alongside the others. He held Riaz's stare; Riaz couldn't bring himself to look down. He didn't want to open that door, reasoning that if he didn't open it, it couldn't slam shut behind him. He suddenly felt like he was in a car about to race off the edge of a cliff; knew that the PSD pair were laying a trap he could see coming but was powerless to avoid.

Fountain looked at the photo, then back at Riaz. The younger man knew he couldn't resist forever, and his eyes flicked down to what he knew he would see.

The corpse was unrecognisable, but Riaz knew it was the strange man called Jimmy Januarie.

He was bloated to practically twice his normal size — and he'd hardly been small to start with. His skin was mottled pale yellow and purple, almost translucent; a distinct network of veins and other waxy subcutaneous mechanics were plainly visible. There were bruises and scratches among his dark blond crew cut, and two gaping black craters where his eyes had been. Riaz felt like he was falling away into them.

The photographs had been taken on the shingle on a beach somewhere — the pebbles were wet and shiny, and a fine layer of moisture was visible on Januarie's rubbery skin.

"This him?" Fountain asked. To Riaz he sounded far away; there was a low rumbling in his ears that sounded like thunder, topped with an intense ringing that, he realised, was just the blood pounding in his head like the waves on the shore.

"It doesn't look like him," Riaz eventually managed in a weak voice.

"That'll be the water. He was submerged for a couple days before he washed up. Gulls or crabs got his eyes."

"Drowned?" Riaz croaked.

Fountain pouted.

"Nope. Only trace water in his lungs. He was dead before he went in. Check out the fingertips."

Riaz shut his eyes for a moment, then tried to scrutinise the photo in a slightly more objective way the second time around.

The fingers of Januarie's hands were raw stumps, mangled almost beyond recognition. They were black with blood and grime.

"The theory we're working to at present—"

"A theory only," Choudhury interjected.

"Right," Fountain continued. "The theory is that someone threw him off Beachy Head — middle of the night, most likely. Only he didn't quite make it all the way down on the first go. He landed on a ledge or an outcrop or something, and spent his last hours trying to climb back up the cliff. Then he either lost his balance, or the cold got him, or both, and then he resumed his journey south. Once he hit the bottom, well . . . You've seen what happens when they land."

"A theory only," Choudhury repeated. "But one the pathologist hasn't dismissed out of hand."

"The point is: it was meant to look like suicide. The fingers tell us otherwise."

"You don't think I . . ."

Choudhury waved a hand and screwed up his face like he'd just sucked a particularly bitter lemon.

"Every contract leaves a trace," he smiled. "I'll ask you again: where's that piece of paper now?"

"Shredded it."

"Now why would you do a thing like that?" Fountain asked.

"I just . . . I thought it was sensitive. Didn't want to leave it lying around."

"What was written on it?" Fountain's tone was growing brittle.

"Hardly anything. Just date, time and place."

"That's it?"

"And the word 'drop'."

"A veritable treasure map," Choudhury said.

"It just—"

"Look, Mr Riaz," Fountain interrupted, placing both his palms flat down on the table. "The boss here is a fair man, and he will say we owe it to you to lay our cards on the table."

"*Some* of our cards," Choudhury said, winking at Riaz.

"I don't always agree with this," said Fountain, "but I think you would benefit from seeing things from our point of view. To wit: you're a high-performing officer whose stats are off the charts. Your district commander probably thinks you are a bit of a star — in fact, I'd hedge my bets that at least a couple of command officers have dined out on your results, particularly when you compare this district with others.

"However, you add that to a very well-placed intelligence source who just happens to pass the first uniformed plod through his door — no offence, by the way — A11 information that shortcuts a ten-month operation, and you have a lot of eyes on you. Especially when said same source is chucked off a cliff."

"I didn't—"

"Look, I don't think you're running informants on the sly, despite your impressive arrest history. If I did, we wouldn't be having this conversation — you'd be in front of a panel and that would be that."

"I didn't—"

"But you should have told someone about that piece of paper. You should have done. You've put several fairly high-ranking noses out of joint, and that was before the source was murdered. The glory stinks of shit now."

Fountain stood up. "A smell that's following you around."

Choudhury got up as well, winking again at Riaz with a vaguely collegiate look that might have said, *Looks like the boss says we're leaving.* It was a look that Lamb might have given, one of camaraderie-through-insubordination. Riaz couldn't read the man at all.

"What happens now?" Riaz managed to call after them in a weak voice.

"We'll be in touch," Fountain said.

"Can I go back to work now?"

"Free as a bird," Fountain said.

"Interesting," Choudhury said, pausing in the doorway, "that you have a photographic memory, but you needed to check your notebook for the deceased's name."

Riaz stared.

There was a slight hiatus as Choudhury's mobile phone rang. The DI stepped outside to take it.

"As to which," Fountain said, holding out his hand. "I want your pocketbook."

For a moment Riaz wanted to say *have you got a warrant?* but he thought better of it, and slowly pulled out the book. It was a bit like losing a limb, stuffed as it was with useful information, tickets, "how to" guides and other items of interest built up over time that made a jobbing patrol cop's life a hundred times easier. Riaz was one of few who arguably didn't need them all, but the thick leather-bound wad in his thigh pocket was comforting in the knowledge that it probably could have stopped a bullet.

Fountain slipped it into his own pocket and made to follow his boss.

"Hey," Riaz called to Fountain. "If you already knew all that stuff, what did you need me for?"

Fountain gave a thin smile from the doorway.

"When you're older," he said, "you'll understand."

* * *

As Riaz wandered back down the corridor in a daze, Lamb appeared and ushered him outside.

"What's up, Pete?" he said, nonplussed.

"Quick word, Airplane."

Lamb lit a cigarette, which dangled from his lips as he shrugged on his stab vest.

"Word to the wise, Airplane. About WPC Knight."

"Who?"

"The new girl. Claudia. Your crew partner tonight."

"Oh. What about her?"

"She looks fine, I know, but I happen to know she's the betrothed of one of our very own senior officers."

"Anyone we know?"

"Ah, that I can't help you with, I'm afraid. But in any case, watch your mouth — anything you say will be the subject of in-depth pillow talk."

"Thanks for spelling it out. Anything else?"

"Keep your hands to yourself."

Riaz rolled his eyes. "What do you think I am, Pete?"

"Look, don't take it the wrong way. But you're a single young man, she's as fit as a fiddle, and I just wanted you to know I've got your back."

"We're not all cut from the same cloth," Riaz retorted, retreating back inside without waiting for Lamb's reaction.

He lugged his kit bag out to the patrol car. He gave it a once-over, and when he shut the bonnet he saw Claudia Knight standing at the back of the vehicle.

"Thought you'd got lost," she said. "Ready to go?"

"Yeah, sorry about that." Over Claudia's shoulder, in the corner of the car park some fifty yards away, he watched the men from PSD get into a maroon Toyota Avensis. "Last-minute appraisal, or something. Let's get out of this madhouse. Got kit?"

She held up a black canvas bag. He opened the boot from the inside for her and got into the driver's seat. He went through the pre-drive checks and was filling out the logbook when she got in beside him.

"Why do they call you Airplane?" she asked as they pulled out of the station.

Riaz turned to look at her. Had she heard the confab between him and Lamb?

"That got out quick," he said.

"Sarge mentioned it," she said.

"After the band," he said. "I don't like Jeff, and so Airplane followed pretty quickly afterwards."

Knight nodded, although she didn't look any the wiser.

"Jefferson Airplane? *White Rabbit?* LSD and sixties psychedelia?"

The radio fizzed in the car.

"Unit please, for an immediate response call to Erica Close — report of a domestic disturbance at that location. History to follow."

Riaz turned to Knight.

"Shall we take it?" he asked.

Claudia smirked. She picked up the receiver to return the transmission.

"Let's go chase some rabbits," she said.

13

After casting the net as wide as possible and setting numerous plates spinning through the urgency of the initial response, the hunt for Reeve became a waiting game. So, Barnes waited. He could have waited in the front room, or he could have waited in the office, or he could have even waited in the pub, but, as was increasingly his wont, he sat on the driveway. He reclined the leather seat of the Rover and listened to the rain drum on the roof.

He hated the feel of a long shift. He could smell the sweat on himself, could feel the layers of grime on his hands that seemed impossible to wash off. The faint smell of liquor from the cells was always at the back of his brain, a smell he would forever associate with seemingly mindless violence. He wondered if, when he retired, he would look back on these gruelling shifts with a kind of romantic fondness, but he doubted it. In any event, he'd have to make it to retirement first.

He would have to go back to ground zero. Look at everything. Listings, jury selection, prison intel, court searches, associates' history, other family connections that might take him in, TWOCs and stolen credit card reports that might map to a likely escape route, hiding places.

Everything.

He didn't want to reinvestigate the manslaughter case, but he might need to commission a fresh pair of eyes. They had a signed complaint and as good as an admission — could this have made them complacent?

Him.

Could it have made *him* complacent?

Eleanor pulled onto the adjacent driveway with Aidan. Barnes looked over, his mind slightly less tightly wound for his driveway meditation.

He slid the window down as she began to fish shopping bags out of the boot.

"Hi, Eleanor," he said.

"Hello, Barnes," she replied, half looking up as she reached in to gather up the groceries.

"Need a hand?"

"No, thank you," she said, as Aidan popped out, school-bag in hand.

"How you doing there, buddy?" he said.

Aidan grinned.

"Very well, thank you," he said, like he'd been practising. He looked over at Eleanor for approval, and she rewarded him with a smile.

"Extra day with Nan?" he asked, and Aidan's smile faltered ever so slightly.

"Go on in, sweetheart. Take some shopping with you," Eleanor said.

"Okay," he said. "Which bag has the cookies in?"

"Not till you've had some dinner."

"Okaaay." He waved at Barnes and bounded into the house. Barnes gave him a salute.

"Sorry," he said. "Did I put my foot in it?"

She shook her head.

"His parents are . . . talking things out. It's better for him if he's away from it."

"I'm sorry," he said.

"Not your fault."

135

"How are things with you?" he asked.

"Otherwise all well, thank you," she said, gathering her bags in the crook of her elbows, politely waiting under the strain to exchange pleasantries. "And you?"

"You know. Can't complain."

She looked to the car and back to the house.

"Why don't you go in, Barnes? You'll catch your death."

He tilted his head. Seven p.m. and it was twenty degrees. She smiled and disappeared inside with her shopping. As she closed the front door, Barnes imagined the kettle, the oven, the TV, all the lights going on.

His phone trilled. It was a text message from Shaw. Col Brennan wasn't coming back to work. Acting DI was indefinite, or at least until the next round of promotion boards.

Barnes drummed his fingers on the dash. Even with no prospect of being promoted to inspector at the time, taking the OSPRE Part 1 exam had nevertheless seemed like a sensible investment. But, in retrospect, he did have to wonder about the logic. After all, his workload had doubled overnight. It was tantamount to volunteering for indentured servitude with a spring in your step and a smile on your face — anything less and that acting detective inspector opportunity could just as easily go to someone else. The boss giveth the acting, the boss taketh it away.

Barnes wondered if he was the first person Shaw had asked, or just the first person stupid enough to say yes. Constable to sergeant on his return from suspension had, as it turned out, been a smooth enough ride, even if it had felt a bit like severance pay — *give him this, maybe it will shut him up.*

The implicit message from Glover had been clear — you'll get stripes, but that's all you'll get. Even backfilling Brennan was no guarantee of anything — the gulf between acting and substantive was a million miles if your face didn't fit.

Still, he had the best part of nine months before the promotion boards. Time enough to make a decent enough shot at being an acting DI to get through it — provided he didn't fluff the interview. Time enough to also, he mused, cock it up spectacularly.

Whatever happened, he had reached his plateau — he knew that. He no longer had the stomach, the spirit or the friends to get to chief inspector, never mind beyond. When he thought of how, in his early years, he'd been promised the earth, promised a gold-paved career staircase straight up to the heady heights of the very top of the service, it was all he could do to suppress a bitter laugh.

You'll go far, Barnes.

That had been a long time ago.

The signpost marked "Potential" had always been ahead of him, but somewhere along the road it had, in the blink of an eye, zipped past and was now firmly in his rear-view.

Barnes wondered how many others there were like him.

There was a tap at the window. Eleanor was standing there, a cling-film-wrapped ceramic dish in her hand.

Barnes hastily wound the window down, catching a waft of floral perfume.

"You need to eat something," she said.

"Oh, Eleanor, that's kind. You didn't have to. I'm very grateful."

"You can thank me by spending some time in your front room rather than out here."

"Deal."

She smiled.

"Look after yourself, Barnes."

As he watched her go, his mind wandered off course ever so slightly. He could almost hear Eve's teasing voice — *I know you like older women, Barnes, but that's pushing it.*

He put the dish on the seat. It looked good. Lasagne, or something.

He put the car in gear.

There was no one in the office when he arrived. He put the lasagne in one of the section fridges and sat alone at his desk, working solidly until the daylight faded around him, leaving just his desktop lamp as the only illumination in the room, apart from an amber streetlight from outside that shone through the blinds and cast hairline stripes across the far wall.

He rubbed the knuckles of his thumbs against the bridge of his nose, a mini cyclone in his brain, reading and rereading the contents of the office whiteboard without really seeing them — crime stats, the duty rota, operational developments, significant forthcoming court dates — eventually he stood up and used the elbow of his sleeve to wipe the board clean.

He grabbed a marker pen and started writing.

HYPOTHESES:
#1 — OPPORTUNISTIC — SUBJECT SPONTANEOUSLY ESCAPED CUSTODY — IMPROVISING PLAN TO EVADE CAPTURE (WHY? NEXT STEPS?)
#2 — PLANNED — WITHOUT HELP — AS ABOVE BUT WITH TRANSPORT/SHELTER/ FOOD ARRANGED AHEAD OF TIME (HOW/WHY?)
#3 — PLANNED — WITH HELP — AS ABOVE WITH SUPPORT AND ADDITIONAL RESOURCES (WHO? WHY? CONNECTIONS?)
#4 — PLANNED — AGAINST WILL — KIDNAP — (WHO? WHY?)

He stepped back for a moment and surveyed the list.

If he'd had a red marker he could have scrawled WHY in an angry vertical stripe across the whole list.

It just didn't make sense. If Reeve had held his nerve he'd have been acquitted in a fortnight. Maybe less.

Avoiding reprisals from the family for a not guilty verdict? The victim was far from being an angel, but Barnes doubted there was sufficient love lost in the inner family circle to necessitate sidestepping justice to save his neck. Barnes knew the characters involved — mother, a brother, a sister, no others — and they didn't have the wit to carry out their own justice without a bit of advertising first: threats, tyres being done, that kind of thing. There had been nothing, and Barnes felt sure Mandy would have been front and centre to tell him if anything like that had happened. More likely that the nearest and dearest would have been channelling all their energy into the compensation claim.

Maybe Reeve panicked. If the stolen Corsa report and the subsequent vicinity fender bender *had* been Reeve, it played to Hypothesis #1. He'd been on conditional bail for the best part of six months, until some skilful manoeuvring by Tate — for reasons that had eluded Barnes, it had to be said — had led to Reeve being remanded in custody eight weeks before trial.

Maybe he just couldn't hack it. He wouldn't have been the first. Running in desperation quite often bypassed logic entirely.

Barnes stepped forward again and added one:

#5 — ABDUCTED BY ALIENS

He shook his head and drop-kicked the marker pen into the corner of the room. It clattered off the lip of the metal wastepaper bin, just as Sofia walked in. She looked over at the source of the noise, then back at Barnes.

"You all right, boss?" she asked.

"Yes, fine. Thanks," he said, looking down at his feet with his hands on his hips. "What's up?"

"Patrol found the Corsa," she said.

"And?" He sat down, interested.

"Dumped it off the A27, on Devil's Dyke Road. It's not ten minutes' drive from the court, even in the middle of the day. Likely he went via Old Shoreham Road then up past Hove Park."

"Torched?"

"Nope."

"Interesting. SOCO?"

"All over it."

"Dog?"

"No point. You're looking at — what? — a three-, four-day lag? And apart from the old geezers in the rough on the ninth, there's no one around to ask, either."

Barnes rubbed his chin.

"So, if it was planned, he'd have had a switch-up waiting. If it wasn't . . ."

"If it wasn't, he could have hitch-hiked. He could have walked back across the bypass towards Withdean and hopped on a bus. He could have jumped in a taxi. He could have walked over the Downs and soaked up the July sun. He could have gone anywhere."

"You know what I'm going to ask, don't you?"

Sofia put her hands on her hips and pouted.

"I'm not doing the CCTV trawl again. Needles in haystacks are an aide's job."

"It's how we'll find him."

"We don't even know it was him that stole it."

"Sofia—"

"You've seen my crime tracker, right? I've got more jobs than anyone in the office, and until we get some courses jacked up I'm doing most of the ABEs for all the other snot-nosed chancers as well."

Barnes raised his eyebrows and let the silence hang.

She exhaled.

"Sorry about that. Look, I'll get the bus and taxi ring-round done, get them to put aside anything they might have. I'll get Monty to check the clubhouse again."

"No, park it. Wait till we have a steer from the SOCO exam. You're right — a needle in a haystack is one thing, but looking for a needle when we don't even know a needle exists is hardly a good use of resources."

Her expression softened a little, and Barnes wondered if the pressure she felt was from him or somewhere else entirely.

"You know we need more people, right?"

"Top of my list."

She turned to go.

"Sofia?"

"Boss?"

"'Snot-nosed chancers'?"

She snorted laughter through her nose without smiling, waved with her back to him, and left.

He sat down, half thinking about actually going back home and calling it a night, but the prospect was as unappealing as it ever was.

He should sell the house. He should move on, in the interests of closure — whatever *that* was. He used to drive past his old primary school on his way to work — he never even looked at it, but he knew it was there. Then they came in and bulldozed it for a new housing estate, and he'd been surprised at his own reaction. Maybe it was because memories alone, without that physical anchor, were a difficult thing to trust; in any case, he knew that if he moved house, he'd feel like he'd lost her all over again.

He peered at the screen. He was convinced Reeve had stolen the car — it was as rash and impulsive as the escape itself. If Reeve had been broken out by somebody else, they would have had transport arranged. And yet if Reeve had worked alone, how did he get the money?

Before shutting down the system, he refreshed the list of incident logs.

A new incident appeared at the top. Barnes recognised the address instantly — Mandy Luis's house.

He was awake in a flash. He checked his watch. The call was still coming in. The front page contained simple text:

"ADDRESS HISTORY: PREVIOUS DV MARKER. EMERGENCY RESPONSE DOUBLE-CREWED UNIT PLUS DOG HANDLER TO ATTEND. REPORT FROM NEIGHBOUR — VICTIM AMANDA LUIS BEING HELD AT KNIFEPOINT BY JAMES REEVE . . ."

Barnes grabbed his jacket and ran out of the office.

14

The first patrol car that arrived at Mandy Luis's house contained PCs Riaz and Knight, having come straight from another call.

Riaz stopped the car in the driveway and shut the blue strobe lights off. The pair ran to the front door.

Both heard the sound of crashing furniture and smashing glass. A grating male voice was barking expletives, punctuated by a female screaming.

Riaz spoke into his radio.

"Sierra-Oscar, Echo-Romeo three-zero-one. Disturbance confirmed. Violent resistance anticipated. Please send backup."

"Dog handler en route to you, three-zero-one," the controller responded. "Has entry been gained?"

"Negative, Oscar. Attempting entry now."

"That's a negative, three-zero-one. FCC directing you to wait for backup."

Riaz did not answer, but rolled his eyes to the heavens. Beside him, Knight looked anxious.

The female's voice was heard again.

"Please! Please put the knife down."

Riaz looked at Knight, then planted a boot against the front door.

The door popped open. Knight and Riaz ran into the front hallway, batons drawn.

"Police! Stay where you are," Riaz yelled.

A shout that began as a swear word and became a guttural scream came from the dining room. Riaz and Knight ran towards it, and froze in the doorway.

Reeve was standing by the patio door, clutching Mandy Luis. The blade of a steak knife was pressed flat to her throat.

"Now, James, just stay calm," Riaz said. "This doesn't have to end badly."

"Fuck you, pig!" he snarled. "Get out of this house now, or I kill her."

"Look, we don't—"

The man howled again, enraged by Riaz's efforts to placate him. Saliva was pouring down his chin, his eyes dilated black like a shark on a hunt. Riaz could smell the drink on him, even from a distance of over ten feet.

"James . . ."

He paused, distracted by Knight's soft voice. Mandy was pulling at his hands, becoming more and more frantic, her words nonsensical through the tears.

"James," Knight began again, "please put the knife down." She turned off her radio, silencing the tinny tones of the radio traffic demanding updates. "We can help you. Don't hurt her."

He seemed to be responding to Knight. Tears formed in his eyes, and then he stuck the tip of the blade into the side of Mandy Luis's neck, under the ear, and ripped the knife towards him, opening up her throat.

Knight screamed.

Riaz was momentarily mesmerised — he had expected to see a geyser of cartoon blood spurting out from her neck, but what he actually saw was the severed end of the artery poking out from the black wound like a snake's head. It spat blood briefly, and then slithered back down inside the wound.

Riaz leaped forward and brought his baton down like a Wimbledon smash shot onto Reeve's arm. The knife was dropped with a howl, and the next two strikes went to Reeve's head. He buckled at the knees, and a fourth strike laid him prone.

Riaz kicked the knife away and handcuffed him, and then he and Knight desperately and pointlessly tried to close the yawning wound in Mandy Luis's neck. The artery was visibly bleeding inside her — her chest cavity was swelling like a water balloon, the torso turning crimson from the inside as the rest of her body turned grey.

A growing cacophony of sirens was audible in the distance, as officers rushed to the house in support of their colleagues. But to Mandy Luis, the sirens sounded tinny, distorted, as if she were hearing them under water.

* * *

Barnes frowned as he pulled into Howletts Close. There seemed to be a remarkable lack of activity, which was often a measure of the calibre of the supervisor. The reassuring phalanx of patrol cars, blue lights and scene cordon tape were nowhere to be seen.

He pulled up outside the house. There were two patrol cars and an ambulance. Neighbours and patrol officers were milling about in the street. Barnes grimaced. No one had a grip on this yet.

He retrieved booties and latex gloves from his go-bag, then locked the car and collared the nearest uniform.

"Where's the scene?" he asked, the lack of niceties inspiring instant surliness in his colleague, who mutely pointed towards the house.

"Wrong," Barnes said. "Get these people back. Get a guard on and get a scene log going. I want the whole street cordoned off."

The uniform made to object, but Barnes cut him off again.

"Where's your sergeant?"

Barnes marched up the path to the front door. He stopped halfway and turned around to the sulking uniformed

144

officer he had just left. He took his warrant card out and held it up.

"For your scene log. Since you didn't ask."

Barnes arrived at the front door as Tam Bates emerged from the house, visibly flustered. The requirements of scene management would have filtered through eventually, just not fast enough for Barnes.

"Tam, who's the PC back there? He's like a tit in a trance . . ." Barnes's voice tailed off. Bates was ashen. Barnes softened his tone a little. "What's happened?"

Bates shook his head. "Reeve . . ."

"Where is he?"

"In the ambulance. He cut her throat. They . . . they hit him on the head. Batoned him. Unconscious."

"Who's 'they'?"

"Couple of mine."

"Okay, Tam. It's okay. We need to lock this place down. I need the street cordoned off, and we need to get the neighbours right back."

"The whole street? I haven't got enough staff for that."

"Relax, Tam. I'll sort out resourcing with the duty inspector. Just get it done. Where are the officers that hit Reeve?"

"In the ambulance."

The last of Barnes's already scarce sympathy evaporated.

"With Reeve? Are you nuts? They're all *crime scenes*. Go and get them out of there!"

Two powerful black Audis pulled up outside the house, and six heavily armed men in protective helmets and face masks emerged.

"Oh great," Barnes muttered. "Time for *Assault on Precinct 13*. Guys, it's okay." He moved back down the path, waving his arms and showing his warrant card. "Party's over. Target's been neutralised."

The team leader tilted his head, as if he were trying to work out whether Barnes was taking the piss.

"Where is he?" he asked.

"Shortly to be en route to hospital. One of the local guys took a baton to his head. He's sparko."

"Who are you?" the team leader asked.

"DI Barnes. This is my command now."

"I'm calling Silver."

"Fill your boots, chap."

The firearms officers retreated to the car and began to remove their kit. They milled about, disappointed that they had missed the fun, their adrenaline pent up and with nowhere to go. One of them got down on the deck and started doing press-ups.

Barnes frowned and turned back to Bates.

"Tam, get your officers at the hospital relieved. Get them back here, and—"

"I walked in, I thought — can't remember the last time I saw a bright red carpet in someone's house. Then I realised it wasn't the carpet."

"Tam, give me your radio."

Barnes realised Bates was in full-on shock. He took him to the edge of the garden and sat him down on a low wall.

"Put your head between your knees and take deep breaths. It'll be okay," he said, looking around for help.

He found it in the form of DC Sofia Johnson. She approached him from the cordon in a thick coat, her Appalachian-dark hair stuffed up under a beanie hat, her warrant card around her neck.

"Sofia? I'm bloody glad to see you. I thought you went home."

"Don't go there," she said. "I don't even want to talk about why I'm sitting at home alone listening to the radio chatter off duty. Sad doesn't even begin to cover it."

"Well, regardless. It's good you're here."

"What do you need me to do?"

"Be nice to Tam, for starters. Then be nice to the armed guys, whom I've just pissed off."

"I can do that."

"Then get the cops out of *that* ambulance and into a fresh one. Then we'll talk. I'm going in here."

"Roger that, guv."

He went to the front door, feeling momentarily reassured by Sofia's unconditional acceptance. She cracked on without question when it mattered.

He looked back at her before entering. She was squatting down in front of Bates, a hand on his shoulder. The sergeant was staring into space, the stripes on his shoulders still crisp and new from the packet.

Barnes stepped inside and saw what Bates meant. At the edges of the living room, the carpet was the colour of ivory, but between the sofa and the counter separating the living room and the kitchen, it was an unrelenting crimson.

There was nobody else in the room. Amanda Luis's body was in the space between the back of the sofa and the kitchen counter. Barnes moved towards her, sticking to the edges of the room. She lay on her back, staring up at him, limbs splayed as if attempting to run for cover. The gash on her neck was an angry black, her dead white face frozen in horror.

The carpet was soaked through with her blood. A police-issue baton lay nearby that, Barnes guessed, belonged to one of the officers who had tried to remove Reeve from his hostage.

Barnes pulled on the gloves and crouched down. He touched the edge of the red kidney-shaped mess that Amanda Luis was lying in. It squelched under his touch and dripped from his finger when he lifted it. Barnes imagined the floorboards below, stained with dark red like varnish.

He stood up. Most cops get philosophical at domestic murder scenes about the senseless end of life. But if Barnes had been baffled by James Reeve's decision to escape from custody, then his decision to end his partner's life was positively bewildering. They had been a stalwart couple — he had tolerated relentless intrusion from her ex-husband; she had stood by him during the investigation and in the slow forests of uncertainty ahead of the trial.

Why kill her? Why did she have to die?

He looked around the living room, trying to pick out anything that could be easily missed in the carnage.

There was nothing obvious at all. A more nondescript living room probably didn't exist. Armchairs, television, coffee table, photographs dotted around the wall and on the mantelpiece of the fake fireplace. The only conclusion he could draw was that it didn't look like they had children — something he pretty much already knew.

Barnes stepped out of the living room and back into the hallway. He suddenly needed air. His eyes were stinging and he realised he'd been mouth-breathing. He made to go outside and noticed, for the first time, a suitcase with a holdall perched on top of it right by the front door. With his gloved hand he gently tried to lift them, and stumbled backwards when they came up easily.

They were empty.

"What the hell?"

He went back into the living room and looked again at the photographs. Mostly shots of Reeve and Luis as a couple on days out — Beachy Head, Cooden beachfront, what looked like Hever Castle. There were a couple of older ones of a couple dressed for the races — Amanda's parents, he presumed.

He picked one up off the coffee table — Reeve standing behind Mandy outside the Houses of Parliament with his arms wrapped around her, her hand touching his forearm.

Barnes squinted — they were both beaming, but the smile didn't quite reach her eyes.

The arms wrapped around her — a possessive gesture?

Her hand on his arm — subconscious — *let me go*?

Was it possible the relationship wasn't quite as rosy as hitherto portrayed? It was a sketchy theory based on just a picture, but it couldn't be discounted. It would need corroborating.

Barnes looked over at her body and imagined her screaming: *What more corroboration do you need!*

The picture was full-length — had they gone with a friend? Or asked a passer-by to take it?

Barnes put it down. Could have just used the timer.

He went outside and stood for a moment on the tiny front lawn. He pinched the bridge of his nose and tilted his head to the sky, trying to banish the visceral imagery dominating his brain in favour of the logic and reason that he was supposedly being paid for.

His concentration was short-lived, however. A tremendous caterwauling from somewhere at the end of the road, followed by muffled shouts and scuffling feet on concrete, interrupted his thoughts.

He walked out of the garden and peered down the road. There seemed to be some ruckus involving a crowd on the scene perimeter, but it was fifty yards away, so all he could make out was yellow jackets and general movement.

He grabbed his radio and demanded a sitrep on talk-through.

"All good here, boss," replied one of the constables on scene guard. "Jean Tully's just screamed that one of the local crusties tried to touch her up on the cordon. All sorted now."

"Someone taking her complaint?"

"Guessing you've never had the pleasure, sir," said the constable, stifling a snigger. "No, she's been locked up for section 5 and assault PC."

"And the crusty, so-called?"

"In the wind, I'm afraid. I'd have liked to get his side of it."

"Are you serious?"

"Sir, if there was an assault I'll eat my hat."

"What'd he look like?"

"Tall, about forty, thick beard, parka with the hood up. That's about it in the dark. He lolloped off towards the woods."

Barnes made a mental note that the constable hadn't paused to get the description off somebody else. He'd seen him himself.

"Sir? You still there?" said the constable.

"I'm here. What's your name, officer?"

There was a reciprocal pause.

"Lamb, sir."

"And I think you were saying an assault suspect — sexual or otherwise — got away in front of a cordon full of cops."

"Yeah. But at least it's quiet again."

* * *

By the time Shaw arrived — at the same time as the press — Barnes had pulled together enough of the initial scene management to give his boss the reassurance that had been absent when he himself had arrived.

Scenes-of-crime officers were bustling in and out of the house under the watchful gaze of their senior. A coroner's officer had arrived, as had the Home Office pathologist. The cordons had been pushed back to encompass the whole street, much to the vexation of the other residents. All in all, Barnes thought as the press rolled up, they now at least *looked* like they knew what they were doing.

15

Riaz and Knight sat in silence, the ambient sounds of the A&E department chattering in the air around their heads.

They were sitting in a broom cupboard of a room that was usually used by family liaison officers to console bereaved relatives. The attempts to decorate it in a less clinical manner, one that offered some comfort to the distraught families, were token at best. The sofa was a charity shop donation in a floral print, vases of small purple flowers adorned filing cabinets and the coffee table was decorated with leaflets from various support services. These seemed to have been indiscriminately chosen — the drug rehabilitation, bereavement counselling and child abuse advice lines had all been lumped in together.

Riaz stared at these for a moment, then his eyes rose to meet Knight's. She was pale, solemn, but calm — although her eyes were a little glazed. Like him, she was, he knew, replaying the moment that Amanda Luis's throat had been opened up.

Reeve was still unconscious, cuffed to a trolley in the resus bay while he was treated. Knight and Riaz had been relieved by four PSU officers, and were now awaiting a ride back to the station. The DI — some bloke Riaz didn't know — had sent instructions for them not to drive, not to do anything. They were scenes, the DI had said, and they needed to be carefully controlled. No washing. No disposing of anything.

Riaz looked down. He could hear Knight breathing. His hands were caked with blood. Most of it belonged to Mandy Luis, but some of it was Reeve's — Riaz had been surprised when the third baton strike had opened up his head.

Blood encrusted his nails and cuticles like the toils of a lifelong labourer, and when he flexed his hands, opening out the grooves and hollows in his palms, white cracks appeared in the red like dried paint.

Riaz knew the Force's support mechanisms would soon be galvanised into action. Support from welfare, supervisors, counselling sessions, critical incident debriefs — it would all come tumbling forth with precision to ensure the officers were properly looked after.

But Riaz knew it would all be too little, too late. These were the crucial moments, the moments when you were left alone, not knowing what to do, knowing there was plenty you couldn't do, alone with your thoughts — these moments and what happened during them could shape and influence the rest of your life.

Knight was still staring at him.

"Anything like this ever happen to you before?" he asked. His voice was a ragged croak. From shouting? Or was there blood on the back of his throat? It felt like it.

Knight shook her head, but that was enough. The tears began to come. She held her palms up and covered her face.

"Hey, don't cry," Riaz said. "You'll wash away all the evidence. You heard the DI. We're *scenes*."

Knight coughed a laugh through the tears. Riaz got up to sit next to her. He deliberately wedged himself close to her. He could feel her warmth.

"You did a good job, Claudia."

She tried to smile. "You too, Airplane."

A uniformed sergeant appeared in the doorway. An older man, in his fifties, with squares of grey at the temples. Riaz didn't recognise him.

"Riaz? Knight? Come on. DI wants you back at the station."

"Where's Bates?" Riaz asked.

The sergeant looked solemn. "He's had a bit of a wobble. I've been pulled over from Hastings."

There was silence in the car on the journey back to the patrol centre. Riaz sat in the front. Now, alongside the sergeant, he saw the warrant number on his shoulder, underneath his stripes, and, like the flash of a camera, remembered that his name was John Callaghan.

Riaz could tell from Callaghan's expression that he was not uncomfortable. He had experience and was not searching for something helpful to say. He knew sympathetic platitudes and small talk would be pointless.

At the patrol centre Callaghan let them out. Riaz made to walk in the front doors, the way he had done hundreds of times in his three years as a patrol constable. Callaghan stopped him.

"Sorry, Riaz. Not that way."

"What are you talking about?"

"I'm to stay with you, and you can't go that way. DI doesn't want you taking the same route as other officers. Cross-contamination. There's a route marked out. Follow me."

They followed Callaghan around the side of the building to the locker room, a prefab single-storey hut separated from the main patrol centre by a small concrete yard.

Inside the hut they were met by a plain-clothes officer. Riaz didn't recognise her either.

"You been pulled over from Hastings too?" he asked.

The plain-clothes officer didn't answer. Despite the low artificial lighting, she wore enormous sunglasses, partially hidden by a mane of thick walnut hair. She was chewing gum and clutching ten or so brown paper evidence bags. With her was a short, dumpy woman wearing a scene suit and a nose ring. Callaghan slipped out of the locker room without another word.

"You the DI?" Riaz asked.

The chewing stopped.

"Hardly. DC Sofia Johnson, CID. SOCO needs to swab your hands. And some other bits." She looked at Knight.

The SOCO with the nose ring produced a number of exhibit bags and swab kits from a flight case.

"You need to be separated, really," she said.

"I'll go make some coffee," Riaz said.

"I'll get the coffee," Johnson said. "You sit over there." She made for the door.

"Is this really necessary?" Knight asked.

Johnson stopped and turned. "You're scenes," she shrugged.

Riaz glared at her, but said nothing. He sat on a large crate.

The SOCO laid out a large paper mat, and Knight stood on it. The SOCO clucked softly and sympathetically while she worked at taking swabs of the blood from around Knight's hands, face and neck. She took fingernail scrapings and hair combings. The sounds she made were gentle — largely meaningless, but Riaz realised that it was helping. Eventually she rolled up the paper mat and laid out a new one.

"Get as much of it as you can," Riaz said while she swabbed his hands. "I've got blood from both of them on me."

"Any idea which is which?" she asked.

"On my hands is mostly the victim's. Neck and above, probably his. Probably his," he repeated.

Johnson returned with coffee in mugs that Barnes recognised from the patrol kitchen — one with a yellow smiley face and a blue one that read, "KEEP CALM AND LET THE COPS HANDLE IT!" Johnson smiled broadly at Knight as she handed her a cup.

"All done," the SOCO smiled, and breezed out.

"Can we wash now?" Knight asked.

"Certainly," Johnson said. She held up the paper evidence bags. "For your uniforms. Put one item in per bag. One shoe per bag only. Don't seal—"

"DC Johnson, I've seized and bagged clothing before," Riaz said.

"Your belts can go in as they are. No need to take all the bits off them." Johnson acted as if she hadn't heard. "We need jewellery as well."

Riaz looked down. He was wearing only a cheap digital watch. He stole a glance at Claudia's hands. She had a gold band on her ring finger, the small diamond just visible under the dried blood. She began to slide it off.

"You got something you can put on?" Johnson asked.

Knight and Riaz exchanged glances.

"I haven't," Riaz said. "I change into my uniform at home."

Johnson produced a cellophane bag containing a blue tracksuit. Riaz recognised it as having been borrowed from the cell block — the tracksuits were regularly given to prisoners who had their clothing seized for forensic purposes.

"Are you serious?" he said.

"Just until we can get you some of your own clothes. When you're done, leave the bags here and report to the DI."

Knight and Riaz went their separate ways to the male and female sections of the locker room and shower and reunited ten minutes later. Knight had washed her hair. It was still wet and she hadn't bothered to put it back up. Riaz hadn't realised it was quite so long. She was wearing the T-shirt and jeans she had travelled to work in.

"Looks like we've got an escaper," she said when she saw Riaz in his tracksuit.

"Funny," he replied. "Feel better?"

"Loads," she said.

"Shall we go see the DI?"

They were interrupted by the ringing of Knight's mobile phone. She pulled it out, looked at the display and then answered it.

"Hello?" she said softly, moving far enough away from Riaz that he could not hear the conversation, although he got the gist. She kept saying she was fine, a hint of protest in her voice, and glossed over the details of what had happened.

Riaz edged closer. Knight held up a finger. He remembered what Lamb had said and imagined some jockstrap on the other end of the phone, blowing and blustering and promising to use all his influence to make sure she was all right. She muttered something like *see you later* and ended the call.

"Sorry about that," she said as she walked over.

"After you," he said.

They crossed the yard to the patrol centre. The DI's office was in the farthest corner, and as they walked across the open-plan office all the other officers stopped what they were doing and watched Knight and Riaz in silence as they walked across the floor.

"Feel like I've been summoned to the headmaster's office," Knight whispered to Riaz.

They loitered outside the closed door of the DI's office. After a moment or so, Riaz knocked.

"Come!" called a voice after a moment or two.

The two of them walked in and stood uneasily in front of the desk, behind which sat a slim man in a well-cut suit, tapping a pencil on the edge of the desk. His right foot rested on his left knee. Riaz thought he would have been quite good-looking, if not for his slightly grey complexion and watery, very tired eyes.

"You can sit down," the man said. "I'm DI Barnes. I don't think I know either of you."

Riaz thought he was right. He knew the district detective inspector was a relatively new arrival called Barnes, but that was all he knew, beyond the rumour that the guy had a funny first name.

The DI called Barnes stood up and shook hands with them. He would have been about six-two had he stood up straight. His shoulders were hunched forward, giving him a slight stoop. Riaz initially put him in his early forties, but then realised he was quite a few years younger.

Riaz and Knight sat down at a small circular meeting table while the DI poured them some coffee from a cafetière on his desk. The office was another whitewashed plaster-board broom-cupboard. The corkboard behind his head featured only a large map of the district. A stack of files was balanced neatly in his out-tray, ready for sending to the Crime Management Unit to be archived. The only view from the window was a solid metal fence and a stack of wooden pallets belonging to the factory depot next door.

The DI was meticulously tidy — the desk was clear apart from the cafetière, a computer screen, his notebook and pen and two framed photographs, both of an attractive, dark-haired woman. There were three quick ways to tell a lot about person, Riaz mused. Bumper stickers, slogan T-shirts and the photographs they kept close at hand.

Barnes passed cups of coffee round. He hadn't asked them whether they wanted any or how they took it. Black without frills seemed to be how you drank coffee with the DI.

"You're a serious coffee drinker, sir. You take your booze like this too?"

Barnes didn't answer.

"Have you two made any notes?" he asked.

"No," Riaz said. Knight shook her head.

"Good," Barnes said. "Tell me what happened."

"Shouldn't we . . . be separated or something?" Riaz asked.

"Perhaps," Barnes said. "But if you two had a story to concoct, you've already had a chance to do it. And besides, wouldn't that imply you had done something wrong?"

"Isn't that why we're here?" Knight asked.

Barnes turned to her and raised an eyebrow.

"What gives you that idea?"

Knight said nothing, but gestured at Riaz in his cell block–issue navy-blue tracksuit.

"It's not very becoming, I grant you," Barnes said. "Look, I know you two have had a rough night, and that being swabbed and scrubbed by SOCOs and having your uniform seized gives you a certain perception about how your actions are being viewed. But . . ."

"We're scenes?" Knight offered.

"Indeed you are, and I'm afraid the need to preserve forensic evidence on you is of paramount importance. And as far as people making snap judgments about your actions — well, no one really knows yet what happened. Except you two."

Riaz and Knight exchanged glances. Riaz took a deep breath.

"It was a domestic call. Male subject holding female partner at knifepoint."

"That was the original call?"

"Yes. I guess it was called as an SFI from the off."

"Indeed it was." Where a 999 call made mention of an offender armed with a knife in a hostage situation, Force Command and Control generally classified the call as a spontaneous firearms incident, which meant the deployment of armed officers — along with the authority to use their weapons.

"It was all still kicking off when we got there. I kicked the door in, and he was there holding her by the neck."

"Where was the knife?"

"At her throat."

"Then what?"

"We tried to speak to him. Negotiate. He was wired on something, wouldn't listen. It wasn't possible to reason with him, sir. Knight did better. He seemed to respond to her."

"PC Knight?" Barnes turned to look at her.

"I think that's right, sir, but I agree that he was completely irrational. I think it was the sound of a female voice, rather than the words, that he may have found less threatening." Her eyes flicked to Riaz.

"And then?"

"And then?" Riaz said. "Then he stuck the knife into her neck and cut it open like he was opening the post."

Knight flinched.

"What did you do?"

"I hit him on the head with my baton."

"How many times?"

"Four. It took four to subdue him."

Barnes stood up. "Would you say it was like this—" he mimed an overhead smash like a tennis pro — "or like this?" The mime switched to that of a cricketer bashing a textbook square cut through the covers.

Riaz and Knight exchanged glances.

"The first, I guess. He was a bit taller than me, so . . ."

"And then?" Barnes sat down again.

"PC Riaz handcuffed the subject, while I tried to administer first aid," Knight said. "Once he was under control, PC Riaz helped me try to staunch the bleeding, but it was obviously useless."

"Is there anything else you haven't mentioned?"

Riaz's shoulders slumped a little.

"FCC said no entry to the house by unarmed officers. Broadcast it over the air. We . . . *I* went in anyway."

"Did you?" Barnes said with exaggerated seriousness.

"Look, we could hear them from outside. I didn't know how far away the ARVs were."

"Miles, as it happens. I was there before they were."

"Well, then. I couldn't stand there and do nothing. He was going to kill her."

Barnes said nothing. Riaz realised what he'd said.

"I know he killed her anyway, but at least we tried to stop him. I don't know if I could live my life if I'd stood outside and let it happen. I made my call based on what we could see and hear — which was considerably more than someone sitting miles away at headquarters."

"Just so I'm clear — you hit Reeve with the baton *after* he had cut the victim's throat?"

Riaz went cold.

"Are you . . . are you saying I've done something wrong?"

"He's still unconscious. Gone for a CT scan." DI Barnes's face remained impassive. "I just want you to know this whole thing's going to get worse before it gets better."

He stood up.

"Don't speak with any of your colleagues. Make your notes, the two of you. You may confer for accuracy, with my say-so."

"Are you sure?" Knight asked.

"If you were suspected of an offence then you wouldn't be writing *any*thing. Once you've made your notes, go home. Take tomorrow off. A couple of DCs will be in touch to interview you properly."

Riaz and Knight stood up.

"Sir, how bad will this get?" Knight asked.

"PC Knight, from where I'm standing, you did the right thing in difficult circumstances."

Relief crossed their faces.

"Although how much that will count for in the long run, I have no idea."

Riaz and Knight made to go.

"PC Riaz?" Barnes called. "That thing you said about not being able to live with yourself if you'd done nothing. Remember it. I think a jury will like it."

Riaz's eyes widened.

"Just in case," Barnes said.

* * *

Outside, Riaz and Knight walked to their cars. They stopped as they prepared to go their separate ways. The patrol centre was dark now, the slow hum of the mixers from the all-night industrial cement plant opposite the only sound.

Riaz felt a sudden urge to debrief the debrief, but then, with an ache of weariness, he pushed the questions away.

"You okay?" was all he said. "Do you . . . have someone to . . ." His voice tailed off, unsure of how to finish the sentence.

160

She nodded.

"How about you?"

"I'll be all right," he said, not wanting to mention that the only person at home was his mother, and if he did try to explain, she would cluck and coo sympathetically — but without any real understanding of what had happened.

"Don't give me any macho bullshit," she said. "You're not all right. Neither of us are. You don't deal with it now and you'll implode in about ten years."

In spite of himself, he smiled at her insight.

"Look, Claudia, I plan to go home, drink half a bottle of whisky, pass out, and have my hangover interrupted by the wheels of the welfare machine. I'll be fine."

They turned to see four or five officers sprint out of the patrol centre and hop into the vehicles. The patrol cars went haring out of the station, blue lights flaring in the darkness.

"Looks like a good one," Riaz said.

"Call if you need me, okay?"

"You too."

He watched her walk to her car. She cruised slowly out of the car park. He waited until her tail lights were out of sight, then he followed suit, the sirens still audible in the distance.

16

Barnes closed the door to his office and sat down at the desk, rubbing his face with his hands. He hadn't quite slept in the office, but he may as well have done.

He stared at the star-shaped conference phone as if in a trance and compared the time on his wristwatch with the time on the wall clock. They were exactly the same.

They were also perfectly in sync with the phone, which started its gentle trill at exactly nine thirty. Barnes knew it would, knew that anxiously checking the time was a completely unnecessary habit born of the inescapable anxiety that descended in the run-up to morning prayers, albeit the lack of sleep had taken the edge off the usual hyper-awareness. Barnes knew that, across the division, inspectors and chief inspectors alike were in a similar state of tension — a state gleefully cultivated by the chair, Chief Superintendent Gabby Glover.

Whose no-bullshit tone cut in as soon as Barnes accepted the call.

"Good morning, everyone," said the disembodied voice. "Everyone here?"

No answer. It seemed a fatuous question for a conference call.

"Okay," Glover said after a four-second pause. "Let's start with the critical incidents. Who's got command of this domestic homicide? Operation Kansas?"

Barnes cleared his throat and leaned — both unconsciously and unnecessarily — towards the conference phone.

"I've got that one, sir," he said. "It's Barnes," he added.

"Looks messy, Barnes," Glover said. "What's the update?"

Barnes thought of the carpet slicked with Mandy Luis's blood. It certainly was messy, but not in the way Glover meant.

"Op Kansas is the investigation into the murder of Amanda Luis by her ex-partner, James Reeve," Barnes said. "Reeve escaped from court five days ago where he was on trial for manslaughter — that investigation was Op Biscay . . ."

"Yes, yes," Glover said, irritability creeping into his voice. "I don't need chapter and verse. Just brief me on the key points."

"While at large Reeve went to the victim's house — their common-law house — and killed her in front of the two responding officers."

"In *front* of them?"

"Yes. Hostage situation. He was holding her at knife-point, and they attempted — unsuccessfully — to talk him down. He killed the victim, and the officers used baton strikes to subdue him. He's now in a coma under LST guard on the ITU."

"As a result of the batoning?"

"Yes, sir."

"Fucking hell," Glover said, deadpan. He sniffed a couple of times — an indication, Barnes believed, that he was thinking. "Why is this the first I'm hearing about this job, Barnes?"

"Sir, Force Gold was called out for the DSI . . ."

"Never mind that. This is *my* patch. A courtesy call as a minimum would have been nice."

He let the silence hang.

"Understood, sir," Barnes mumbled.

"Presumably, ADI Barnes, if he had escaped from custody five days previously, we'd have been monitoring his partner's house?"

"Yes, sir. Static OP in the street and a RIPA for her phone billing."

"So how, then, did he manage to find his way in without us knowing?"

"OP was part-time."

Glover raised his eyebrows.

"What bit of you thought that was going to be a good idea?"

Barnes knew the correct answer — *because you wouldn't authorise the cost of 24/7 staffing and some decent covert tactics, like proper surveillance* — would have made the hole he was in even bigger.

"Sir, there was no intelligence about a threat to her. She stuck with him throughout the prosecution and had been anti from day one. They were a devoted couple, and she would have helped him get inside the house without detection."

"So devoted that he decided to cut her throat open?"

Barnes said nothing, but felt the heat rising in his own throat.

"Let me summarise, then," Glover said. "See if I've got this right. Manslaughter defendant escapes court during a part-heard trial. He somehow evades our subsequent dragnet with such efficiency that he can stalk his hitherto dog-faithful partner — not only that, but kill her right under our noses. So not only do we fail to prevent his escape, then fail to prevent her murder, but we subsequently put him in the hospital *after* he's done the deed — a bit like shutting the stable door after the horse has bolted. I miss anything?"

"I don't think so, sir," Barnes said, his lips tight.

"Fuck me, the *Daily Mail* is going to have a field day. I think you'd better brief me in person, DI Barnes. Come see me later this morning. I'm free at eleven. Right, next. Who's running this rape in St Leonard's?"

"That would be me, sir," piped up another voice.

Barnes hit the mute button and slumped back in his chair while a similar exchange took place between Glover and the Hastings DI. He had no further updates for this meeting, but he remained online until the bitter end. To do otherwise would have been both sacrilegious and impossible — the conference phone had a tendency to interrupt all conversations to loudly announce — in automated tones — the departure of one of the delegates.

Barnes didn't hear a further word that was said during the conference call. Morning prayers — or the daily management meeting — was a command-led meeting to scrutinise all ongoing incidents of note. The small matter of Op Kansas — and its originating investigation, Op Biscay — was top of the agenda, and despite Glover's supercilious tone, Barnes could see why. It was going to be difficult to keep this one out of the press.

* * *

Glover didn't wait till eleven. The conference call ended at twenty minutes past ten; Barnes's mobile rang three minutes later.

"Sir," Barnes said, pressing the device to his ear.

"Barnes, this can't wait. You free now? I'm in my office."

Glover ended the call without waiting for an answer. Barnes slipped the phone into his pocket and headed out to the car. His was the corner office, and so he had to traverse the patrol centre's entire open-plan office to get to the main doors.

Eyes followed him as he passed — usually because if the bosses had it tough in morning prayers, then they tended to emerge from their offices to fire a rocket up their team's collective backside. It was well known, after all, that shit slides downwards. But Barnes hugged the walls and met no one's eye as he walked out to the car.

The patrol centre in Hammonds Drive was a single-storey building that sat in the heart of the town's industrial core, overlooked by two huge gas containers and an array of tanks in the nearby Finmere Road gas works.

Barnes waited for what seemed like a lifetime for a gap in the traffic and pulled out onto Lottbridge Drove for the short but torturous run to the police station in the town centre.

His already brittle tension was not helped by the challenge of parking. All the police bays out the front of the station were full, and Barnes knew better than to park illegally in a police fleet vehicle. Such images had a tendency to make the *Argus*.

In the end he found a space that was more Meads than the town centre, but he forced himself to walk at a normal pace to Grove Road.

Barnes nodded *good morning* at DJ as he passed the front counter and buzzed himself into the inner vestibule. He climbed the circular staircase to the first floor, his heels echoing in the brown concrete stairwell, and padded across the royal-blue floor tiles to the waiting area outside Glover's office.

When Barnes walked in, Glover was standing at one of the full-length windows in purple rubber gloves, apparently feeding Baby Bio into a small window box bearing flowers Barnes could not identify.

He waited in the open doorway.

"Nice of you to show up," the chief superintendent said, not looking up.

Barnes said nothing.

"Shut the door," Glover said. He put the trappings of his miniature gardening kit on his desk and perched on the edge of it. He gestured for Barnes to sit at the small circular conference table next to it. To the casual observer, the act was innocuous, perhaps even unconscious, but Barnes knew better. They were both sitting — Glover casually, Barnes stiff and attentive — but the height differential was one of an arsenal of calculated psychological tactics that Glover had doubtless spent a lifetime acquiring, presumably at great expense.

Barnes stared at Glover, who held his gaze but didn't immediately speak. He shifted uncomfortably until a thin, lipless smile crossed Glover's face.

"Judge Gavin called the chief. Wanted to know why one of his jurors is dead and how his defendant escaped a secure dock."

Glover snapped off the gloves.

"Judge Gavin apparently doesn't like his homicide trials to crash and burn unless he's the one doing the crashing and burning. Chief could have taken it better. He was three over on the ninth when he took the call and trying to get out of the rough. The only thing that went down a hole was his cigar."

Barnes suppressed a sudden, irresistible urge to swallow.

"There'll be a Gold Group for this, Barnes. IPCC will be breathing down our necks too. That's why I want us to be able to talk before we can't without every single thing being documented or minuted."

"Yes, si—"

"But I'll tell you this — it's going to get worse before it gets better. We could have prevented that woman's death, and, on the other side of the coin, we nearly killed the suspect — some might say pointlessly."

"Sir, I—"

"When I say 'we', I mean, of course, 'you'."

Barnes, preoccupied by his body temperature dropping a couple of degrees, said nothing. Glover's strategic intentions were slowly becoming clear.

"What's the prognosis?" Glover asked.

"For Reeve?"

Glover said nothing, just stared at Barnes as if he could not have asked a more stupid question.

"Not good, sir," Barnes said. "He's still in a coma. They're talking about transferring him to Hurstwood Park Neurological."

"The excessive-force complaint we can wear," Glover said. "It's only a small piece of the pie when you compare it with our failure to protect a victim of domestic abuse."

"Sir, she wasn't—"

"You're not hearing me, Barnes. The chief just wants the genie back in the bottle so he can finish his golf game."

"Yes, sir."

"The officer that batoned Reeve."

"Riaz. Works response. Young lad. Three years in."

"I know that."

Barnes started to feel distinctly out of his depth. Whatever agenda Glover had brought to this meeting, he had prepared for it and had not shared it with Barnes.

"We need to make an example of him, Barnes," Glover said.

"I'm not sure that . . . I think his use of force in these circumstances was justified, sir."

Glover did that stock-still-silence thing again, and Barnes started to wonder if he was doing so to impart thoughts telepathically. If he was, then the thought Barnes read behind his boss's eyes was, *So what?*

"We'll be subtle, Barnes."

"He's a good lad, sir. Very clever. Think he might be on the spectrum."

"Even better. In fact, I might even give him a job up here first, rubbing shoulders with some brass. You know, cushion the blow while his head's spinning, that kind of thing. Tell him we're worried about germinating PTSD or some nonsense, if you have to dress it up."

Glover got up and went to the window, not looking at Barnes's aghast face. He clasped his hands behind his back and stared out at the street.

Barnes stood up.

"I've played this game before, sir, and I—"

"I know you have," Glover interrupted, without looking around. "You do remember what we discussed in this office not five months ago? About that business you and that fuckwit Paul Hadian cooked up a few years back? About the fact that you're lucky to still have a job, let alone your stripes. You remember who *gave* you those stripes, yes?"

Barnes was silent.

"Yes, I thought you might. Acting pips too. They can be taken away in a heartbeat. And that hurts — when you've been acting so long you've got used to people calling you 'guv', everyone just thinks you must have been demoted.

"People have good memories when they want to remember something," Glover continued. "No one will forget your past, either. Not as long as there's someone around to remind them. Now, is there anything you need from me?"

Barnes swallowed — and found his tongue in so doing.

"To be perfectly honest, sir, I'm not staffed for this. I've got a cracked manslaughter trial that's mutated into a domestic murder and a fugitive enquiry. A bit of help from the region wouldn't go amiss."

Glover eyed him for a moment, then walked over to the window, hands clasped at the small of his back.

"Some cheeky prick has parked his Porsche in a police bay," he said, squinting out of the window in an exaggerated fashion. "Do us a favour, Barnes. Write a ticket for the thing on your way out."

* * *

"Your career must be doing well," DJ said. "You look dreadful."

"Thanks, DJ. I look that bad?"

"If I had a pound for everyone that came past here saying good morning, and then left with tunnel vision, I could retire all over again. It's got worse since the new bloke started."

"Great."

"You see a lot from behind here," DJ said, flicking the kettle on. "What's on your mind?"

Barnes let out a deep sigh.

"I'm not sure. You mean the case?"

DJ smiled, and leaned against the counter.

"Whatever's on your mind."

"The case is a strange one. I've got a victim in the mortuary and a killer in the hospital. It's cut-and-dried, and the family isn't creating — probably because there isn't much of one to create — but the *why* is giving me sleepless nights."

DJ didn't say anything, but raised his eyebrows.

"It's not the case I have a problem with, though, really. It's . . . everything else," Barnes said, waving a hand in the general direction of Glover's office. "All the extraneous bullshit. All the politics. And feeling shit all the time. You have the word 'acting' before your rank and they hold you to fucking ransom with it . . ."

"Who'd have thought you could weaponise ambition, eh?"

Barnes snorted.

"You could fit all my ambition in my little finger, these days."

He sighed again.

"Sorry, DJ. You don't want me to rant."

"Trust me, that wasn't a rant."

"How are you, anyway?" Barnes asked.

"We're good here. We're all good. Listen, if the *why* is that hard to come by, it might be because you're looking too hard."

"You could be right," Barnes said, sipping the coffee which DJ had handed him.

"You get out much?"

He could have used any words, but what he was asking was, *How are you coping since your wife's death?*

"Not much, if I'm honest. Tried to get back into the running, but . . ." He tapped his gammy leg and then patted his belly. "Routine helps, though. If it wasn't for the work . . ."

He stopped, suddenly aware of what he was implying. DJ must have noticed it too.

"You ever notice," DJ said, "how some people think listening and giving advice are the same thing? It drives me mad."

Barnes got up to go.

"Thanks for listening, DJ. For asking how I am. It's been a while."

"Any time. *Nil carburundum illegitimi*, as they say. You remember that time I called the sergeant's desk and you answered?" DJ said. "I came through to the wrong number, but you still tried to help me."

"Yeah?"

"Most others would have said *not my problem* and hung up. Don't change, eh?"

Barnes gave him a crooked smile.

"Listen, Deej," he said, shrugging his jacket on. "You worked Op Vestry and Op Hexagon, right?"

"In rapid succession. Managed to get the kitchen *and* the bathroom done on the overtime."

"How did they — you — finally get him? Acosta?"

"Hunch, persistence and luck. In that order. And it was 'them'."

17

Why did he do it?

Barnes used the token effort at housework as a means of stimulating his thought processes, which, by and large, was a complementary relationship. Running the hoover over the lounge, folding laundry — or, in this case, finishing the dishes in silence — were tasks that all seemed to be grist to the mill of his grey matter. And the house got clean. Not that it ever really got dirty. You had to be home for that.

His thoughts were interrupted by a knock at the front door. Barnes dried his hands on a tea towel and opened it to find a nervous-looking boy toeing his front path.

"Hi, Aidan," Barnes said, scanning the street before bringing his eyes back to the boy's. "Are you okay? Is Eleanor . . . is your nan all right?"

"I'm sorry to bother you," Aidan mumbled in recital. "Please could I have my ball back?"

"Your ball?"

"I kicked it into your garden."

Barnes relaxed, and gave the kid a grin.

"Of course you can. Want a biscuit?"

Aidan shook his head mutely.

"Okay, well, come on through."

He opened the door and stood aside — Aidan stepped in and stood awkwardly in the hallway. Barnes led him through the house and into the garden, making nonsensical chit-chat as he did so.

The ball was new — a bright, fluorescent orange thing with geometric designs and logos stamped all over it. It was nestling like a trophy in the middle of the lawn — upon seeing it, Aidan pushed past Barnes on the decking and pounced on the ball with relief, like it was the lost treasure of Atlantis.

"Any others while you're here?" Barnes said from the deck.

Aidan gave a cursory sweep of the square garden.

"I don't think so."

"Well, if I find any, I'll throw them back."

This time Aidan led the way back in — Barnes watched his head turning this way and that, taking in the sole cup and plate on the draining board, the scattered photographs of Eve — and he wondered if the questions that were forming would find their way to the surface. No toys, no mess, no evidence of anyone at all besides Barnes's entirely functional existence.

"I was worried you might be angry," Aidan said on the doorstep.

"Angry?"

"Mr Wade gets angry when the ball goes into his garden."

"Does he now? Well, Mr Wade has clearly forgotten how important it is for Premier League footballers to never miss training. Are you a Gooner?"

Aidan screwed up his face.

"Spurs."

"Good man."

Aidan gave a confused smile. Barnes reached out to ruffle the boy's hair, then stopped himself for reasons too numerous and nebulous to name.

The boy gave a funny little bow, then scurried off, orange prize tucked under his arm.

* * *

173

Barnes leaned forward on his elbows and pushed his drink around the table. The same could not be said of his friend Hamilton Tate, who had downed half his pint within a minute of sitting down. He was ahead of Barnes by about three to one.

"Come on then, officer, where are you in the hunt for Mr Reeve? My conviction rate is in dire need of shoring up, and the fact that you keep letting my defendants escape isn't helping."

Barnes groaned inwardly. Tate was in a playful mood — although he was admittedly well lubricated.

"Well, I suggest you try and book yourself onto a floater. Reeve's could be what you call a vacated trial."

"I'll say. You haven't found him, I take it."

"Oh, we've found him."

Tate's eyebrows shot up.

"There's a holding press release. Details very scant — just enough to keep the rags at bay."

"That generally means the police haven't a clue."

"Funny. You want to hear it from the horse's mouth, or what?"

"*Mea culpa*, detective. Please continue."

"Mandy Luis is dead. Reeve confronted her at the house. He cut her throat. The two officers that arrived took their sticks to Reeve, and he was taken comatose to hospital."

Tate's drink froze halfway down his neck. He slowly put the glass down.

"That's the abridged version," Barnes said.

"I . . . I don't understand," Tate said, the shock having penetrated his cocksure mask slightly. "Why did he do that? I thought they were a pretty tight-knit couple."

"Your guess is as good as mine," Barnes said. "It made no sense that he tried to escape in the first place, much less the fact that he subsequently decided to end the life of the woman who stuck by him throughout the investigation and trial."

"A woman who, one might say, was indirectly responsible for him being incarcerated in the first place."

"I don't think that's quite fair. The *relationship* may have been indirectly responsible, but that's love, isn't it?"

"My God." Tate scratched his chin and stood. "Excuse me a moment. Get another round in." He fished out a fifty-pound note and dropped it on the table.

Barnes picked up the note and looked at it. He knew Tate well enough to know he wasn't showy — at least not with Barnes — but he found it equally difficult to believe that this was simply pocket change for the barrister. Maybe it was. Barnes looked around him. The bar was filling up. He would make his excuses soon. Tate apparently had a big session on the cards, and Barnes didn't want to get sucked into it.

Tate came back and sat down.

"Is this why all you lawyers only drink in this pub? Anywhere else, they'd think you were passing a fake. I guess they don't bat an eyelid here."

"Your tone is bittersweet, officer."

"I certainly don't remember the last time I saw a fifty, much less held one."

Tate leaned across the table and swept his thick blond locks back over his head with his hands. They were the same age, Barnes thought, thirty-five or thereabouts. That age when you were either getting serious about setting your stall for the future, or you already had more miles on the clock than your calendar let on. Barnes knew which side of the fence he fell on — Tate had no lines, no grey, and none of that watery translucence that age and stress brings. In fact, he thought, if Tate was the portrait, then Barnes was Dorian Gray.

"Look at yourself, Barnes," Tate said, looking left and right conspiratorially. "You know as well as I do that you're wasted in the police. You could have so much more." Tate's voice was thick with promise.

"Do you mean the fifties?" Barnes nodded at the cash on the table.

"You know why I left, Barnes? The police service just wasn't *fast* enough for me. I felt like a bird in a cage. The rank structure and job opportunities were all too rigid for me to flex my muscles."

"You're too good for the police. Is that what you're saying?"

"Call it what you like. But you can calculate, with a reasonable amount of accuracy, where you will be and how much you will be worth when you hit retirement age. Don't you find that depressing?"

Barnes suddenly found Tate's insight to be like a fish-hook inside his cheek. He remembered the ambitious fire he'd had in his early service, and also how he'd pissed it all away.

"You know as well as I do that I'm going no further, Hamilton."

"Exactly! Now for me, I could make partner, I could own my own practice — the sky's the limit."

"You're not wrong." Barnes leaned forward and brushed a speck of white from Tate's nose. The lawyer gave him an exasperated look. Not even slightly worried.

"My advice to you? Get some books, go to night school, get your law degree. We could work together."

"I'm heading off," Barnes said, tapping his nose. "I've enough on my plate without having to make association disclosures to ACU. The forms are monstrous."

"Well, thanks to your colleagues my schedule has suddenly cleared, so if it's all right with you I'm going to stay and party."

"Alone?"

Tate winked. "You know me better than that, detective. You could join me, you know."

Tate's eyes burrowed into him.

Barnes stood up and put on his jacket. He opened his mouth to speak, but then just nodded and turned to go.

"*Carpe diem*, Barnes," Tate called after him.

Barnes walked to the doorway, where he stopped and turned. Tate was already on his feet and had sidled up to a pinstriped associate. If he didn't already know her, Barnes thought, then the guy truly had balls of brass.

Barnes tried not to feel that he was being supercilious, but although he knew all too well the reasons why he had side-stepped into a life of unassuming austerity, he nevertheless felt like Tate was accusing him of cutting off his nose to spite his face. As he watched the young barrister's hand slide to the woman's rump, he did just wonder. After all, she was a cracker.

* * *

Why did he do it?
    Why did he do it?
    Why did he do it?

The moon cast blues and blacks all around the bedroom as Barnes lay in the milky half-light, eyes fixed on the ceiling, palms flat on the mattress.

He thought of what Tate had said. Cocaine aside, there was no real reason why he couldn't have hung around a little longer and tried to be a little more sociable. He was, after all, technically single.

He thought of what DJ had said. The whys shouldn't be that hard, and if they were, you were looking in the wrong place.

He rolled over on his side and looked down at the grey space where his wife used to sleep. Barnes imagined it was still indented with the shape of her body. He'd thought about replacing it, maybe even getting a single bed, but he spent so little time there, it seemed pointless.

Eventually he gave up and padded downstairs to the phone.

"Morning, Comms. ADI Barnes here. I need—"

"Sir. Permission to interrupt," said the controller on the other end of the phone. Barnes recognised the voice — Colin Hind was like DJ's malign twin, a retired cop whose toxic brand of cynicism, insubordination and laziness had infected the entire control room. "You do know it's two thirty on a Thursday morning, yes?"

"I do."

177

"Normally it's us calling you in the middle of the night. Something must be very wrong."

"I need a logistics log created. Link it to Op Kansas, the Mandy Luis murder."

"Hold on—"

"I want the crime scene reopened. We searched the house, but I want it torn down. I want wall cavities, floorboards, foundations, the lot."

"Do you—?"

"She was killed for a reason. The *way* she was killed — that was someone who wanted something from her, and she didn't want to give it up. I want to know what it was."

"Okaaaaay. Anything else?"

"Yes. I want the night-turn senior SOCO called out, and a search team jacked up for daylight. We'll need a couple on scene guard, and I'm going to need some plant to excavate the garden."

Barnes heard a distant throaty laugh in the earpiece, in some dark corner of the control room.

Hind cleared his throat.

"I can create the log, tag it for briefing, send it to the SOCO queue and do the callouts. The rest is up to you, I'm afraid, sir."

"You can ask the night-turn sergeant for the scene guards, though, right?"

"I can ask, but I imagine she'll be straight on the phone to you."

"Do what you can, but don't hurt yourself," Barnes said, so earnestly that Hind either missed the sarcasm or it just glanced off his rhino-hide exterior.

"You're going to be pretty popular, guv," he said. "Why don't you just go back to bed?" He clicked off the line.

Barnes stared at the phone for a moment, feeling a sort of detached numbness in his brain that was masking the anger he might normally have felt.

He knew even attempting sleep was pointless, so he drove to Eastbourne's District General Hospital and parked in one of the spaces outside the Accident and Emergency

Department reserved for emergency service vehicles. He stuck a laminated notice on the dash that bore the police crest and the words "RUTHERFORD BARNES — DISTRICT DETECTIVE INSPECTOR". It carried no legal weight as far as parking enforcement was concerned, but he would have been interested to have it tested in open court.

Before he got out of the car he reclined the seat ever so slightly, just to ease some of the pressure on his gradually growing stomach. His frame was still slim, but there was now a definite absence of creases on his shirt front where the stomach stretched the material.

The benefits of five miles a day, six days a week, at less than seven minutes a mile, had quickly disappeared after the crash. He'd had the physio, and the rehab, and the pain meds, but all he could manage these days was a mile-long hobble once or twice a week.

Running had given him all the things the health editorials promised — a chance to clear his head, get a handle on things, remove stress and avoid things like depression. Now, with his dicky chassis making him draw a line under his running habit, he could feel these things creeping in insidiously.

He cut through the main A&E department and headed for the ITU on the first floor. The corridor was lit with an unreal blue tinge that made him think of acetone. The smell of disinfectant fighting a losing battle against vomit was heavy in the air.

He found himself thinking about the bottle of single malt on his kitchen counter. There, he knew, was the real insidious treachery — the fact that his exercise had decreased in direct proportion with the increase in his alcohol consumption. From being a serious teetotal runner to thinking about his next drink with as much neutrality as if working out a shopping list — there was no pleasure in it; that had passed. His last remaining stained-glass window of self-deception was the fact that he didn't make special trips to the shop to buy the stuff; the bottles and six-packs now just slid into the trolley — harmless, just part of the weekly shop.

He frowned to himself. He had been raised to place faith in science, making him agnostic by default — this Christian guilt was completely out of character. Despite everything, he still drank for pleasure.

Didn't he?

The ITU was silent apart from the twittering of the various machines and gasps of artificial breathing. Barnes held his warrant card up to the ward clerk, who glanced at it long enough to register total disinterest, and walked over to the patient.

As he approached the bed his pace suddenly slowed, the urgency of his step staunched by some childhood fear of dead bodies suddenly coming to life.

The man had a gaunt, ratty-looking face, with a tattoo of an iron cross on his forearm and five-day growth on his face like a scattering of grey iron filings.

He was utterly still, the only life coming from the rhythmic chirp of the machines surrounding his bedside, and the rise and fall of his artificially inflating lungs.

Apart from a black, swollen left eye, much of the damage done to the patient was not visible. The large dressing on his head already needed changing. It was covering an apparently significant wound — red was beginning to seep through the gauze, like a blob of jam in a bowl of semolina. His head was swathed in bandages, his hands clasped. He looked peaceful, as if he had been laid out in a casket ready for his final deliverance.

Barnes frowned. There were three things troubling him about the image presented to him. Firstly, the officers who were meant to be guarding him were not here. Secondly, two tubes — that Barnes assumed should have been attached to the patient's cannula — were hanging loose off the pump.

But the third and most troubling thing was that the man in the bed, whose peaceful countenance Barnes now regarded, was not James Reeve.

Not by a long shot.

18

Barnes walked over to the nurses' station, where a solitary nurse sat engrossed in reports, the top of her head illuminated by a pale blue halo from a desk lamp. Stray brown strands of her hair glowed like filaments in a light bulb.

"Where are the officers that were with that patient?" Barnes said. His voice shuddered as he tried to keep it under control; even so, it was loud in the otherwise silent ward.

The nurse jumped and looked up at him. He held up his warrant card with a slightly quivering hand, and recognition appeared on her face, although it didn't displace her obvious irritation.

"Password?" she said.

Barnes shut his eyes. "Lighthouse," he said, after a moment's thought. "The officers . . ."

"Yes, I heard you. They left an hour or so ago."

"Did they say anything?"

"I wasn't here, but Sister said they told her a new risk assessment had been done and they were no longer needed."

"Did you . . . did anybody check that?"

"I'm not sure why you're asking *me* that, but does he look dangerous to you? The only thing he's guilty of is stealing oxygen."

Barnes couldn't suppress a smile. That was a police neologism if ever he'd heard one. The nurse was only young — maybe late twenties — and he wondered if she was married to a cop. He couldn't see a ring, but that didn't mean anything in this place. Barnes suspected jewellery had a tendency to slip off in the most awkward of locations.

"Do you have a swab?" he said, his mind returning to the small fact of identity theft being as likely as oxygen theft at that moment.

"A what?"

"A buccal swab. I need to swab him."

"What for?"

"DNA."

She frowned. "I'm not sure. Hold on."

She got up and went to a small cupboard mounted on the wall. She stood on tiptoe and rummaged around inside for the best part of a minute, removing tongue depressors, syringes, oxygen masks, a blood pressure monitor and a handbag.

"Anything will do," Barnes said. "Even a toothbrush. Or a cotton bud. I just need to—"

"Nothing in here. That kind of thing will be in the treatment room. Hang on a sec." She made to go.

"It's okay," Barnes said. "Thanks. I've got a kit in the car. I'll go down and get it."

"Are you sure? I could—"

"Honestly, it's fine. I should do it properly for the sake of a few minutes. Especially as I have a horrible feeling that this is one of those times where doing it properly is going to be very necessary."

The nurse sat down again. "I'm Annie," she said.

"Thanks for your help, Annie. I'm Barnes," he said, giving her a smile. Then he turned on his heel and left the unit.

The faintest curtain of daylight was stretched over everything as Barnes went back to the car. The pre-dawn air was warm. The fronds of carefully planted shrubs that lined the hospital grounds were dark against the mauve sky.

There was a go-crate in the boot of the car, containing scene tape, traffic cones, gloves, an early-evidence rape kit, wet-print ink packs and a bounty of polythene evidence bags. Barnes rooted around until he found a buccal DNA swab kit and a couple of the exhibit bags.

He shut the boot. At the main entrance, something made him pause. He turned to look back at the car and checked his watch. Half three. Over by the entrance to the emergency unit was a lone patient in a white gown, complete with drip stand, smoking like her life depended on it. In the sallow artificial light from the ambulance bays, she looked like a ghost.

Besides her, there was no one else around. There was a light breeze coming in from the south-west that was making the shrubbery whisper. Barnes put his trembling sixth sense down to meteorological anomalies and stepped inside the hospital's main foyer.

As he climbed the stairs to the second floor, it vaguely occurred to him that the trembling sixth sense was what caused cops to pull over certain cars and find them stolen, to stop someone loitering on a corner and discover them preparing to rob a shop, to investigate things that were somehow not quite right, and to be rewarded by the uncovering of criminals hard at work.

It was a buzz, no doubt, Barnes thought as he stepped onto the second floor by the south bank of lifts and turned into the main corridor. It made him think of that young constable — Riaz. He was a good officer, and could go far, provided he wasn't permanently sidelined by the current investigation.

The tall, dark figure emerging from the ITU was wrong — his pace, his gait, his clothing, the time of night — it was all wrong. Barnes froze in the corridor as he weighed up his next move.

Barnes had never been shot at before, and, despite his vocation, his brain became a vacuum for rather longer than he would have liked. It took him a good second or two to work out what was going on.

At first — like an idiot, he would recall later — he thought it was a sudden thunderstorm. The muzzle flash was startlingly bright, but the sound of the explosion was deafening in the corridor, an obliterating bass thump and resonating crash that seemed to fill his head.

He thought he actually felt the compressed air whistle against him as the round torpedoed past his head and embedded itself in a yellow, wall-mounted machine that dispensed pre-pay phone cards.

A shrill ringing met Barnes's ears as he got himself together, but the shooter was already at the far end of the corridor, having put his head down and sprinted the minute he pulled the trigger. There was a moment's hesitation while Barnes's instinct for self-preservation wrestled with his obligation to run towards the danger, but it filtered through that a better chance for apprehending an armed suspect might not come again. He could count his blessings later.

He stuffed the swab kits into his pocket and ran — limped — to the end of the corridor, yanking his radio from his belt as he did so. He jabbed the red button on the top of the handset, which broadcast an emergency status-zero call — officer needs urgent assistance — and interrupted all other transmissions as a priority call.

"Shots fired, Eastbourne DGH," he yelled into his radio. "Male offender, six foot, dark clothing. Foot pursuit, second floor. Heading from the ITU to the . . . north stairwell."

The corridor, on this level, led more or less directly to the north bank of elevators and stairwell. Barnes slowed his pace for a second. Beyond the lifts were four surgical wards, and there was nothing to suggest an armed man had thundered into one of them to seek refuge. In any case, none of them featured a way out, and so Barnes hedged his bets and opted for the stairs.

On the ground-floor elevator bank the offender had the option of charging west down the main corridor and out through A&E, hanging a right and into four more dead-end orthopaedic wards, or carrying on down to the basement level and out through one of the delivery entrances.

The last option was the most likely, but Barnes felt sure he would have been able to hear the man if he had continued running down the stairs. As it was, he could hear nothing. He muted his radio and stood for a moment with a hand on the guard rail, his leg twinging, the blood pounding in his ears, straining to listen for noises out of place — screams, thundering footsteps, sounds of violence.

None came.

The shooter could have gone to ground somewhere in the hospital. It was well and truly out of hours — there would be any number of offices and clinical stores and treatment rooms that would afford excellent hiding places.

Barnes took tentative steps down the stairwell to the basement level. He stepped out into the dimly lit elevator bank and held his breath.

The floor was utterly silent.

To his right, immediately underneath the orthopaedic wards, stretched a corridor that led to the restaurant and pharmacy. Beyond that the north exit door led to a staff car park and the unlit expanse of land that lay between the hospital grounds and the neighbouring college. There was a small staff smoking room just before the exit.

If the man had not gone this way, his only other option was back towards the south exit, which opened out onto the staff residences. This would involve traversing the main corridor, effectively doubling back on himself and back through the medical wing past the physiotherapy clinic.

North would get him out of the building quicker, but the intensive care unit was closer to the south exit. Had Barnes not disturbed him, this would, in all probability, have been his favoured route. Both options avoided the front of the hospital and thus the areas of heaviest footfall, even out of hours.

Barnes moved back towards the main corridor. He tried not to dwell on the fact that the mortuary lay to his right. The place was secure, however; his armed quarry was not getting in there unless he was wheeled in, and so Barnes moved back towards the area where, two floors above him, a round with his name on was lodged in a vending machine.

He inched forwards, eyes straining in the gloom created by the artificial night lighting, taking shuffling steps so as not to betray his presence to anyone else. The corridor stretched away before him — the pathology lab on his left, plain white walls with no escape routes to his right.

With his quarry out of sight, the enormity of his near miss began to descend upon him, and his steps became ever more reticent as fear began to spread through him like a deep freeze.

Beyond the pathology lab the walls on the left became windows leading out onto black gardens. Barnes's hand went back to his radio, more for comfort than anything. He couldn't hear the chattering voices, but he could feel them vibrating in the set. In terms of protection, he had the radio, a small torch, handcuffs and a tiny canister of incapacitant. The man had already fired. He could — and probably would — fire again, especially if cornered. Barnes had no doubt that the control room inspector was desperately trying to get him back on the air, doubtless to tell him to withdraw, take cover and report.

Which suddenly seemed like a sensible plan. Unaware that he was doing so, Barnes moved to the right and hugged the edge of the corridor, his back sliding over the white wall, his eyes trying to fix on a point in the gloom ahead of him.

At its end the corridor turned right ninety degrees. To reduce the risk of collisions there was a convex mirror mounted high on the left-hand corner wall, but in the half-light it was impossible to see clearly.

Barnes got to within ten feet of the end of the corridor and froze.

Footsteps.

Coming towards him.

He crouched down low and focused on the convex mirror. His hand went to his radio; then, for all the good it was going to do, he decided he'd be better off with his hands free.

186

Why is it always me? he thought as the dark figure passed by. He launched himself from his crouch and thumped into the man in a low rugby tackle.

The man took the hit with a *whoof!* sound, and the momentum carried them into the opposing wall. Barnes's fingers got caught between the man's weight and the wall, and he yelped with pain.

The man was already starting to exclaim; Barnes brought his knee up into his midriff and knocked the remaining wind out of him.

He went to the floor a dead weight and curled into a ball. His face had contorted with pain, and he managed "*What the . . .*" through clenched teeth. Barnes flicked his torch on and deduced within half a second that the man at his feet had probably not fired a gun at him in the last five minutes, or indeed ever. The jangle of keys and the crackle of the radio at the man's belt caused Barnes to think for a moment that he might have been a colleague, but then he saw the pale-blue short-sleeved shirt and NHS logo, and realised that he had actually floored a night porter on his rounds.

Barnes crouched down and took the man's arm.

"I'm the police. There's an armed man in the building. I thought it was you. I'm sorry. Do you understand?"

The porter allowed Barnes to help him to his feet. He nodded understanding, but wasn't quite up to talking. He was a small, sinewy man with spectacles and a bald head, and navy tattoos sleeved his forearms almost down to the wrists. The name badge on his breast pocket said DUNCAN.

Barnes opened his mouth to apologise again, but he was interrupted by footsteps and shouts from above.

Barnes froze, unwittingly clamping his fingers down on Duncan's shoulder as he strained his ears to listen. Several sets of footsteps, running from south to north. It was too soon to expect the cavalry — they were good, but not that good. Barnes's eyes roved above him like spotlights, as if sheer will could bring them to penetrate the layers of plaster and concrete above.

It was no longer a pursuit. It was a search.

"How many of you are there?" Barnes said, unable to keep the alarm from his voice.

"Four. And a team leader," the porter wheezed, leaning back against the wall. "That's me."

"Sorry about that. Listen, get your team to all the exits and keep them on their toes. Cops are on their way. Keep an eye out."

The porter shook his head. "One . . . one of us needs to go to . . ." He jerked his thumb at the sound of the activity from above. "Cardiac arrest."

It was only then that Barnes realised the porter's bleeper was going off. He caught the words *"Crash team . . ."* from his radio, and realised that their position on the corner down here in the catacombs was two floors directly below the ITU.

He left the porter clutching his stomach and ran towards the stairwell.

"Get them to the exits. Don't get shot."

It was fatuous advice for a cop, let alone a minimum-wage civilian armed with nothing more dangerous than a torch and a bunch of keys, but Barnes consoled himself with the fact that, in certain situations, some people could surprise you.

He bolted up the stairs to the second floor as fast as his protesting leg would allow. He was just in time to see a flash of white from the coat of the doctor bringing up the rear of the charge. But by the time Barnes burst into the ward proper and saw the activity around Reeve's bed, with doctors and nurses clamouring to tend to the rapidly deteriorating patient, Barnes knew it was too late.

He edged closer, the formerly steady chirps and beeps now riddled with urgency, the arms of a doctor locked tight as she pumped the chest of the man in the bed as if she were trying to cure a misfiring engine. There was a pillow on the floor, spotted with blood.

Barnes turned his attention to a secondary tableau — the nurse called Annie was on the floor by the nurses' station, being helped into a sitting position by a colleague. Blood dripped from a wound in her scalp.

He moved over and squatted beside them.

"What happened?" he asked.

"In case you hadn't noticed, she's been assaulted," the colleague snapped. "She's not quite up to talking."

"I need to know," he said in a quiet voice. "Annie?"

"A man," she said. She was clearly in pain, but her eyes were clear. "Came in here. Just after you left. Hit me with something hard. Then . . . I don't know."

"Here, hon. Press this against your head," Annie's colleague said, handing her a compress. "How many fingers?" She held up a hand.

Behind them, the continuous whine of a flatline was a sudden counterpoint to the decline in activity. The crash team started snapping off gloves. The lead clinician called out the time.

"Is he . . . oh, God. Is he dead?" Annie said, her voice rising half an octave.

"Listen, this is not your fault," Barnes said.

He stood up.

"It's ours. It's . . . mine."

19

It was too soon, and they both knew it.

Too soon to get back in a patrol car, too soon to go racing around Eastbourne, tense with anticipation at whatever the next call might bring.

There had been little conversation to start with — both were all too aware of what had happened the last time they had patrolled together.

It was an early shift, however, and the first couple of calls had been relatively innocuous — fender bender and a burglary report — and after an hour or so the pair started to relax.

Then a 410 came over the air.

"Echo-Echo two-zero-one, attend 359 Seaside. Report from neighbour that they can hear a child crying inside the address. Informant has knocked on the door but with no answer. Mother's car is on the driveway."

Riaz acknowledged the instruction and spun the car around, feeling Knight's eyes on him. He didn't meet her gaze. Calls like this could mean any number of possible explanations.

Seaside was a long, straight road leading east out of Eastbourne town centre. It ran parallel to the seafront and diverged inland where the seafront parades followed the coast.

Number 359 lay opposite the Archery Rec, beyond a tranche of takeaways, second-hand shops and ethnic cafes. The house was a tiny end-of-terrace cube with a view of the rubble next door that remained following the demolition of the Roselands working men's club.

Riaz parked and they approached the front door. Knight knocked while Riaz took a step back and scanned the face of the row of houses. A net curtain twitched at the house next door, and an anxious face peered down at them. Their informant, no doubt.

Knight's knocking yielded much the same result as the neighbour's. She pressed her ear up against the front door.

"I can't hear anyone crying," she said.

The curtains of the front room were drawn, and the small crack where they met showed nothing but darkness.

Riaz wedged the letterbox open with his baton.

"Hello?" he called. "Is anybody there? It's the police."

Nothing. Riaz inhaled deeply through his nose, concentrating his senses on any untoward odours.

He found them. Excrement, he thought, and a faint tang of rotting meat.

"Anything?" Knight asked.

He didn't answer, but instead turned to meet her gaze. She swallowed and went to the living room window.

She returned a second or two later.

"Blowflies in the window," she said.

Riaz stood up and planted a boot against the front door. The frame splintered, and a piece of metal clanged to the floor on the other side.

Two more kicks and the door flew open. The Yale lock flew out of the frame and spun across the grimy brown lino-leum that just about covered the hallway.

The smell hit them both as they stepped inside. It was like a thick curtain, cloying in its warmth.

Riaz felt a sharp pain in his wrist. He looked down and saw Knight's hand gripping his arm. He looked at her. Her breathing was shallow, her eyes wide. The hand on the arm had been unconscious.

The crashing open of the front door had prompted a small voice to start crying from somewhere near the back of the house.

Riaz and Knight moved forward to the kitchen. The crying got louder as their footsteps moved closer.

They reached the kitchen doorway and stood shoulder to shoulder. At first, they could not see the child — the room, little larger than two phone boxes put together, was piled high with crap.

The counters were stacked with dirty dishes that had been there for months. The floor was invisible, caked as it was in rubbish — cigarette ends, beer cans and soiled nappies.

The boy could not have been more than two. He was naked and grimy, huddled in a corner, staring up at them with bright, scared, red eyes.

His face was wet with tears, which had caused the dirt on his face to smudge and stain.

Riaz moved forward a step, whereupon the toddler mewed and scrambled over an overflowing rubbish bag.

Knight put her hand on his shoulder. Riaz stepped back, and as Knight moved forward towards the boy, making soft, comforting noises, Riaz left the kitchen and moved through each room of the house.

The living room was as squalid as the kitchen, with every conceivable surface and piece of furniture littered with old food, soiled clothes and nameless rubbish. Riaz wondered if the smell permeated the walls through to the neighbour's house.

There was nobody in it, however, and as Riaz climbed the stairs he knew he was not going to find a dead body. Had the child's mother been here, the boy would almost certainly have been found with her body. The boy alone in the kitchen suggested he was likely alone in the whole house.

Three minutes later, after a search of the upstairs rooms, Riaz's theory proved correct.

He went downstairs and sifted through the pile of post. By comparing the postmarks on the letters with the date of an opened letter on a shelf in the hallway, Riaz guessed that the boy must have been alone in here at least four days.

He went back into the kitchen, wondering how the kid had survived. As he walked in, he saw Knight cradling the child, cooing to him. Her eyes were brimming with tears.

He looked at the floor, and saw something he hadn't noticed first time around, but which gave him his answer about how the child had survived.

On the floor was a line of digestive biscuits, like a trail of breadcrumbs, each with a single bite taken out of it.

Riaz stared at them for a second, and, just as he felt his eyes begin to sting, the control room called up, asking him to report to John Callaghan. Sergeant Tam Bates had been staring at his bedroom wall for the best part of a week, and John Callaghan's temporary stint as substitute had been extended further.

Riaz made sure Children's Services and CPT were rolling, and then called in.

"CID have an arrest tasking," Callaghan said on the phone. "Rape suspect. Go straight there, okay? Don't wait for the radio to get busy. And mind your Ps and Qs — the perp is a lawyer or something."

"We have to be polite?" Riaz said.

"Just don't forget the caution. And tell the control room when you leave, when you arrive, and what route you've taken. Give them your odo readings too. You know what lawyers are like — the journey between the scene and custody is a black hole they just love to fill with bullshit in a courtroom. Full details on serial 0167, okay?"

Riaz drove, while Knight read the tasking on the MDT. It was only a couple of pages long, a scant arrest plan put together by the night DC that sought to ensure, among other things, that no hairy woodentop would forget to seize the perp's clothes as evidence.

"He's no ambulance-chaser. He's a barrister. Callaghan was right. Don't cock it up," Knight said.

"You want to say the words?"

"Don't mind. I trust you."

"What is it, domestic or something?"

"Doesn't seem to be," Knight said, scrolling through the log again. "Office party gone wrong, maybe."

"Better get him before he wakes up properly, then. You know what lawyers are like."

* * *

Hamilton woke suddenly, the early morning sun warm through the glass of the large bay windows in his Victorian Meads apartment. He was lying flat on his back, but felt like he was falling. Whatever he had consumed along with the scotch, it had done a good job on him.

He got up and moved gingerly to the bathroom. He gazed at his reflection in the mirror while he urinated, and noted he was in a vest and boxer shorts. He hadn't been so wasted as to sleep in his clothes, which he supposed was something, but he had no memory of getting undressed. In fact, he had little memory of anything. He didn't remember getting home.

"Shit," he said, peering closer at the mirror, where a scratch on his neck and a red welt under his collarbone had caught his eye.

He went back to the bedroom, intending to check his phone, but was delayed en route by a wave of nausea. He steadied himself on the wooden bedpost, but by the time he had picked up the device, he was again interrupted. This time, by a loud, sharp rapping at the front door.

"Who's that?" he muttered to himself. Hangover or not, it was early by anyone's standards.

He shuffled to the front door, noting through the frosted glass that there were two people at the door, all dressed in black.

The possibility that they might be Jehovah's Witnesses evaporated in the time it took to answer the door. He registered first that they were cops, secondly that both wore devices on their stab vests that were blinking with a steady red light.

Being a generally pro-police lawyer — not to mention an ex-cop himself — Tate didn't react with the same blend of suspicion, defensiveness and worry that most people did when the cops turned up unannounced.

That is, until the male officer opened his mouth.

"Mr Tate? Hamilton Tate?" the male officer said, moving himself into the doorway without waiting for Tate's reply. He looked Asian. "I'm PC Riaz. This is PC Knight."

The officer called Riaz didn't get his handcuffs out, but he did make sure he was right in Hamilton's personal space — presumably in case the lawyer was about to make a run for it.

"I'm afraid you're under arrest, sir."

"I'm what?" Tate finally found his sandpapery tongue.

"On suspicion of raping a female adult. Last night, at the victim's home address. You're going to have to come with us, I'm afraid, but we need to come in first."

While PC Riaz gave him the caution, Tate let fly in protest.

"You mean the girl from the pub? She was like a banshee! Look at my neck. And I've—"

"You'll have your chance to give your side of it later on, on tape, with all the usual rights and safeguards," PC Riaz said. "But you spoke over me just now. Let me just say again: you don't have to say anything. Okay?"

Tate closed his mouth. His brain had kicked in about the same time as PC Riaz had effectively cautioned him for a second time. He was a human first, a lawyer second.

"We need to come in," Riaz said again, moving inside the flat. He still didn't handcuff or otherwise lay hands on Tate, but there wasn't a spider's leg between them.

"Any kids here? Pets? Wife?"

"Just me," Tate mumbled.

The three of them moved in formation like a land crab around the flat, so Tate could be witness to the search and any subsequent seizure. As it was, it was a brief search for two reasons. One, the size of the apartment. And two, it couldn't have been easier.

They found the clothes the lawyer had been wearing the previous night — which was more than he had managed — carelessly discarded on the sofa. They found his phone on the bedside table. And on the lounge coffee table, they found his wallet, keys, cigarettes — and a small baggie of cocaine.

* * *

Riaz placed the plastic tray inside the microwave, deliberately putting the cardboard sleeve in the bin in a manner that meant he did not have to read the ingredients.

Bagging, tagging and writing up had taken several hours — Riaz had seized the brief window of opportunity to eat before another call pulled him away.

Such were the perils of shift work. At 2200 hours on a busy late shift, or close of play on an early turn when the calls hadn't stopped and there had been no time to eat, the pull of the fast food stop or the microwave meal was just too convenient to ignore. The light of the vending machine out in the garage was like a hallowed beacon in the gloom, and it had heard the confessions of many hungry cops at four in the morning.

Riaz disappeared into his own thoughts, and began to hum while watching the LCD timer count down. He didn't hum any particular tune, but imitated, without drawing breath, the steady drone of the microwave as it worked.

He noted to himself that the drugs they'd found were not particularly helpful to the lawyer's case. He didn't otherwise have an opinion on the rape investigation, but his experience to date did lead him to think that surprised protests by a suspect were usually indicative of something.

The ones that knew you were coming — well, they never said a word.

Lamb walked into the kitchen.

"Christ, that microwave's loud," he remarked.

Riaz stopped humming and turned to look at him. The microwave resumed its normal volume. Lamb frowned. He opened his mouth to say something, and then stopped himself and changed the subject. "I'm afraid you're saddled with yours truly for the rest of the shift."

"How come?" Riaz said, reaching inside the oven and burning his fingers on the molten plastic.

"Claudia's been dicked with the prisoner handovers."

"Oh, great."

"Hey, I know I'm not as good-looking, but at least you can fart in the car."

"You're a charmer, Pete. You eaten?"

"Yeah, had a little pizza not long ago."

Riaz glanced at him. Lamb's little pizzas often took two people to deliver them.

"Okay, I'll eat this and be with you. Any taskings?"

"Not so far, my friend." Lamb moved closer and assumed a conspiratorial tone. "Anyway, what a thing, eh? Can't believe it."

"Can't believe Claudia's been given the prisoners?"

Lamb looked at Riaz like he was stupid.

"No, not that. You haven't heard?"

"Heard what? What are you talking about?"

Lamb inched closer.

"Someone topped James Reeve in his hospital bed."

"*What?*"

"Only it wasn't James Reeve at all. It was an imposter. Couldn't make it up, eh? Anyway, I'll see you at the car."

And then he was gone.

Riaz's brow knitted with anxiety as he tried to assimilate the casual, almost cheerful disclosure by his outgoing counterpart. An *imposter?*

He forgot about his food and stepped out into the corridor, then doubled back and peered out of the kitchen window at the car park. Post-1600 hours it had thinned out considerably and it wasn't hard to run a quick inventory of what was left.

197

There. Over by the gate. The same bloody maroon Avensis. Same index. The PSD double act were here somewhere.

Riaz stepped out into the corridor. It was empty. Where the hell were they?

He thought about it. Likely waiting for him in one of the offices, so he headed towards the gents and then slipped into the main office by the NPT entrance.

He peered around a rack of radio chargers and saw the DI — Barnes — by the entrance to the briefing room. He caught Riaz's eye and mimed stirring a large bowl with his finger, mouthing *go around*. Then he disappeared into the briefing room.

Riaz did not need to be told twice. He headed out the side entrance and around to the briefing room annexe. Barnes had pushed open the fire exit doors and he ushered Riaz in.

As Riaz stepped over the threshold he had the sudden horrible thought that Barnes could well have been the facilitator of his downfall, and that Fountain and Choudhury would form the welcoming committee.

But only Barnes and Claudia were there. She was sitting down, looking pensive. The DI stood in the middle of the room, hands on hips.

"PSD are circling," Barnes said.

"Don't I know it," Riaz said.

"Sit."

Riaz did so. Barnes showed them a photograph.

"Is this the man that stabbed Mandy Luis?"

Riaz exchanged glances with Knight.

"No," Riaz said, after a beat.

Barnes slapped the edge of a table with an open palm. "Goddamn it!" he muttered, addressing the ceiling.

"Who's that?"

"*This* is James Reeve," Barnes said.

"Then who did we . . . ?" Claudia said.

"Well, we couldn't get near him for prints and DNA all the while he was in the ITU," Barnes said. "Now he's dead we can pretty much do what we like with him."

He drummed his fingers on the arm of the chair and eyed them both.

"You never met James Reeve?" he said.

"Nope," Riaz said, while Knight just shook her head.

"What about the rest of the team?"

"You'd have to ask them," Riaz said. "I wasn't around for the Op Biscay call. Neither was Claudia."

"Did you recognise him when you confronted him?" Barnes asked.

"No," Riaz said. "Comms just said his name was on the history marker. He had no ID on him. I guess we just assumed. The only person who could tell us otherwise was Mandy, and she wasn't really in a fit state to say anything."

Claudia winced.

Barnes looked around the briefing room. A small gaggle of mosquitoes was circling unenthusiastically around the white strip light. The heat of the day radiated through the brickwork as the evening drew in.

"Let's go for a drive," Barnes said, suddenly springing to his feet. He headed for the fire exit; Riaz and Claudia exchanged glances again, then slowly got up to follow him, going wide around the outside of the building to avoid bumping into the two horsemen of the apocalypse.

They took Barnes's car, heading out of the patrol centre and south towards the Sovereign Centre. Barnes drove them along Royal Parade, the sea air doing little to break the thick summer drizzle.

"It's hot," Riaz murmured.

"Don't knock it," Claudia said. "You want to try some of the smog uptown."

"That what brought you here? Bit of sea air?" Barnes said, looking over at her.

"Partly," Claudia said. "That and 7/7."

She looked out of the window.

Riaz shifted uncomfortably in the rear seat. He stretched an arm out along the parcel shelf and looked out the rear windscreen.

He felt Barnes eyeballing him in the rear-view.

"I'll have you back in a jiffy," he said, cranking up the air conditioning. "I know you're late off."

"Don't hurt yourself, boss," Riaz said. "I'm in no rush. But I would like to know where we're going."

"I think better when I'm moving. And better still when I have other brains to bounce things off."

"Why would you need our brains?" Claudia asked. "I mean, we're just plod. You're the detective."

Barnes looked at her.

"That's the last thing you are," he said. "You're more than responders or witnesses. You are *actors* in this case, however much you don't want to be."

They passed Princes Park and drove along Marine Parade, where the sky was like a purple blanket stretched across the seafront guesthouses, with a few diehard guests gathered in the glass-fronted dining rooms like silver-haired hothouse flowers.

"So, if he wasn't James Reeve, who was he?" asked Claudia.

"Chris Jenner," Barnes said. "Twenty-eight years old. Regular bottom feeder. Heroin addict. Don't think he's been in town long — most of his convictions are up Salford way. Spent more time in prison than out of it, but his longest stretch was three months, and that was for commercial burglary. What does that tell you?"

There was silence. They passed Treasure Island, where the minigolf course was shrouded in darkness and the silhouetted pirate ship's flag hung limply in the still air.

Barnes turned off the seafront and headed west through Roselands. The journey took them into Hampden Park — and to the terraced shoebox once shared by James Reeve and Mandy Luis.

They got out of the Rover and stood on the kerb, facing down the building. The windows and front door were boarded and there was construction fencing around the perimeter, with the small patch of lawn snarled up into a churn of mud. Blue-and-white scene tape was wrapped around the outside, and it lay dark and silent, as if the soul had evaporated from it.

"There's not much left of it," Riaz said.

"I tore it up," Barnes said. "Everything but the rear garden."

"How come?"

"I ran out of money. Division wouldn't cover the resourcing. Said it was a fishing trip."

"And was it?"

"Partly. But that's what detective work is. Partly."

"Why did you bring us here?" Claudia's voice was strained.

"I want you to *think*."

"Think?"

"Don't worry, I'm not going to ask you inside. But take yourselves back. Think. Mandy Luis is attacked by Chris Jenner. The neighbours report the disturbance. The history marker mentions previous domestic violence and that James Reeve is an escapee. You've never met him before, and he didn't correct you when you called him James. Then, what with his being carted off to hospital, the delay in identifying him feels like a reasonable error, no?"

"Wait, wait," Claudia said, pinching the bridge of her nose. "Previous domestic history? I thought her and Reeve were thick as thieves."

"It wasn't him. It was before him," Riaz said. "Her ex. The guy Reeve killed. The trial. Tommy Gayle. The history information referred to her previous relationship."

"Right you are," Barnes said. "So, an honest mistake. The marker never got weeded after Gayle died. And the neighbour that called it in made the same assumption. But it doesn't answer why Jenner attacked her in the way that he did. I mean, what did you think when he killed her? That level of rage?"

"Domestic," Riaz murmured.

"Exactly. But no."

Riaz looked at him, then turned to face the house, examining it like an unforgiving surveyor.

"Maybe it *was* domestic," Claudia said. "Maybe her and Jenner were over the side, and he saw Reeve's absence as an opportunity for them to be together. Maybe she had no intention of doing so."

Her eyes glistened in the gloom.

"God knows what the neighbours must think," Riaz said.

"Can we please just go?"

"Well, that's kind of the point," Barnes said.

They headed back into town, past the hospital and along the old Lewes Road, passing where the Lottbridge Sewer abutted the Tutts Barn allotments.

"Quicker to go down Cross Levels," Riaz remarked.

Barnes said nothing.

They headed over Whitley Bridge, just as the last Ashford train of the evening began its slow journey out of the Eastbourne terminus. It groaned its way underneath them, a grinding ache of steel and sparks and filth, heading back over the Levels towards Hampden Park, where the East Coastway Line split like a zipper and the train would fork right towards Hastings and beyond.

Barnes took them back onto the seafront, heading up towards Beachy Head. They stopped at St Bede's, at the mouth of Helen Gardens, and Barnes got out of the car.

The sky had darkened over the Channel, and Hotel-900, the police helicopter, rattled slowly overhead, its powerful Nightsun scanning the black waves.

"Couple of weeks, traffic will be as bad up there as it is down here," Barnes remarked.

"The air show," Riaz said, seeing Claudia's blank expression.

"It'll be quite something," Barnes said. "That's assuming they can resolve the sponsorship fiasco, of course. You working it?"

"If I'm working at all, then I'll take it."

Barnes buried his hands in his pockets and looked out to sea.

"I practically knocked that house down because one motive for Chris Jenner losing his shit and killing Mandy is that she had something he wanted, and wouldn't give it to him."

"Like what? Drugs? Money?" Riaz said.

"I don't know. Whatever it was, I didn't find it — suggesting an affair theory is just as plausible. Whatever his reasons, a murder like that — in front of two cops, no less — tells me he was in very bad shape. He snapped."

"That makes it sound like her fault." Claudia folded her arms.

"Noted. You're right," Barnes said. "What I mean is: you don't just promote yourself from petty theft to murder, unless your circumstances materially change."

"And did they?" Claudia said. "He could have just always had it in him."

"What I know is: prison went from being just an occupational hazard to somewhere he was going to spend the rest of his life. At least, it would have been — until someone finished him off in his hospital bed."

The helicopter's staccato rotors grew fainter as it headed out to sea, then it rounded the headland in the direction of Beachy Head and disappeared.

"I have to ask you — because someone else will, sooner or later: where were you both when he was killed?" Barnes said.

"On duty," Claudia said, without hesitation. "Rest day overtime. Late turn responded to the call. We got turned out early to staff the search."

"And you?" Barnes eyeballed Riaz.

"Home," Riaz mumbled.

"You live alone, right?"

"He lives with his mum," Knight said.

Barnes looked at her, and then back at Riaz.

"You want to drag her into being your alibi? The way I hear it, she's pretty infirm. Slipping out for an hour unnoticed would be no great feat of subterfuge for you."

Riaz tensed as his blood rose, but didn't answer.

"Don't worry about it too much. You'd need to be dirty to get hold of a firearm, and you haven't been in long enough."

"Can I have that in writing?"

"I don't think it will count for much."

"What kind of gun was it?" Claudia asked.

"Shotgun. Legally held and stolen, most likely. We're cross-referencing it with burglaries in the region, but the list is surprisingly long.

"Imagine it, though: you persuade a control room operator to stand down a police guard, then walk in and smother your quarry with a pillow. *Then* you let off a round at a cop with the shotgun you brought with you just to make good your escape. What does *that* tell you?"

"Balls of brass," Claudia said.

"And then some."

"Definitely not an imitation?" Riaz said.

There was a pregnant pause.

"The round missed my head by about four feet. It definitely was a real bloody gun," Barnes said.

Fair enough, Riaz thought.

"And if Mandy Luis's murderer was not James Reeve, that means Reeve is still out there," Barnes continued.

Claudia's eyes widened.

"And someone killed the woman he loved? He's going to be mad."

"Mad enough to let off a shotgun at a cop?" Riaz wondered aloud.

They took turns staring at each other, just as Hotel-900 appeared overhead again. It hovered over the sprawling Gothic site of All Saints Hospital, encased as it was by construction fencing and arc lighting. The hospital proper had been mothballed a couple of years previously, and while the main building and chapel stood largely untouched — if dark and mournful — the rest of it was an impassable peat bog of churned mud and half-laid foundations.

"They're turning it into flats," Riaz explained. "Periodically get people breaking into the site to steal plant or copper. Usually it's just kids. Remote monitoring. Last time I was here I tore my trousers on the fencing, and then some geezer in a control room in Canterbury barked at me through their PA system. I nearly had a heart attack."

"Survived three wars, but couldn't keep out the developers," Barnes said.

Riaz and Claudia looked at him.

"Come on, I'll get you back."

20

The Avensis had gone by the time they returned to base. Riaz managed about another hour of his shift, but the noise in his head was like a constant, unrelenting whine. He could concentrate on nothing and when he felt the anxiety in his stomach become the beginnings of panic, he told Callaghan he had a migraine and drove slowly home.

He wasn't in the least surprised when, the second he got in, his phone trilled — a low, inoffensive chirping. He couldn't stand shrill noises or clever loud ringtones.

"Hello?"

"This is DS Phil Fountain."

For a second Riaz wondered if the man knew what he was thinking. He couldn't stop himself from wandering over to the window. He peered out at the boardwalk below.

"We popped in to see you. Where did you go?"

"I'm not at work. I . . . didn't feel well."

"Pity. Did you wonder how we identified him so quickly?"

"What?"

"There were four days between the late Mr Januarie handing you that bit of paper and his body washing up on the beach, in the middle of which you dismantled a drugs OCG single-handed and off duty."

Riaz wondered if the man sounded mildly impressed.

"In the intervening period between then and now you have also, it seems, killed a man."

Hearing it in these terms caused a feeling like icicles breaking from the ceiling and plunging into his stomach to hit Riaz. He found himself taking deep gasping breaths, and forced himself to listen.

"Listen, we know what it's like," Fountain said, all pally now. "You scoop up a body from the bottom of the Head and find three more you hadn't bargained for. They sit in a queue waiting for the — frankly overworked and underpaid — Coroner's Office to get around to identifying them. They couldn't get prints off your man — something to do with his mangled fingers — but the DNA match came back pretty quick. Want to know how?"

Riaz closed his eyes. Through the open window, he heard the sea.

"He'd been reported missing the day before. Reported by the cops."

He paused. A gang of seagulls screeched outside as they tussled over some unidentifiable feast splattered on the boardwalk.

"Turns out we'd been to his house, found signs of a struggle, and circulated him as a misper. The cop on scene had the presence of mind to seize a toothbrush. Why were we at his house?"

Riaz heard him breathing.

"The reason we were at his house was, he didn't turn up for jury service. The trial judge took a dim view of that, and demanded that an early-turn unit go and get him out of bed. Guess whose trial it was?"

Riaz closed his eyes. He knew the answer to that one.

"James Reeve," he said quietly.

"Correctamundo!" Fountain said. "How weird is that? He escapes, kills his partner . . ."

"That wasn't Reeve. It was somebody else."

"In either case, he didn't survive an encounter with you. Let me know if that piece of paper turns up, eh?"

"I told you: I shredded it."

"It's a miracle what they can do with that nowadays," Fountain said, and hung up.

Riaz dropped the phone and sat down heavily on an armchair, trying to concentrate on his breathing.

He gave no thought to the notion that another man in the same situation might have spent a fruitless evening rifling through the laundry and upending the bins. But Riaz didn't function that way.

He knew exactly where the damned little piece of paper was.

He went into the bedroom and retrieved it from between the pages of the Bible on his bedside table. He'd heard tell of full PSD ops squads kicking in the doors of their own to execute search warrants, hoovering up the contents of a life within four walls in the space of a morning. He hadn't yet suffered the same fate, and wondered briefly if he'd been fortunate that they'd been reasonably upfront with him.

He scoffed to himself. He was young in service, but he wasn't that naïve.

He pulled the paper from his pocket and unfolded it. In scrawled biro was written:

DROP, 22 JULY. 10 A.M. THE OLD FIRE STATION, 29 CAVENDISH PLACE

And then, underneath that:

LIGHTHOUSE

Riaz went to the kitchen and lit the hob. He ignited the cursed scrap of paper and dropped it into the sink.

He was momentarily alarmed when the thing caught and the flame kicked halfway up the wall. It burned away quickly enough, but the smoke alarm trilled so loudly and suddenly that he audibly yelped, reaching up to punch it quiet.

It took several attempts, and only when it was finally silenced did he become aware that there was someone knocking at his door.

In the other bedroom, his mother groaned in her sleep.

"For Christ's sake!" he shouted. He felt on the verge of a full-on panic attack. Things were flying at him like meteorites on the motorway. In a convertible. Unexpected things, things that were not part of his usual routine and which served only to distract, disrupt and destroy.

The knocking was not forceful, however, and he heard Claudia's voice from the hallway.

"Airplane? Are you in there? It's Claudia."

He answered the door in a swift movement.

She caught the look on his face. "That bad, huh?" Her eyes dropped, and he realised he was shirtless.

"Come in. Sorry, I'll put some clothes on."

She sat down on the edge of the sofa, back straight, hands flat on her knees. She was in full uniform, and her utility belt dug into the soft leather.

"You single-crewed?" he asked, pulling on a T-shirt as he emerged from the bedroom.

"Yes. Squared away one of the prisoners; the rest aren't fit till morning, which is handy. I've got my own cases to progress."

"I just couldn't face it, Claudia. I'm more of a hindrance than a help today."

She flushed. "That's not what I meant. As far as I knew, PSD were there to suspend you. I just . . . I wanted to make sure you were okay."

"Well, I'm not. But thanks." He was pacing in front of the other sofa.

"Are you? Suspended, I mean."

"Not yet. But—"

The radio mounted above her breast burst into life.

"RUNNERS! I'VE GOT RUNNERS, COMMS. HOLLY PLACE, BACK OF McCOLLS . . . THEY'RE THROWING BEER AT ME . . ."

Claudia grinned, but Riaz flinched like he'd been tasered. She caught the look on his face and hurriedly turned the radio down. Riaz's mum groaned again from the bedroom. Claudia glanced over at the closed door.

"Sorry about that. Getting busy out there," she said. "Are you sure you're okay?"

"I never said I was in the first place."

She held her hands up in front of her. "Okay, okay. I'm sorry. I need to go, anyway."

She stood up and looked around. "Where's your bin?"

"Kitchen," he said, looking out of the window.

She walked over to the small, open area that was demarcated from the living room by virtue of a white melamine counter. If she saw the smouldering flakes of ash that had once been Jimmy Januarie's intelligence, she didn't say so.

"Whoa, Airplane," she said, holding up the empty white plastic bin, upside down. "No one in the world has a kitchen bin this clean."

He looked over at her but didn't speak. She dumped her gum in a wad of tissue and put it in her pocket.

"Feel bad dirtying it. Why would I not be surprised if every other bin in the place looked the same?"

Still nothing.

She walked to the front door, and he finally got up and hurried over.

"Claudia, I . . ." he began.

"Jefferson!" croaked an elderly voice from the bedroom.

Claudia gave him an understanding smile.

"I'd better go. Mum has an early appointment. I've woken her up, which means my name is mud."

"It's okay," she said. "Go help her. Just don't suffer in silence. Call me if you need me, okay?"

"I will."

"Maybe see you tomorrow? Night shift. Nice and quiet."

"I hope so."

"And, so you know for next time, I have one sugar in my tea."

"I didn't make . . ." He faltered, seeing she was teasing him.

She walked off down the hallway towards the lift. She turned her radio back up as she went.

Another burst of activity, the walk became a run, and she was gone.

* * *

The dense humidity of the previous evening hadn't dissipated overnight — even at eight in the morning, the air was thick with it. Barnes stood at the sink, a single cereal bowl sliding around in the soapy water. He idly wondered about selling the dishwasher. He never used it.

He heard Aidan's voice from outside, counting keepy-ups as the football bounced around the garden, and frowned, wondering what he was doing there on a weekday, before remembering it was the school holidays. The sound of the kicking was like a metronome, prompting Barnes's mind to retreat further into itself, the domestic chores causing an almost Pavlovian urge to run for the car and get to the office.

As a half-bitten compromise, he suddenly remembered that he still had to tell PC Riaz the good news about his posting. Last night hadn't seemed appropriate, not with PC Knight there.

He wedged the phone under his ear as the call connected, and plunged his hands back into the sink. Riaz answered almost immediately, tension in his voice.

"PC Riaz. It's DI Barnes here."

"Hello, boss."

"You all right?"

"Yeah, thought it might be PSD. They called last night after I got in."

"Well, you evaded them at the nick — stands to reason they'd follow up. If they really want you, they'll get you. By the same token, it might be months before you hear from them again, so don't get your hopes up."

"Oh, great."

"Then again, it might not," Barnes added. "But in the meantime Division are still looking after you. What are you up to? You sound like you're in a wind tunnel."

"I was just out for a run. Had to get out and do something. I just feel like I'm waiting. I'm in for nights later."

"No, you're not."

"I'm not?"

"No. We have a new proposition for you. Working in the divisional commander's office. Doing projects and the like."

Barnes swallowed as he realised he wasn't selling it particularly well. The ball continued to bounce steadily outside. Aidan was doing well.

"Bagman, sounds like." Riaz's voice was flat.

"It's non-op, I grant you," Barnes said. "But it's eight-hour days, no more nights, weekends off. And it'll get you exposure to a bunch of stuff — and people — that will look great on the CV. You think about the next rank?"

"All I'm thinking about right now is keeping my job."

"Fair enough," Barnes said. "It might be good for you. A break from the frontline. Given what you've been through . . ."

"You're thinking I might crack up?"

"I'm no psychologist, but the last couple of weeks are going to have an impact. You get referred to Occ Health? Want me to do it?"

"Callaghan sorted it," Riaz mumbled.

"Good. There's no shame in it these days."

"That's a relief," Riaz said, a faint note of sarcasm creeping into his voice.

"Look, I know you're a thief-taker, and the pace will take some getting used to," Barnes said. "But no career is static. Try to enjoy it."

"Do I get a choice?"

"It's from the big man himself," Barnes said, and hung up.

The bouncing stopped. A raised voice from the garden. Barnes frowned and dried his hands on a tea towel. If

Eleanor was the perfect neighbour, then the cantankerous Mr Wade, on the other side, was her polar opposite. He had a pathologically low tolerance of young children — Aidan had already confirmed that he'd had the misfortune of encountering him.

Barnes was polite whenever he saw him, because Mr Wade had lost his wife as well, albeit ten years earlier. (Three of them, bereaved, all living in a row.) But he didn't like him. He was fat, rough, and he drank. Barnes suspected Mr Wade had been the subject of more than a couple of 999 calls in his time.

The voice got louder. And there were tears. Aidan's.

Barnes went out onto the patio and peered over the fence. Mr Wade was in Aidan's garden, holding his ball. Without any further thought, Barnes hopped over the fence and wedged himself between the boy and Mr Wade. Aidan grabbed Barnes's legs.

"What's happening, Mr Wade?" Barnes asked, trying to keep his voice light and chipper, his stomach broiling inside.

"What's it got to do with you, *Mister* Barnes? Suffice it to say, if this ball comes over my fence again, I'll puncture the fucking thing."

Barnes took a breath. *Into your overgrown cesspit of a garden, you mean?*

"Mr Wade, could I please trouble you to mind your language? I'm sure he won't let it happen again . . ."

"Yeah, he said that the last hundred times."

". . . but I don't see quite why you need to come into *his* garden to have this conversation. You've upset him."

"He ain't seen the half of it," Mr Wade snarled.

Count to three, Barnes. One . . . two . . . three . . .

"Mr Wade, please leave the property now."

Mr Wade took a step forward, and then dropped the ball onto the patio.

Aidan, still sniffling, broke away from Barnes and ran to get his ball. He hesitated as he got closer, because the ball was still inside Mr Wade's personal space (*his fighting arc*,

213

Barnes thought), but Aidan inched forward and grabbed the football.

He should have left it. Barnes should have told him to leave it, told him that he would buy him a decent World Cup replica. Because then what happened next wouldn't have happened.

It was a deft, wristy move that belied Mr Wade's lumbering dough-ball size. With a low snarl that took Barnes straight back to that sick childhood fear of being castigated by a strange adult, he brought his right hand around from the left side of his waist, and backhanded Aidan across the face.

The boy's head snapped upwards and he flew backwards onto the patio like he'd been hit by a car. There was a second or two of stunned silence from all concerned, then Aidan started bawling properly.

Barnes felt electricity surge through his body, could feel the silver shine of rich oxygen streaming into his lungs. Every vein in his body stood out, his hands felt heavy by his sides, and he knew he could not stop himself. This energy had to go somewhere, and keeping it in was not an option. He understood now why the firearms officer did those push-ups.

Even as Barnes moved towards Mr Wade, he saw the consequences playing out. The suspension, the tribunal, the dismissal. Maybe even a criminal prosecution. All over the headlines. As he advanced, though, he knew he was prepared to risk all that — and, if he found himself jobless and with a conviction for violence, he would do it again in a heartbeat.

Mr Wade didn't budge, didn't retreat. There might even have been a small smirk on his face, knowing he had successfully goaded a cop.

The smile didn't last long, however. Barnes — an inch or two taller — brought his forehead down onto Mr Wade's nose in a swift strike. Mr Wade's nose exploded in a bloom of red, and as his hands flew to his face, Barnes, side-on to the boy's assailant, placed both hands on Mr Wade's shoulders for purchase on his target, and brought his good knee up into the doughy solar plexus.

Mr Wade doubled over, and Barnes rounded off the trifecta by dropping his elbow down onto the nape of Mr Wade's neck. The connection made a dull *thud*, and Mr Wade was laid out prone on the patio, the blood oozing onto the lemon-yellow paving slabs that Aidan often said looked like fondant fancies.

21

Riaz pocketed his phone and opened the car door. The wind he had managed to block by getting in the car rocked him again as he walked back across the cliff top.

He hadn't wanted to tell the DI where he was. He wasn't yet staring down the barrel, but a cop in his position on top of Beachy Head would generate more attention than a masked armed robber in the middle of the day.

He wasn't quite sure what had pulled him up here. His mother, with an ironclad sulk on at having her sleep disturbed the previous night, refused absolutely to allow herself to be driven to her appointment, instead opting to assert what was left of her shaky independence by getting the bus — despite Riaz's protests. This had left him at something of a loose end.

He crossed the road by the pub and headed across the vast green expanse. The day was blue and clear, the sun warm on his back, but the wind was cold and crazy like a banshee. It didn't matter how warm it got down there on the surface, it only ever seemed to be cold up here.

He picked his way carefully across the cliff, trying not to lose his footing in the myriad ruts and dips hidden by the long scrubs of wild grass.

He made it to the edge of the cliff and set his feet, his hands on his hips. No one should trust their balance up here.

The sea was a band of impossible blue, as if someone had swept a huge paintbrush across his field of vision. Kayaks and yachts far below him looked like tiny toy birds with their feathers streaming out behind them. He couldn't see the candy-striped lighthouse, but imagined it down there, a beacon from another age — a final, scrabbling chance for sailors to make a grab for life before they were dashed to pieces on the bladed white rocks.

"Hi there." The voice came from just behind him. It was cheerful, light.

Riaz turned. He hadn't heard the man approach. He was heavy and red-faced, but was trying hard to control his breathing and put on a calm exterior.

Riaz knew they always walked if they were making an approach to someone. They never ran. He recognised him immediately, and was only mildly irked that the chaplain hadn't recognised him in turn. Even if he hadn't known who he was, the hi-vis jacket, torch, crucifix and home-knitted fisherman's jumper were a bit of a giveaway.

"Hi." Riaz tensed slightly. He knew what was coming next.

"You all right?"

"Fine, thanks. Just admiring the view."

"It's beautiful, isn't it? Those colours."

"I know," Riaz said, trying hard to reciprocate the banter in order to keep it as exactly that. "Makes me want to be a painter."

"Well, why not? It's never too late to start."

Clever hook, thought Riaz.

"Yeah, maybe you're right," he said.

"What do you do?" the chaplain asked.

Just asking, Riaz thought. Just trying to keep me talking. Only doing his job.

"I'm a cop," he said.

The chaplain didn't falter. "Thought I recognised you. Gabby, right?"

Despite himself, Riaz grinned. He wasn't going to fall for it. The chaplain knew damn well his name wasn't Gabby.

"Close enough," he said. "You're Colin, yes?"

"That's me."

"Busy day?"

"Always busy," Colin said. "Always work to do."

"I guess you don't need me here gumming up the works, then."

"Busy doesn't mean anybody cares any less," Colin said. Riaz wanted to make a wisecrack, but something about the earnest look on Colin's face stopped him.

"Well, I'll leave you in peace," he said, tapping his watch. "Got to get my ten thousand steps in."

"You be at peace too," Colin said.

Riaz jogged back to his car. He looked over his shoulder at Colin the chaplain, in case he was following him or talking into his radio, but he was already taking a slow walk in the other direction. Clearly Riaz had passed the test.

The chaplain's words stayed with him as he drove back home along the seafront, taking the snaking S-bends of Dukes Drive at a crawl before he dropped down onto King Edwards Parade and past St Bede's School.

Busy doesn't mean anybody cares less.

You be at peace too.

He leaned forward and switched off the radio, listening to the gulls screech as he drove. The road narrowed as he passed the pier, and he tuned out the stop-start drive as he slowed to a crawl to navigate coachloads of tourists, pedestrians and cyclists.

As he slowed for the millionth zebra crossing, his eyes drifted from Princes Park across to the open car park outside Fort Fun, where a couple of learner motorcyclists in shiny hi-vis vests were practising U-turns and emergency stops.

His eyes came to rest idly on a surfer pulling a board up the shingle towards the surf club, a split-level timber-cladded cube nestling in an unmade gully that passed for a car park.

The surfer turned around so she was facing the road, and he did a double take as he realised it was Claudia.

"Hey! Claudia!" he waved, calling out of the open window. She didn't hear him — though a couple of German students passing the car got a shock — and he idled impatiently while the steady stream of octogenarians finished traversing the zebra crossing.

He pulled ahead and turned into the car park with more eagerness than he cared to admit, doubling back towards the corner fence that abutted the surf club, roaring to a stop next to the learner motorcyclists.

He hopped the fence and ran along the promenade, still waving.

She had arrived at the surf club by the time he reached her and was preparing to stow the board. She stopped pulling it; her body tensed slightly as she registered the bloke running straight for her, but her face broke into a smile as she recognised him.

"Airplane!" she said, her face flushed from exertion. "What are you doing here?"

"I was just passing . . ." he said, then stopped, suddenly, thinking it might have looked like he was following her. "I was just going home."

She had pulled the wetsuit to half mast, the sleeves tied at the waist to keep them from flapping about. She wore a blue vest top underneath bearing a red-and-yellow "S" logo, and her shoulders flexed with the effort of lugging the board. They were caked with sand and salt, and brown with the kind of tan that you could somehow only get at sea. She didn't look the type to spend time lounging about on a deckchair. Her dark hair was soaked with sea water and hung in tails around her neck.

"Superman fan, huh?" Riaz said, pointing at the logo on her chest.

"It's Supergirl, actually," she said. He felt heat rise in his face. "Were you out for a run?"

She looked over at the road, then down at his clothes, as if answering her own question.

"No, not exactly," Riaz said. "Just out . . . enjoying the air. Then off to pick up Mum."

He started to feel uncomfortable, then realised that what he had taken for suspicion on her part was actually concern.

"Are you okay?" she asked. "You haven't been sitting around just thinking about everything, have you?"

"It's kind of hard not to. Especially when you live alone. Well, more or less."

"I live alone," she said.

"You do? I thought . . ."

"Thought what?"

"Nothing."

"No kids, no husband. Gives me all the time I want for this kind of thing," she said, waggling a finger at the board.

"Yeah, but what do you do in winter?"

"Chess tournaments," she deadpanned. "Seriously, you need to find something to occupy yourself. Don't you have any hobbies? No, wait. Don't answer that. Do you want to get some lunch?"

He very much did.

* * *

They went to the Caravel, one of several ultra-modern waterside restaurants and cafes that were popping up along the seafront, in an attempt to gentrify, modernise and generally shift the focus away from the salt-decayed B&Bs that were by turns holiday accommodation and halfway houses.

It was a sprawling, split-level timber-clad affair, with a huge terrace overhanging the prom. Riaz had seen it go up, but had never been inside, and, as tall, sweating glasses of some sweet and fizzy drink pimped with ice and lemon were brought to the table, he felt himself relax a little. He tried to decide whether this was down to the view of the Channel, the inviting-looking drink or the woman sitting opposite.

"How are you doing?" she said, sucking her straw.

"Okay, I think. What about you?"

"It wasn't a pleasantry. I'm asking. You don't have to give me the answer you'd give your neighbour. Don't forget, no one else experienced what we did. Nobody."

He thought about the chaplain, and the invisible siren that had drawn him up to Beachy Head.

"I'm okay," he said again. "I'll feel a lot better when I know if I still have a job."

"You tell your mum about what happened?"

"Not yet. She wouldn't understand. She's got enough on her plate."

She nodded.

"Listen, I'm sorry for being a dick last night," he said. "There's . . . there's just so much *noise*, you know?"

"I know. Don't worry about it."

She held his gaze for a moment.

"So, what else does your pre-nights routine consist of? Xbox?" she asked.

"Actually, I'm not in for nights."

"Oh?"

"I have a new job, apparently. With the big boss."

"What is it?"

"I have no idea. That DI phoned me this morning, told me not to come in for nights."

"Barnes? The one that took us out for the Magical Mystery Tour?"

"Yeah. What do you think of him?"

"I liked him. No, that's a bit strong. I trusted him. Instinctively."

"Yeah, me too, I think."

"Why did he call you?"

"I think he was just passing the message," he said. "He certainly didn't sell it too well. But then, a career detective could never sell a job counting beans."

"Is that what it is?"

"I get the feeling they want me off frontline. Plus . . ."

A waiter approached with two plates of food. Riaz shifted in his seat uncomfortably, weathering the interruption as the plates were set down and various other niceties took place — adjusting cutlery, refilling glasses, blathering about specials.

"Go on," she said.

He waited until he was sure the waiter was out of earshot, then leaned across the table.

"I'm in trouble for something else. Not just batoning that clown."

She dabbed at the corner of her mouth with a napkin, even though she hadn't eaten anything yet.

"What . . . do you mean?"

"You know Ty Godden?"

"Your off-duty heroics?"

"That's him. Well, I got some intel off a witness. Good intel. I didn't hand it over, but went after him myself. Stumbled straight into a surveillance op. And now the source is dead."

She twirled her straw in her glass, and didn't speak for a long time.

"How much trouble are you in?"

"It feels like a lot. But I haven't been suspended, so maybe not."

A beat.

"Did you do anything wrong?"

"I failed to hand over the intel, and by acting like Captain America I nearly compromised a UC. But that's it. I swear."

"You know I think you did the right thing at the house, right?"

She didn't say *the bloodbath*, or *when he sliced Luis's throat open*. She didn't need to.

"I guess."

"It's important you know that."

"Thanks."

"You were going to tell me about your hobbies."

"That would be a short conversation."

She exhaled heavily through her nose.

"I wasn't kidding before. It's bad enough sitting around moping after what happened with Reeve, but now you've got PSD breathing down your necks, there's even more of a reason to not sit at home staring at the wall."

"I just . . . I don't know. I don't have much else but work. And Mum, obviously. But I just . . . count down my days off until I'm back at work. I'd work every day if I could."

"Look, I get it. You're young in service, you've got the buzz of the chase and fighting in the gutter, all amplified tenfold by some of your — frankly amazing — results and big cheeses blowing smoke up your backside. And that's fine. Shoring up division-wide performance is fine. Until the job falls out of love with you."

He hadn't heard it in such bald terms before. Just because you love your job, it doesn't mean your job will reciprocate.

She apparently caught the look on his face. "It might not be forever. A thirty-five-year career is full of peaks and troughs. I've been doing this seven years now, and if you don't keep one foot outside work, it'll take the car, the house and your Bee Gees back catalogue when it finally throws a hissy fit."

He snorted with laughter.

"Do you have any suggestions?"

"You ever tried windsurfing?"

* * *

His maiden outing was a clumsy, rigid affair, hampered by his own self-consciousness and embarrassment at the gulf between his infantile thrashing about and Claudia's own graceful efforts. He was tense on the board, and by the time they were through he ached all over. She was a good teacher, however, and he gradually forgot his own neuroses as he managed to concentrate, and a couple of hours flew by unnoticed.

"Not bad," she said, as they hauled the boards back up the beach.

"Don't be funny," he said. "I was terrible."

"I've seen worse maiden voyages," she said. "You'll get it. If you come back," she added.

He stared at her. A couple of low-flying jet fighters ripped overhead before being swallowed up by the horizon. Claudia nearly jumped out of her skin.

"Getting warmed up," Riaz said. "You'll get a lot more of that before the air show proper."

"Good to know," she said.

"Thanks for the lesson," he said. "I enjoyed myself."

She met his gaze for a moment, then slapped the board heartily.

"Well, better get these babies stowed," she said. "Some of us have to work tonight."

They got changed, and she came over to his car as he was getting in. The Supergirl shirt was still a feature, but she had tied her hair back and had pulled on some Levi's.

"Listen," she said, leaning on his door sill. "I meant what I said before. If you find yourself howling at the moon or just staring at the walls, text me or something. Just don't do it alone. It's a mistake. Trust me. I've been there."

He said nothing, but prompted her to continue with his eyes.

"I'll tell you about it, one day," she said. "Good luck in the new job. If your replacement is a clown I'll be lobbying for your return."

"I'm being replaced?"

"I bloody well hope so," she said. "We've barely enough to parade minimum as it is. Be safe. Don't cut yourself on the paperclips."

He watched her as she walked off to her car.

22

"So, who is he?" Shaw asked.

Barnes stood in front of his boss's desk and thumbed through the intelligence profile, the pages still warm from the printer.

"Chris Jenner. Street name 'Ratman'. Identified from DNA. Twenty-eight years old, born Wavertree. Previous for ABH, shoplifting and burglary. Looks like he's a bit of a freelance street dogsbody — muscle, transport, that kind of thing. Some intel to say he was the driver for a string of countywide knifepoint corner shop robberies last year, but nothing concrete. Most of his violent convictions are domestics and pub brawls."

"And murder?"

"Nothing like it. This guy is your out-and-out loser. Violent streak, but he's certainly no contract killer."

"What about associates?"

"The list is as long as your arm. On-off girlfriend, who's been on the receiving end of his knuckles more than once. There was a child, scooped up by Children's Services in the time it took to cut the cord. Other than that, he's directly or indirectly linked to practically every other shitbag in Eastbourne."

"Any names jump out at you from that list? Reeve? Luis? Our original victim? What was his name . . . Gayle?"

"Not so far, but there might be some middlemen we haven't uncovered yet."

"So no motive."

"Plenty, but all conjecture at this stage. My experience, that level of violence is generally reserved for the heart, not the head. Revenge, jealousy, rage. There was nothing businesslike about it. The preferred theory has to be that he perceived she had done him some wrong."

"She wasn't a social worker, was she?"

"No."

Shaw cupped his chin in his hand and frowned.

"Sir . . ." Barnes cleared his throat. "With respect, we are not resourced for this."

"Meaning?"

"Meaning the case of Tommy Gayle's homicide by James Reeve was straightforward enough, even if it didn't have a hope in hell of getting home. Reeve escaped inexplicably in the midst of the trial, then you add to that the murder of his long-term partner by Jenner while Reeve is at large. Jenner survived his arrest — just about — but someone armed came to the hospital to finish the job, orchestrating the removal of his police guard and shooting at a cop in so doing."

"Are you saying that—"

"I'm not done. One of the jurors for Reeve's trial failed to show the day he escaped. He had assaulted his neighbour the day before that, and gave the responding officer good intel about a drugs drop, unrelated to the assault. Said officer acted on this intel, netted two keys of brown off duty, undercutting Op Liphook, a ten-month FCDU operation, in so doing.

"This same officer was the one that nearly killed our friend Jenner while arresting him, and has been placed on light duties since. Meanwhile, the missing juror washed up on the beach a couple of days after going missing. Supposed to look like a suicide, but Tony Sarwan is convinced the injuries are consistent with someone who was quite happy with this mortal coil for a few more years yet.

"This says to me that there are quite obviously more than a handful of organised elements to this. Jenner and Gayle were both bottom feeders, but they earned a living somehow. Which meant they were getting paid. I can't join the dots yet, but I need access to all the intelligence. I need tech. I need some covert assets. And I need twice the staff."

Shaw eyeballed Barnes from under his frown. A knot of muscle flexed in his fatless jaw.

Barnes sighed.

"Ed, look, I know there are some who would just suck it up and not make waves, but the divisional commander has already marked my card, so I don't really feel like I have much to lose. In any case, I've been burned too often to have the promise of promotion hanging over me like the sword of Damocles. I don't equate 'acting' with 'omerta'. I want some justice for Mandy Luis. I want to find James Reeve alive. Results need investment. Just ask Kevin Keegan."

Shaw sat back in his chair and exhaled.

"You're a good man, Barnes. I admire anyone who puts the needs of the victim ahead of their own career. But there are some torrid times ahead. You know that, right? You're too smart not to realise the global credit bubble's going to burst at some point in the next five years. The belt's already tightening."

Barnes gave a sour smile.

"Okay, I tell you what, Barnes. Firm up your theory. If you can give me some tangible links to organised crime, then I'll take it to the region. Okay?"

"Fair enough." Barnes went to go.

"Hold on," Shaw said. "I need to serve you with these."

Shaw dropped a bundle of papers on the edge of the desk like they were on fire.

"What's this?" Barnes asked, walking back over to the desk.

"Reg 15. PSD are investigating an assault complaint. Made by your neighbour, I gather. ABH injuries. Sounds like you gave him a right going over. Allegedly," he added.

"Am I suspended?"

"No. Not yet, anyway. I'll let you know if Glover changes his mind."

"Keeping his powder dry would be my guess."

"Whatever that means. Len Spearing is teed up as your Fed rep. Give him a call and go vent. I guess there's life in your dicky leg yet."

Shaw returned his attention to his computer screen, a faint look of disgust on his face. Barnes eyed him for a second, then tucked the papers under his arm and walked out.

* * *

Barnes was not visiting Tate in a professional capacity, and so he endured the ignominy of joining the regular queue of visitors to HMP Lewes. Behind him, a young woman with a pushchair was barking at a snotty five-year-old boy.

Barnes looked round. She had lank, greasy hair and her yoghurt-white complexion was sprinkled with red spots. When she wasn't yelling at the boy she was fiddling with the infant in the pushchair.

She caught him looking.

"Fuck you looking at?"

He raised an eyebrow, his mouth set in a scowl.

"You look like filth to me," she said, and turned back to the child; despite her appearance, she had somehow managed to achieve the right note of contempt and disinterest.

"Think I'd be queuing with the pond scum if I was a cop?" Barnes had left his warrant card in the car.

The search of a similarly emaciated-looking creature in front of him was concluded, and Barnes was beckoned forward to stand under a search arch.

He saw Tate sitting waiting for him in the visitors' hall. He caught the barrister's eye and held up his hands to allow the screw to search him.

The screw waved him forward. Not taking his eyes from Tate in the distance, Barnes shot his cuffs and nodded his head behind him.

"Check the nappy," he said to the screw, and stepped into the main hall.

He sat down at the table. Tate had a black eye, and he sat slumped in his chair, like his spirit had been broken.

"I'd hate to see the other guy," Barnes said as he sat down.

"Don't turn around then," Tate answered. "He's at seven o'clock, trying to cop a feel off his missus."

"Just tell me you gave as good as you got."

"I did, as a matter of fact. Southpaw Tate, that's me. You learn quite a bit about yourself in prison."

"That's very philosophical. You're hardly a lifer."

"Ah, but the day is yet young."

Tate's usual spark, front or otherwise, had clearly been stripped from him. Barnes tried a more sympathetic approach.

"You see your brief?"

"Couple of times."

"Who's defending you?"

"Marco Daniels."

Barnes was impressed. Even in police circles there was a grudging respect for Daniels, the relaxed barrister who always looked like he'd staggered in from the surf club when he was in court. His laconic drawl and blond beach-bum hair-cut had lured many a prosecutor into a false sense of security.

"That's who I'd want," Barnes said.

"He tends to only represent cops and lawyers. Apparently there's more than enough work to keep him busy."

"What did he say?"

"He can't believe they've brought a prosecution. He reckons it's someone with a grudge. That would make sense."

"Hamilton, the SIO deliberately took this out-of-county. Local CPS aren't running this show. Besides, *you've* run with skinnier cases."

Tate planted both of his palms on the edge of the table and leaned across it, suddenly earnest.

"Barnes, this is all bullshit. She . . . she was like a bloody banshee. Christ, she was *wild. That's* why we both have injuries. But there's no way we did anything she didn't want to do. She's stitching me up good and proper."

"Why would she do that, Hamilton?" Barnes tried very hard not to make his voice sound accusatory. He had deliberately distanced himself from the investigation, but he did know that the girl — a trainee lawyer from London — had alleged that Tate had fed her drugs and drink and then taken advantage of her while she was intoxicated. The balance had been tipped by her injuries and the scratch marks on Tate's body.

"That's the question that's occupied my mind since I've been here." He sat back in his chair and sighed heavily. "It matters not. It's the drugs that'll fuck me. It boils down to my word against hers, but the art-school juries in this part of the world are going to think: if he's bad enough to do coke, he's bad enough to rape someone."

"You don't know that."

"Even if I'm lucky and get them onside, the possession charge will stick. They found traces in the baggie — which was in my jacket — and matched it to the stuff on the table. I might not do any more time, but I'll never work again."

Barnes didn't say anything. Reassuring platitudes seemed pointless.

"Anything else to report?"

"Got a bail app next week."

"I still can't believe you're here in the first place. They think you're a flight risk?"

"Believe it or not, my career as a lawyer is what did it. Marco offered to surrender my passport — among other things — but the DJ seemed to think that my money, connections and legal knowledge could get me out of the country under the radar. Ridiculous."

There was a guttural curse from another table, and Barnes suddenly felt truly sorry for his friend.

"Listen, Hamilton . . ."

"What? One day I'll look back on this and laugh? I hope so, chum, I really, really hope so. It's a game, Barnes, and the odds are tipped in her favour. When that jury retires, they'll forget half the evidence. It will come down to whose face they like best. If it gets to trial."

There was a beat.

"What do you mean?" Barnes said.

"I mean — it might not get to trial. She might change her mind. The CPS might drop it. Stranger things have happened."

Tate stared at Barnes, unblinking.

"I suppose they have," Barnes said.

Tate stretched out a hand and touched Barnes's forearm.

"I don't need sympathy, Barnes. I need someone to help me. Can you help me, Rutherford?"

A curious buzzing feeling swept over Barnes's shoulders.

"We're friends, yes?" Tate said, his eyes wide. "I value our friendship. More than anything. Help me get out of here, Barnes. Anything it takes."

"Anything?"

Tate sat back in his chair and resumed a more casual tone.

"Well . . ." he said. "Marco will stall as long as possible. Means I've got to suck it up in here, but at least I'll have a shorter sentence after conviction."

He was right. In the event of conviction, time served on remand counted as double off your eventual sentence.

"You're being remarkably pragmatic about the whole thing."

"Believe me, Barnes, it's all I can do to keep from howling at the moon."

A screw called time on the visit. Barnes gave his friend a perfunctory handshake and walked out to his car. He had intended to tell Tate about the curious identity crisis of the man in ITU that everyone had hitherto thought was James Reeve, perhaps with a view to seeking his friend's critical input, but that had gone out of the window the minute he saw the state Tate was in.

As he pulled away from the foreboding flint walls of the prison, he took a deep breath, and felt immediately guilty. He could just drive away, which was more than Tate could do.

He knew what Tate had been asking him, even if he hadn't said the words. And, in his position, he knew he could derail the whole case with ease and minimal risk of detection.

In the moment, Barnes thought, breaking the rules is never tempting. What you have to think about is this: in the end, when you look your Maker dead in the eye, and He says — when the chips were down, did you put your friends first? Did you do everything you could . . . ?

Barnes sighed and turned the radio up loud.

23

Mandy Luis's funeral was held on a Wednesday.

July had become August, and dry sunshine had given way to thick curtains of almost subtropical humidity. Barnes headed out of town in the Rover, which was fast becoming such a staple of Eastbourne CID that the local criminals knew it better than the marked cars.

He crawled along Seaside, the driving sheets of rain slowing the perpetually thick train of traffic even more than usual. At the Princes Road roundabout he spied the green-and-yellow Battenberg squares of a paramedic response car. It was parked just off the roundabout on a small apron marked with chevrons that would undoubtedly have been an exit directly out of town were it not for the wide and wet expanse of the Langney marshes beyond.

The paramedics did not park here to eat lunch or read the paper — although some undoubtedly did. They were tactically stationed to be in the optimum location to respond to a call. The positioning was far from random; detailed analysis of the times, days, seasons, types and locations of incidents that might necessitate an ambulance had been painstakingly undertaken over a substantial period in order to predict when and where such things might happen, with the responders placed accordingly.

Barnes caught the eye of the paramedic in the driver's seat as he passed. The guy was young and square-jawed, and was neither reading the paper nor eating lunch. He was watching the traffic intently with his elbow on the door sill and his fist pressed against his mouth.

The static positioning of the ambulance responders was an increasingly familiar sight, but for some reason the sight chilled Barnes today. Maybe it was the solemn gaze of the guy behind the wheel, but clearly someone somewhere thought that at some point during the morning someone in the nearby radius would face sufficient danger as to warrant an ambulance, and that such an eventuality was so inevitable that there was nothing to do but sit and wait for it. That, and the fact that people would, in all likelihood, do nothing to change their routines even if they knew.

Barnes, ignoring the cold shudder that passed through him, drove on. The cops had a bit of catching up to do with their green-suited colleagues when it came to predicting where they might be needed at any given time, but they might eventually get there.

He turned into Hide Hollow, a wide, sweeping road that led up and around the Langney residential estates before bisecting the Pevensey marshes and leading to Westham and out of town.

Barnes pulled into the crematorium. He had driven past on other days where the attendance of mourners was such that cars spilled out from the car park and lined the verges on both sides of the road.

That wasn't the case today.

Barnes parked and walked up to a sign listing the day's services. There were ten in all, including Mandy's. That's express ritualising, Barnes thought.

The other services were for people with names like Phyllis, Ivor, Alfred — names that might conceivably belong to people who had reached the natural end of their lives.

In Barnes's experience, deaths like Mandy's — sudden, unnatural, violent — often attracted a high number of mourners, but unless they were all late, attendees for her service were conspicuous by their absence. Sometimes the acknowledgment of a life cut short was too hard to bear.

He stood outside, the sun warming his face and making the brightly coloured collections of flowers even more vivid, watching an infrequent procession of vehicles enter the car park. A white Range Rover with tinted windows. A small silver hatchback. A gunmetal hearse followed by a similarly coloured limousine.

The hatchback parked and an elderly couple walked away from the chapel, down towards the cemetery. One of them was holding a stuffed toy. Barnes looked away.

The Range Rover followed the snaking driveway down from the road and parked as close to the chapel as possible, causing a slight hiatus as it blocked the drive. It pulled half onto the grass to allow the hearse past, its massive tyres grinding the lawn into mud. A man got out, holding a phone to his ear. He wore sunglasses and a grey three-piece suit the same colour as the hearse. He walked around in circles while he took the call.

Amanda Luis's coffin was festooned with flowers. On both sides the blooms were arranged to spell out "MANDY". Not "Mum" or "Auntie" or "Daughter", and Barnes wondered if there was a correlation between this fact and the number of mourners.

"A terrible tragedy," said a voice from behind him.

The rake-thin vicar had a clear foot on Barnes, which meant Barnes got the coffee-and-cigarette breath full bore when he turned around.

"Indeed," said Barnes.

"Are you family?" He seemed eager.

"I'm afraid not. I'm . . . police," he answered, debating for a second whether to keep it under wraps. "I'm investigating . . . this."

"I could have guessed. You look a little out of place."

"I do?"

A coach pulled up on the main road outside the crematorium, and thirty or forty silver-haired men and women tottered down the driveway to the chapel. *That* was a bit more like it.

"We see the police quite a lot, and their presence at funerals in a professional capacity can sometimes light the touchpaper. Particularly when answers are still in short supply. My name's Michael," the vicar said, extending a bony hand.

"And what's your assessment of this family?" Barnes said, returning the shake.

"Well, it's difficult. You know, when you have shock and confusion to contend with on top of pain. People often don't want to hear about the Lord working in mysterious ways any more than they want to be asked where they were on the proverbial night in question."

"I don't plan to—"

"It's okay, officer," Michael the vicar said, waving a hand. "We're both here because someone died."

"Indeed," Barnes said. "But, after today, your job will be done."

The hearse came to a stop down the side of the building, and Barnes realised that the funeral for Mandy Luis was being held in the smaller Family Chapel; the steady parade of mourners that had alighted from the coach were headed for the Main Chapel, and the funeral of someone else entirely.

He hurried around to the side of the building, where the undertakers were sliding the coffin out of the back of the hearse. There was a gaggle of about fifteen people standing around the vehicle, all adults, separated into groups of ones and twos. Range Rover man was there, with his arm around a young woman who, despite being dressed in black, looked like she had come straight from the office.

Range Rover's phone wasn't out, but this didn't last, and while the undertakers stood around the back of the hearse he tried, as discreetly as possible — one-handed, eyes cast furtively downwards — to reply to a text message. His efforts were in vain, however; there weren't quite enough undertakers to go around, and in an awkward moment he found a number of eyes suddenly on him as he was roped into being a pallbearer.

The coffin was carried into the chapel under Michael's watchful eye, and Barnes, deciding that the woman from the office now looked a little lost, walked over.

"Hi there," he said. "I'm so sorry for your loss."

"Thank you," she said, smiling as she held out her hand. "You're . . . ?"

"Well, I'm actually the police officer investigating Mandy's death. My name's Barnes."

"It seems inappropriate to ask for ID," she said, after a pause.

"It seemed inappropriate to show it. But you can verify my credentials easily enough."

"I'm Laura. Mandy was my cousin," she said, in a small voice. "I guess I'm the next-of-kin."

"I did wonder," Barnes said. "Other than her partner, I've struggled to find much in the way of family."

"Is that why you're here?" she asked.

"Partly, I guess."

"Well, you're welcome," she said.

Clearly she hadn't yet had the pleasure of Chief Superintendent Glover's rhetoric. Plenty of time for that, however.

"No other family? Parents, kids?"

"James was all she had in the world. We were a similar age, so we got on pretty well, but we weren't *close*. Her dad is — was — my mum's brother."

Barnes realised that they were the only two still standing by the rear of the empty hearse.

Just, in fact, as Range Rover man popped his head out.

"Laura? You coming in?" His eyes flicked from Laura to Barnes and back again. His eyes were wide and hard; Laura must have noticed the challenge bubbling to the surface, and she grabbed his arm and escorted him back inside the chapel, muttering about Barnes being the police.

* * *

The service was muted. Michael majored on Mandy's achievements, and merely hinted at the nature and sudden arrival of her death. He certainly avoided any suggestion that the Lord worked in mysterious ways, implicit or otherwise.

Barnes stood at the back, despite an abundance of vacant seating. The twenty or so mourners were scattered around the chapel, maybe in an unconscious effort to create the illusion of there being more in attendance than there actually were. Barnes wondered if there was such a thing as a mourner-for-hire, a contingency to minimise the embarrassment of the end of really lonely lives. A bit like the Oscars, he thought.

The chapel was cool and dark, and Barnes blinked in the baking sunshine after the service was over. He slipped on some sunglasses and looked at his watch. The whole service had taken less than twenty minutes.

He looked around for Laura, but couldn't see her. He did, however, notice Range Rover man sitting alone on a bench, sneaking a crafty fag.

The bench was several yards away from the chapel, on a pristine patch of lawn in the centre of a figure-eight of vivid summer blooms. Range Rover man was sitting forward on the bench, his legs apart, forearms on his thighs, fingers steepled together. The smoke from his cigarette curled upwards from between his fingers as he studiously regarded the ground.

Barnes sat down next to him.

"She said you're a cop," Range Rover man said, without looking up.

"She'd be right."

"Good job she told me. She tells me I'm the jealous type."

"Did you know Mandy well?"

"Nah. Only what I got from Laura, really. We saw her every couple of years or so, usually when someone got the guilt around Christmas and wanted to bring all the family together. Somehow, though, I'm the one that ended up paying for all this." He waved an arm around the crematorium, still looking at the grass. "Are these things means-tested or something?"

"Within families, I think they probably are."

"I *hate* funerals. A thirty-six-year-old man should not have been to more than two or three. I've been to seven."

"What did you make of her?"

"Very quiet. Pleasant enough, but frightened of her own shadow. Suffered from anxiety or something. Funny, we saw more of her once she got together with that James fella. Came out of her shell a bit."

"How long were they together?"

"Good few years." He flicked the cigarette and finally sat up straight. "What d'you make of it all, then?"

"To tell you the truth, I was expecting someone to have slapped or sworn at me by now."

"Yeah, you're getting a time of it in the papers. And it only takes one family member to do the dog-with-a-bone thing and those headlines never go away. You should count yourself lucky she didn't have kids. Or parents."

"I still intend to solve her murder, whether I've got a complaint up my backside or not."

"Solve? The geezer's dead, isn't he?"

"Not quite. And there's a bit more to it all than that."

"Oh yeah?"

"No one could have predicted it. She stuck by him through the trial, and everything else indicated they were very happy together. If he'd threatened her, or if she was in any way worried about her safety, we'd have done something more. The *why* is eluding everyone at present, myself included. But that doesn't mean I won't stop trying."

"The trouble with cousins and people like that is they just don't care enough. Me, I think it's a bit shameful how she got cut while you were already looking for the bloke, but I ain't going to write to my MP about it, you know?"

"Is Laura going to be free for a quick chat, do you think?"

"I dunno. She was pretty cut up during the service."

Barnes turned his head and looked over at the chapel. "She was?"

The undertakers were climbing back into the hearse, while the attendees for the next service in the main chapel were turning out in a good number, and were spilling down the side of the crematorium. It was impossible to tell who was here for Mandy's service and who wasn't.

"Not sure where she is now. Her mum's buried here, though. She might have gone off to visit."

He stood up.

"Do you want to give me your card or something?"

"I'm afraid I don't have one."

"Cutbacks, eh? Ah well, I'll find you if I think of anything."

And Range Rover man sauntered back to his Range Rover, pulling his phone out as he walked. Barnes watched him go, distracted momentarily by the low thudding gargle of a helicopter as it rumbled overhead towards the seafront.

If you'd asked him why, Barnes probably couldn't have given an immediate answer. But he leaned forward, unfolded a polythene evidence bag from his jacket pocket, gloved it over his hand like a diligent dog walker about to recover a particularly substantial deposit, and picked up Range Rover man's discarded cigarette end from where it was still smouldering in the brilliant green grass.

24

Riaz, having lain awake most of the night, reported for duty the following morning in his standard operational uniform — boots, black combat trousers and a black top that was somewhere between a football top and a T-shirt.

Unlike the patrol centre, Eastbourne Police Station was eerily quiet. Riaz's boots echoed around the circular stairwell in the centre of the building, the turret windows fighting a losing battle against the cold, dark concrete walls.

Riaz toed the dark blue carpet outside the divisional commander's office, at one end of what was collectively entitled the Command Suite. The door burst open just as he was starting to wonder how to best announce himself.

Gabby Glover was not what Riaz had been expecting. He was short, completely bald, and the slight lisp combined with a rather softly spoken voice gave him an oddly effeminate demeanour. Despite this, he pumped Riaz's hand like he was dribbling a basketball, while his smile stretched as widely as it could without baring teeth.

"Constable Riaz," he said. "Good to meet you. This'll make a change from rolling around in the gutter with the drunks."

"I like being hands-on, sir," Riaz said, not intending to sound argumentative.

"And that's a good thing," Glover replied. "But it can't all be fun and games if you want to get on. At some point you have to grow up. Get serious."

"I guess that depends on whether you think promotion is everything, sir." Riaz inwardly kicked himself. "I don't, personally."

Glover looked sideways at him, chewing the inside of his cheek.

"Come on through," he said. "We'll kick that naïveté out of you soon enough. Besides which, you'll get your Friday nights back."

Riaz followed the chief superintendent through to the same high-ceilinged corner office that, he imagined, had witnessed many an officer had been on the receiving end of a top-drawer roasting.

"This is my office," Glover said. "You're through there." He pointed at a connecting door, beyond which there was a small vestibule with a photocopier, kettle and filing cabinet; beyond that was a second office with three desks.

Riaz had stepped forward into the vestibule when Glover called him back.

"Constable, you're strictly non-op now. That means white shirt, tie and shoes. I don't want GI-fucking-Joe up here."

Riaz swallowed. "Understood, sir."

"Good. Any questions?"

"Well, yes. What do I do?" Riaz spread his hands in front of him.

"You pay attention," Glover said, and slammed the door shut.

* * *

Barnes stood with his hands in his pockets, looking down at the stack of green case files on his desk.

The pile was like mould growing in a damp house; every time he cleared it — which he did regularly, with the monotonous diligence that came of having very little home life — it grew again within days.

Usually, he didn't mind. The part of the job that demanded a meticulous eye for detail, when the storm and chaos had settled and the investigators stepped in, was what he enjoyed most about policing. To him, it was therapeutic.

But today he was anxious. And the reason for this was the file on top of the stack.

This was the original green crime file, rather than the court copy bundles, and so it was comparatively slim, but it still gave most dictionaries a run for their money. It was dog-eared and worn already, with myriad red ink stamps and file routing logs littered across the front.

Amid the scrawls were the charge and defendant details — the part that was holding Barnes's attention and making his stomach turn cartwheels:

R v Tate, H.
Charge[s]:
1. Rape
[s1 Sexual Offences Act 2003]
2. Possession of controlled drug of Class 'A' (cocaine) with intent to supply to another
[s5(3) Misuse of Drugs Act 1971]
Plea and Case Management Hearing: 4 September 2006

Barnes ran his finger over the file. Hamilton had been unlucky with the drugs charge. Straightforward possession would have been bad enough — and easier to prove — but adding intent to supply made things a hell of a lot worse, sentence-wise.

Barnes shook his head. Find a scumbag with fifty wraps, a sales ledger and portable scales and the CPS would still play it safe and bump a PWI down to straight possession, but find a lawyer — a *cleanskin*, no less — sharing a snort with a colleague and it was a bad day at the office. In Barnes's view it was constructive PWI at best. They were pulling out all the stops for Hamilton, of that there was no doubt.

Retrieving the file without raising suspicion had been easy enough. A couple of days beforehand, DC Sofia Johnson had received details of a bail app for one of her cases with less than 24 hours' notice. The bail app clashed with the trial of a man who had taken a heated iron to the face of his wife of twenty years — a case Sofia had been preparing for earnestly for some time.

It had been relatively straightforward to seek an opening to assist her — as with any minor adjustment to her schedule, the rest of the office had been alerted to the latest transgression by a volley of colourful invective. Barnes had offered to cover her bail app for her — she'd been grateful, if a little surprised. The DI was offering to step in personally to assist? Barnes had qualified his offer by saying that what he actually meant was that he would *task someone* to cover the hearing.

He would have to watch that. Anything out of the ordinary could arouse suspicion. In any case, he hadn't tasked anyone, but had simply driven straight down to the Criminal Justice Support Unit — the prosecution admin office — to retrieve the file.

No one in the CJSU had given him a second look. There were always detectives in the office looking for files. Barnes had rooted around in their massive pile of outbound files — finding both Sofia's and the case file against Hamilton.

And now it was on his desk.

He took a slow, reluctant drive back home, parked on the driveway and got out, taking a moment to look up at Eleanor's house next door.

Just on the off chance.

It was dark and silent. Barnes wasn't even sure what the time was.

As he walked to his front door, Eleanor's porch light went on and she appeared in the doorway, hands clasped.

"Hi," he said.

"Barnes . . ." she swallowed. "I need . . ."

Suddenly he saw the look on her face.

"What's the matter, Eleanor?"

"Look, I'm grateful that you stood up for Aidan. Part of me wants to be glad you did what you did."

"Oh, now look . . ."

"But I must ask you: please don't speak to him anymore. He . . . he was quite troubled by such a level of violence."

"The poor lad. Tell him I'm sorry . . ."

"I will, when the time is right. He is quite afraid of you now. As much as he is of Mr Wade."

"I'm sorry," Barnes croaked.

"Go inside, Barnes. Get some rest," she said, slender fingers on the door as she went to push it closed. "I hope you're not in too much trouble."

Barnes stood facing the closed door for a moment, then walked across the driveway to his own front door. He stepped inside, silently capitulating to Eleanor's last request of him. He loosened his tie, slipped off his shoes and sat heavily in the darkened front room, an amber curtain radiating in from the outside street lights.

He fumbled for the remote, pointing it behind him, and some late-night radio station whirred into life, giving him a dose of Massive Attack.

That'll do, he thought, sliding a little lower in his seat. He opened the stolen case file on his lap.

Barnes flicked through it. The OIC's name was Walsh, and he had done a fairly tidy job. There was an indexed transcript of the victim's video interview, a record of Tate's interview, Riaz's arrest statement, enquiry log, the SOCO and lab statements, CCTV stills — not to mention a sequential collection of bookend witness statements that would serve to create a tight narrative of what happened that night, including the run-up to the offence itself and the grim aftermath. There were working copies of the interview tapes and CCTV discs in numbered envelopes stapled to the back, while Walsh had even provided a time-stamped statement of his complete involvement, including what CCTV he had personally watched and Tate's demeanour in interview. It was largely hearsay, but it would show willing to prosecuting counsel.

The music gave way to a phone-in dedications segment. The DJ's voice sounded like it was coated in treacle.

"*Harry, we've had such a tough year. I could never have got through it all without you. You've stuck right by me through thick and thin. Here's our song. All my love, Michelle.*" The dedication segued into "Never Too Much" by Luther Vandross.

Barnes twitched.

He idly noted that Riaz's arrest statement, far from being the bare minimum please-don't-summon-me-to-court narrative of many similar, was extremely detailed. Barnes hoped the lad would exit his own personal maelstrom long enough to carve out some semblance of a career.

He picked up the victim's interview transcript. He wasn't interested in the details, but wanted to know some of the background.

She worked at an affiliate firm of Tate's, based in London, and was on some kind of exchange with another lawyer, apparently with a view to relocating to the coast and taking up a permanent role alongside Tate.

Needless to say, she had put that idea in the bin and had apparently gone back to London.

"*Helen, you mean everything to me. Thanks for being amazing. Happy anniversary, Derek,*" the treacle-voiced DJ said, followed by "I've Got the World on a String".

He read on. The drugs were all Hamilton's, she said, and she hadn't touched any. Barnes flicked to the back to see if the toxicology backed this up. It did — her samples showed small amounts of alcohol but no drugs; by contrast, Tate's made for sobering reading. Barnes wondered if he was reading the verdict right there.

Walsh had included in the file a sort of biography of the defendant, which included career highlights and notable cases alongside his police record. It appeared to have been cleaved from police intelligence, Tate's interview record, defence correspondence, disclosure statements and what appeared to be character references from a couple of his colleagues, albeit nobody too senior. Barnes wondered how the complainant felt about *that*.

The bio was a nice touch — handy for the jury, and showed that the prosecution had nothing to hide. Barnes noted that, during his brief police service, Tate had worked on the outside enquiry team for Op Hexagon, as well as Op Vestry, Op Lighthouse and Op Cathode, playing more than a bit part in putting away a number of villains — including, among others, Anjou Acosta and another individual called Stratton Pearce, who, by all accounts, was Acosta's capo.

Tate had received a commendation for rescuing a suicidal woman who had waded into the sea. He had also managed to land a caution for possession of Class A during the interval between his police career ending and his law career starting. So not *quite* a cleanskin. Both episodes were news to Barnes, and, although he considered Tate to be a good friend, he found himself wondering just how much he actually knew him.

He sat in the sudden silence and rubbed his cheek, thinking. It wasn't enough to just dispose of the file. There were copies of everything. The forensic samples were probably all still at the lab, and so some additional effort would be required to lose them. There were working copies of all media on the file, with the masters no doubt tucked away in a police property store somewhere — and likely not in Sussex. CCTV wasn't a deal-breaker, as Tate's defence had been one of belief in consent, while losing the statements wouldn't help either, given the plethora of copies — it would just cause the witnesses to be revisited to have their statements taken again.

Barnes didn't see how it could work. Tate's barrister would need to cry foul on the existence of copies and insist the originals be presented in court for corroboration — and then cry foul again when they couldn't be located. At worst

— depending on how you looked at it — this would simply delay things for witnesses to be revisited and samples to be hunted down. At best, the judge would either lose patience with the Crown's inability to get its house in order and throw the whole thing out the window, or realise Tate had friends on the other side of the thin blue line. This might actually result in considerably more scrutiny being exercised than the level currently in play. In either case, there was a side possibility that Walsh may or may not get stuck on for losing the file — or worse.

There was a slim possibility that the victim could be bribed into retracting her complaint — or better still, admitting she lied — but it would have to be a hefty sum to cover the damage to her career and reputation, and who the hell would fund that?

Barnes shut the file, feeling for a moment like he was closing it on his friend, but then thought: if one of your closest friends is a rapist, is he actually your friend?

"Fiona, this one is for you," the DJ crooned. "*Can't wait to taste freedom and get back home to you. All my love always, Hamilton.*"

"I Drove All Night" followed. Barnes put the file down, stood up and stared at the radio accusingly. "Hamilton" was not a particularly common first name, and Barnes suddenly felt that both the dedication and the song choice was exactly the kind of insidious threat a suspected rapist might make — and enjoy making.

After a moment of scrabbling around trying to find the number, he called the radio station. The bored-sounding producer, who doubtless had to deal with all manner of weirdo callers at this time of night, refused to tell him anything except that calls to the studio weren't traceable, until Barnes said he only wanted to hear the names that had already been broadcast out into the public ether a matter of moments before. He told her it was a police matter, and she relented, even though she clearly didn't believe him.

The dedication was to Fiona, from Harrison. Not Hamilton. Harrison.

Barnes turned the radio off and squeezed the bridge of his nose with his finger and thumb.

He looked at his watch, then back at the file on the seat, and made his decision. He didn't feel anywhere near ready for bed. He knew what was going to happen next.

As if he was on the outside looking in, he watched himself get up and pull a bottle of Bombay Sapphire from the tiny icebox above his fridge. The bottle frosted up as it hit the air, and the syrupy gin slid into a tumbler. Barnes swirled it around, wondering what coalition of willpower and further distraction would need to prevail for him to pour it away.

More than he had in him, he knew that. He knew full well it was only the alcohol, the music and the piece of judicial contraband that was stopping him from opening some old photo albums of Eve and sliding away into a black hole. He just didn't feel able to be that honest with himself.

His phone chirped from the front room, and he put the tumbler down before going to answer it.

"DI Barnes?"

"Yeah. Who's this? I'm not on call till tomorrow."

"This is not a call-out. Forgive me, Mr Barnes, I'm so terribly sorry to disturb you at such a time, but—"

"But what?"

"But . . . well — and you'll forgive the presumption — I just think you're a little like me, insofar as the call of work can enable a U-turn on *many* an ill-advised path."

Marlon Choudhury, and his theatrical countenance. Barnes had barely given him a second thought since their introduction outside Hove Crown Court, but now fear and paranoia flashed through him as he glanced guiltily at the file. It was surely impossible for Choudhury to be watching him, wasn't it? Barnes managed to rationalise it away, but he wouldn't put much past the old bastard.

"I thought you might like to know that we are closing the Donald Wade case."

"Which case?"

"Your neighbour. I believe you broke his nose last month."

"His first name is Donald? And what do you mean, you're closing it?" Barnes tried to keep the relief from his voice.

"Remarkably quick, no? I took many things from my time in the capital, and one of them was the amount of time it takes for misconduct matters to drag themselves along the rumbling walkway to closure. There's just no reason for it, Mr Barnes, and I've seen too many of my colleagues punch their own ticket rather than allow the wheels of justice to turn."

Barnes pinched the bridge of his nose and sat down. If he didn't, he was likely to forgo the tumbler and drink straight from the bottle.

"In your particular case, there are three elements that have allowed me to conclude matters, the IPCC's desire to set up camp in my office notwithstanding.

"First, you were off duty. Secondly, it was one clean strike to the face, which — pre-emptive or otherwise — is consistent with your claim of self-defence. Both of yourself and another — a seven-year-old lad, in fact. It was quite clear you had only the welfare of a vulnerable person at heart — a point which he was generally happy to corroborate."

"You interviewed Aidan?"

"And finally," Choudhury said, appearing not to have heard. "Finally, Mr Wade has declined at this stage to pursue a formal complaint."

"That *does* surprise me."

"Having met the odious little man twice, I'm minded to agree."

"So why would he not—?"

"My best guess would be that he would prefer to retain the dubious power of being able to hold you to ransom with it until the end of time. It's also possible that he worked out that the loss of your livelihood would more or less give you carte blanche to carry on where you left off, only without any of the professional constraints that held you back last time.

In short, if you're not a cop any more, what's to stop you going back for round two?"

"I see."

"I must warn you, though — I would see any attempt to remonstrate with him in future as grossly incongruous to your position, even in the face of extreme provocation. There comes a point where the lack of any formal complaint almost becomes a moot point."

"Well, I appreciate you letting—"

"In the meantime, don't let's lose sight of what is essentially good news: the matter is finished, and you may come back to work. No prejudice — no *sub judice* — whatsoever. And I shall leave you to your evening, what's left of it."

"I was just off to bed."

"As was I, Mr Barnes. A most sensible idea."

"Goodbye, DI Choudhury."

"Actually, just one more thing. A slightly impudent observation, in fact. If I may?"

"I guess."

"It's perfectly okay to grieve."

Barnes stared at nothing.

"Mr Barnes? Are you there?"

"Let me ask you something," Barnes said, slowly. "Where exactly are your touchlines in all of this?"

"I'm not quite sure I—"

"I've got what started as a relatively straightforward manslaughter case. Then my defendant escapes, facilitated by at least one impressionable court jailer with either a few dirty banknotes in his back pocket, or threats and intimidation, or both. Then one of my jurors is thrown off a cliff, but not before he's passed intel on an undercover drugs sting to a patrol cop.

"Said same patrol cop then responds to a call at my fugitive's girlfriend's home, arriving just in time to see a skag-addled shitbag out-of-towner gut her like a fish. This shitbag gets put down by a couple of baton strikes — quite rightly, in my view — and carted off to hospital.

251

"While he's in ITU someone engineers the removal of his police guard just long enough to put his lights out with a pillow, and lets off a farmer's nostrils at yours truly in order to make good his escape. You can't tell me that wasn't an inside job."

"Mr Barnes, I—"

"Not only am I running point on every single act of this godawful space opera so far — as well as investigating my own section 17 Firearms Act offence, despite being the one singed by a .410 slug — but in the middle of this, my prosecuting advocate is remanded in custody for rape, which may or may not be incidental."

"Barnes . . ."

"The whole thing stinks to high heaven, and I just wondered whether your sole involvement is going to be limited to the kid that bashed Chris Jenner around the head with a stick."

There was silence on the line.

"I understand," Choudhury said after a moment.

The phone went dead. The dial tone became the dead space of the pips of the empty line, and Barnes clicked the red "call end" button.

He stared at the phone for a moment, and then went into the kitchen. He took hold of the gin bottle, emptied the contents down the sink, and threw the empty in the recycling box.

He walked to his car, drove back to the patrol centre and parked in a far corner of the site, just under the windowsill of the DCI's office.

Then he slid over to the passenger seat of the Rover, reclined it and slept.

* * *

He was awoken at some nameless hour by a tapping at the window. He sat up suddenly, cramp in his bad leg and a dull ache in his left love handle. His eyes were gritty, his crotch and armpits felt sweaty and his tongue felt as if he had been licking envelope seals all night.

He fumbled for the keys in the ignition and slid down the window. Sofia, by contrast, looked sharp as a tack, with a dark brown trouser suit, enormous opaque sunglasses and her shiny chestnut hair hanging loose somewhere down the middle of her back.

"Sofia . . ." Barnes croaked.

"Come on, boss, look sharp."

"What's happening?"

"Reeve."

"Reeve?"

"The real one, this time. We've had a sighting."

25

Barnes followed Sofia into the patrol centre in a daze, only to be ushered back out when she grabbed some car keys off the board and spun a U-turn back out of the door.

"What are you doing?" she said.

"What do you mean? Coming in to run it," Barnes said.

"Come on, jump in," she said.

"Wait, where is this sighting?"

"Seafront."

"He's *here*?"

"Come on."

They jumped into an unmarked Focus and headed out of the patrol centre, taking a shortcut across the Wickes car park.

The Focus featured neither a light bar nor sirens, but that didn't stop Sofia driving as though it did, jabbing the horn and flashing the headlights as she went, tearing through the Admiral retail park like a woman possessed.

"Subtle," Barnes said, clinging onto the ceiling grip.

"Come on, get out of the way!" Sofia yelled at the world, before sticking on the hazard lights for good measure.

Three RAF Tornadoes tore overhead in a scream, making Barnes jump. They banked in formation and flew towards Holywell, dwindling in the distance until they looked like dragonflies silhouetted against the impossibly blue sky.

"What's the information?" Barnes asked, trying to keep his lunch in.

"Sighting from the public. Someone at the air show. Recognised him down by the Western Lawns from the media release and called it in."

"Who's running it?"

"FCC, far as I can work out."

"That'll be subtle as a barn door," Barnes said, grabbing for his radio. "Sierra-Oscar, DI Barnes, permission?"

"Go ahead, DI Barnes," said the controller.

"All units on the Reeve sighting — silent approach. I am deploying with plain-clothes officers — we just need someone to keep eyeball on the perp and talk us in. Marked units plot up at the perimeter of the air show footprint and keep him from getting out—"

"That's a negative, DI Barnes," said the controller, stepping on Barnes's transmission. "Report states subject has a firearm. ARVs en route. FCC has command."

Barnes shut his eyes and swallowed the yell he was about to emit. He could practically feel the stress on his heart. Another twelve days off your life expectancy, thank you very much.

"Comms, who's the caller?" he said, with exaggerated calm.

"Member of the public."

"Do they still have eyeball?"

"Caller offline, DI Barnes."

"Could someone give them a call back, do you think?" Barnes said, just about able to part his teeth.

"We've been trying for about ten minutes," the controller said. He didn't say, *We are not as stupid as you think*, but then, he didn't really need to.

"Try the MDT," Sofia said, lurching onto Royal Parade.

Barnes jabbed at the small screen on the dash and then rooted around in the glovebox for the keyboard, before finding it in the door pocket.

"No batteries," he said, holding it upside down.

"Honestly, if it isn't nailed down . . ." Sofia said.

Barnes found a biro and used it to jab the incident number into the tiny on-screen keyboard. It was painfully slow.

"You're going to have to slow down," he said. "I'm going to throw up."

"Ordinarily, I'd say no chance," Sofia said. "But I think you're about to get your wish."

They snarled to a crawl along Royal Parade, where there were as many people on the road as the pavement, and then stopped completely at the road closure.

"Police!" Sofia yelled at the two prop forwards in hi-vis jackets standing in the road, thrusting her warrant card out of the window. "Move the barrier!"

One of them lumbered over.

"I'd happily move it for you, love," he said. "But I don't think it will help you much."

He pointed down the road. Beyond the barrier a crowd cling-filmed in a heat shimmer stretched across the road from the building line onto the beach. Rows of food vans, market stalls and floats lined the promenade.

"Dammit!" she muttered, smacking the steering wheel in frustration.

"I've got the number," Barnes said, shutting off the MDT.

"Better use it. We're going to have to ditch the car."

"Are you serious?" Barnes said. "The sighting was the Western Lawns. It'll take forever from here."

She thought for a moment.

"I've got an idea," she said, looking over at the barrier behind the two marshals.

* * *

They pedalled along the seafront on the mountain bikes Sofia had commandeered from the bemused marshals.

Sofia had stopped yelling "Police" fairly quickly. It took all their powers of concentration to weave and wobble through the crowd.

"This," Barnes called to her, "is precisely why police whistles should be brought back as mandatory issue."

At the pier the crowds were practically shoulder to shoulder, forcing them to dismount. There was a burst of noise from their radios. Sofia grimaced as she held hers to her ear and tried to listen.

"What's happening?" Barnes said.

"ARVs on scene. They're searching on foot."

Barnes dialled the number as they pushed the bikes past the statue of William Cavendish and onto Grand Parade. A Chinook grumbled above them, its rotors thundering like all the percussion orchestras in the world playing together. It made Barnes's guts shake.

"Anything?"

"It's just ringing out."

"No way he'll be able to hear it in this racket."

Barnes looked at her. She met his gaze.

"Come on," he said.

"Why would he come back here?" she said as they hurried through the crowds as best they could. "His ugly mug is all over the papers, and he decides to not only come back to town, but on the busiest day of the summer."

"I don't know," Barnes said.

"What's the description again?" she asked.

"Black hoody, grey joggers, trainers, handgun in his waistband," Barnes said.

"How the hell are they going to find him?"

Barnes stopped pushing the bike as the low rumble of more aircraft grew in volume from the east. Hundreds of heads turned upwards in unison, like a ripple of petals opening on a flower.

The noise grew. Barnes leaned in towards Sofia.

"Look for the person not looking up," he said, pointing overhead to where the Battle of Britain memorial display was proceeding stoically across the pale blue sky.

He tried the number again as they pushed on.

"What if he's looking for someone?" Barnes said.

"He's picked the wrong day to look for *any*body," Sofia said.

"Maybe. But maybe not. If you know the cops are after you, but you need to come back, this crowd is the perfect cover. Particularly if you have unfinished business with someone."

"Like who? The man that killed his partner is already dead."

"I don't know. But he's got the gun, hasn't he?"

She stared at him as Barnes tried the number again.

"Nothing."

The crowd grew denser as they approached the bandstand, and they were forced to abandon the bikes.

Beyond the bandstand the crowd was a static swirl of bright colour from the lifeboat station up the sharp incline towards the Wish Tower, while the Western Lawns were spotted with a sprinkling of blues, reds and greens from windbreaks, tents and umbrellas. The crowd was almost impenetrable, but movement was at least standing out.

"Look," Barnes said, touching Sofia's shoulder.

She looked to where he was pointing, not immediately understanding, then she nodded. About fifty yards away, directly ahead of them, a pair of large men in enormous black coats moved slowly through the crowd. A second, similar-looking pair were inland by Wilmington Square, outside the TGWU Centre, at their two o'clock; another pair stood at their ten o'clock, on the seafront where the prom split and snaked around the Wish Tower slopes.

"Firearms," Sofia said, and moved forward again. "They're putting a wide containment on."

"Hold on," Barnes said.

Three Spitfires and a Hawker Hurricane paraded majestically out to sea, before circling slowly around to head back along the length of the shoreline, from Holywell to Langney Point. Barnes mused that they could have done with some music to score their journey.

As the aircraft passed overhead, Barnes forced himself not to look up. He scanned the crowds as the spectators craned their heads. His eyes flicked to one of the AFOs. The officer touched his ear and Barnes saw his lips move.

"They've seen something," he said to Sofia.

They moved forward again. The AFOs began to converge on a single point where the crowd was thickest, on the apron of concrete separating the promenade and the lifeboat station.

The AFOs began to move faster. Barnes shoved his radio to his ear but heard nothing — the firearms teams were operating on a different channel, one Barnes was not privy to.

He gave an update anyway.

"Comms, DI Barnes. Possible sighting. Am with ARVs. Stand by."

He shoved the radio back in his pocket, missing the acknowledgement. Urgency like static electricity tensed his limbs — he wanted to run, but he had no idea where to.

As the memorial parade began to dwindle in the distance, the crowd began to move around at the edges. Like crumbs falling off a biscuit, they spilled into the road, onto the beach, back to their tents. Barnes wasn't sure if the planes would be coming back. Didn't they take off from Shoreham?

The AFOs weren't slowing down, however. As the crowd continued to disperse, their full-length countenance was even more incongruous. Their weapons were not on display, but with the black overcoats, combats and boots they stuck out like flies on a birthday cake.

Barnes felt a twinge of fear. They were obviously looking to put themselves between whoever they could see and the rest of the crowd, but Barnes had a horrible feeling they were going to show out any minute now.

A tinny announcement echoed from a series of PA speakers, inviting the crowd to show their appreciation for the Battle of Britain display. The crowd obliged, in droves — and, in so doing, stopped moving.

Barnes strained his eyes.

There.

He zeroed in on him, right by a row of yucca separating the car park from the pavement. Thin, grey-looking, stooped. He matched the description, and despite a good chunk of weight loss, Barnes recognised him instantly.

James Reeve.

"There!" Sofia shrieked.

Bizarrely, Barnes's first thought was: *What exactly did she see in him?*

His second thought was: *The info is good. He matches the description. He's here.*

And he's holding a gun.

Reeve clocked the AFOs at the same moment, and broke into a run — mercifully, across the road towards the mouth of Carlisle Road, which took him away from where the crowd was at its most dense.

There was a shout. The AFOs moved in formation to box him in, flicking on dice-band POLICE caps as they surged forward.

Carbines appeared in the hands of the armed officers. They were levelled at Reeve.

"Armed police! Drop the weapon!" It was less shouting than baying. Bemused onlookers in shorts and sunglasses stood nearby, taking in the tableau in the middle of the street while their ice creams dripped over their fingers.

"No!" Sofia shrieked again.

Reeve didn't immediately obey. The gun hovered by his side. If he didn't drop it . . .

There was an explosion, and Reeve doubled over, clutching his gut.

Then he pitched forwards onto the warm tarmac, and lay still.

26

As it turned out, Reeve was dropped by a painful but entirely
non-lethal baton round fired by one of the AFOs – just as
another AFO had been levelling his carbine at Reeve's torso.

Barnes and Sofia tag-teamed the phone calls — Barnes
to Shaw and the media desk, Sofia to the legal rep and custody to make it quite clear that they wanted to get into Reeve
tonight. The AFOs cleared the weapon quickly — it was a very
real-looking imitation.

The initial flurry eventually abated, and Sofia gathered
up her papers to head downstairs to the cell block. Barnes
followed, and they walked in parallel down the wide Georgian
corridors to the stairwell.

"They're in two," the custody sergeant — Stu Nippers,
parachuted in from Hastings on overtime — called from
the office, and Sofia headed across the corridor leading up
from the garage into the interview room. She looked at him
sideways as Barnes stayed on her heel.

"You're coming too?" she said. "Since when does a DI
help with interviews?"

"Since my substantive rank remains DS. I'm acting,
remember. Two jobs for the price of one."

"Want me to see if Monty's free to help?"

"That's okay. My curiosity would only get the better of me."

They passed through the double-door sandwich airlock into the interview room. One of two such rooms, every inch of its fabric soundproofing was caked with layers of grime that locked in the sweat, booze and tobacco odour of a thousand desperate prisoners.

James Reeve sat facing the door, his brief off to his right. He didn't look up when they came in, and instead kept his focus on the tiny styrofoam cup that he rolled gently in his fingers. Fingers of steam drifted up to the velour ceiling.

Sofia began the preamble, during which their prisoner's eyes remained on his cup, the brief's eyes remained on his notepad, and Barnes's eyes remained locked on the prisoner.

His rights duly covered, Sofia asked him for an account of what he understood by his arrest and the events leading up to it, and got "No comment" in response.

She exhaled sharply through her nose and folded her arms. Barnes thought she probably didn't realise she was doing it — he could practically hear her thinking, *So it's gonna be like that, is it?* Most cops, he mused — even the most experienced — found it hard not to get pissed off by a "no comment" interview.

The tone of the interview set, Sofia relayed a narrative of events as she saw them, inviting Reeve to interject if she had anything wrong. She took her time, and Barnes kept his eyes on Reeve.

He had definitely lost weight. There were dark patches at his cheeks and cords visible in his neck. His hair was untidy — an all-over number one grown out to the tune of almost four weeks. He just looked generally grubby — although a custody tracksuit would do that to a person — but, again, Barnes found himself wondering what Mandy had seen in him.

"As you don't plan on answering my questions, I'm gonna take it back to brass tacks," Sofia said.

Reeve shrugged with his hands. A drop of muddy liquid spilled onto the melamine table.

"You do know it is an offence to punch a court security guard, vault a secure dock and run out into traffic partway through being tried by a jury of peers? Right?"

Reeve pursed his lips. "No comment."

"Where did you go?"

"No comment."

"What have you been doing for four weeks?"

"No comment."

"Why didn't you turn yourself in?"

"No comment."

"Who have you contacted while you've been unlawfully at large?"

"No comment."

"How has your business survived?"

"No comment."

"Did you steal a Vauxhall Corsa from Wilbury Grove, Hove, on the day you escaped?"

"No comment."

"Why did you have a gun today?"

"No comment."

"What kind of gun is it?"

"No comment."

"Were you going to cause someone harm with it? Threaten someone with it?"

"No comment."

"Who's the someone, James?"

"No comment."

"Who's the someone?"

"I said: no comment."

Sofia sighed and sat back. "James, for the second time, you don't have to say anything. It's your right not to answer my questions. But I just want to be clear: you escaped Crown Court during your manslaughter trial, you stole a car, and then, having evaded us for almost four weeks, you were arrested in possession of a very real-looking firearm. And you've got nothing to say to me?"

Reeve remained silent.

"James, you are looking at charges of escape from lawful custody, ABH, aggravated TWOC and an S16A firearms offence. And that's without the original manslaughter charge. Whatever else happens, you'll never get bail again, even for littering. You've got *nothing else* on your sheet: retained firefighter, local business owner—" she eyeballed the brief, who kept his eyes on his notepad — "and you have nothing to say to me?"

"No comment."

"James, you might feel like a big man right now, telling me to go fuck myself with my questions, but when these interviews are played back in court you won't feel half so clever. So just to reiterate: you don't have to talk to me, but you try giving a jury an explanation after these tapes are played to them. You'll squirm like a lab rat."

Barnes privately defied anyone to explain the caution any better. The brief shifted in his seat and opened his mouth.

"Um . . ." he began.

"How did it feel when you found out Mandy Luis was dead?" Sofia asked.

Barnes flinched, but Reeve kept his eyes on his cup and remained silent for a moment, his breath whistling through his nose.

"No . . . comment," he said.

Sofia sat back. "All yours, boss," she said, keeping her eyes on Reeve, who slowly shifted his own gaze to Barnes.

"James, just one question," Barnes said. "Why did you run? Everybody thought your odds of acquittal were fifty-fifty at *worst*. DC Johnson has already outlined the charges you might be facing. An acquittal would have kept you your clean sheet. So, why?"

Reeve stopped rolling his cup. He set it down on the table and tilted his head. "How do you decide who's gonna get these?"

"What?" Barnes said, momentarily thrown.

"These hot drinks. You must get murderers and rapists and all kinds of psychos in here. So how do you decide who gets a steaming hot drink in a room less than five foot square?"

Barnes and Sofia exchanged glances. Sofia's thumb went to the red panic alarm strip that ran the circumference of the room. It hovered there while Reeve drank the remainder of the contents.

"I think we're done," said Barnes.

* * *

They took Reeve down to his cell and left the station for some air. The sun had fallen away, creating an orange backlight in the sky for the tortoiseshell streaks that could have been clouds or the remainder of the air show's vapour trails.

"Want to get a beer?" Sofia said.

Barnes looked back at the station.

"He isn't going anywhere."

He eyed her. "No. But I'll have a coffee."

"Even better. I won't have to get a taxi."

She winked, and they crossed the street to Bibendum, the three-storey red-brick pub that acted as the unspoken gateway to the area known as Little Chelsea. The terrace on the edge of Grange Road was packed with the dregs of the air show visitors straining to catch the last of the sun as it filtered across the Saffrons and behind the Downs — which meant that the inside was incongruously quiet.

Barnes took a table in what a frosted window told them had, many years ago, been the Saloon Bar, while Sofia got the first round in — a pint of Stella for her, and a frothy coffee for Barnes. He recognised some of the faces at the other tables from the station — two from Finance, and a group of five or so from Neighbourhoods who appeared to be gathering for a birthday, or a retirement.

"I miss working at Grove," Sofia said. "Think they miss us?"

A chorus of laughter erupted from outside.

"I'm not so sure," Barnes said.

Sofia shrugged and took a gulp of her pint, meeting his eye over the rim of her glass.

"This feels a little weird," she said.

"What does?" Barnes said.

"Me being the only one drinking." She pondered it. "Still, if it means you can drive me home, I'll take that."

"What did you think of him?" Barnes said, only half listening.

"Reeve?" She shook her head. "Couldn't get his number at all."

"There was something not right about the whole thing."

"I know, right? It's like he's a totally different person."

Their eyes locked for a moment.

"You've met him before, right?" he said.

"You know I have. Me and Craig did the interviews."

"And?"

"Oh, it's definitely him. And if it wasn't, custody would be on the phone the minute he got put through LiveScan."

He nodded slowly.

"I just wanted to know what he'd been doing while he was on the run. He had nothing to lose. He's getting a bunch of charges regardless. If he'd done something he didn't want us to know about, his brief would have told him not to incriminate himself."

"Who knows?" she said. "You know what these scumbags are like. They'll tell you nothing just because they can."

"That's true of proper criminals, but he isn't. Not really."

"He escaped his murder trial and avoided us for a month. He looks like one to me."

"Think about it," Barnes said. "You have a rush of blood to the head, smack a court officer in the chops and leg it. You steal a car and avoid getting snared by the initial response. Then what? Everything points to it being an impulsive act. You had no plan, so you just survive and focus on keeping your head down. He must have desperately wanted to contact his friends and family — particularly Mandy."

"Then she was killed."

"So at that point you start thinking: what's the point of anything? What keeps you going at that point? He had no kids or other family that we know of."

"I don't know. The survival instinct can be pretty strong when it wants to be."

"Revenge, maybe?"

"On who? We already had Chris Jenner, the man who murdered his common-law wife."

"He came back to town with a gun."

"An imitation. He could have had it for any number of reasons. He's been on the run for four weeks with no source of income. He could have been using it to steal."

"Maybe. He could also have had it for protection."

"I guess," Sofia said. "He's been homeless for a month, so anything's possible."

She sank her pint. "Anyway, what do you think we'd be talking about if we weren't talking shop?"

"Huh?"

"You and me. If we had to pick, say, a non-work subject. What would we pick?"

"I'm not very good at—"

"I'm not saying we have to. I'm just curious to know what we might talk about. You don't strike me as one for small talk."

Barnes wasn't sure if it was some kind of subconscious Jedi mind trick or just natural biology, but as she spoke he noticed her hands for the first time. They were smooth and elegant, with long, slender, naked fingers that, wrapped around the pint glass, seemed somehow simultaneously incongruous and defiantly feminine.

He opened his mouth like a guppy, closing it again when his phone began to ring. It was a brief conversation, and he kept his eyes more or less on Sofia for the duration.

He put the phone on the table. Her eyebrows went up.

"Custody," Barnes said.

"Should I be getting you to predict the lottery numbers?"

He shook his head. "He went through LiveScan. It's definitely him. They were calling because he's asking to speak to me."

"What about?"

"I'll find out in about ten minutes."

He looked at his watch and fixed his gaze on one of the scrolled pelmets over the double doors as he mentally ran through his to-do list.

"I can go, if you're busy," she said.

"No busier than any other day. Besides, it's not like I have to rush off."

"Don't I know it."

They stood up to go. The last of the sun was melting away behind the horizon, but the drinkers on the terrace showed no signs of throwing in the towel.

They paused for a moment on the corner of Grange Road and South Street as the town hall bonged eight on the hour.

"Let me go," she said. "I need to read him the charges anyway. If I speak to him while you finish up, then we might even get to finish our conversation. The non-work bit of it," she added.

He chewed it over.

"Okay," he said. "But if it's anything more than asking the time, come get me."

"I am but a messenger," she said, spreading her hands.

They turned up the alleyway that led behind the station — Sofia headed on into the custody garage, while Barnes peeled off to climb the rickety death-trap fire escape that led over the garages and into what had, not so long ago, been the CID office.

"Sofia?" he called.

She turned around.

"Thanks."

Her face crinkled into a smile that he thought he hadn't seen before, and then she disappeared into the gloom. He climbed the fire escape, the bolts creaking under his weight and blowing out white puffs of masonry dust from their sockets, and he thought: maybe getting rid of this place is long overdue.

The former CID office resembled a storeroom these days, but it still looked and smelled like the old area control room it had once been. A couple of workstations were still hooked up — Barnes walked over to one, thinking at least they now had permanent digs in somewhere where the dominant colour wasn't brown.

He heard the screaming as he sat down. It was a shrill, high-pitched shriek of pain and horror. It was female, but other than that . . .

He turned and ran out, half-falling, half-climbing back down the fire escape. He sprinted across the surgery car park to the descending shutters as fast as the jarring in his leg would allow, ducking underneath them and into the garage before they rolled shut completely.

The garage was empty, but he could hear a commotion on the other side of the cell block walls.

It was another three sets of doors with keycode entry pads before he could get anywhere near an answer, and he ran down the corridor to see Nippers and a gaggle of officers kneeling around Sofia's prone form. One of them was Gabby Glover.

"What happened?" Barnes yelled.

"Prisoner," Nippers shouted without looking around. Barnes looked to see two more cops fighting with Reeve as they tried to stuff him back into his cell. "He chucked his coffee over her."

"Fuck's sake, Barnes," Glover said, looking up as he pulled on some latex gloves. "Will you go call an ambulance?"

* * *

After the ambulance had left with Sofia and Nippers had sealed off the corner of the cell block, Barnes went to the custody office.

"I need to speak to him," Barnes said. He was full of nervous energy, bouncing from foot to foot. Nippers looked him up and down.

"No can do, boss. As it is, we're going to have to shout the charges through the cell hatch," he said. "Besides, it would get you nowhere."

He pointed at the CCTV monitors. Reeve was pacing his cell, pausing periodically to scream expletives at nothing.

"Did he say anything? At all? At any point?"

"'Die, you fucking bitch.' I may be paraphrasing."

"Did he say why he wanted to speak to us? To me?"

"Just something about having important information."

"And it was just a trap? He asked for me — Sofia came. Was the boiling water intended for me? Or was he pissed off that I didn't come myself?"

"I know you're upset about your colleague, boss, but you're asking questions I don't think I can answer."

"How did he end up with a boiling drink in the first place?"

Nippers said nothing, but eyed Barnes from underneath a grey monobrow that shifted like a suspension bridge in a heavy wind.

Barnes took some deep breaths, and turned back to the monitor, where the fuzzy, monochrome image of Reeve continued to barrel around his cell.

"It's not him," he said, eventually. "It can't be."

"Boss, it is. You know it is. He's been printed and swabbed, and you only have to look at him. Your informant made the right call."

Barnes had a single image of Reeve throughout the investigation imprinted on his mind. Waiting patiently at home to be arrested, in interview, at the charge desk, throughout his trial. Stoic, impassive, emotionless.

He looked back at the monitor. This wasn't the same man.

It couldn't be.

And yet, it was.

27

Barnes took the hexagonal stairwell at a slow climb, the mud-coloured stone walls smooth and cool under his palm, his footsteps echoing up into the ceiling as he rotated around the lift shaft that even he had, of late, considered using. This would surely mark the beginning of the end, because it was a death trap.

He pushed the double doors out onto the main floor. Early evening on a Sunday, and the place was deserted, even with the surplus troops laid on for the air show. He'd started to double back on himself towards the former CID office when he saw the door to the command suite open. Jefferson Riaz was at his desk, holding his chin, his brow furrowed in a look of concentration.

Barnes wandered over and pushed open the massive oak door.

"Boss got you working weekends, huh? So much for my sociable hours promise."

Riaz looked up and pushed his chair away from the screen. He tilted his head. "Last weekend it was crunching numbers for some urgent performance meeting. This weekend he's Gold for the air show and needed someone to carry his bag. Next weekend . . . some funny-handshake meeting or other, I think."

"I'm sorry."

Riaz shrugged. "On, off, doesn't really make any odds. It's not like I have a wife and kids to rush home to."

Barnes raised an eyebrow. "No one at all?"

"Just me and my mother. Believe that?"

"Is she . . ."

"She's not a well woman. I have certain . . . responsibilities. But they apply whether I'm on duty or off. So, like I say, it makes no odds."

Barnes perched on the edge of the opposite desk and examined a biro.

"He's going to fuck you, you know."

Riaz's face was impassive. "I wondered why he wanted me up here. Me, of all people. I thought it was just to keep me close and out of trouble while the IPCC sniff around. I figured there was more to it, I just . . . are you okay, guv? You look a little pale."

Barnes shook his head slightly, like it was a tremendous effort. "James Reeve. We got him."

Riaz sat forward as if he'd been stung. "You did? How? When?"

"Just now, on the seafront. Some air show punter recognised him from the paper and called it in."

Riaz shook his head and thumped the table lightly. "Shit. I could have been there."

"Surprised you didn't have your radio on."

"I did when I first started up here, but the boss didn't like the noise. It's now gathering dust in my bottom drawer."

"Don't feel bad. He had a gun on him, so you'd have been sidelined anyway. ARVs responded and put a baton round into him."

"Where did he get a gun?"

"Wish I knew. He didn't feel like telling us. At least not in interview. Then we got a phone call saying he wanted to

272

talk, so Sofia went down to his cell. Turned out all he wanted to do was chuck his coffee in her face."

"Jesus. When was this?"

"Just now."

"She okay?"

"Too soon to tell. Ambo's just carted her off to hospital."

"You didn't go with her?"

"Standing room only, with the boss in there too."

"Gabby? He was going home, last I heard."

"Well, he was doing a good job of first aid when I got there. Must have heard the screams on his way out." Barnes shut his eyes. "It should have been me. He wanted to see me. Sofia offered."

Riaz frowned.

"What?" Barnes said.

"He's facing a bunch of charges, right? And now you're gonna add, what, GBH to the list?"

"At least."

Riaz shook his head. "It doesn't make sense."

"If I had a pound for every time someone said that to me . . ."

"But it doesn't. You know better than me, but if he'd been convicted, he'd have got maybe five years? Served half of that?"

"Maybe less."

"And that's a big if. The odds were on his being acquitted, no?"

"I know what you're going to say."

"Well?"

"I've been driving myself crazy trying to work it out. And everyone that could tell me something about it either ends up dead or stonewalls us completely."

"He must have felt it was his only option. Caught in the middle of a justice sandwich."

"Huh?"

"Well, the victim was a shitbag, right? Meaning his friends and family probably were too. He might not have fancied walking out of court a free man."

Barnes was silent. It was nothing he hadn't already considered.

"It stands to reason that they probably had people inside too. Anjou Acosta as a minimum. You're in trouble if you're convicted, and you're in trouble if you're acquitted. So you make your own luck and scoot out the middle."

"I could buy that, but I don't buy the way he collected extra charges while he was on the run. He was practically shopping for them. GBH on a cop from the confines of your cell was the two-for-one special. If you want prison that badly, why not just see out the end of your trial?"

Riaz shrugged. "Who knows what a desperate man will do?"

Barnes shook his head again. He didn't have an answer for that one.

Riaz eyed him. "You look like you've given up, guv."

"I don't know where else to look."

"Back to the beginning and start again, I guess. Like all those cold cases."

"Those cases tend to be more about 'who' than 'why'."

"Your attention has been all over the manhunt. Now you've got him. You can start to look at the whole picture. What about the scene?"

"The house?"

Riaz nodded. "Mightn't hurt to go back to square one."

Barnes looked up at the ceiling. "I practically knocked it down. You know that. There was nothing to find there besides Ikea photo frames, empty suitcases and bloodstained foundations."

"Well, associates, then. There has to be an intel log hidden somewhere linking one to another . . . Hang on. Suitcases? What suitcases?"

"Suitcases. The suitcases by the front door. They were empty. No idea why."

"There were no suitcases when I was there."

The temperature in the room seemed to drop slightly. The sound of the air show PA carried faintly on the breeze, zigzagging back to town from the seafront.

"What do you mean? They were right by the front door."

"Not when I was there, they weren't."

"You wouldn't even have seen them going in."

"Maybe not, but I would have on the way out."

"How can you be sure? You were rather preoccupied."

"Guv, my memory has led to me being on PSD's employee of the month wall. I may be no good at this stuff—" he gestured at the performance report in front of him — "but I can tell you categorically there were no suitcases by the front door of Mandy Luis's house when Claudia and I attended."

Their eyes locked for a moment.

"Shit," Barnes said. "Then . . ."

He spun round and booted up the machine opposite Riaz. It was almost deliberately slow.

"*Come on come on come on . . .*" he muttered.

"What are you doing?" Riaz said.

"Looking for the scene logs," Barnes said.

Riaz stood up and moved around to Barnes's shoulder. "You have it online?"

"Got one of the secretaries to transcribe it."

"Sounds like a fun job."

"It's mind-numbing, but extremely useful. One of these days we'll invent something that will allow us to type a log straight onto the database, rather than producing dog-eared rain-sodden scene logs in court that are like poppadoms from being dried on a radiator . . . here we go."

Riaz moved closer. "What are you hoping to find?"

"Anything that stands out. Here . . . first names on the log are you and Claudia. Clever lad."

"Huh?"

"The kid on scene guard. I tore him off a strip for not checking my ID but looks like he had the good sense to add everyone that got there before him retrospectively. Starting with you two."

They exchanged glances briefly.

"So," Barnes said. "Everyone who entered the scene between you and me. Sergeant Tam Bates, PC Karlie Tann, PC Hannah Vanderwal, PC Darren Cork, PC Pete Lamb . . ."

"Wait, hold up. Pete was there?"

"Looks like it. Hang on, let me find the statements. Here: your skipper went in first and the rest of them did a cursory search to clear the building, then they all retreated outside and locked down the neighbourhood. Why the surprise? You're all on the same section, aren't you?"

"Yes, but he was meant to be on annual leave that day."

Barnes shook his head. "How do you *remember* this stuff?"

Riaz shrugged.

"Anyway, it might not mean anything," Barnes continued. "Plans for a hot date could have gone out the window and he decided to come in, save his hours."

"Either way, you're saying there were empty suitcases by the door when you turned up, and I'm saying they weren't there when I left, then we're saying that one of this lot must have put them there."

Barnes stared at him.

"Aren't we?"

"I guess," Barnes said.

"There's a hell of a lot of theories floating around this job, guv. You're going to have to grab one and nail it down."

Barnes rubbed his temple. The kid was right.

"Speaking of Pete, does he know yet? About Sofia?"

Barnes frowned. "No. Why would he?"

"They're dating."

"They're *what*?"

"Actually, they might even be closer to an item."

"Shit." Barnes stared at Riaz. "She was there too."

* * *

276

Barnes drove to the hospital, trying not to calculate how many times he had been there in the last twelve months. He crawled through the sun-baked metal caterpillar that represented the exodus of air show traffic along the Lewes Road towards Rodmill roundabout.

The kid had needled him, both because he had politely and obliquely given Barnes a kick up the backside, but also, Barnes thought, as he eventually cleared the roundabout and headed onto Kings Drive, because he was right.

Riaz had reframed Barnes's considerations around the case now that Reeve was in custody, and, in so doing, had given him food for thought. Not necessarily new food for thought, just food for thought that might otherwise have been further down the list of priorities.

Just like Eve used to.

The realisation that his prowess as an investigator — not to mention his career generally — owed considerably more to her existence than he'd ever given her credit for caused his breath to stall in his chest, and he had to pull over briefly onto the Esso forecourt.

Trying not to think about things just meant the pile of stuff leaning on the closed door was simply building up. He'd have to let it in sooner or later, or it would burst in at a time of its own choosing when it finally got too heavy.

He got out of the car, suddenly worried that the simple act of finding a parking space in the hospital car park might be beyond him. He filled up, and then tucked the vehicle behind the car wash, out of immediate view, and crossed the road by the Rodmill pub, heading along the tree-lined pedestrian entrance into the hospital.

He had hoped that, for a Sunday evening, A&E would be quiet, but it was its usual state of carnage. On production of his warrant card, Barnes ascertained that there were four casualties from a serious town centre RTC in Majors — two of whom were conscious and letting the world know it — and an old lady who had been mugged on her way home whom they were trying to stabilise before sending her to theatre.

Sofia was already on a ward. There wasn't anything they would tell Barnes, other than they wouldn't be operating until much later.

He headed slowly upstairs into the surgical wing through the main corridor, noting that the shotgun-damaged yellow phone card machine was still there, swathed in a token criss-cross of red-and-white tape.

He hovered in the entrance of the ward, where he was pointedly ignored by the clerk, two nurses and someone with a stethoscope around their neck whom Barnes presumed must have been on work experience.

He scanned the scribbled names and bay allocations on a large whiteboard. Sofia had her own room near the ward entrance, and so he doubled back the way he had come. He had timed his visit as dinner was being served, and just about managed to keep his stomach in check as he faced the aroma of stew laced with disinfectant and faeces.

His own comparatively trivial personal issues with both the frequency and nature of his visits to Eastbourne DGH were sidelined when he was confronted by the nurse.

"Help you?" The challenge may as well have been *friend or foe*?

She looked like she was in a hurry, a wad of patient notes clutched to her bosom, but she took the time to stop and accost the loitering visitor, practically barricading the door to Sofia's room.

Despite himself, Barnes started to stutter and stammer an explanation, before realising he recognised her.

"I know you. Annie, right?"

She frowned and tilted her head, then recognition spread across her face — albeit not a particularly warm shade of recognition — and she exhaled heavily through her nose.

"You're the policeman."

"The one responsible for you being bashed over the head. How is it?" he asked.

"Don't feel bad. You're indirectly responsible at best. And it's getting there, thanks," she said, fingering her forehead.

"How are you? That's a genuine question," he added — and it was. They had both suffered at the hands of an unknown stranger — small talk seemed trite in the extreme.

She thought about it. "I'm . . . doing okay."

"Any nightmares?"

She shook her head. "Not so far."

"That's good."

"How are *you*? I didn't realise he shot at you until I saw it on the news."

"I'm okay."

"That's a genuine question."

He smiled.

"Fair's fair," she said.

"Okay, well, honestly? I think I'm just holding it together until the investigation is over."

"Sorry to say, I could tell that just by looking at you. This investigation? My case?"

"I think your case is the outer layer of a very large onion, but yes. Truth be told, I want it to be over, but I'm dreading it at the same time."

"How's it going? The investigation, I mean. I'm surprised I haven't heard back from anyone yet."

Barnes swallowed. "Heard back?"

She raised her eyebrows. Barnes noticed that they formed an almost perfect arch when she did so.

"Yes. I gave my statement, but didn't remember anything, so I can't have been of much use. Then details started to come back to me. Not much, you understand, more like the edges being filled in."

"You . . . you happen to remember what your assailant looked like?"

"Only a little, but that's why I called your office. He was big, and I think he had camo combats on. The main thing was his hair. He had it all piled up in a topknot, and not a very tidy one. He had a thick beard too. Made me think he'd been camping in the jungle for a month."

Barnes's notebook was out.

"You say you called us about this?"

"Yes, I left a message with a DC. Female. I forget the name, sorry."

"No, it's not your fault, it's ours. Mine."

She gave him a half-smile. "That's what you said last time."

"Annie, we'll need another statement from you. Soon as you can."

"You have my number," she said. "And when your investigation is all done, you can tell me whether you were right to dread it being over." She made to go.

"Listen," Barnes said, "thanks for . . . you know." He indicated Sofia's room with his notebook. "Giving a shit."

"That's okay. No one else was going to do it." She indicated the ward clerk and prepubescent doctor with her stack of notes. "She's your . . . ?"

"Colleague," he said, after a moment. "And I appreciate that."

"You should put a cop on the door."

"She is a cop."

"Well, cop or not, she's still pretty defenceless, and — my experience — an injury like that on a woman is almost always going to have been caused by a man."

"Well, it was, but the one that did this is in custody."

"Maybe so, but there are always others," she said, and walked off to the desk.

He stared after her.

"Barnes?" Sofia's voice sounded small and hollow. "Is that you?"

He stopped staring after the nurse called Annie and entered Sofia's room.

She was half sitting up in bed, propped up against a stack of pillows, the end of the evening August sun filtering through the vertical blinds. Were it not for her heavily bandaged eyes and the strange-looking plastic shield around her face, she would have looked almost serene.

"Oh, God," he said, and sat down heavily on a chair. He grasped her hand and squeezed it. "Sofia . . ."

"It hurts, Barnes. It hurts so much. I heard the plastic and the eye registrars arguing about who should take priority. I might not get my sight back. They were talking about grafts and . . ."

Her face tried to contort under the plastic shield as her chest hitched with anguished, wracking sobs.

"It should have been me. It should have been me. Why didn't you let me go?" Barnes said. He wanted to ask her, *What did he say?*

He wanted to ask her, *Why did he do it?*

He wanted to ask her, *Are you dirty?*

He wanted to ask her, *Why didn't you tell me a key witness called us with new information?*

But none of it seemed right. Not right then, anyway. And so he just held her hand until she calmed down enough to talk.

As it was, he didn't need to ask her anything.

She told him all of it.

28

Several times during Sofia's story Barnes was galvanised with urges like electrical pulses — the urge to call PSD, the urge to call Shaw, the urge to arrest her.

In the end, he did nothing. The story was punctuated by bouts of wretched sobbing, and in the end, he just sat back in the bedside chair and held her hand while she delivered her confession.

There are always others.

He was awoken a couple of hours later by the sound of running footsteps. At least two pairs of footsteps. Heavy, approaching.

He jerked upright in his chair in time to see a porter and security guard thundering past Sofia's room. They headed out of the ward and into the main corridor. Barnes caught a clip of chatter from their radios as they passed: "Assistance A&E . . ."

He got up and followed, groggy and aching from sleeping in the chair. He staggered out into the corridor. It was dark outside — he'd slept for a couple of hours at least.

Once he stopped weaving like a drunkard, he picked up his pace and hurried down to A&E. It would have been easy enough if he didn't already know where it was — he would have just had to follow the screaming.

He arrived in Majors to find a security guard and two uniformed cops pinning what appeared to be another uniformed cop to the floor, who was furiously wriggling and yelling. More cops were running in to assist.

"What the hell is happening?" Barnes yelled.

"This lad's mother got mugged. The kid who did it is over there," somebody said.

Barnes turned. The yelling on the floor was being mirrored by more yelling from the opposite bay, where a skinny youth with a zero-cut and purple eyes was protesting about the outrageous behaviour of the cop who had seen fit to attack him while he was defenceless and naked save for the flimsy surgical gown.

The black shirts parted long enough for Barnes to get a glimpse of their quarry. He muscled in when he saw Riaz's contorted face.

"Enough, enough!" Barnes said. "Let him up. He's calm. You're calm, Jefferson, right?"

"Yes, I'm calm," Riaz shouted. "Get off me!"

The cops slowly eased off him, and Barnes helped him into a sitting position.

"Have you seen her?" he said, rubbing his shoulder. "Have you seen what those scumbags have done to her?"

"Go and sit in the family room. I will handle it."

"Go and look. It's a fucking—"

"I said I will handle it! Go! You." Barnes pointed at one of the other uniformed cops. "Go sit with him."

"I've . . . I've arrested him," said the cop.

"No, you bloody well haven't," said Barnes. "Whatever words you've said, you can damn well unsay. You two—" he pointed at two more cops — "go and arrest that clown. And then get him out of here."

He pointed across the room, where the kid with the zero-cut had stopped protesting, yanked out his cannula and was now attempting to creep unnoticed out of the exit doors.

Barnes debriefed the remaining uniformed cop. It transpired that Mrs Riaz had been hobbling home when she was set upon by a small group on the boardwalk that led to her flat. She put up a fight, and they laid into her to take her bag. They escaped in a stolen Fiesta, which the driver, off his head on rock, wrapped around a lamppost in Silverdale Road half an hour later.

Riaz had made his way to the hospital from Grove Road after getting the call, and, through miserable coincidence, the two hitherto separate incidents had been joined up when Mrs Riaz had been wheeled around for an X-ray and had made an on-the-spot confrontational ID of the main perp as he was arguing with one of the nurses. She had called for her son, who had lost his shit.

When some semblance of order had been restored, Barnes apologised to the charge nurse — who reciprocated, on the basis that he had no idea the two events were connected — then went to where Mrs Riaz was sleeping on her trolley, apparently having been helped there with a dose of something or other that Barnes felt he might need to procure himself.

She was a small woman with soft papery skin hanging on a narrow frame, and she was a mess. Two black eyes, a swollen jaw the colour of a summer fruit pudding and a spread of black-and-purple bruising running from her right buttock down to her ankle. Barnes's hand went to his mouth. No wonder Riaz had reacted the way he did.

He pulled the curtain closed and went to the tiny room set aside for those families who needed to process earth-shattering news away from the main gaggle.

Riaz sat there on the two-seat vinyl sofa, staring at the bare pea-green wall four feet opposite.

The cop sitting with Riaz was staring at the floor, his left leg jiggling nervously. Barnes made eye contact and flicked his head towards the door. The cop slunk out without a fuss.

Barnes sat down heavily, the vinyl imitating his own sigh as he did so. They sat for a moment in silence, the ambient noise of A&E beyond the door filling the space.

"They got the bag back," Barnes said, eventually. "Found it in the car. Looks like most of it is still in there."

Riaz said nothing.

"They're going away for a long time," Barnes said. "Jefferson, I'm sorry. Do you want me to drive you home?"

"Did you see her?"

"I did."

"Why would anyone do this?" Riaz said, his voice small and cracked. "That woman never hurt a single living thing. And these . . . animals, they . . . "

"They're going to prison."

"Are they? They'll plead not guilty, because why wouldn't they? That means my mother worrying about having to give evidence six, nine, twelve months down the line. If she survives that long. Meantime, the house gets spray-painted and the car gets torched."

"Jefferson . . . it will be okay. She will be okay."

Riaz's shoulders began to gently shake.

"When you've got yourself straight, I need to share something with you," Barnes said. "Sofia, she . . . She's compromised."

Riaz stood up. "I'm going to sit with my mother."

"I'll keep this investigation myself. She will get justice."

"You'd better be right about that, or I will kill them all. That's a promise."

"I'll pretend I didn't hear that."

"Do whatever you need to."

"Is there anything you need me to get? Anyone to call?" Barnes said. "What about Claudia?"

Riaz stopped in the doorway, and turned. "We're all outcasts. Who are you trying to impress?"

* * *

Barnes left the hospital and started walking back towards the petrol station, but before he crossed the road something occurred to him, and he turned and walked back along the hospital's service road towards the Rodmill roundabout, past the aged Armco barrier, block-printed with "DISTRICT

285

GENERAL HOSPITAL" in blue lettering, past the yellow "KEEP CLEAR" hatching that stretched back from the roundabout — a mitigation against the design flaw that meant a departing ambulance would otherwise catch a tailback more often than not before even getting warmed up.

Barnes hugged the kerb and then joined the cycle path that cut back behind Cross Levels Way and ran parallel to both the road and the back of the hospital, separated by a dense line of foliage and a grass bank several feet high.

He walked for a few hundred yards, then his leg started to twinge as he reached the northeast corner of the hospital site. The hot smell of industrial laundry dryers drifted like smog through the air, and the incinerator chimney fingered the sky like an enormous, scorched cigarette. Between the trees the brown aluminium cladding of the clinical stores and the red brick of the psychiatric department were visible.

He turned and pushed his way through the waist-high undergrowth, and scaled the bank, sliding awkwardly down the other side and just about regaining his balance before he tumbled into the road.

He took a moment to rub his leg, then followed the white line, moving slowly towards the college and hugging the verge so as not to be taken out by a passing car. The evening air was thick with warmth, and although the sun was still spreading over the edges of the horizon, it was more night than dusk.

And then he saw it.

His breath caught in his chest, and he realised he hadn't actually been back to the scene of the crash since that day — the day Eve lost her life in a jumble of metal. There hadn't seemed any point, but now he was here, it was like stepping back in time, a portal to the past where all his memories and spent emotions were concentrated in the one spot. He imagined he could see the faint tyre marks on the road, wondered if the collection of glass fragments and pieces of old bumper swept to the side of the tarmac were from that day, fantasised that forensic opportunities could still be retrieved from this fossilised crime scene.

The 40 mph sign was practically a marker to the location of the impact, of the exact spot where Eve had been alive one second but not the next. Even thinking the words of the fact of her death was like a concession to some huge, obscene reality.

He frowned. There was a fresh bunch of tulips wrapped around the metal cylinder, the brittle skeletal remnants of previous offerings still there underneath them.

A car whistled past him. He suddenly felt bad for not having come to this lonely place before and — with a frantic edge to his movements — tore down the dead flowers so only the tulips remained. There was no card or message — Barnes figured it must have been her mother who left them, although this strip of road was hostile to pedestrians, and he couldn't see the elderly lady navigating the bank.

He kicked the brown remains into the foliage and turned to go — and saw PC Claudia Knight standing there. She grabbed his arm to stop him from stepping back into the road.

"Sorry! I didn't mean to scare you."

"Claudia? What . . . what are you doing here?"

She frowned. "You called me."

"To meet Jefferson at the hospital."

Her eyes roved over his face, and then the lamppost, and the dead brown flowers at his feet. The frown softened.

"I saw you walking out as I pulled up. I wondered why you weren't heading to your car and . . . I followed you."

Barnes took a deep breath, feeling naked and exposed, as if he had to explain himself.

"Is this . . . why you're so sad?"

His breathing came heavier, his eyes filled and the back of his throat stung, an orgasm of grief threatening to erupt from his body.

"Jesus, don't . . . please don't be nice to me," he croaked. "I . . ."

And then he stopped, for he knew his voice would betray him.

She held out a hand.

"Come on. Come out of the road."

* * *

He allowed himself to be led back through the brush to the cycle path, and back towards the hospital, leaving the strange and lonely marker behind him.

Back on familiar territory, he managed to compose himself a little, and briefed Claudia on what had happened to Riaz's mother. Her hand went to her mouth as he spoke.

"He just needs . . . a friend," Barnes said.

"I just came from the scene," Claudia said. "I've been doing the house-to-house."

Barnes bristled. "And?"

She pulled out her notebook. "Neighbour saw most of it. Driver was the main instigator. The poor woman fought to keep her bag, and . . ." Her voice tailed off. "She should have just given it up. Driver put the boot in even after he'd got the bag off her. The neighbour heard one of the others say 'That's enough.' Pulled him off, by all accounts."

"Anything else?"

"Yeah. It wasn't just a street robbery. They found the address and keys in the bag, and did the apartment as well." She lowered the notebook. "It's a mess."

"I'm not sure Riaz knows that yet."

"It's okay. I'll tell him."

She put the notebook away and headed to the hospital entrance.

"You coming too?"

"I need to go piece this thing together," Barnes said. "But before I do, I want to look each one of these pricks in the eye."

They separated in the main foyer — Barnes turned left towards A&E, while Claudia continued straight on into the medical wing.

The driver was lying impassively on his trolley, a glittering of cuts across his face. His eyes seemed heavy, and they flicked dolefully up to Barnes as he pulled the curtain back, flanked by the two uniformed cops guarding him. There was a fresh bandage around his middle that was already starting to show red seepage.

"Any idea how long we're gonna be here, guv?" one of the patrol officers asked. "Two escorts per DP doesn't leave us much to answer calls."

Barnes ignored him and left the cubicle.

Perp Two was either asleep or unconscious. Perp Three was in quite a bit of pain, and was writhing and cursing as a nurse attempted to do his obs, while the two cops assigned to him looked on with grim-faced, gum-chewing righteousness.

Perp Four was sitting on the chair in his cubicle. He was staring at the ceiling with his fingers laced. Unlike the others, Four still had his own clothes on, but a large dressing was stuck to his forehead. He didn't even look at Barnes. Barnes stood for a moment in the cubicle entrance. They all were sallow-looking, skinny kids in their twenties, but the red-eyed desperation of the others didn't seem to be present in this one. At least, not to the same extent. There seemed to be a degree of intelligence in the face of Perp Four, and Barnes knew that this one had been the one to pull the driver off Riaz's mother.

He didn't dwell on the fact, however, because as he went to the nurses' station, something occurred to him. A memory, a flash of recognition.

He went back to the driver. He didn't break stride this time, but marched straight in, leaned over the driver and dropped his knee on the bandaged wound.

The driver screamed. Before the uniforms pulled him off, Barnes hissed in his ear, hot and loud: "Why . . . aren't you . . . in *prison*?"

ACT THREE

29

"Airplane . . . Airplane." Claudia gently tugged at Riaz's sleeve. "Come on. You need to rest."

"I'm not going anywhere. I can rest here," he mumbled, his breath sour. The slow, steady chirping of the array of machines with their esoteric lights was oddly comforting. That contrasted with the ache in his neck and the complete dead numbness below his right elbow. An electric shock of pins and needles flowed like a river back into his arm as he sat up and the blood gushed back into it.

The night outside the window was like a black curtain. The arc lights of the hospital glowed, somehow reassuring in the knowledge that they would never go out, that the place never closed.

He stared at his mother. The tubes had made her lower chin jut out, as if she were pouting. The low light softened the injuries, somehow, and Riaz couldn't tell if she were asleep, unconscious or dead.

"Airplane . . ."

He remembered Claudia was in the room, and turned to look at her. She was still in uniform, the radio winking on her lapel. She looked tired.

"Claudia . . . you don't have to stay here. You need to rest."

"We both do." Her voice was soft. "Come on. Let your mum rest. One good night's sleep, and I'll have you back here before breakfast."

He turned back to his mother.

"You want to be here when she wakes up, I get that. You won't miss it. I promise. She needs to sleep."

He wanted to protest, but he felt himself yielding as she gently pulled him out of the chair.

He rested his head on the window as she drove him home. The silence and steady motion were comforting.

"I'll take you to mine," she said.

He lifted his head off the window. The discomfort was like a sudden shooting pain in his bowel.

"Yours? But isn't—"

"I live alone, Airplane. Well, besides the cat. I have a spare room. En suite. I won't even know you're there. Can't promise the inverse, though. I like to sing in the shower."

She looked over at him, encouraging him to join in the joke. He didn't reciprocate, and her face clouded in a fog of awkwardness.

"Take me to my place. Please."

"Whatever you say. My place is closer to the hospital. Just saying."

"I know. It's not . . . I just need my own space."

"I get that. Just . . . look, prepare yourself, okay?"

"What do you mean?"

"They burgled the flat too, Jefferson. They found your mum's house keys."

"You . . . you're welcome to stay," he said, apparently not having heard her. "I have a spare room too."

She didn't say anything, didn't take her eyes from the road.

She parked up underneath the boardwalk, and they climbed the fashionably functional steel staircase to the high-rise apartment blocks. The tide was out, and the smell of the mudflats drifted over from the lock.

Riaz let them in, and the lift ascended in silence. He leaned against the wall, as if standing tall was just too much effort, his eyes staring at something way beyond the lift doors. Claudia edged over and gently took his hand.

He knew someone was in the apartment the moment he unlocked the door. He could sense the sounds of shuffling and the nameless clicks and thuds of items being moved.

DS Phil Fountain was over by the glass balcony doors, lifting and overturning the sofa cushions with blue-gloved hands.

"Welcome home," he said, not taking his eyes from his work. "I'm glad you're here."

"What the hell is this?" Claudia demanded.

"If you were expecting SOCO, they've been and gone. This is a search warrant," Fountain said, still not pausing his search. He ran his fingers down the side of the sofa. "Despite the ransacking, you must have the cleanest apartment I have ever seen, PC Riaz. Those bins look brand new and unused. I haven't found anything yet, but my suspicions are working overtime. If you're UC, you need a better legend. Eat some pasties once in a while. Just to put something in the bin."

"He's on the spectrum, you fucking idiot," Claudia said.

Fountain finally straightened up. "'He's on the spectrum, *sergeant*,'" he said.

Claudia folded her arms. "How do morons like you end up in PSD? Aren't you supposed to be the last bastion of ethics and professionalism? Role models or some crap?"

"Claudia . . ." Riaz said, "It's okay."

"Like hell it is."

"What, exactly, are you going to do about it, Constable Knight?"

Fountain walked over and pressed the warrant into Riaz's sternum. Riaz flinched.

"I'd say your only trump card is to pick up the phone to your lover. Who, it has to be said, has already been briefed. As has the Fed."

Claudia bristled. Riaz sensed her fists clenching. He lightly took her wrist.

"Claudia . . . he's goading you. An arrest for obstruction would make his day. You'd be out on your ear."

Fountain smiled thinly, stepped back again and resumed the search.

"Civil lawsuits are a dish best served cold," Claudia said.

"See you in court, then, I guess," Fountain answered, his attention back on the sofa.

Riaz frowned. "What exactly are you looking for?"

"It's all there," Fountain said.

Riaz studied the warrant. "This just says 'articles in connection with a misconduct investigation'."

"Misconduct investigation?" Claudia said. "What sort of misconduct?"

Fountain stopped again and gave a big sigh, as if explaining himself were some enormous effort of philanthropic courtesy.

"Mr Riaz, I firmly believe that the intelligence that led you to Ty Godden and a holdall full of heroin came to you by decidedly unethical, possibly even illegal, means. And I'm going to prove it."

"But I told you the source."

"A source who ended up dead. And when I'm done here, I'm going to do your car, the communal bins downstairs, your bank statements and your phone records."

"This is . . . wait. Are you here alone?" Claudia said.

Fountain smiled tightly, like someone about to blow a trumpet.

"Oh no," he said. "My ops team is already downstairs in the underground car park. I'm actually about done. Nice place you got here, Jefferson. For a point-three PC, that is. Let's hope you aren't living beyond your means."

He snapped the gloves off and headed out the door.

When the apartment door had slammed shut, Riaz surveyed the living room. The search had left it untidy — but then, by his standards, anything less than showroom perfect was untidy. It certainly could have been worse.

He caught Claudia's eye, and they both hurried to the bedroom.

"Bastards," Claudia said in the doorway.

The bedroom had been properly ransacked, but there was no way of knowing whether this was because of the burglary, the search warrant or a combination of both. The mattress had been pulled off the bed and was lying across a chest of drawers. A triple wardrobe had been completely emptied, the contents discarded across the pile floor, and the weight of all the doors being open had caused it to come crashing forwards.

"Maybe we should go to your place after all," Riaz said, trying to suppress the sudden feeling that the disarray had caused in him — like there wasn't enough oxygen in his lungs and no amount of gasping would help.

"He's fishing," Claudia said. "If he actually had anything, they would have put the bracelets on you the moment you walked in."

Riaz looked at her. For the first time the gulf between them in terms of time served was obvious — her seven years to his three. Her eyes roved about the room as her mind worked.

"What?" he said.

"There's another possibility," she said. "I don't want to speculate, but if they really thought you were in over your head, if they actually thought you had ongoing criminal associations, the search might just have been a smokescreen."

"What do you mean?"

She stared at him, and let him work it out. His eyes widened.

"You're saying they've bugged the place?"

"I don't want to sound paranoid, but it does depend on how heavy the shit you're into is."

"I'm not into any shit!" Riaz protested.

She held up a finger. "Listen, I believe you. But there's no smoke without fire, and something's got his dander up. You know that as well as I do. Look, I'll help you tidy up, then we'll go to mine, open a bottle of wine and you can tell me everything. We can try to work out if he's putting two and two together and making ten."

* * *

296

An hour later Riaz sat awkwardly on the sofa in Claudia's living room, perched on the edge while he regarded the untouched glass of Merlot in front of him. Claudia's own glass was already at half mast, with a faint lipstick mark at the rim.

Riaz took the time to drink in the contents of the front room while he waited for Claudia to finish in the bathroom. The sound of the shower pummelling the enamel was loud, almost drowning out the Super Furry Animals album she had put on.

There were artefacts from her life everywhere. A purple-and-yellow windsurfing sail was pinned to the far wall, acting as a sort of canvas backdrop. An acoustic guitar hung on the wall next to a sprawling ivy plant, while large acrylic canvases showcasing wild galactic efforts were encased in frames on the wall. The room told the story of a single person whose personal life was as busy as her work life.

He tried to call the ward to see if his mother had woken up, but got no reply. Riaz stood up to look at some photographs above the television. There was one of Claudia's passing out parade at Hendon, one of her receiving some bravery award, pictured next to a handsome, smiling woman that Riaz took to be her mother. One of her skiing. One of her backpacking in a desert somewhere. One of her bungee jumping in New Zealand. One of her *busking*, of all things. No intimate others anywhere.

The shower stopped, causing an inexplicable bolt of anxiety to shoot up Riaz's spine.

Claudia emerged from the bedroom, her hair wet and combed, a towel still around her.

"Sorry," she said, hurrying across the wooden floor of the living room to grab some clothes from an airer. "Back in a sec."

She went back into the bedroom and appeared a minute or so later, this time in a Batgirl T-shirt and jeans.

She sat next to him on the sofa, grabbed her glass and tucked her feet under her backside. She smelled of tea tree and vanilla.

"Wow, that's better," she said, indicating the bathroom with her head. "Help yourself."

"I'm okay," he said. "Maybe later."

"You call the hospital?"

"No one's answering. Listen, there's something I didn't tell you about the intelligence."

She stiffened slightly and set her glass down. "I was waiting for this. Something you haven't told PSD?"

"Something I haven't told anyone."

"I'm listening."

"Jimmy Januarie. He wrote down the date, time and place of the drop on a piece of paper. I told Fountain this. I told him I got rid of it."

"And did you?"

He nodded. "I burned it. But there was something else on that paper."

"What?"

"A word. 'Lighthouse'."

She mulled this over, and then picked up the glass again. "What does it mean?"

"I haven't a clue."

"And you've told no one else?"

"No one."

"Why are you telling me?"

"I . . . I don't really know. I guess . . . you're the only one I trust. And . . . I need your advice. I don't really know how much danger I'm in."

She swirled the wine in the glass while she thought.

"It could mean anything," he added.

"That's what troubles me," she said. "You did the right thing keeping it to yourself. Suppose you blurt it out to someone who does know what it means? You could compromise yourself. I don't trust that Fountain, and if you can't trust PSD, who can you trust?"

"Well . . ."

"How did Jimmy Januarie come by the information?"

Riaz shrugged. "No idea. Best guess, he overheard the Tully clan shooting off their collective mouth."

"And, what, he gave it to the first plod that walked through his door?"

"More or less. He didn't trust the proper channels."

"'Lighthouse' is a code or something, right?"

"Seems to be. It wasn't a location . . . I don't think."

"Did he overhear that as well? Or did it come from somewhere else?"

Riaz shrugged for the second time in a minute.

She swirled the wine again. "He lived next door to them, right?"

"Right."

"He was also a juror in the trial of James Reeve?"

"Coincidence?"

"Which bit?" She frowned. "You don't think it's a bit odd that he was picked for jury service at the same time he overheard his neighbour crowing about a drugs drop?"

"Not impossible, given his address. The two cases aren't connected, anyway. The only common thread is . . . is . . ."

"You."

"Me," he said, in a small voice. "I responded to the call that led to him giving me that intel, and I responded to . . ."

He didn't finish the sentence. He didn't need to. Claudia's eyes glistened momentarily, and she finished her glass, pouring another in quick succession.

"What are you saying?" he said.

"I'm not saying anything . . . yet," she said. "I'm just figuring things out."

"I kind of assumed . . ."

"What? That CID would have been over this already? They may well have done, but it doesn't mean they arrived at any answers. They're maxed out, anyway. Fresh pairs of eyes won't hurt . . . will you please have a drink? I'm going to do the whole bottle on my own, at this rate."

He started slightly. He'd completely forgotten about his glass. He reached for it and took a gulp. She topped him up and put the bottle down.

"So, what order did it happen in? He lived in that house for . . . what?"

"Not long. About a year, he said. He moved down from London for sea air, is what he said."

"And the Tully lot?"

"Permanent coastal fixtures, but they've moved around a lot. They have to put them somewhere long enough for them to generate an ASBO complaint, then they move them off into a new address."

"The neighbours must love that."

"Well, when Anjou was around they were a lot easier to evict. The knife-throwing circus act kept the bar pretty low."

"So, when did they ship them into that address?"

"About two months before Mr Januarie biffed her on the nose."

"Okay. So assume he'd have had, what, two weeks' notice for jury service?"

"Maybe. More like six. I think it varies." He eyeballed her. "How would they have known he'd been summonsed for jury duty?"

"They wouldn't, necessarily," she said. "But what if someone else did?"

"Like who?"

"Like whoever at the council is responsible for finding an address for shitbag families who have to be rehoused every five minutes. And besides . . . hold on, we need to draw this."

She jumped up and grabbed some sheets of paper from the back of a small printer by the television, and a couple of marker pens from a drawer.

"CID will have done this . . ." said Riaz.

"If CID have, then they haven't shared it with you, have they?" she said, her back to him. "Besides, CID don't know about 'Lighthouse'."

She didn't wait for an answer, and instead started arranging the paper on the coffee table. "So . . . you responded to Januarie's assault complaint on . . . when?"

"Jean Tully was the complainant, actually, but . . . nineteenth of July."

"The intel he gave you. How much notice was it?"

"Three days. Twenty-second of July. A Saturday."

"Reeve escaped two days before." Claudia drew a thick black line and started punctuating it with dots to represent specific dates. "You and I . . . responded to the sighting the same day. Then everything goes to shit, and somebody kills Chris Jenner in his hospital bed. Somewhere in among all this, Jimmy Januarie goes missing."

"From what PSD told me, he was reported missing when the trial judge ordered a patrol to check his house when he didn't show up for jury duty. Twentieth of July. The day Reeve escaped."

"And then his body was found on the beach two days later."

She worked this out on her fingers, and scribbled *20 July* on the paper at the end of the row. Then she sat back and stared at the paper.

"You're telling me Jimmy Januarie washes up dead exactly three days after he gives you some Class-A drugs intel? And James Reeve escaped practically at the same time? The same week you and I watched Mandy Luis get murdered?"

She flung the marker pen, and it clanged on the glass.

"You can't tell me this is all coincidence," she said.

"*Lighthouse*," he said again. His voice was almost a whisper.

"What?"

"*Lighthouse*. I have to tell the DI. Barnes."

30

Barnes arrived back at Grove Road and parked out front. A sheet of rain whipped across the building.

A dark form was huddled in the doorway of the heavy wooden front doors. The figure was prone, and the assortment of sleeping bags, blankets and other itinerant belongings suggested it wasn't in a hurry to move.

Barnes stood there in the rain and flashed his badge.

"Police. You're trespassing. Clear off."

It was not an uncommon sight — the deep recess of the Georgian doorway often proved a convenient shelter to many — and many other times before, Barnes had just let it slide. Once, during a particularly bad storm, he had even opened up the front office in the early hours and allowed someone to sleep on the hard blue chairs in the vestibule while he worked on a file.

But not tonight. There were thorns in his blood, and this poor unfortunate was on the receiving end.

He knew he would feel bad later — particularly as the man said nothing, made no eye contact, just gathered his things and shuffled off without protest in the direction of the railway station.

Barnes watched him go, distracted momentarily by the man's curiously upright gait, then walked down the adjacent loading ramp and let himself into the station via the basement locker room, illuminated only by the sickly yellow arc light over the ordnance pit.

His feet echoed through the silent building as he climbed the stairwell, flicking on lights here and there as he went. The patrol centre was a hive of activity round the clock — not so its town centre counterpart, whose pockets of 24/7 operational functioning were like candles sputtering in a nine-to-five rainstorm.

He headed towards the old CID office, the narrow partition walkway at odds with the cavernous stone of the main corridor.

He opened the door. Opposite him, the outside streetlights refracted a spatter of rain against the enormous windows. In the darkness, his eyes went straight to a tiny blinking red light on one of the desks, and the slow curl of smoke rising next to it.

He flicked on the light.

"Good evening, DI Barnes."

Marlon Choudhury sat in front of him, hunched forwards, one enormous leg draped over the other, his hands laced around his knee, his churchwarden's pipe between his teeth.

"You're not supposed to smoke in here," Barnes said, after he had recovered from the initial shock.

"I would hazard a guess, DI Barnes, that there are many things that go on in this room that shouldn't," Choudhury said. "And yet, here we are. Have a seat."

Barnes pointed at the red light on the desk phone.

"We have company?"

"The once-eminent and now-disgraced advocate, your friend Mr Tate, joins us on conference call from the confines of Her Majesty's Pleasure."

"Hamilton's on the line? How did you engineer that?"

"Last time we spoke, Mr Barnes, I did tell you that I understand."

"Hamilton? Are you there?"

The ambient noise of a prison payphone queue was suddenly audible, and then Hamilton spoke in a low croak.

"Hello, Barnes."

Choudhury removed his pipe and smiled broadly, just as Barnes had started to wonder when the grin was going to make an appearance.

"Regard us," he said. "The resistance!"

"Is that so?" Barnes said.

"We need to compare notes," Choudhury said. "As a matter of some urgency. I imagine Mr Barnes has the most time on the agenda. What's top of your worry list, Mr Barnes?"

Barnes looked from Choudhury to the phone and back again.

"I don't have long," Hamilton said.

Barnes slowly sat down in a chair near the phone.

"I suppose top of my list is how Ty Godden, remanded in custody after being arrested by PC Riaz in possession of a holdall containing enough heroin to serve up a gram with chips in every B&B in Eastbourne, managed to regain his liberty long enough to rob and burgle the arresting officer's mother and turn her into blackberry crumble."

There was silence. Choudhury looked, momentarily, deeply concerned.

"Even as I'm speaking, I think I know the answer," Barnes said. "Sofia picked up the investigation. Lose the file, miss the committal deadline, ignore a bail app — the whole thing gets thrown out. It's easy enough to do."

Lord knew he spoke from experience.

"It was a bail app," Tate said.

Barnes stared at Choudhury, who looked back at him with a gaze that told Barnes he already knew.

"Hamilton . . . please tell me . . . not you," Barnes managed after a heavy silence.

"It was a bail app," Tate said again. "CPS instructed me to oppose it and asked Sofia to document the police representations. I didn't, she didn't. As you say, easy enough to do."

"Oh, Jesus. Why, Hamilton?"

"A more pertinent question might be: what now?" Choudhury interrupted. "As counsel says, he is pressed for time."

"I'm all ears," Barnes said.

"I take it your investigation into Mr Godden took account of the fact that he might not exactly be employee of the month, post-arrest."

"Of course it did. Within minutes of taking delivery of two keys of wholesale heroin he managed to practically surrender both himself and the drugs to the police. At best he's incompetent, at worst he's an informant. He hasn't got many friends."

"And looking at a sentence in the region of double figures, no doubt. He'd have been rather vulnerable, no?"

"Vulnerable in, vulnerable out. Even in prison I'd call even money on Anjou either protecting him or sticking the shank in Ty himself. Sofia tried a cell intervention. Several, in fact. He told her to fuck off. Said he isn't a grass. Said he could do the time. *Et cetera.*"

"Did he?"

"He did."

"But did he? Or did she simply *say* that's what he had said?"

The thought had occurred to Barnes as the words left his mouth. He eyeballed Choudhury.

"Notwithstanding the fact that his assertion of serving his sentence like a good little street oik is probably the bare minimum that his fraternity expects, it doesn't detract from the fact that he now owes both his supplier for the drugs he lost and whoever put the money up for him to purchase it. He isn't having a good month."

"Where are the drugs now?" came Tate's voice from the phone.

Barnes fixed Choudhury with a stare. "They were taken under armed escort to a bonded warehouse. You'll forgive me if I don't give you the postcode."

"Barnes, I . . ."

"That will probably turn out to be a rather canny move," Choudhury said, interrupting Tate.

"We do function in your absence," Barnes said, folding his arms. "Look, I just came from Sofia's hospital bed. She'll live, but she will be scarred. She's vulnerable. She told me everything."

"Which is what, exactly?" Choudhury asked.

"I can't help feeling that I should let Hamilton answer that," Barnes said, figuring the wily old DI probably already knew the answer. "I've had a confession from Sofia, I've got strong suspicions about her boyfriend PC Pete Lamb . . ."

"My ops team is on their way to pick him up right now," Choudhury interrupted.

". . . and I've just learned the dirty duo is actually a trio."

Tate exhaled heavily into the phone, distorting the sound coming out of the loudspeaker.

"How did it start, Hamilton?" Barnes said. "Was it before you left the job?"

The ambient prison noise again, and then Tate began to speak. His tone was nasal, his breath coming in a careless snore from the back of his throat.

"I was using. Not much, nothing heavy like smack, but Class A nonetheless. Cocaine on my rest days, mostly. If I'd had a hard duty, then between shifts as well. I was studying for my law degree at the time, and . . . well, burning the candle at both ends. Not enough time in the day, not enough money in the bank, not enough fuel in the tank.

"It started pretty innocuously. I owed my dealer six hundred quid, and as a part-payment he asked me to run a car through the box, see if there was a marker on it. Then it was another, and another. Then it was a small favour to check someone out on the system — supposedly to establish suitor potential for a friend's daughter — then . . . well, you get the idea.

"PSD were starting to look, and I don't blame them. As luck would have it, my degree and a job offer came through just before the cuffs went on."

"I believe the phrase is: you jumped before you were pushed," Choudhury said.

A pattern of rain smacked across the windows, as if carelessly flung by some avant-garde painter. Barnes made the idle observation that his leg throbbed more when the air was damp. *Shit out of luck living by the sea, then, aren't you?* he thought.

"And Sofia?"

"Sounds like you know more about that than I do," Tate said. "Bad apples spoil the whole barrel, but they don't generally work in cahoots. Too much at stake. As far as I knew, the Ty Godden bail app was just a bit of incompetence on her part that made my bit easier."

"What about due diligence?" Barnes asked. "Didn't your new firm get the download from PSD prior to taking you on? As a criminal *lawyer*?"

"If they ever did, I never got to hear about it. I moved around a fair bit until I was called to the bar. Maybe it got lost in translation."

"I must concede, as reinventing yourself goes, it was decidedly impressive," Choudhury said.

Barnes wanted to ask about Tate's character references. Wanted to ask why those particular cops had put pen to paper. Wanted to know about the significance of Op Hexagon and Op Lighthouse, the swansong cases he worked before he wriggled out of a full misconduct probe. But he couldn't, because then he would be incriminating himself in the attempt to lose Tate's case file — notwithstanding the fact that he'd had a touch of the seconds and put the bloody thing back.

Did Choudhury know? Did the old bastard know, and that was why he was here at all, brokering Tate's confession? Just so no further conspiracy could pass between them?

"Hamilton . . . Reeve. The escape. What happened?"

"I wish I could tell you. I knew there was some kind of undercurrent, but it was never directly in my line of sight."

"What the hell does that mean?"

"You've looked at Tommy Gayle's form. He was street muscle. A Grade-A scumbag."

"Yes, he was. He was hardly the kind of commodity that warranted the risk that comes with interfering with a Crown Court trial. He was expendable. Replaceable."

"But he was connected. He collected in Eastbourne so the organisers upstream didn't have to get their hands dirty."

"Upstream? Liverpool? Manchester?"

"And some others, but they are the heart of the matter."

"While the south coast, it seems," Choudhury said, "is the necrotic toe."

Barnes looked at Choudhury, and then moved closer to the phone.

"What happened at the trial, Hamilton? Did somebody make sure it ended up in your lap? So you could take a dive?"

"I can see why you would think that, but the truth is nobody wanted it. You know that. I didn't need to take a dive, because the case was doomed from the start. Nobody thought it had a cat-in-hell's chance of a conviction, and so there was nothing to do except go through the motions and wait for the verdict.

"And besides, let's say, just for the sake of argument, that Tommy Gayle's employers *were* desperate for justice. They could do that just as easily on the streets or in prison, so it mattered not whether he was convicted or acquitted."

Barnes already knew this.

"So Reeve made his own luck."

"Probably. But I don't know. That's the truth."

"And the girl?"

Tate didn't immediately answer. The sound of men jeering and shouting was plainly audible. One told him to hurry it along.

"Hamilton?"

Tate came back on the line. "Sorry. I'm on borrowed time here. What did you say?"

"What about the girl?"

"Honeytrap. It was a set-up from the off. That's why I asked—"

"Honeytrap is a term for blackmailers," Barnes said, cutting him off. "Blackmailers, private investigators and middle-aged men who cheat on their wives. This was rape, Hamilton."

"It's alleged rape until the verdict comes in," Tate said. Barnes could practically hear him shrugging. "She was a plant, whichever way you cut it. The final piece of leverage."

Barnes sat forward in his chair.

"Leverage for what? From who?"

Tate sighed.

"From the . . ."

More jeering. The sound of Tate being jostled.

"Hamilton, who is controlling it? Who has been blackmailing you?"

Tate didn't answer. It sounded like he was front and centre at a boxing match.

"This is ridiculous. I can't hear a bloody word he's saying," Barnes said to Choudhury. "Hamilton, I need to see you. Can you get me in to see you?"

The jeering crescendoed, and there was the sound of a short, violent argument on the line. Hamilton was jostled off the call, a man said, "*He'll call you back, girls*," and then the line went dead.

Choudhury leaned forward and clicked off the loudspeaker. The silence filled the cavernous office like a cloud. Barnes sat back in his chair and pulled his hands slowly down his face.

He hauled himself to his feet and retreated to a workstation. Not the partitioned corner box that had once been the DI's office — that was full of boxes — but the corner of the main office that had once belonged to the duty DS, and one which had remained empty since the day they had asked him to act up.

Choudhury watched him go. Barnes sat down heavily with the odd feeling of security that comes with sitting in the corner of a room. At least here one could see all the vultures as they circle.

"A troubled man," Choudhury said.

Well, nearly all of them.

"You have an ops team?" Barnes said.

"I do now," Choudhury said. "The days of Professional Standards detectives sitting in offices eating custard tarts while waiting to be furnished with dirty case files are gone. Now, we go out there and we find them."

"How did you engineer that little conference call?" Barnes said.

"Not difficult. You just have to have the idea. Then it's a case of making some calls."

"I'm not talking about the practicalities. When did he get the sudden urge to reveal a lifetime's corruption?"

"It's all in the timing, DI Barnes."

"I need to see him. Before his trial. That thing about the Reeve case just landing in his lap because nobody else wanted it — bullshit."

"Possibly. However, if the infection spreads beyond more than even a small handful of cells, then it's good business sense for each individual to know no more than what is within their own sphere of influence. Plausible deniability in the supply chain, if you will."

"Whatever. He knows more than he's telling us, I'm sure of it."

"Are you surprised?"

"That he's bent? You know, deep down, I'm actually not."

"You are good friends?"

Barnes didn't reply. He was distracted by a piece of paper lying atop the keyboard. A single piece of white A4, with the word "LIGHTHOUSE" written on it in black marker pen.

Riaz.

Had to be.

He picked it up and held it lightly by the edges in one hand. The teetering stack of packing boxes meant Choudhury couldn't see it.

Another swell of rain. The strip lights flicked off and back on again, so quickly Barnes wondered if he'd imagined it.

"What are your people arresting Pete Lamb for?"

"We are not arresting him, DI Barnes. We are simply inviting him in for a conversation. You might call it a shot across the bows. As a tactic it is considerably more effective than it might be with your usual customers — an anxiety-riddled police officer can be surprisingly verbose."

"I'll rephrase: what's your interest in him?"

"What's yours?"

Barnes opened his mouth to retort further, then exhaled through his nose.

"He responded with the rest of his section to Mandy's murder. Except he should have been on leave. I think he might have interfered with the scene."

"Really? Why on earth would he do something like that?"

Barnes screwed up his face.

"Can't be sure. All I know for sure is that someone put two empty suitcases by the front door between Claudia and Riaz responding and the scene being locked down."

"Strange. But useful. You may or may not be interested to know that Mr Lamb has been on our radar for some time, but more for general red flags — drinking too much, spending too much, friends of friends who could best be described as unsavoury, hare-brained side enterprises. Sometimes the line between reasonable standards of off-duty behaviour and expecting people to lead a good Christian life is a fine one."

"You lead a good Christian life?"

Choudhury beamed.

"It makes no sense," Barnes said. "I don't even know it was him — all I know is he shouldn't have been there, and that he's dating one of my DCs, who has practically just spilled her guts to me about a career of backhanders, dubious associations and out-and-out sabotage."

"From her hospital bed."

"Indeed." Barnes squeezed the bridge of his nose and screwed up his eyes. How could this not reflect on him? How many others in his team were rotten to the core?

"The truth, revealed in a moment of vulnerability. As with Mr Tate."

Barnes eyeballed him. "Is this where you tell me you already know about her?"

"Assume not."

Barnes took a deep breath. "Sofia's a good cop. She and I have been colleagues for about eighteen months. She joined CID after me, from Intel. Bob Baker was her skipper, rather than me, but, obviously, when they gave me the acting pips I got the whole team.

"She's a good, solid worker. Catches the criminals off guard with the whole 'fifties Italian movie star' thing, then swoops in with that potty mouth of hers and they don't know what's hit them — they all want to be her best mate. Gift of the gab doesn't even come close. The lawyers can't stand it.

"I never would have said she was dirty. This has blindsided me completely — of course, now I know, it seems obvious. No one can be that chummy with the shitbags and not risk flying too close to the sun."

"Alas, a common trade-off. How embroiled do we think she is?"

Barnes picked up a pen and tapped it against the edge of the keyboard. "I wish I knew. The only thing I know for sure is that she had to do no more than ignore the memo asking for reps for Ty Godden's bail app, and he was free to stomp all over a defenceless old lady when he shouldn't have seen daylight before the age of forty."

"It starts small, DI Barnes. A blind eye to this, a small favour for that. Once you've put your job on the line, scale is almost irrelevant. They've got you over a barrel, and they know it."

Barnes stopped tapping. He looked Choudhury dead in the eye. "Who are we talking about, Marlon?"

Choudhury stood, swept his gaze around the office and headed for the door. The beige partition walls were some kind of ancient corduroy/velour hybrid that might once have been white. Choudhury poked it with his finger.

"There's no sense of permanence here, really," he said.

"Just as well. Is that meant to be an analogy for something?" Barnes said.

"This is prime real estate, DI Barnes. I can't imagine it will be too long before they start selling off the family china to some enterprising developer."

"Why would they do that?"

"There are always tough times ahead."

"You may be right," Barnes said.

"Good night. We will speak again." He opened the door. "Oh, by the way. Those suitcases you mentioned. Are you quite sure they were empty?"

31

They found Sofia's body under Golden Jubilee Way, lying between the Willingdon Upper Sewer and the ballast of the naked railway line that ran through the Levels like a zipper.

She was still in her hospital gown, her arms twisted out awkwardly behind her, explosions of blood from her nose, ears and mouth that suggested, even to the layperson, that she had struck the cold ground with huge force.

The road arced in a bridge over the railway line, and the only way the response officers could get to her was to head into the housing estate that abutted the railway line, park in Percival Road and pick their way across the wasteland. A marked 4x4 arrived from Lewes and was able to get closer, and the blue strobe lit up the huge concrete underbelly of the flyover like a nightclub ceiling.

Barnes, numb, watched from the apex of the flyover. She was a tiny blotch of white against the dark expanse of the Levels; the static, taunting tableau, with the black, rolling sprawl of the South Downs on the horizon, was at complete odds with the scramble in his mind.

He stared, and stared and stared and stared, in utter disbelief.

She looked so cold. The wind was always fierce across the elevated highway, and even after the warmth of the day it could chill you to the bone in minutes once darkness took hold.

Her foot moved. Almost imperceptible at this distance, but he caught it, gripping the barrier and squinting into the gloom.

There. Again. Her leg was moving. Holy Christ, she was alive.

"Hey!" he screamed at the two uniformed response officers conducting a cursory search around the body. "Hey!"

His voice was lost on the wind.

He bolted back down the road to where the flyover descended, and cut down a dirt access road leading down towards the tracks, scrambling and stumbling as he pelted down the steep grit incline in the darkness, his leg screeching in protest, barking into his radio for an ambulance, intermittently yelling at the cops in the distance as he did so.

He just about managed to get to the body without turning an ankle, and he fished in his pocket for his warrant card as one of the cops turned and raised two hands.

"This is a crime scene—"

"DI Barnes. She's alive! I saw her move."

"Guv . . ."

"Goddammit, let me past. Why isn't there an ambulance here? Have you checked her vitals?"

The two cops looked at each other uncomfortably.

"Guv, I don't think—"

Barnes finally shouldered past them, and stood on the ballast over Sofia's still body.

From the fall or some other blunt force trauma, he couldn't yet know, but the extent of the injuries to her face and head made it obvious she was beyond help. Even if they had wanted to give rescue breaths, there was barely a mouth discernible.

The white of the flimsy gown flapped lazily around her legs, taunting him. From a distance it had played tricks on him.

Despite this, the temptation to cover her with something was almost irresistible, in the same way you would shelter an abandoned baby from the elements. He knelt beside her and lightly touched her calf. She was stone cold, but shades of irrationality were swirling around him like laughing mists.

He stood again, and took a huge breath, trying to get some oxygen in his blood. He was the ranking officer here. He could go to pieces later.

"Guv . . . who did this?"

Barnes finally tore his eyes from the body and fixed on the young patrol constable. He was young, but not so young that he thought he was invincible, that the evils the job contained didn't always play by the rules, didn't always leave you alone when you booked off duty and shut the front door.

"I don't know. It'll be okay, though." He rested a hand on the constable's shoulder. "It'll all be okay. Now, let's turn the tables a bit, eh? Put the balloon up?"

"You bet."

Barnes started making calls. Within half an hour the Force SIO, Ops Department, Scenes-of-Crime and Home Office pathologist were rolling. An intelligence cell, media liaison and search team were similarly stood up. Barnes's last call was to Force Gold. For any murder investigation, the divisional DI would become an extraordinarily busy but completely reactive addition to the inquiry, with the most significant contribution being the immediate mandatory surrender of all their DCs. This would be no different, and Barnes wanted his ducks in a row before he briefed the boss — particularly as he had no suspects. Not only that, but this was the murder of a serving police officer who had already been assaulted by a prisoner, and Barnes felt that someone with more braid on their shoulder than he should be the one taking the slow walk up the driveway to tell her family. That meant someone having to get a chief officer out of bed, and Barnes assumed — rightly, as it turned out — that this privilege belonged to the Gold Commander.

Blue lights and scene tape duly installed, he flipped the phone shut and trudged back across the broken ground. He slowly ascended back up the dirt track and headed back over the bridge to where he had left his car in a gravel trap in the lee of a Daihatsu truck with A-frame hoarding on the back advertising no-fee gym membership.

Barnes looked at the billboard, the wind whipping his tie like a kite tail; oblivious cars raced past him and onto the flyover, studded in their progress by the overhead lights; the black Downs looming up on the horizon like the earth's constant, a reminder that although one of his own had been cut down early, the few extra years denoting the natural end of a life made no difference to Nature.

What now? Who to tell next? What act of responsible leadership could he demonstrate, right at this moment? What was the right thing to do?

He dragged his hands down his face and promised himself a drink before his mind tried to consume itself.

He opened the car door and collapsed heavily into the driver's seat. He pulled the door shut, and the cold of the wind was momentarily halted. Barnes took a moment in the relative quiet to compose himself.

In so doing he became aware of a hard lump underneath his backside, pressing into his coccyx. He frowned and reached around behind him, his fingers closing around a hard, cylindrical object.

He flicked on the interior light and held the item up in front of his face.

A roll of cash, wrapped as tightly as it could possibly have been and held in place by a thick, blue elastic band.

It was almost exactly the same as the roll he had found in Stuart McKinnon's locker.

32

Barnes made some calls when he got back to the office. It was no accident that only the exhibits officer had access to the exhibits store — if he wasn't immediately available, however, it made life slightly troublesome.

Monty Beck was one of two late-turn DCs, and he had seized the opportunity of the post–air show lull to finally execute a search warrant on the address of an Alliance & Leicester cashier whom Beck suspected of being the inside man for a number of high-value cheque frauds.

He was interviewing the cashier at Hastings nick when Barnes called. Barnes left a message with the custody officer, then realised that Monty wouldn't have heard about Sofia yet. He rebadged the message, asking the custody officer to lead with the news about a seriously injured teammate as being the reason for the urgency, rather than the fact that Barnes desperately needed to get into the exhibits store.

"You duty, guv?" the custody officer asked, as Barnes was about to hang up. Nippers had long gone home.

"Not exactly. What do you need?"

"One of the shits from the old lady robbery has come back from hospital. He's had his rights. Wants his mother told. Figured we're holding them all incommunicado — just need an inspector to sign off on it."

"Which one is it?"

"Ty Godden. Mum is Jean Tully. Stepfather Anjou Acosta. You want to hold his rights?"

Barnes chewed it over, then a thought occurred to him. "No. Endorse the custody log. I'll do it."

"You will?"

"Yep. In person. On my way there in five. And Baz? That old lady is a cop's mother."

He hung up and had just pulled his tie off when Monty Beck staggered in, wide-eyed and pale.

"Boss . . . is it true? About Sofia?"

Yashid Hinton and Craig Furness followed suit, followed by a couple more DCs from one of the other sections. Two of them were in casual clothes, and Barnes knew that they were not rostered to work today. One may as well have been in pyjamas. Barnes felt like he hadn't seen any of them for weeks.

They formed an unnatural line at the end of the office, all staring at him expectantly. He stuck his chin out towards them, jaw grimly set, and silently beckoned them all towards him with a two-fingered pistol gesture.

He perched on the edge of a desk. A couple of them sat down.

"Sofia's dead," he said. A couple of them gasped. One began to cry, and Barnes suddenly realised how real it all was. "She . . . someone removed her from the hospital. She was found an hour or so ago under the Golden Jubilee bridge."

"Oh . . . my fucking God," Monty said, rubbing his brow with his knuckles. They turned white with pressure, and he began to sob also.

"Boss, how did it happen?" Yash's voice was steady — unaccusing, but brittle.

"From what we know so far, it looks like someone posed as a porter. Collected her from the ward in a wheelchair and walked out a side entrance with her."

"I mean . . . *how* did it happen?" Yash said. "Was there no one guarding her?"

Barnes was able to manage a slight shake of the head. "They hadn't arrived yet."

A couple of them exchanged glances. Monty dropped his hands. His face was grey. "What now?" he said.

"There's something you need to know," Barnes said, scanning the faces of his ashen audience. "Sofia was dishonest. Bent."

There was a ripple of disquiet.

"Those are strong words, boss," Yash mumbled quietly.

"It's not spurious," Barnes said. "And I know you won't want to believe it. But she admitted it to me. She was in over her head."

"Admitted it to you?" Monty said. "Admitted it how?"

"From her hospital bed."

"You were there?"

Barnes stared at Monty. He hadn't timed this well. He should have broken the news of her death, and then saved the rest of it for later.

"Are you asking me if there were any witnesses? I know what you're getting at, Monty, but believe me, I didn't want to believe it either. She and I responded to the sighting of Reeve. We interviewed him together. He . . . he asked to speak to one of us in the cell. Sofia went, and he threw boiling coffee in her face. She . . . she was distraught, and told me about her part in Op Liphook."

"Which was what, exactly?"

"Sabotage by omission, mainly. Ignoring new lines of enquiry. Looking the other way. Deliberately failing to submit the court file for committal on time. Easy to do, and difficult to prove."

"Look, boss . . ."

"Deliberately, Yash. That's the reason Ty Godden was out on bail. That's how he was able to rob and burgle Jefferson Riaz's mother."

"I don't believe it."

"There's strong evidence to suggest her partner is involved too."

"Pete?"

"PC Pete Lamb. PSD Ops are about to scoop him up, if they haven't already."

Yash and Monty glanced at each other.

"They're not."

"They're not?"

"They asked us to back them up. He's not at home, didn't show up for work, not answering his phone, and . . ."

"That doesn't surprise me. He's missing, ladies and gents."

There was a heavy silence.

"I've got three ways of looking at this. One, you've lost a colleague and you need time to deal with that. Two, you're professional, impartial investigators, and even when Major Crime breeze in here and take root, they're going to need you on board and involved. That being the case . . ."

He scribbled something on a Post-it note and walked over to Yashid.

"This is the nurse who got tonked on the head the night Chris Jenner got smothered. She remembered some details about the guy's description. She called Sofia to tell her. Sofia took the call and then promptly forgot about it."

For the time it took to walk over to Yash, Barnes thought about the fearlessness that the nurse called Annie had shown outside Sofia's hospital room, and the way her eyes had bored into him, and he thought about keeping this particular action to himself. But he didn't. He pressed the Post-it into Yashid's hand, keeping his eyes locked on him.

"Go take her statement. Get an image done as well."

"The e-fit people aren't on until eight."

"I don't want an e-fit. Those things look like inflatable sex dolls. Get a proper sketch artist in there with you. The guy from East Dean is good. He might even not complain. He's one of those rare people that will actually get out of bed for a matter of life and death."

321

"Okay," Yashid said, stuffing the Post-it into his back pocket. "What was the third thing, boss?"

"The third thing . . . I can't discount the likelihood that one or more of you are at risk of imminent threat. One and possibly two cops have been taken out by . . ."

He faltered.

"By who, boss?" Yashid said.

"I don't know," Barnes said, thinking of the roll of cash in his car. "I don't—"

"The ones you want never get their hands dirty," Yash said. "They're like sodding ghosts."

Barnes slipped off the desk and turned to go.

"They just offer up their cannon fodder to take the hit," Yash said.

Barnes stopped, and turned. "What . . . what did you say?"

"Cannon fodder. Throw the cops a bone, surrender your expendable foot soldiers, put more distance, more obstacles between you and justice."

Barnes barrelled over to the door. "Monty . . . come with me."

"Where are we going?"

"I've just thought of something. Call it a hypothesis. But first we need to get into the exhibits store."

He didn't wait, but trotted off down the corridor.

* * *

Nothing.

Not a single damn thing.

Barnes and Monty had practically ripped the suitcases into shreds, expecting to find a coded message, a confession in blood or a secret map to the lost city of Atlantis.

But there had been nothing.

Barnes felt flat. He had surmised that Marlon Choudhury didn't ask questions he didn't already know the answer to, and on that basis felt sure that he would find a clue stitched into the lining or rolled into the handles.

The drive across town was clear, but he took it steady, holding the speed limit, settling his mind and shutting out any scripted patter. Seaside stretched out in front of him, a long straight boulevard lined with streetlights like a runway. Barnes imagined getting up enough speed to leave the town twinkling below him, and where it might take him if he could.

As if making a genuine attempt to act out his flash-fantasy, a pair of headlights suddenly filled his rear-view mirror, hovered there for a second, and then a Subaru roared past him with a blast of the horn and a middle finger out of the passenger window.

Barnes thought about putting out an AD on the car via the control room, but the index was partially obscured by a massive spoiler, and in any case the car was practically out of sight before he could memorise the whole thing.

He turned off at the Langney roundabout and headed along Langney Rise towards the crematorium. Bailey Drive was surprisingly lively for late on a Sunday night. The night was warm despite the ever-present threat of rain — several front doors were open, casting beams of light out into the road from both sides, like the opposing laser cannons of council gunships. The sweet tang of liquor infused the still air like a cloud.

He stopped outside Jean Tully's house — and noticed the Subaru that had cut him up a few doors down, engine idling.

He walked to the front door and gave it a couple of dull thuds with the bottom of his fist. He turned to look at the Subaru as he waited. The low sound of a thumping woofer could be heard from inside the car, but beyond that, the opaque windows were giving nothing away.

"Who is it?" the voice barked from the other side of the closed door.

"Police, Jean."

A moment's silence. Barnes turned and regarded a stack of car tyres and a washing machine spewing its innards on the threadbare patch of lawn.

"What do you want?"

"I'm not here about the misappropriated Littlewoods parcels. They'll wait till another day." He poked at the dirty yellow uPVC door. The hinges bore the smashed hallmarks of more than a few search warrants. "It's about your son. Ty."

"What about him?"

"Just open the door, will you?"

Barnes heard the sound of thudding as heavy items were moved — presumably to clear a path to the front door — but there were no sounds of panicked whispers, frantic footsteps or toilets flushing. On that basis, Barnes gave himself reasonable odds on being granted an audience.

The door creaked and was yanked open. The whole thing looked like it might collapse inwards, frame and all.

"Yes?"

Barnes hadn't clapped eyes on her for some years, but Jean and her clan had been a relative constant in his career — directly or indirectly — from the day he had joined up. He mused that the same was likely true of most of the cops in Eastbourne.

The last time he'd seen her she'd had a head of lank dark hair, but now she was as bald as an eggshell. She was tiny, maybe five foot tall, with papery skin stretched taut over bone, untroubled by any fat in between. Her mouth was constantly pursed, and — besides a solitary fang overhanging her lower lip — the darkness in her mouth suggested her teeth were either very bad or missing entirely.

"DI Barnes, CID," he said, holding up his warrant card. "Can I come in?"

She shrugged and headed back into the tiny house. She made a throwaway gesture as she passed the door to the front room — her back still to him — which Barnes took as an invitation.

He walked into the front room, trying not to recoil. It stank of cigarette ash, urine, stale weed and very old socks, and — based on the haphazard arrangement of dirty bedding — slept at least four. Empty plastic three-litre bottles of cheap own-brand cider contained floating colonies of cigarette ends, while storage seemed to be given over to an array of black bin liners, whose contents Barnes was content to leave to his imagination. He prayed to God there were no children living here.

The only concession to homeliness was a bookshelf containing hundreds of DVDs, and an enormous flat-screen television with a framed photograph on the top.

"Want tea?" Jean said from the doorway.

Barnes turned, amazed at the offer. If his rank had impressed her, it was marginal.

"Why not?" he said. She disappeared off to the kitchen, and Barnes heard a match being struck as the gas hob was ignited.

He inched over to peer at the photograph. It was some years old, showing Jean with a number of her kids on a sunny day at the beach. Ty was on the far right, aged maybe eleven, still in school uniform. He had a long-departed, healthy plumpness about him, and the smile was one of genuine happiness. Barnes felt something sting behind his eyes, and he tried not to think about what had happened between then and now.

Tucked into the corner of the frame was a passport-photo-cum-mugshot of the absent partner — a moustachioed, scowling Anjou Acosta. Barnes had never personally had the pleasure, but a town centre episode three years previously, involving a windmill impersonation with two kitchen knives, had put two firearms cops and a police dog in the hospital.

"Here."

Barnes turned and took the plastic beaker of dishwater from Jean's outstretched hand.

"Thanks," he said, knowing that there was no way this muck was going to touch his lips.

He kicked a couple of stuffed bin bags off the only piece of furniture in the room and sat down. Jean resumed her place leaning against the doorway.

"Just how much trouble are you in, Jean?"

"Don't know what you mean."

"Look, I figure that you want me out of here sooner rather than later, which will be helped along nicely if you don't just play the guppy the whole time. This is as close to off the record as I get."

She stared at him balefully.

"My theory is: young Ty, probably with his goodly mother behind him, managed to manoeuvre himself into a position where he could act as a distributor for a large consignment of wholesale heroin. An area manager, if you will."

She twitched, and looked past him out the window, searching for some sign of a fit-up. Barnes didn't look round, but he could hear the Subaru, still idling.

"Off the record," he said again, holding up a palm as if stopping traffic. "I'm just thinking out loud."

She seemed to relax a little.

"Unfortunately, he wasn't quite equal to the task. Your late next-door neighbour came to us with information about Ty's enterprising — and my guess is that he came by this information by means of nothing more sophisticated than overhearing you lot gobbing off over the garden fence. Celebrate with the old White Lightning, did we?"

He nodded towards one of the plastic bottles serving as an ashtray.

"So young Ty managed to keep his hands on a hold-all full of gear for less than the time it took to get himself dressed that morning, before getting himself arrested in possession of said holdall."

Jean's chin started to tremble with anger — at Barnes's accuracy, or her wayward son's idiocy, he wasn't sure.

"He's looking at serious time, Jean, but somehow he managed to get bail. Bail with conditions. The usual conditions imposed by the court, plus — I imagine — some others imposed by both the wholesaler, to whom he owes a great deal of money, and whoever fronted him the cash. Not to mention a ring of pissed-off street dealers, who now have demand they can't meet.

"So, the first thing he does when he gets out is try to make good on his debt. Unfortunately, he doesn't really have the wit to pull this off in the most lucrative way possible either, and opts to rob and burgle an old lady — an old lady who happens to be a cop's mother. Oh, that's what I came to tell you, while I think of it. He's in custody. He wanted you told. He was out for about two days before getting himself arrested again."

He paused.

"He's not very good at this lark, is he? His stepfather must be thoroughly ashamed."

There was practically steam coming out of her ears. She sucked her teeth with derision. "You'll get nothing from me."

He smiled broadly, feeling like Marlon Choudhury. It was a comfortable suit of armour. "Even if I said I was taking your complaint? As a victim of crime?"

"What?"

"The day Mandy Luis was murdered in her own home, you were on the cordon with a bunch of the other rubber-necks. You were there pretty quickly, I might add."

"So?"

"So you complained that someone assaulted you while you were stood there. Sexually."

"And?"

"And you reported this to one of the cops standing on a point. I have since developed a few concerns about the integrity of said cop. A cop who is now missing."

A flicker in the eyes, like the headlights of a passing car briefly lighting up a dark room. She swallowed.

Barnes sat forward. "There was definitely someone there, because he was seen. By police officers. He lolloped off into Hampden Park."

"So?" she said again.

"Were you really assaulted, Jean?"

She was nervous, and used hostility as a defence, switching it on and going from cold to hot in an instant, in a way that Barnes had seen many times before.

"You can't talk to me like that!" she yelled. "I was fucking touched up! I read the papers. You have to believe me. It's the *law*. Pigs like you aren't allowed to tell me I'm making it up. I'm going to complain about you. I want your fucking number."

Barnes didn't flinch. "You can have all that, Jean. Make your complaint. My job is to investigate impartially. I'm afraid some people do just make shit up. What I want to know is: what really happened?"

"Listen, you fuckin—"

"Where were you touched?"

"I . . . on my fucking fanny."

"Over or under clothing?"

"What?"

"Did he put his hands inside you?"

"You dirty fucking—"

"What did he say to you?"

She went pale, and the yelling stopped.

"Did he make lewd remarks? Did he tell you to keep quiet? Not to look round?"

Her mouth was clamped tight. Her breath shot out of her nose in jets.

"Were you really 'touched up', as you put it? Or did this man come up behind you and say something that put you on edge? Something that meant you wanted to suddenly draw attention to yourself, to scare him off? What better way than the righteous screaming banshee act?"

"I want . . . a solicitor."

"You're very welcome," Barnes said. "But as I am here speaking to you in your own home as a victim, rather than a suspect, I'm afraid you're the one that would have to pay for it. Unlike Ty, who is, right now, lapping up the full gauntlet of rights that the Police and Criminal Evidence Act affords suspects who are unlikely to see daylight for several years.

Unless one of these wholesale nutcases gets to him in prison, of course. It would be like shooting fish in a barrel, but in some cases cancelling his ticket might be easier than doing the time. Lord knows it isn't uncommon."

She said nothing.

"What did he say to you, Jean?"

Still nothing.

"Tell me what he said."

"Fuck off," she mumbled, like a surly teenager.

He stood up. "Right you are," he said, glancing down at the untouched beaker. "Thanks for the tea. Good luck with . . . well, with it all."

He straightened up, buttoned his jacket, telling himself that the feeling of fleas up and down his back was just his imagination, and headed past her.

"So what is this about? You gonna offer protection or some bollocks?" she said, when Barnes had his hand on the greasy front door handle.

Barnes turned. His eyebrows went up. "Protection? You and your family? Oh no, don't misunderstand me. I have no interest in protecting you. The wholesalers can have you, and you can take your chances."

She looked genuinely surprised. "But . . ."

"Why would I, frankly?" he said. "All I'd get in return is some information of dubious origin about the identities of certain drug kingpins, and I don't need you for that."

"You're not allowed to do that."

Barnes thought about the comment. Irritatingly, her sullen monotone had struck a chord with him. Much of his — of any — policing career depended on what was *allowed*. The book on the rules of engagement was labyrinthine, and ever-shifting.

But he didn't let the mask drop.

"Technically, you're right. If I got wind of an actual, specific threat to your life I would be obliged to act on it. But I don't have anything. Right now I'm simply hypothesising about how this is all likely to play out."

He stared at her for a moment, and then smiled.

"Well, like I say. Good luck with it all."

He left the house, letting the front door slam just as she opened her mouth to say, "But . . ."

He walked down the three broken flagstones that passed for a path and stopped when he reached the pavement. The Subaru was still idling by the roadside, the same low thump of bass coming from a woofer hidden in the back, but a small crowd of youths had gathered around it. The driver's window was halfway down, and the driver appeared to be holding court with the gaggle. They were talking in low tones, not showy or furtive, just going about their business in the same way that old men in a park might play dominoes.

Barnes took half a step towards his car, and then stopped and turned back.

You're not allowed to do that.

He strode over to the Subaru, warrant card aloft.

"Police," he barked.

Nobody scattered, so clearly no drugs in hand. The group by the driver's window begrudgingly parted to let him through.

Barnes stuck his warrant card through the open window.

"Police," he said again.

"Yeah?"

Two eyes gleamed at him in the gloom. The interior of the car was all blue dash lights in the darkness, with a warm aroma of scented freshener and aftershave. No smell of weed. These boy racers wouldn't take the risk.

"You cut me up on Seaside. It's all on video. Minimum: that's seizure of your car right now and a couple of hundred quid to get it back. Minimum."

The driver said nothing, just stared at Barnes. Like many kids of his age, he knew the drill. Knew exactly how much interactions of this nature relied on your cooperation, and how much harder complete passivity made life for the cops.

"No comment," he said. The eyes said, *So do it.*

"How do pricks like you get a licence?" Barnes wondered aloud. "Where does driving like a complete cunt fit in with all that? You must have been a delight to teach. Did your instructor live to tell the tale?"

The eyes gleamed brighter and narrowed. This cop was officially acting out of order. That was a small amount of ammunition in his favour. On another day this might have given him cause for deference, because a cop with a loose tongue was likely to have loose fists too, but Barnes was all alone, and the driver had numbers on his side.

"What did you say?" the driver said.

"I called you a cunt," Barnes said. "And I'm going to take your car."

"The fuck you are."

Barnes straightened up. The group slowly closed around him. Barnes heard a couple of front doors opening in the distance.

How many misdemeanours does the average criminal get away with in their lifetime? Barnes wondered. *We lock them up for, what, one per cent of all their undeclared sins?* For the recidivists, less. And yet, an otherwise unblemished twenty-year police career could be torn down in a heartbeat with a poor choice of text message.

The real difference was, the criminals just didn't care what they did or didn't get away with. Cops were the inverse. They spent their whole time worrying.

Maybe it was time to worry a little less about what he could reasonably get away with.

The blade – a non-issued, unsanctioned, but nevertheless extremely handy lock knife that featured in many a cop's kit bag – appeared in Barnes's hand from nowhere. This tore up the rules of engagement. The group froze. A cop with a blade was something else. They weren't sure where this was going.

Barnes turned and pushed through the crowd. They let him pass — it looked as if he had given up and was heading back to his car.

He passed the front bumper and then spun on his heel. He whipped his arm down and plunged the blade into the tyre. The driver's door opened.

331

"What the . . ."

Barnes walked around to the other front tyre and locked eyes with the driver. Another swooping crouch, and a second tyre was consigned to history by the blade.

He stood up, and for a moment there was no sound but the stereo hiss of the deflating rubber. Then there was tutting and the sucking of teeth and muttering ("Fuckin' bang out of order, bro . . .") from the group, who began to inch menacingly towards Barnes. Any sudden movement would galvanise one of them into rushing him, and that would greenlight the rest of them, and so Barnes held the knife out in front of him, backed slowly away towards his car, and kept eye contact. This seemed to arrest the slow, zombie-like advance. He didn't know what they saw in his face, but he did know that if he had to use the knife, he would. Maybe they knew that too.

In any case, he reached his car without incident and spun a quick U-turn in the road. He sped out of Bailey Drive just as a couple of beer cans clanged on his rear window.

He glanced in the rear-view and saw the flurry of activity as a second car pulled up alongside the crippled Impreza. There was a mass decanting of occupants as they set about their pursuit. They were like dogs, Barnes mused — static when he was actually within reach, and only now, when the chase was on, did they leap into action. He wondered what they would do if they actually caught him.

He decided not to wait to find out and spun out back onto Hide Hollow, killing the lights as he did so. He raced past the crematorium, and before he got to the double roundabouts, turned into the long service road that led down to the cemetery itself, just as a pair of headlights appeared in his rear-view. He reversed away from the road and up onto a grass bank, tucking the car in the bosom of a sprawling willow.

The sound of the pursuing engine screamed into range a couple of seconds later, and he saw the shadow of a sports car race past. A few seconds more, and his hurried attempt at hide-and-seek would have been spotted. He heard the engine shriek off into the distance.

He had hoped to feel exhilarated, even liberated, but he didn't. He couldn't shake the sense that his phone was going to ring any second, that his behaviour would filter through in double-quick time and that Marlon Choudhury, vanguard of Professional Standards, plus some high-ranking admonisher would be waiting on his doorstep before he'd even had a chance to get home.

He did feel dirty, however. Once you take a bung, you can't give it back, can't put the genie back in the bottle. This wasn't quite the same, but it was cheating, whichever way you sliced it. You played by the rules, and if one day you didn't, then the slow burn of time was the only thing that might make the branding fade.

33

Feeling as if he were in the eye of the storm, he wondered what Jean Tully would be doing now, and the lull gave him a sudden idea.

He locked the car and hopped over the fence that separated the service road from the crematorium proper, which kept him away from being spotted by marauding boy racers on the main road. He traversed the grounds, parallel to the road, and after a few minutes reached the other side. He followed a path that snaked through neatly tended trees and eventually led to the end of a cul-de-sac round the corner from Jean Tully's house.

He walked to the mouth of the cul-de-sac, got his bearings, and from there worked out which house was Jean's. He went back into the cul-de-sac, counted chimneys, and then climbed ungracefully over a fence into what he thought was her garden — though, if he'd had any doubts, they would have been cast aside in the face of the array of junk strewn about the place. The rear garden was a carbon copy of the front, with the burned-out husk of a former London cab taking centre stage.

He stood for a moment, staring at her house, knowing that if he allowed himself to mull over exactly what the hell he was doing for too long, he'd give it up and get the hell out of there. Something was driving him, and it was, he thought, the fact that by the time you've got a warrant, or set up an observation post, or mobilised a surveillance team, you could have missed all the fun. One thing Barnes knew: the things people did immediately after the cops had shaken their tree often told you all you needed to know. It was just that the cops were seldom around to see it.

Barnes picked his way carefully through the garden, bracing himself for any sudden variables — an unexpected visitor, an outdoor fag break, an unhinged dog. He looked over at the fence. The house next door was shrouded in darkness, and Barnes remembered it was the former abode of the late Jimmy Januarie. It didn't look like anyone had succeeded him. Barnes imagined Jean Tully and her clan crowing in the garden about Ty Godden's promotion to the Premier League, and the ill fate that was to become of the poor bastard who happened to overhear it.

A square of yellow light suddenly framed the brown lawn from the curtainless kitchen window. Barnes pressed himself flat against the rear wall of the house and held his breath.

He chanced a look by craning his head to peer through the patio door. Jean appeared in the kitchen just long enough to flick her roll-up into the sink and refill her beaker from a bottle of cider in the fridge.

He watched her. She was focused on her task, but she spun around as a shadow fell across the kitchen doorway.

"Hello, Jean."

Rather than being able to actually discern the words, Barnes inferred them from intonation, syntax and environment. The voice was deep and baritone and rumbled through the glass.

Barnes couldn't see its owner, but he marvelled at the sudden fear on Jean Tully's face. He had only ever seen her operate on three settings: bilious rage, sullen indifference or righteous scorn — to see her without her authority-repellent shell was quite something, and Barnes wanted to fix his eyes on the character that could invoke such a display.

"We need to talk," the voice said.

She started to blather — a mix of stuttering faux-hospitality and general expressions of innocence, but something silenced her, and she left the kitchen, presumably to entertain her second visitor in half an hour.

Barnes inserted the same blade that had disabled the Impreza into the patio doorframe; the glass wobbled in the frame and then popped open without a fuss. Barnes wondered how many hits it had taken, both from inside and out.

He stepped into the dark kitchen. Jean and her houseguest were in the front room. He inched forwards. The adrenaline was firing through him. Here was a big fat piece of intelligence, a new lead, that hitherto nobody had any idea about, and if he hadn't had a sudden rush of blood to the head he'd have been no more the wiser than anyone else.

You do the right thing and walk away, and you never find out what you missed. Or you stick around, claim the prize and worry about the rules later. Barnes figured, after the episode with the Impreza, the latter was a moot point.

He had no intention of forcing a confrontation unless he had to — not least because he was unlawfully on the premises — but at a minimum he needed to hear what was being said and get eyeball on the new guy.

He crept forward as quietly as the sticky linoleum would allow, wincing with every step, before finding himself a dark recess to the left of the kitchen door that put him within earshot and gave him a narrow aperture through which to see what was happening in the front room. It wasn't a widescreen view, but he could see Jean's knees where she had pressed herself into a chair. Her visitor, meanwhile, was standing and pacing intermittently, which put him in and out of Barnes's sight lines.

The visitor was massive. He wore a black jacket that was wrapped tightly around arms thicker than loaves of granary bread, and a woollen ski hat from under which long braids fell like tentacles. Barnes caught a hint of sweat and some kind of musky aftershave.

He was only able to make out fragments of conversation, and only when the visitor was in view.

". . . where your son is . . ."

". . . in over his head . . ."

". . . all mouth, no trousers . . ."

". . . get Anjou . . ."

". . . tut, tut, tut . . ."

Throughout all of this, a constant undercurrent of Jean Tully babbling eight types of bullshit, apparently without drawing breath.

This stopped when Barnes heard the unmistakable sound of a knife being unsheathed, and the conversation did too. He couldn't see the visitor, and surmised that he was right up against Jean Tully, with only the blade between them.

Barnes craned his neck to look — and nudged a carrier bag filled with empty beer bottles with his toe.

He looked down in horror; when he looked back up, a pair of bright yellow eyes bore down on him from the hallway.

"Hey," the visitor said, quietly. "Join us."

Barnes inched forward, screaming silently at his own stupidity, and took up position in the doorway of the front room. The visitor seemed satisfied with this. There certainly wasn't anywhere for Barnes to sit.

"He's old bill!" Jean shrieked, anticipating the question. She bounced up and down in her seat excitedly. "I didn't know he was here! He's sneaked in! No warrant or nothing! Do him! It'll be self-defence. He's trespassing."

She was silenced by the blade being pointed again in her direction, the visitor pressing a finger to his lips as he did so. Evidently, Jean Tully's raucous screeching was universally unpopular.

"That right? You a copper?"

Barnes stuck his jaw out in what he hoped passed for defiance, but he was unduly distracted by the knife. It was a huge, unblemished, ornate thing, with a double tip like the devil's horns.

"You alone?" the visitor frowned, peering past Barnes into the kitchen. "Whatchu doing here?"

The visitor aimed the blade horizontally at Barnes, uncurled his index finger along the blade and levelled it with his sight lines, like a snooker player lining up a long pot.

"Well, she's right. It would be self-defence. You're probably thinking: do I have it in me? Taking out a copper?"

"And do you?" Barnes croaked.

"What you need to understand, officer, is that you are paid to worry. I'm not. The point at which you hesitate is the point I will slide this piece of ice between your ribs. Yeah, there's prison. Yeah, there's your mates with the guns who might shoot me. But there's a fuck-ton of kudos. There aren't many that can say they've killed a copper, and it's a club I'd pay a high price to join . . ."

Barnes had felt more or less completely detached since he'd decided to double back to Jean Tully's house. Like he was having an out-of-body experience, watching himself slash those tyres. But now, this rational acknowledgement of the irrational caused sudden cold flames of fear to lick up inside him. He found himself thinking about his arrangements, thinking that death would silence him inside a glass box where he would be forced to impotently watch the small handful of people that still had an interest in his life make a hash of trying to piece its story back together.

The man inched towards him. The leather of his jacket creaked. Now Barnes was aware of the fear, it seemed to pin him to the doorframe, forcing him to lock eyes with his executioner. His peripheral vision did not extend to Jean sitting next to him, but he could hear strange, wet, smacking sounds coming from her lips, and he wasn't sure if she was physically relishing this shift of karma or if she was too fixated on her own fate. In either event she was almost certainly using this brief stay of execution to formulate some kind of escape plan.

Barnes stared deep into pinprick pupils, and tried to imagine this man stealing a porter's uniform, kidnapping a wounded police officer, throwing her in a van, throwing her off a bridge. Tried to imagine him bundling Jimmy Januarie into a car and throwing him off a cliff in the dead of night. Tried to imagine him scaring bottom feeders like Ty Godden and Chris Jenner, scaring them badly enough to commit horrendous acts way beyond their ken.

It was all too easy.

"You kill me, your drugs stay gone," Barnes suddenly blustered. "For good. I can help you get them back."

The man frowned at this apparent disclosure of suggestibility. He lowered the blade slightly. Then he grinned, flashing a gold incisor.

"Nice try, officer. I ain't interested. You ain't bent, anyway. Any fool can see that."

"You don't—"

"Ssh. Sssh," the man whispered, as if soothing a baby. Then he took a step back, bringing the blade down to his hip.

Then he blinked. He blinked twice, three times, a rapid fluttering as if something had short-circuited in his brain.

Barnes noticed the tiny red dot on the man's forehead a split second before he sank to one knee, the blade clattering onto the hard, grit-dusted floor. Then he sank to the other knee, and tumbled forwards in a heap, his mouth forming an inelegant attachment to Barnes's shoe.

It took Barnes several seconds to process what had happened, and several more to unfreeze himself. It also took considerable mental effort to arrive at both the logical conclusion and a suitable course of ensuing action.

He slid down the doorframe and wriggled on his belly over the floor to the patio door, which was now wide open. He could see nothing in the garden but managed to assume that the shooter hadn't hung around, and so he pushed on through the garden and into the service road. He stopped by a row of lock-ups and strained to listen — footsteps, engines, anything.

But all he heard was silence.

* * *

"Point-two-two, most likely," the Crime Scene Manager said. "No exit wound, tiny entry wound. No doubt bounced around in his head like a pinball before coming to rest. Shot came from behind you, shooter in the wind well before you got yourself together. You remember hearing anything?"

Barnes eyeballed him, and shook his head, his lips pursed. He didn't remember hearing anything except the revolting smacking of Jean Tully's lips, but that didn't mean there hadn't been some enormous explosion. His brain just hadn't registered it.

"Not a thing."

"We need your clothes. I've got a tracksuit in the van."

Much as it pained him, Barnes had gone back into the house to check on Jean Tully's welfare, and had then radioed for help. There were now arc lights and exhibit markers all over the place, with white-suited experts piecing together the jigsaw. The CSM seemed almost disappointed to have a living eyewitness.

"I need to know whether he killed Sofia," Barnes said, pointing at the mound of dead grey flesh on the floor. "In the fullness of time, I also want to know if he did Jimmy Januarie and Chris Jenner. But my team need answers, and they need them yesterday."

Barnes walked out the front and bagged his own clothing under an umbrella of blue strobes, catching sight of his erstwhile pursuers — having given up and returned home — idling past on the other side of the cordon. Distance and darkness made it impossible to pick out any of the vehicle's occupants, but something told him they were not part of this, and he felt a strange swelling in his breast.

He pulled the tracksuit top over his head, and made the slow walk along the road back to his car, swirling in some strange void between victim, witness, suspect and law enforcer.

34

The morning light streaming through the bars of Hamilton Tate's cell was bright, turning the walls into a shade of yellow that was almost more primrose than bile. Although the concrete walls were cool, Hamilton could smell the heat from the outside like a rising tide and suddenly, desperately wanted to feel the day on his skin.

He imagined what his freedom would taste like, what that moment would feel like when the stone box opened up to reveal some magnificent auditorium, a canopy of blue stretching away into infinity.

And how many years he would have to wade through to get there.

For a brief, moronic moment, he had actually thought he could do the time. He figured with a plea and lots of remorse he might get ten, out in six. If he kept a trial at bay for as long as possible to maximise the amount of remand time off his sentence, and then threw in an eleventh-hour guilty plea, blaming the change of heart on poor legal advice, he might even be out in five.

He had even crafted some gilt-edged fantasy in his mind, where he played chess in the yard by day, read Shakespeare by candlelight and dug a tunnel using a teaspoon while making meaningful, long-lasting brotherhoods with a close circle of misfit lifers.

That romantic notion had gone right out the barred window when the cell door thudded dully shut behind him, closely followed by a stabbing out on the wing after a dispute over a burner phone.

He wondered if the world would generally be lighter if he had just pleaded guilty. Not in that tactical, carefully timed, survivalist way, but a genuine guilty plea. Real guilt. Real remorse. Not a plea just to the court, but to society, mankind, his Maker . . . his victim. He wondered how many brutalised families would have traded a twenty-year sentence for a real, deep-seated *sorry*. He wondered how exhilarating that would be. It wasn't something he'd seen much of in a short, intense legal career, but . . .

But the problem was, he didn't really think he was.

Guilty, that is.

At least, not of that. If he truly had hurt her, he was sorry, but he didn't believe he had done anything wrong, really, and the minute you started introducing qualifications and conditions to contrition, it ceased to have meaning. *Sorry you didn't like being hurt* as opposed to *Sorry I hurt you.*

It was almost a moot point, however; the fact remained that he was dirty. Dirty inside, dirty out. Susceptible to cash, suggestible to omissions, persuadable by shortcuts and technicalities.

No one would complain if he threw himself on his sword in the dock and asked for a lifetime of corruption to be taken into consideration along with rape and supplying class A. It might raise a few eyebrows, but they would get over that.

What the hell, he thought, *this is as close to guilty as they're going to get.*

Hamilton was mildly perturbed to note that his cell was not short of choice when it came to ligature points, and the whole thing was going to be depressingly easy to orchestrate — on a technical level, anyway.

He spun some sheets and carefully looped them through an aperture between the cell door and the frame, using the hinge to lock the sheets tight.

The rough cotton was surprisingly cool and soft against his skin. He pulled the makeshift noose snug and felt his eyes bulge in their sockets. Instinctively he sucked air through his narrowed windpipe — despite himself, he knew his survival instincts were kicking in.

He wedged his fingers between the noose and his neck, like some kind of final failsafe, and propped one foot up on the edge of his bunk, intending to push himself off — but, as it happened, fate played its part, and his foot slipped off the edge of the bunk.

His entire weight was suspended from the neck in one sudden movement. Panic fired through him as he gasped airless breaths through his closed airway.

Although the door hinge was technically low enough for him to stand, the woollen socks on his feet slipped on the smooth concrete floor.

Unable to gain purchase, his feet scrabbled and slipped on the floor, kicking like a trapped insect, as his desire to live suddenly superseded all.

A face appeared at the hatch, and his oxygen-deprived brain was able to just about send notions of relief and thanks through his body.

But the guard just stared.

No frantic movements, no jangling of keys, no yells for help.

He just watched, impassive, and waited. He peered down through the hatch, his jaw set in grim recognition.

Ten seconds, twenty seconds, thirty . . .

Just before Hamilton's brain became soup, relief was followed by confusion. Then, as his lungs finally gave up and he drowned, as the edges of his vision began to blacken, like thick, opaque tunnels of ink spreading from the outside in, the prison officer pulled out his keys and finally began to call for help.

But, by then, it was too late.

* * *

Barnes would not have been surprised to find a welcoming committee on his doorstep, but the street was quiet.

He was exhausted, and the thought of shutting the door on the world was suddenly appealing, but as he opened the front door he immediately realised he wasn't alone. If only he had a weapon on him. As it was, he had nothing besides a bunch of car keys — the blade having been ditched in a public bin somewhere near the Sovereign Centre — which he tossed carelessly into the bowl by the front door and marched into the lounge.

He wasn't entirely surprised to see Marlon Choudhury sitting in his favourite armchair. In fact, it was almost a relief.

"The vulture on my bedpost," Barnes said. "I suppose you have a warrant."

"I do, as it happens," Choudhury said. "It's been in my drawer for the best part of a fortnight. I'm rather hoping it won't be necessary — I was merely trying to lessen the impact on your neighbourly reputation."

"By breaking in?"

"Why don't you have a seat?" Choudhury said. "You've had a busy night."

Barnes, too exhausted to argue, flopped onto the couch opposite, only dimly aware that he had never actually sat on it before.

"I feel like a lab rat," he said. "I've been poked, prodded, swabbed and generally forensicated. My phone's been seized and my clothes bagged. I will never see that suit again. I liked that suit."

"Ciro Citterio, two for one?" Choudhury said, smiling.

"Hardly the point."

"As to which . . ."

"Am I a suspect?"

"A suspect for what?"

"They've done everything except ask me what happened."

Choudhury smiled, and laced his huge fingers in front of him.

"That's why you're here?" Barnes said. "To take my statement?"

"Mr Barnes, not so long ago you asked me where my loyalties lay. You asked me to roll my sleeves up."

"And?"

"You should be careful what you wish for. I am now leading this investigation."

"I'm very pleased to hear it."

"What happened?"

Barnes sighed. "Every time I leave the station I'm faced with a wall of silence. People would rather go to prison or kill themselves than talk. I questioned Jean Tully — lawfully."

"Lawfully?"

"Well, on the pretext of a Code C notification. And then I went back again to observe her."

"Unlawfully."

"I was trespassing in her house. That's it." Barnes didn't mention the tyres.

"Is it?"

"The pathologist will tell you there are no friction burns on that entry wound. That was not a close-range shot. I was standing right in front of him."

"So you say."

"What does Jean Tully say?"

"'Fuck off.' But she'll come around."

"You ID him yet? Our dreadlocked friend."

"A matter of time."

"He was going to kill me. I've absolutely no doubt. But he's not the guy that shot at me in the hospital. Build, height, gait, hair — all wrong."

"I did wonder. There are a couple of other interesting developments, however."

Barnes edged slowly forward on the seat. "Go on."

"The working hypothesis is that DC Johnson was thrown from the Golden Jubilee flyover."

"That was *my* hypothesis, yes."

"SOCO found fibres snagged on a bolt at the apex of the bridge. An early comparison suggests that they came from the donkey jacket worn by the deceased."

"Just to be clear: which deceased are we talking about?"

"Mr Hairy Knuckles. The one at Jean Tully's house. The one taken out before your very eyes."

"He killed her. Sofia. It was him. I believe it," Barnes said, more to himself than Choudhury. His eyes began to sting. "What else?" he added quickly, as a means of getting himself back in the blocks before he unravelled completely.

"Hotel-900 did a flyover of the scene. Thermal imaging revealed a tidy hydroponics setup in the loft. About fifty plants, which isn't bad for a house that size. Lord knows what the neighbours must have thought."

"She in custody then?"

"Oh yes."

"Sorry I missed that."

Choudhury pursed his lips. Outside, engines began to start and dog walkers exchanged pleasantries as the morning began to get going. Barnes could already feel the promise of heat that the new day was going to bring, even with September just around the corner.

"We have yet to confirm, but indications are that the .22 rifle that took out Dave the proverbial Rave was most likely stolen in the same burglary as the shotgun that was unloaded at you at the hospital."

"It's . . . it's the same guy," Barnes whispered. "He's still out there."

"So it would seem."

Choudhury stood. Barnes hauled himself up and opened the door to show his uninvited guest out just as

Eleanor's front door opened and Aidan bounced out in his school uniform.

Barnes frowned. Was it that time already? He looked at his watch — not seven yet. Barnes wondered how the boy managed getting up at such an hour, and, in his own eyes, whether the demands of his private education would be worth it. Aidan caught Barnes's eye as he opened the car door, and Barnes offered a small wave.

Aidan seemed to hesitate, then he reached into his bag and pulled out a sheet of paper. He bounded over to Barnes, pressed the paper into his hand, and then ran back to the car. He got in and shut the door just as Eleanor left the house.

Barnes watched them go. On the drive home his most prominent thought had been, *Where do I go from here?* The new day played his night's activities back to him on fast-rewind, and he shut his eyes momentarily. The fact that Choudhury knew some of it was something of a relief, but it had been such a bonkers night that . . .

Quite without warning, his legs lost their strength and he slid down the doorframe, his hands gripping the uPVC as he went, as the images of the knife in his face and Sofia's ghost-white body suddenly flashed into his mind.

He got himself together after a moment, then stared down at the drawing. It was of two smiling people playing football in a big stadium — one was small with yellow hair; the other was tall, wearing a policeman's uniform.

* * *

He was still looking at it ten minutes later when the doorbell went. He thought briefly about pretending he wasn't home, then carefully tucked the drawing on the mantelpiece behind a scented candle he'd never bothered to unwrap, and answered the door.

Riaz stood there, fists thrust deep into the pockets of his maroon hoody, baseball cap pulled low over his eyes, a duffel bag slung across his body.

"I'm sure that the fact everybody seems to know where I live is all fair and above board," said Barnes.

"Claudia told me."

Barnes's eyebrows went up — *none the wiser.*

"I knew she was seeing someone in the job," said Riaz.

"It isn't me, I can assure you."

"I know. I thought it was, but it isn't."

"Glad you agree."

"It's Glover."

Barnes mulled this over for a moment. "He wouldn't have been my first guess."

"That's putting it delicately," Riaz said. "He was walking up her driveway just as I was leaving. Stopped just long enough to serve me papers. At first I thought he'd gone there just for that."

Barnes realised that the young officer's conclusion had not been a welcome one.

"You coming in, or what?"

Riaz shook his head.

Barnes looked at him properly. "You going somewhere?"

"Well, I'm not staying around to be hung out to dry, so I guess I must be going somewhere."

"What about your mother?"

The younger man tensed. "They'll call me if there's any change. But it could be weeks. And I'm not going far. Just far enough."

Barnes pushed the door open a little wider. "Come on. I'll put the kettle on."

Riaz hesitated. "I'm also homeless."

Barnes frowned.

"I can't go home. They haven't released the scene yet. In case she dies. Which is hilarious, because PSD have already torn it to pieces."

"Look, Jefferson, I can't second-guess your entire life on the doorstep. It's just a cup of tea."

Barnes walked back into the kitchen and left the door wide. Riaz waited a few more moments, and then followed him in.

Barnes made tea and passed Riaz a mug. The younger man nodded at the morass of papers scattered across the circular dining table.

"You allowed to bring your work home with you like that?"

"I don't advise it, but not for the reasons you're thinking of. This job will swallow you whole if you don't keep one foot outside it."

"You suggesting I take up squash?"

Barnes shrugged. "Whatever works for you. The point is: suspension is not fun. There are some who might see fourteen months on full pay as a bit of a touch, but I can assure you, it isn't. You'll just wake up each day wondering whether you're going to get the phone call. You might even be pragmatic about fearing the worst and line up another job — but that's only fine if you can say for certain that you can start in three months. What about six? What about nine? What about: I have no idea? Do you see what I'm saying? It's like the world's worst check-in queue."

"I haven't been suspended."

Barnes sipped his tea. Riaz carried his mug over to the table and sat down.

"Whose decision was it not to release your house back to you?" Barnes said. "Last I heard, that was my investigation."

"That's what I thought too. I got a phone call from the DCI."

"Shaw?"

"Maybe he thought you had too much on your plate. There aren't many PACE rights notifications that end up in murder."

Barnes exhaled heavily.

"That's why you're here? You want your house back?"

"If she gets discharged she'll have nowhere to go back to. She'll be homeless. Assuming she wants to go back there at all, of course. I'm half expecting her to want to go back home to Georgetown."

"*Lighthouse*," Barnes said.

349

"What did you find out?"

"Nothing, yet."

Riaz looked disappointed.

"I've been a little busy," Barnes said. "Hoovering up dead colleagues and the like."

Riaz grimaced at the tasteless comment, then put his mug down and started looking at the papers on the desk. Barnes watched him as Riaz scanned, assimilated and arranged the papers in order with the efficiency of a secretary on fast-forward.

It was far from being an idle activity — Barnes could *see* Riaz absorbing every detail and cross-referencing them with the filing system inside his head, and he realised he was excited. After last night, he had thought about thanking his lucky stars, drawing a discreet line and going back to bed, but, of course, in the moments when an investigation suddenly burst into life, you just had to go with it.

Barnes's heart was thumping and there were butterflies in his stomach as he edged forward towards the table, eager with the promise of insight, simultaneously kicking himself for not making more of this young man's ability.

"Scene guard . . . initial response . . . escaper . . . hospital . . . sighting . . . imposter," Riaz muttered as he rifled through the paperwork.

Eventually Riaz held up a document. Barnes peered at it. It was a printout of the incident log for the anonymous 999 call about the sighting of James Reeve during the air show.

"Did you ever get to the bottom of who reported the air show sighting?"

"Not exactly top of my list of priorities."

"You didn't call them back?" Riaz said.

"Well, no," Barnes said, feeling about as stupid as he ever had in his career. "Why would I? It was a sighting of a wanted person. They weren't a witness. I asked the control room to put in a callback to say thank you, but that was it."

"And did they?"

"I never followed it up. Why would I?" he said for a second time. He realised he was beginning to sound petulant, and set his jaw.

"Try it now," Riaz said.

Barnes did.

"It's ringing," he said, putting his hand over the mouth-piece of his mobile.

They listened to it ring — four, five, six times. After twenty rings Barnes hung up.

"Try it again."

"I will. Later."

"Where was the sighting?" Riaz asked.

"Opposite the TGWU. We were moving west, and had got about as far as the lifeboat station. We saw him about the same time as the AFOs."

"Good spot."

"It was surprisingly easy. When the displays flew over, the only people not looking up were cops, pickpockets and him. Especially there — it's the best place to get a view. There were so many tents on the Wish Tower Slopes it looked like paint-by-numbers, and . . . Jefferson? What's the matter?"

Riaz was focused on the printout. He had grabbed a red marker pen and began circling the phone number furiously.

"I've seen this phone number before," he said, holding the printout aloft again.

"Seen it? Seen it where?" Barnes said.

Riaz frowned. His eyes drifted off to the window as he accessed his internal hard drive.

"Front office," he said, eventually.

"Front office? Grove Road? Whereabouts?"

"Handwritten . . . on a notepad. With a bunch of other stuff. Which sort of makes sense. Control room tried a few times to put in the thank-you callback, couldn't get through, so they asked front office to try. It isn't that uncommon, and . . . Boss? Barnes? You okay? You look a little pale."

Barnes dropped his mug. It smashed on the tiled floor, but he was already running for the hallway and fumbling for his car keys.

35

Barnes hurtled along Royal Parade. The morning sun was already warm; despite being on the cusp of September, the summer showed no sign of abating, and the promenade was busy with joggers and dog walkers.

He swung into Cavendish Place and pulled up outside the Old Fire Station, scattering a trio of seagulls pulling apart some bulging bin bags. The front door was open, but Barnes quickly realised this didn't mean much. Two of the top windows were without glass, and as he stepped carefully into the entrance hall, he looked up and saw that most of the first floor was missing, as was a portion of the roof.

There were two notices adorning the once-proud Edwardian pillars that flanked the front door — one from the council, and one from the fire service. The building was a skeleton, and its days were clearly numbered. The likelihood of anyone being here was remote; nevertheless, Barnes racked his baton and gingerly stepped up the staircase, expecting his foot to go through it at any moment.

"Police!" he barked. "Make yourself known!"

Only the cacophony of squalling seagulls above the open-top roof answered him.

At the first-floor landing he kicked open the door. The floor that remained was no more than four feet wide all around the perimeter, and unless someone was hiding in the precariously perched wardrobe on the far wall, the room was empty. He certainly wasn't going to traverse the edges to check — it was a ten-foot drop to the concrete basement.

He resumed the climb. The door did not yield to his kick on the top-floor landing, and so he raised his baton above his head and yelled "*Police!*" again.

He tried the handle. It turned, and the door popped open. A stream of sunlight beamed through the roofless ceiling, flooding the room with warmth. The room looked as though everything had been hurriedly moved upstairs when the floor below had given out — there was a sofa, a couple of cots and a kitchenette in the far corner. The floor appeared intact — certainly it seemed to be bearing up under the weight of the furniture — but Barnes didn't fancy testing the load limit.

Besides, it was clearly empty. He closed his eyes and tried to imagine the tension at the deal that Riaz had intercepted outside, throwing nearly a year's worth of intelligence gathering down the toilet. Who would have been here? At a minimum, Ty Godden and the undercover. It seemed likely that Jean Tully's dreadlocked assassin would have been here as well, but who else?

He picked his way back downstairs and stepped out onto the street. He got a quizzical look from someone in a tie exiting the grey industrial block opposite that housed a car rental company. He flashed his warrant card, and the man in the tie set about washing cars.

Barnes looked up at the first floor of the car rental place. Had an obliging sense of community spirit meant that they had permitted use of their offices by a nameless police operation? Barnes imagined a makeshift command centre up there, with a strike team ensconced around the corner, ready to deploy on a barked radio command, had Jefferson Riaz not got there first.

Maybe.

Barnes thought about going over and asking the man washing cars that very thing, but he decided against it.

He had something more pressing to tend to first.

* * *

He headed down Cavendish Place, over Whitley Bridge and then along the Avenue, looping around the one-way system and up Grove Road.

He parked outside the Saffrons and walked back down to the station, the adrenaline starting to catch in his system like spark plugs firing up.

The oak double entrance doors had just been opened, and the foyer was empty. He buzzed himself through into the back and went into the office.

There was no one there. Barnes figured it was likely to be a short-term absence, and so he went straight to the window that DJ usually occupied.

He found the jotter pad that DJ used religiously, and flicked back through the pages. Working on an assumption of a page a day, he worked backwards until he found the one he was looking for.

He found the phone number almost straight away. It was at the bottom, circled twice, standing out between a doodle and a driving licence number. "SERIAL 419" was written above it.

He suddenly smelled tobacco and aftershave, and turned to see DJ in the doorway, drying his hands on a paper towel.

"Deej?" Barnes said from the doorway. "You're in early."

There was a tremor in his voice he was unable to conceal. DJ looked over, smiled and flicked on the remainder of the office lights. Barnes squinted.

"You've had a night," DJ said. "When was the last time you slept in a bed?"

Barnes snorted.

"Coffee?" DJ said, spooning instant into a couple of mugs.

"Why not? Black treacle," Barnes said, thinking for just a moment that if they maintained the pleasantries like they always had, he might not need to get round to why he was there.

Barnes sat down while DJ flicked the blinds up behind each counter position.

"You don't open till eight," Barnes said.

"I was awake early. I'm always awake early. Why not let the public benefit?"

"You don't sleep?"

DJ held Barnes's gaze for a moment. "I sleep fine. I just don't need much of it."

Barnes said nothing.

"I'm retired, Barnes. You know what that means?"

"I'm not sure I'll get there."

"You'll get there. And when you do, you won't want to sleep through any of it."

Barnes took a long slurp of coffee, watching his own hand carefully to make sure it wasn't shaking. The coffee was thick and bitter, and he grimaced.

"You're awake now, eh?"

Despite himself, Barnes laughed, and then coughed.

"Policeman's coffee. Nasty stuff," DJ chuckled.

They shared the joke and then Barnes moved in as their laughter tailed off.

"Do you remember Hamilton Tate?"

DJ licked his lips and set his coffee down, his eyes on his mug. "I do. It was in the news. Cell suicide."

"You gave him a character reference. Last month."

"A moot point, now," DJ said, holding Barnes's stare expectantly.

"Were you going to appear for him?"

"How do you know I gave him a reference, Barnes? That case went out of county. You seem a little . . . wired."

The point of no return had been reached. They both knew it. Barnes slowly raised the pad. "What's this?"

"It's my notepad. It isn't private. Just as well."

355

Barnes tapped the phone number with his finger. "This phone number. What is it? Where did it come from?"

DJ made a show of squinting at it. "Says right there. Serial 419. I couldn't tell you why I've got it. Not without looking."

"I think you do."

DJ tilted his head. The desktop radio set suddenly spat into life. A nasal-sounding controller was hawking for a unit to respond to a report of a suspicious-looking homeless man wandering around the pier.

"I feel like I should have someone with me, all of a sudden," DJ said, turning the volume down.

"Don't give me that. Look it up, if maintaining the pretence makes you feel better."

"Pretence?" DJ's eyes widened. "Look, I don't know what you're getting at, Barnes, but I can assure you—"

"Look it up."

DJ moved over to a computer, and brought up the incident system. He suddenly looked visibly upset, and Barnes tried to banish a twinge of doubt.

"There. Serial 419 of the twentieth of August. It was your capture of James Reeve. You asked the control room to put a thank-you call in to the caller. They tried but got nowhere, so they passed it to me."

The doubt doubled. It was a perfectly plausible explanation — one that Riaz had already predicted.

"And?" Barnes said.

"And nothing. I tried it a few times, but it just rings out. You know me, though, Barnes. I'm nothing if not thorough. Don't like leaving unfinished tasks. So I kept it on the to-do list."

Barnes went for his remaining trump card.

"Tell me about Op Lighthouse."

"You know why I respect you as a detective, Barnes? I get the feeling you don't ask questions you don't already know the answers to."

Barnes stared at him; DJ's shoulders seem to slump a little.

"Few years since I talked about that job."

"Good time to start."

"What do you want to know?"

"Who was on the team, for starters?"

"Me, Colin Hind, Stu Nippers. Tony Sarwan was lead interviewer; Hamilton Tate was on the OET."

"Who SIO'd it?" Barnes said, half knowing the answer.

"Gabby Glover. Tony Shillingford was office manager."

"Shillingford? Where do I know that name from?" Barnes said, suddenly thinking it might have been a good idea to have Riaz tag along.

"Career DS. He got posted over to West before your time. Been in the press a bit lately. PSD caught him embezzling from his elderly burglary victims to plump the pension."

Barnes was stunned. "His trial was running at the same time as Reeve's," he said, flicking through his notebook. "The jailer — McKinnon. He was intimidated by a couple of heavies the day of the prelim."

DJ shrugged. Barnes slowly put his book down.

"Tell me about Hamilton."

"He was brand new. Full of piss and vinegar. Someone thought he was incredibly hot shit and that an attachment to a homicide enquiry would do him some good."

"What happened, Deej? He asked you and Colin Hind for a character reference. He didn't ask me. Why would that be?"

"You tell me. Maybe the two of you weren't as chummy as you thought."

"Maybe. Or maybe he knew he couldn't count on me to bend the rules. Or maybe he figured you owed him something."

"The kid was a car crash waiting to happen. He would rather have drama — any drama — over boredom. You know the saying: give them enough rope, they hang themselves."

Barnes's fists clenched on the table, and he willed himself to keep them where they were. Decking thirty-eight years of loyal public service on the countdown to his second retirement just wouldn't play well.

"Poor choice of words, DJ," he said, through gritted teeth.

The wrong reaction would have led Barnes to start swinging, but they were interrupted by a short man in glasses who wanted to produce his driving documents — and mount a brief, one-man protest about how he hadn't been doing anything to warrant the attention of the traffic officer on the day in question. DJ was all soothing charm and jovial reassurance, and the man left the station positively buoyant. Despite himself, Barnes was impressed.

DJ turned back from the service window. "Getting to my busy time, Barnes. You want to do this later?"

"You single-crewed today?"

"Helen's on at ten."

"I won't keep you," Barnes said. "Op Lighthouse."

"You know about it?"

"It was a homicide inquiry, I know. Fifteen-year-old girl, caught in the crossfire of some drugs rivals' turf war. Four convicted, and commendations all round for the investigation team."

DJ folded his arms.

"And yet," Barnes said. "I can't help feel there's more to it than that."

"Well, you can't rely on intuition in court, Barnes. But, my God, it does get you looking in some dark corners."

"The question is: are they the right corners?"

DJ looked at his watch, then up at Barnes from under a thick white monobrow. "I suppose if we keep this informal, then anything I say is inadmissible."

"Getting you — or anyone — to court is a long way down a very rocky road. I need people to talk to me first, and every time I try people end up dead. I'm starting to get a bit of a complex."

DJ smiled. It was cold. "I gave thirty-plus years to the job. I joined at just the wrong time — my pension wouldn't quite cover the mortgage, so I had to come back. A small deficit is like a snowball rolling down a hill — give it a year and it's an avalanche. You know what I'm talking about."

Barnes shook his head. "I'm just lucky to have a job, frankly. I don't plan to ever retire."

"Not a bad strategy. Because even after you clear down the mortgage, there's still university to pay for, and weddings, and deposits on a first house."

"Please don't tell me you're bitching about having to provide for your children, DJ. Not to me."

"Far from it. But what I am saying is that I'm prepared to protect my investments."

"Enough to kill?"

The smile went from cold to reptilian.

"Now you're putting words in my mouth. But you won't ruin this for me. They'll carry me out of this police station in a box. You too, I'd wager — in a hundred years or so, but by then no one in my family will need to worry."

"Op Lighthouse."

DJ folded his arms. "Enough of this. You tell me whatever crackpot theory is on your mind and I'll try to give you a grunt now and then when they start coming in to sign on for bail."

Barnes picked up the phone and tried the number on the notepad again. He put it on loudspeaker and let it ring. Twenty, thirty times.

Nothing.

Barnes accused DJ with his eyes.

"Control room called me. They wanted me to keep trying."

"It wasn't your old buddy Colin, was it? That would have been a coincidence."

"What's on your mind, Acting DI Barnes?"

"I've read the investigation report — or at least, what I can find on the system. The paper case file is in a container archive somewhere, growing mould."

DJ shuffled in his seat.

"Or is it?" Barnes said. "Two crime gangs wanting to do each other out of some territory. One slights another, then there is retaliation, and it becomes a tornado from there. But around here, those wars seldom happen in public view. So how does an innocent come to be in the midst of it?

"You had intelligence about threats and intimidation. Mysterious visitors in the dead of night collecting debts. Witnesses to volume crimes suddenly going quiet. People disappearing.

"But no one would talk to you, am I right? People wanted it to stop, but not so badly that they wanted to get involved."

"A frustration you recognise, I'm sure," DJ said. "Albeit none of my witnesses killed themselves."

"And why is that, I wonder?" Barnes said. "I have little doubt that whoever the knuckle-dragging nutcase is that got taken out by a sniper less than thirty-six hours ago, he and another approached a young jailer called McKinnon on the first day of Reeve's trial — the same day as Tony Shillingford's prelim.

"Your four defendants: Mark Hicks, Stratton Pearce, Michele Braggia and Anjou Acosta."

"Not to mention Shaun Whitton and Duquesne Kenley. They were acquitted."

"Pity. Looks to me like you had a straight flush. So what was it? Tainted jury? Disclosure manipulation? Just good old-fashioned coercion?"

DJ visibly bristled. "I'll have you know that case was as tight as they come. All above board, all done within the rulebook. And justice was done."

"Then why the fuck is the op name being passed around in the night six years later!" Barnes shouted.

A couple that looked like tourists had entered the foyer; when they heard Barnes's raised voice, they left again.

"You're losing me customers, Barnes," DJ said.

"Are any of those surnames going to come up when I start cross-referencing them with my dead bodies? After all, you seem to have the monopoly on . . ."

Barnes's eyes suddenly widened.

"My God. You offered her up. It was manipulation."

DJ's breath was coming in heavy jets through his nostrils.

"She wasn't just in the wrong place at the wrong time, was she? You made *sure* she was. No one would stand in a witness box and talk about threats and intimidation and all the maybes, but kill an innocent girl and suddenly everyone wants to talk to you. Tap into that righteous outrage of the moral majority. That's it, isn't it?"

"You don't have a clue what it's like," DJ said. "Why do you think our conviction rate was so high? We did what needed to be done to get the bastards locked up. You sit around complaining about why people won't get involved, why they won't come forward. Well, we didn't just sit back and take it. We made our own luck."

"And an innocent was murdered."

"She wasn't bloody innocent. She was Jean Tully's daughter. One in a long line of wretched juveniles spawned for the sole purpose of keeping us busy, of keeping their banshee of a mother in drink."

"She was a fifteen-year-old kid."

"A fifteen-year-old kid who was halfway to being an alcoholic and gave at least two cops Hep C by trying to claw their eyes out."

"So she . . . she was Ty Godden's sister?"

"Half-sister. Older than him by a few years. Christ alone knows who the father was, but Anjou was the stepfather-of-the-moment. He was a brute, even by her standards. He tried to burn the house down once — with her in it — and was already on bail for wounding her. Used every knife in the house to practise his William Tell routine."

"On bail?"

"She wouldn't make a statement," DJ said, eyeballing Barnes. "But he knew he'd sailed close to the sun."

"He . . . he was working for you, wasn't he?"

DJ said nothing. Barnes used the silence to follow his own line of thinking — DJ could have thrown him off course, but the choice of destinations was rapidly dwindling.

"He was looking at the rest of his decent years in prison, so he became your inside man. He got the shortest sentence of the bunch — just enough for the others to believe he wasn't a grass. Was he complicit in his stepdaughter's murder?"

DJ shook his head. His eyes were red. "He didn't know what was going to happen. The strike was supposed to happen well outside town — we just let it run all the way to his house. So we didn't offer her up, to use your words. We just picked a time and place where the likelihood of collateral damage was practically inevitable."

"Collateral damage, and that's that? You can't make an omelette, *et cetera*."

"All four went away, with three still inside."

Barnes frowned. "Anjou is out?"

"He only did four years. Any longer and he wouldn't have been particularly interested in cooperation."

Barnes chewed this over for a moment. It was a history buried deep, with its own brand of twisted justice that someone else would have to arbitrate over. But the thread connecting the past and the present was a single word, passed by a dead man to a cop on a scrap of paper and then consigned to history.

"And Hamilton?"

"What can I tell you? We looked after each other. No matter what. When people say 'do the right thing', the right thing is always to protect your own. You want to know why he came to me for a character reference and not you? He knew I would say yes without hesitation."

Barnes stared at him, suddenly feeling that there was considerably more than a generation of service between them.

He stood up. "Parking your skewed principles for the moment, I still want to know how your case connects to mine."

DJ shrugged. "It's not rocket science. The whole family is shit. They're probably connected to half the active caseload at any one time. It's what a management consultant might call a 'hub and spoke' model. You're far from special, Barnes."

Barnes searched for a closing jab, but nothing came to mind. The controller was still hawking for a unit to respond to the pier. Barnes turned and left the office, leaving DJ sitting alone at the service window.

* * *

He paused on the steps of the station and breathed in the morning air. It was warm, and the smell of coffee drifted up from one of the myriad cafes further down Grove Road. The air seemed loud with the day's activity. Vans were unloading, patients were converging on the surgery and customers circled the ancient second-hand bookstore, exhausting the bounty of choice before venturing inside.

His foot hit something soft. There was a grubby blue sleeping bag laid out across the steps. He tutted. Likely belonging to one of the homeless. Maybe even the same guy he'd barked at the other night.

A pang of guilt hit him. He'd been out of order. He bent down and carefully folded the bag up into a corner of the doorway so as to reduce the trip hazard.

He headed back up towards the Saffrons, his mind crackling with electricity.

DJ was right. Old cases, criminally active families, networks of relationships — they all impacted on the future, and the ripple effect could never be fully quantified. It was maybe no more than that.

Then: Anjou Acosta working for DJ — with or without Jean Tully's knowledge. Tully's daughter: live bait, mown down in the crossfire. And a solid case. Tony Shillingford running the actions under Gabby Glover.

Now: Jimmy Januarie wanted Jefferson Riaz to know about Op Lighthouse, through the curtain of a drugs drop. An undercover in place. Two men trying to intimidate a court jailer — one was almost certainly his dreadlocked assassin. Could the other have been Tony Shillingford, the former DS? Two apparently unconnected court cases starting on the same day. Someone nobbled in Listings? Or a smooth-tongued advocate casually suggesting potential dates to the court — with no better alternatives on the table, they got their way.

Dead cops. And Jefferson Riaz. The head of a scapegoat on a spike outside the town hall, or were PSD's concerns about a burgeoning splinter intelligence enterprise well-founded?

He didn't know.

What he did know was that the kid had a mind that any detective would dream of, and it had brought him nothing but trouble.

The attack on his mother — random? A little "fuck you" to the cop trying to extricate himself from a shitstorm? Or was he getting close to something, and someone needed to divert his attention elsewhere?

Something?

Someone.

He kicked out at a stray branch on the pavement in anger. All this confusion, all these unanswered questions, and the only actual real-life criminal he had his hands on was a dead dreadlocked body, who was likely little more than an enforcer. Him, and a sketch-up of a mysterious bearded man who had burgled a farm for a .22 and a shotgun and had discharged both in less than three months.

He swore and dug around in his pocket as he realised he had forgotten to ask Shaw to release the house as a scene, which had left Riaz homeless, to use his own — rather melodramatic, Barnes thought — turn of phrase.

He stopped dead.

The phone clattered to the floor.

Homeless.

How long had he been in with DJ? Half an hour?

The sleeping bag on the steps was there when he came out.

But not when he went in.

A homeless man in the midnight rain, sloping off to the train station on Barnes's command.

364

A makeshift camp among the flowers in Hampden Park, not a hundred yards from the cordon where Jean Tully complained of assault.

A rainbow of windbreaks and tents on the Wish Tower Slopes, right on top of where James Reeve had been sighted and then flattened by armed police.

36

Barnes stumbled to his car, almost took out a moped as he performed an inelegant U-turn outside Caffyns, and sped down Blackwater Road towards the sea. The gridiron of long, straight boulevards that intersected the spread of enormous Edwardian buildings allowed a decent run, and he stepped on the accelerator, the whine of the engine drawing stares from passers-by.

He wrenched the Rover around the college, narrowly avoiding a returning hockey team as they crossed the road, and popped up onto Carlisle Road by the brutal grey structure that housed the Congress Theatre.

The end portion of Carlisle Road that led down to the sea was one-way, and Barnes toyed briefly with ignoring the No Entry signs and ploughing straight on against the traffic, steaming past the restaurants and ice cream parlours.

He just about kept his head, however, and, after an interminable wait at the junction with Compton Street, pulled away past Wilmington Square's neat lawns and onto the seafront.

He dumped the car like he'd stolen it, and ran across Grand Parade to the Wish Tower Slopes.

He stood for a moment, knowing he was close, but suddenly unsure of where to start. In his mind, the area could be contained, mapped and searched by one man. The reality was that the towering height of the TGWU, the wild expanse of the Channel, even the wide sprawl of Grand Parade, were enormous.

He ran over to the slopes, trying to pick out obvious spots of colour from the tents that had festooned the seafront during the air show, but all he saw today was an apron of green.

He ran down to the lower promenade, pulling out his phone. He dialled the number again, letting it ring, spinning round and round on the spot as he strained to listen.

He spotted a bin and jogged over, the number still ringing in his ear. He peered inside at the contents, noting it was near full, and didn't appear to have been emptied since the air show.

He squatted down, the number still ringing, and planted his ear to the green painted iron.

Nothing.

He stood up, briefly making eye contact with a bemused-looking jogger, and ran to the next bin, where he repeated the exercise. Sweat broke out across his brow as the sun started to get going.

He continued in this vein towards the pier, telling himself it wasn't a fool's errand — the phone was still live, still in Eastbourne, and this was not a speculative exercise — he was following a trail of breadcrumbs.

Wasn't he?

Another bin.

And another.

And another, frantically scanning other likely locations as he ran between the bins — a phone-sized niche in the rockery around a flower bed, underneath a shiny blue bench, tucked behind the open door of a beach hut.

His radio muttered in his other pocket. The control room was still looking for a unit to respond to the complaint of the vagrant on the pier.

Grateful — and not for the first time — that he had never become one of those CID officers that instantly consigned their radio to their locker the second they left Response, Barnes called up and offered to take the call. The controller accepted gratefully, though the confusion was apparent in her voice as to why the district DI was taking a nuisance call. Barnes didn't dwell on it, but it did make him think back to the slashed tyres. They might yet come asking about that, or they might not.

You get away with something you shouldn't have, and it will come around one way or another.

On the one hand, it was a long shot, but on the other, his gut was telling him something. Most lines of enquiry come to nothing — you follow, then if you get nothing, you move onto the next one. A good cop knows when a trail goes cold, and this one wasn't cold — yet.

He ran to the pier, drawing more stares from the promenade's foot traffic — the only one in a crumpled suit, the only one clearly not there for leisure, the only one running like his life depended on it.

The smell of deep-frying donut batter hit him as he reached the pier entrance. He paused for a moment on the mosaic-tiled floor, his hands on his knees, his breath coming in snatched rasps.

A number of other stalls were preparing their wares for the day's trade, but footfall was low. Barnes looked at his watch. Not quite nine. It would be opening soon.

He climbed over the largely ineffectual chain that barred the entrance, flashing his warrant card at a quizzical cleaner spreading a sopping mop over the timber boards of the pier floor proper.

"Comms, DI Barnes," he said.

"Go ahead, boss," the controller answered.

"Show me at scene. Who's made the complaint?"

"Looks like maintenance staff of some kind."

"Got a telephone number, please?"

The controller went with the telephone number, and Barnes inhaled sharply.

It was the same number.

He called it again and shut his eyes, trying to concentrate. It rang ten, twenty times. Nothing.

He moved up toward the amusement arcade, stood under the faded, salt-blasted lettering of the "Funtasia" entrance sign, and tried the number again.

Nothing.

He moved out of the sun into the darkened vestibule of the arcade's main entrance doors.

He dialled the number.

There.

A faint trilling, deep in the gloom.

His pulse doubled.

He moved into the main arcade. Garish rides, games and slot machines stood silent and dark. A musty odour rose off the dark, swirling patterns of the worn velour carpets.

The trilling became a fraction louder, then rang off.

He dialled it again.

A stereo ring — the tone in his ear, accompanied by a tinny, muffled chirping from somewhere in the gloom.

But a little louder.

He moved over to the source of the sound, when the muffling stopped and it echoed up into the curved, cavernous ceiling, accompanied by a small square of flashing light from the device's screen.

A device that was attached to an arm.

The man moved forward out of the shadows — the sun was still rising through the eastern windows, and the figure was shrouded in gloom, as well as being partially concealed by a bank of arcade machines.

Barnes killed the call, and silence descended on the arcade.

37

"You took your time." The voice was dry, as if it had not been used in a while.

Barnes edged forwards into the room — the man was over the other side of the room, about thirty or forty feet away, in front of the windows and little more than a silhouette. Barnes tried to force his eyes to adjust to the gloom after the blinding daylight outside. They did, slowly, and he was able to make out a broad figure, maybe six-three, aged about forty-five. He had a shipwreck beard and a mass of hair piled up into a bun on the top of his head, with worn combat shorts and a camo sleeveless vest.

As the tableau gradually sharpened into focus, Barnes noticed another smell surpassing the otherwise oppressive reek of the carpets.

He sniffed. Petrol.

There was a can at the man's feet, along with a collection of twisted rags.

"That's far enough," the figure said.

"I guess you must be my maintenance man," Barnes said, stopping a good twenty-five or so feet away. There was a bank of fruit machines between them, like a makeshift line of defence.

Barnes nodded towards the array of amateur pyrotechnics. "What was your next move going to be? Sending up smoke signals?"

"More or less," the man said. "If you didn't bite this time around."

"You know, you could have just called my office."

The man scoffed with laughter. Barnes saw a streak of saliva sputter out from his lips and catch the light from the windows behind him.

"A suicide mission," he said. "You don't make yourself invisible for a year and then march into a police station."

Barnes pulled himself up to perch on the edge of an air hockey table. "If this were the Cold War you'd have put a coded funeral notice in the *Herald.*"

The laughter stopped. "Don't make fun of me. I've kind of lost my sense of humour in the last twelve months."

"Okay. Sorry."

"Those theatres you work in — investigation, manhunt, arrest, court. Those are just stops on a Tube map. The rest of the time we have to live in the tunnels."

Barnes swung his legs. "It occurs to me that you loosed off a couple of 12-gauge shells at my head in the not-too-dim-and-distant past. Not to mention a .22 slug that singed my earlobe."

"Bring any backup?"

"No. I figured I wanted to meet the real James Reeve."

The man was silent.

"Assuming that's actually your real name, of course. Is it?"

"No."

"What is?"

"It doesn't matter," he said quietly, more to himself than to Barnes. "I saved your life with that .22 slug."

"And I'm grateful," Barnes said. "So, you want to come in? Is that it?"

"Whatever way you want to phrase it, the short answer is — no way."

"Then why are you here?"

"You need to ask? You're going round in circles. Two dead cops and a wall of silence."

"Two?"

"PC Lamb's body is going to turn up at a waste transfer station in the next week or two."

Barnes's legs stopped swinging. The words hung in the air and echoed up into the ceiling.

"So what are we doing here, exactly? If my theory is correct, you're committing some kind of criminal treason by coming up for air. There must be an endgame."

"Tell me your theory, and I'll tell you how close you are."

"Strictly speaking, it isn't my theory, but I'm the only one crazy enough to give it any plausibility."

The man shifted in the gloom, and disappeared briefly from view. Barnes craned his neck and hopped off the table. He needed to get a bit closer to him, to facilitate conversation if nothing else. He couldn't even get a proper ID on him. It was like being on the baseline at Wimbledon and trying to have a conversation with the umpire.

He swallowed. If his theory was right — or thereabouts — then James Reeve had every reason to be pissed off at best, unhinged at worst. It wasn't anything he hadn't already considered, but the petrol can and array of makeshift detonators had *blaze of glory* stamped all over it. Barnes wondered what else he had hidden behind there.

Maybe he should be a little more circumspect.

Reeve reappeared. His hands were empty. "I'm listening."

"Eleven hours and twenty-eight minutes," Barnes said. "That was the time between the first response to Tommy Gayle getting thumped in the head and the early turn patrol to come back to arrest you for murder. There was an intervening visit, but you were out for a walk. At two in the morning."

"A bloody long walk."

"I've got precious little evidence, but the storyboard I can't dislodge from my brain goes a bit like this:

"Either you or Mandy — or maybe both — were valuable, in some way, to someone important and not very nice. Maybe they came to see you both after Tommy checked out. *We're sorry, Tommy was a bad lad, he shouldn't have put you in that position, figure we owe it to you to make things right*, or words to that effect.

"They nominate one of their cleanskin foot soldiers to take the fall. He doesn't complain. After all, it's a win-win — kudos, loyalty points, probably a relatively light sentence, even a small possibility that the CPS won't run with it. Besides which, he'd end up buried in the foundations of a new build if he said no.

"So you make yourself scarce, he assumes the role of James Reeve, just sitting quietly in the lounge, drinking your tea and eating your Rich Tea biscuits until the cops work it out and come back to put the bracelets on. He's fully briefed, ready with his story of self-defence and provocation, ready to plead remorse, take one for the team.

"Everyone has to play their part for it to work, of course, but the main thing is the *cops have stopped looking*. They have their perp walk, they have their trial, they have a detected homicide on the books — whatever enterprise was ticking along prior to Tommy Gayle's demise can now continue uninterrupted.

"But the faux James Reeve leaping out of the dock and making a bolt for freedom wasn't part of the game plan, was it? Nor was a juror upsetting the applecart with some intel on a drugs drop. Nor was what happened to Mandy. Nor was—" Barnes traced a line in the air with his finger, running it from Reeve's head to his feet and back again — "what appears to be a never-ending life of exile and banishment."

Reeve didn't respond.

"Wow," Barnes said. "It sounds even more nuts when I say it out loud."

For a moment, there was only the sound of Reeve's breathing, and a whirring from somewhere deep within the building. It allowed Barnes's thoughts to catch up with him.

"And, look: I'm sorry for your loss," he said. "For Mandy. Genuinely."

A sound like a hyena's bark burst from deep within Reeve's chest and echoed up into the ceiling.

"Am I right?"

"More or less," Reeve said, his voice thick with emotion.

"Then fill in the blanks for me," Barnes said, unable to stop his guts from doing a little leap at confirmation of his hitherto-leftfield theory. He'd consigned more plausible hypotheses to the wastepaper basket long before this stage. "Preferably with some bloody names."

"Names?"

"The meathead at Jean Tully's house, for one."

"I only knew him as Roland. He was an enforcer. Horrible piece of work. Liked to use that Rambo knife to cut nostrils open."

Barnes made a mental note to run a national check on the *Chinatown* MO when he finally extricated himself from this tableau, in the hope of accelerating the ID. It then occurred to him that that *when* might actually be *if*.

He manoeuvred himself a little to the right, so he was closer to the window and the abundance of daylight fighting to get in. He was slightly closer, slightly more square on to Reeve — better, but not much.

And it didn't go unnoticed.

"What are you doing?" Reeve said.

"Just trying to see a little better," Barnes said. "Mind if we flick on a few lights in here?"

"No lights."

"Well," Barnes said, spreading his hands, "given the complex subterfuge you've indulged in to get me here, I would say the floor is yours."

"You were a lot less wordy before. Verbal diarrhoea now."

"Sorry. My mouth gets a bit clever when I'm nervous. Anyway, before what? When?"

Reeve sniffed hard. Something *thwacked* on the back of his throat. He swallowed.

374

"She used to do their books," Reeve said. He let the sentence hang.

"And?" Barnes said. "James, it's fair to say I'm all ears. Please proceed."

"Mandy. She was a bookkeeper. Did an apprenticeship. Was going to do her degree, become an accountant. Set up her own practice. She used to help run the camera shop." His voice became wistful.

"I take it she was pretty good?"

"At keeping book? Oh yeah, you could set your watch by her. Had a calculator in her brain. She was good. Too good."

"Caught the eye of someone."

Reeve nodded in the gloom.

"She was washing all the dirty cash through the shop, and it was coming out pristine. It was a clever front, really. Tell someone a camera is worth five times its actual value, nobody really questions it. Put a hundred-pound camera and a thousand-pound camera in front of an amateur, they can't tell the difference. So dicky invoices were no real drama."

"How did that come about?"

"Through Tommy. They met in a pub, years ago. Had been together a few months when he realised she was useful. Once she was in, she couldn't get out."

"Until you came along."

"He nearly killed her, once. Tied a dressing-gown cord around her neck. She threw him out, but the trade-off was: you have to keep doing the books. If she'd refused, they'd have finished the job with the cord. But because she agreed, she had their protection. Tommy got put on a leash."

"Which, from time to time, he liberated himself of."

"One too many times."

"So how did the two of you meet?"

Reeve didn't immediately answer. Barnes imagined his eyes narrowing in the darkness.

"You working the negotiators' playbook? You know all this already."

"Maybe I do. But I'm willing to listen. How often are you going to get that?"

"We met at group. One of these church things — different addiction every night. I was there for the drink, she was going to some battered-wife rehab group. Survivors, they call them. I went on the wrong night."

"Surprised she wanted to get involved with another drinker."

"I said the same thing. I was twelve years sober. She said: 'I want to be the reason you manage another twelve, not the reason you fall off.' Soon as she said that, I wanted to marry her."

"Then what?"

"Tommy used to come around, shouting the odds. Twice, three times a week in the beginning. Then it tapered off. But every time he did it, she got a little more frazzled. We reported it, of course. Got the usual — alarm, marker on the address, even had a camera there for a little while. For all the good it did.

"Then the night I . . . the night he died, I'd gone out on a shout."

James Reeve the retained firefighter. Reeve the community hero, Barnes thought. This is the evidence-in-chief he never got to give.

"We received a few calls. Block of flats on fire. Sent five pumps. Turned out to be a hoax."

"Tommy?"

"Who knows? I got back and there he was on the driveway, acting like a prat. I tried to talk him down, but he was spoiling for a fight. So he got one."

"One punch."

"It was a few punches, but on both sides. We were hugging for most of it, getting in these little rabbit punches, body shots. Then he took a step back, just to reset. Left himself open, only for a second. But long enough for me to clean his clock. Straight uppercut. He went down, hit his bonce on the kerb, and game over."

"You almost sound pleased about it."

"I'm not gonna lie. When someone makes your life a misery, when they know the cops can't do anything, when your partner is a nervous wreck forever looking out the window, it does feel quite nice to wrestle back a bit of control over your own destiny. Feel a bit more like a man than a spare part."

"Aren't you a bit old for playground bravado?"

"Playground, my arse. Fucked if I was going to let him be the last man standing. Me on the deck and him free to have his way with her? No way. What kind of future husband would that make me? I'd turn in my grave."

"So you meant to kill him."

Reeve didn't immediately answer. His eyes gleamed in the darkness. If Barnes could just get the other side of the bank of fruit machines between them . . .

"Even if I said yes," he said slowly, "it would be inadmissible. I'd be incriminating myself, and you haven't cautioned me. The truth is: I'm glad the prick is gone. But I didn't mean to kill him. Let's not forget: *he* came to *my* house. *He* came looking for it."

"And then?"

"Then . . . then it got really weird. The first car turned up, I was waiting in the lounge like a good boy, knowing they were coming, knowing they would need to lock me up. They turn up, they say: he's having his head glued, no big deal, we're a bit strapped tonight for numbers so we'll invite you in for an interview once we know if he wants to make a complaint or not. They were all pretty reasonable about it, actually. Then off they toddled."

Barnes took an involuntary step closer. Reeve seemed not to notice.

"Then what? Someone else visited, didn't they?"

"They sure did."

"Who? Who was it, James?"

"Two of them. Roland, and the main guy. Youngish, good-looking. Not rough like some of the street men. Bit of charm about him. Wore a long coat. Roland was a cock — he would just walk around your kitchen like he owned it. The other guy, he owned it sitting still. And he did it with style."

"Give me a name, James."

"Wish I could."

"Look at some pictures?"

"If it means coming to a police station, no way. Anyway, I'd bet my topknot that he's a cleanskin."

"A sketch likeness, then."

Reeve shrugged. "I can try. It was almost a year ago."

Barnes exhaled heavily. "Go on."

"Well, it's like you said. He told us Tommy had died — Christ knows how he knew before the cops — and that he felt responsible. Said it wasn't right that I go down for something like manslaughter. What he meant was, of course, he wanted to keep Mandy sweet."

"So he offered someone up."

"One of his lackeys — a James Reeve lookalike, supposedly, though I couldn't see a likeness. Someone briefed and ready in the wings to cough to it as a means of getting his stripes. A cleanskin — guilty plea, show of remorse, looking at maybe four years for involuntary manslaughter."

"Mandy went along with this?"

"If it meant keeping me out of jail, then yes. Plus there wasn't much time to think about it. He said: now the prick's dead, the cops will be back any minute. You'll need to disappear for a little while. Pack a bag, and get out."

"What, was this substitute waiting outside in the car or something?"

"More or less."

"And did Mr Handsome not think that the cops would come back and realise James Reeve had suddenly grown a foot?"

"I said just that. He laughed. Said not to worry. He said the chances of the same patrol coming back were zero. Not only that, but it was close to dawn, which meant close to shift change, which meant the very last thing the night turn patrols would want to do would be to start nicking people as the sun's coming up.

"Mandy said: won't the cops that have already been here have gone back to report? Noted my description? Given a photograph to their day shift colleagues? Me and the guy *both* laughed at that one."

"Well, you may have been right," Barnes said. "But that is still cojones of steel."

"You think? He got to drive away into the new day. Everyone else did the hard yards. Mandy said: the cops will at least ask for ID, surely. This guy apparently already had some. In my name. What do you make of that?"

"I'm not sure," Barnes muttered. "What I do know is that I'm sure you're describing my main man, and I have no way to identify *or* find him."

"That's your problem."

"So what happened to you?"

"I did what he said. I packed a bag, grabbed some camping stuff, walked off down the road at four thirty in the morning, and have been playing musical bloody tents around Sussex ever since."

"You didn't go to see her?"

"I couldn't. There were strings, mate. It wasn't just a case of keeping my head down. I had to liquidate the business, relinquish the savings and basically sign a contract of indentured servitude in blood to keep her safe. Pay for my own exile. The carrot was: once their put-up guy was safely at Her Majesty's Pleasure and all the hoo-ha had died down, I could resurface. Cops forget all about you once the trial's over. Media too. A year absolute tops, he said."

"But."

"But the prick jumped the dock."

"I take it that wasn't part of the plan."

"Too bloody right."

"Why did he do it?"

"I wish . . . I wish I knew," Reeve said, his voice hitching slightly. *Careful*, Barnes thought. *We're building up to the tough part of the story.* "I've spent a year thinking about nothing else. Touch of the seconds, couldn't face doing the time after all, couldn't face bumping into Anjou inside. Saw Januarie in the jury and realised the whole thing was stacked against him. Saw a way out from whatever mess he'd made of his life."

"Then what?"

"The handsome prick put a bounty on him and let Roland off the leash. But I hunted him down first."

"And called it in during the air show."

"It was that or bash his head in with a rock."

"How did you find him?"

"Does it matter? By crapping himself and making a run for it, all bets were off. Roland sent that skinny prick Jenner to collect the washed cash from Mandy, knowing she wouldn't have it, knowing that if he came up empty-handed he'd go the same way as countless others. And she paid for it."

He was breathing heavily through his mouth. *Careful*, Barnes thought again.

"So, after deciding that disconnecting his IV wasn't enough, you smothered him."

"An eye for an eye."

"And fired a shotgun at me."

"Nothing personal."

"And clobbered a nurse in the process."

"That was an accident. I feel bad about that."

"For the working-class hero thing, you're racking up quite the body count," Barnes said. "Murder, attempted murder and ABH as a minimum."

"Now you see why I don't want to come in."

"You were on the cordon. You were camping in Hampden Park. You threatened Jean Tully."

"Nothing could threaten that mangy little banshee."

"Maybe, but where does she fit into it? Where does her next-door neighbour fit into it? He was a juror at your decoy's trial, and he got thrown off Beachy Head for his troubles."

"PC Pete Lamb, the snake. He was your common denominator. He was bent as they come."

"He doesn't have the reach to attempt jury-tampering. Or the wit, for that matter."

"He didn't need to."

"What do you mean?"

"Jimmy Januarie was *already* nobbled. Before he got anywhere near jury service."

"What? By whom?"

Reeve looked surprised. "Who do you think? By your lot."

Barnes's blood ran cold. "My lot? Cops?"

"Yeah. Easy. Let the trial start, make an approach, offer a fee, get them to keep an ear out."

"Or what? Get them to move in next door to your local shit family?"

"Why not? If the price is right."

"That doesn't make any sense."

"Of course it bloody does. Why wouldn't it make sense? Let me ask you something: how far did you look into Jimmy Januarie's death?"

"What do you mean? I . . ."

"It was homicide, right?"

"How do you—?"

"Did you happen to establish when he moved into that house?"

Barnes felt suddenly light-headed. He steadied himself against a fruit machine. "You're saying, what? Jimmy Januarie was installed in that house to spy on Jean Tully, and then ended up as a juror in your trial?"

"What did you think it was, a coincidence?"

"I . . ."

"How do you think these things work, exactly? You get a crime complaint, take a few statements, make an arrest and everyone's happy? How often does that work? You must know there's more to it than that."

"Of course I do."

"Tommy, Jean, Ty, Anjou, all of them. Even the barrister. There are hundreds of disposable dogsbodies like them in seaside towns all over the country. People like Roland and Handsome let them think they have a chance of bettering themselves, and string them along. These are the names you get on your crime reports, because everybody knows them. They're part of the town's fabric. And they're wound so tight they don't talk. Fear keeps them loyal.

"So if you're trying to bring someone like that down, you have to get creative. Install a London vigilante next door, let them keep their ears open. Then put them on a jury."

"How, exactly?"

"Jury selection, for the most part, is a pretty tight process. Until it goes wrong. They are only human, after all."

"The girl that got arrested?"

"How hard do you think it is to get a drinker drunk? You want to serve on a jury, your history is on display. Find someone who likes a tipple — and likes fighting cops when they do — it isn't hard to manoeuvre one into the cells for the night. Seven pints and a well-timed insult is all it takes.

"Then the judge realises he's one juror down, and has to pay the talesman to find another. Which is no more sophisticated than sending out the court clerk and any other spivs on hand to literally go out into the street and press-gang passers-by into jury service that day."

"And Jimmy Januarie just happened to be walking by," Barnes murmured.

"The question is: was he acting alone? And the safe answer has to be: of course he wasn't. But I don't think Handsome and Roland put him there. I think it was a cop."

"This is going to sound stupid, but why that particular trial?"

"Look, these cases don't come around very often. You'll seldom get them with guns and drugs in their pocket, and definitely not the ones higher up the food chain. The door into a reasonably well-organised gang is a faulty brake light, or not picking up after your dog, or beating up your woman. Tommy beating his chest and coming off worse was a golden opportunity."

"At the risk of sounding like a broken record, who the hell are we talking about?" Barnes almost yelled.

Reeve nudged the can with his foot. Barnes heard the petrol slosh around the sides.

"The undercover?" he said. "At the old fire station? Where Airplane caught Ty Godden? That was you?"

"No," said a voice. "It was me."

Barnes spun around on the spot. If he'd been armed, he would have levelled his weapon and possibly even pulled the trigger. He was wound tighter than an overtuned harp.

Standing behind him, her fingers trailing along the air hockey table, was Claudia. She was dressed in a black Adidas hoody and jeans, with all of her hair stuffed into a baseball cap.

"Claudia?" Barnes said. "What the hell?"

"You told me you didn't bring anyone," Reeve called. "This better not be a betrayal, DI Barnes."

"He didn't betray you," Claudia said to him. "I followed him."

"Anyone else I need to know about?" Reeve said, picking up the petrol can.

"Everybody just take a breath," Barnes said, holding up his hands. "James, please just relax. Claudia, if you are about to tell me you're bent, I might just push you off the pier myself."

"I'm not," she said. "I came to get him out."

"Get him out?" Barnes began. "You . . ."

He whirled back to Reeve.

"Christ," Barnes said. "You're a cop."

Despite the apparent stand-off, Reeve shuffled his feet. He looked momentarily self-conscious.

Barnes wanted to laugh. Great big chunks of the story fell into place at once. He rubbed his hands down his face, for a moment barely registering either Claudia or Reeve.

"It was a gig," he said, mainly to himself. "You were deployed into the gang. Ground floor. Ingratiate yourself with the girl who washes the money and does the books. Low-hanging fruit, then work your way up.

"But that must have been . . . four years ago?"

"Six." Reeve's voice was flat.

"Six years." Barnes rubbed his chin. "Around the same time Op Lighthouse folded. Were . . . were you on that enquiry?"

"Peripherally. Distant enough to be parachuted in after most of the key players skated on the charges. The four they put away were barely one above street level, with the possible exception of Anjou. It wasn't enough."

"Holy Christ. So some bright spark thought to stick a UC in. And . . . and you . . ."

He stared at Reeve.

"You fell in love with her."

Reeve said nothing. His eyes gleamed.

"They must have loved that. So what were you, persona non grata?"

"Permanent exile would be a better way of putting it."

Barnes's mind was racing. "Her funeral?"

"At least five of them were Crime Squad."

"Not called NCS any longer. It's the new lot, as of a few months ago. SOCA."

"Plus a couple of AFOs," Reeve said, ignoring the correction.

"The cousin? Laura?"

"I'm guessing you didn't spot the sidearm. Mandy doesn't have a cousin."

Barnes whistled. "All in the hope that you might show at the funeral."

"Not me. My so-called decoy. But yes."

"That would explain why it was like DEFCON Three when I tried to put her boyfriend's dog end through FSS for a profile. Jesus. And you were never compromised? Roland didn't know?"

Reeve shook his head firmly. "Never. My cover was always intact. But they thought I'd gone rogue. So what do you call that?"

"A cop and a hard case, I'd say."

384

"Oh, very good."

"And Mandy?"

He shook his head again, more circumspect this time. "She . . . she never knew. It's the one thing I'm grateful for. I was going to tell her, once we were away."

"Away? The suitcases by the front door?"

"That was me," Claudia said. "I was trying to get a message to James, that we were standing by once it was safe for him to come up for air. I knew both sides would be watching, but I didn't know that . . . that . . ." Her voice tailed off.

A painful sob escaped Reeve.

"And Chris Jenner?" Barnes said.

"He went round to collect the clean takings," Claudia replied. "She didn't have it. He flipped, knew he was a dead man if he went back empty-handed. So he took her out instead. A defenceless, innocent . . ."

Reeve produced a long, metal screwdriver. Barnes took a step back, instinctively stretching out an arm to the side to prevent Claudia from coming any further forward.

"She was all I had!" he bellowed.

"Got a Taser or something?" Barnes said to Claudia, out of the corner of his mouth. "I've got nothing."

"Of course I bloody don't," she answered.

Reeve approached the front of a fruit machine by the window. Barnes took a couple of tentative steps forward and squinted to try to work out what he was doing. He'd closed the gap between them, but only by a couple of feet.

The back of the fruit machine was facing into the room and there was a handwritten sign taped to the back: "OUT OF ORDER". Reeve squatted down and used the screwdriver to lever off the rear panel. It looked like a well-practised manoeuvre, and the back came away cleanly.

Several bundles of pristine bricks of cash tumbled out onto the grimy carpet.

"The escape fund," Reeve said, in a voice that was hoarse and too loud for Barnes's liking. "She used to skim a little and stash it here until we had enough. That last lot was the final payment. She was going to await the verdict and then meet me at the airport. She wasn't counting on the silly prick vaulting the dock."

"And from then on, a vigilante crusade," Claudia murmured out of the corner of her mouth, loud enough for only Barnes to hear. She took a tentative step forwards.

Barnes ignored her.

"And Jean Tully? She was on the cordon, rubbernecking. You were camping out in the woods in Hampden Park."

"She was in my sightlines. She's of the same ilk as every other chancer that wants to get promoted by the London gangs, except she's the Fagin doing the brokering. With her own kids, no less. She was push, push, push, her whole miserable life. Roland handed out the punishments, but *she* kept them on the leash. *She* kept them wound tight. *She's* the reason Chris Jenner went banzai and ended Mandy's life."

"So you told her you were coming for her."

"Or words to that effect."

"Well then, why not take her out with your sniper rifle the same time you took out Roland? Your charge sheet already has murder and attempted murder on it. What's one more body?"

Barnes felt Claudia's glare.

Reeve shrugged. "You were in my way."

There was a heavy pause. Everything was muffled by the sound-deadened arcade — the gulls, the waves, the increasing footfall on the pier's boardwalk. The silence felt like a thick blanket of stale air that had been shut away for a decade.

"And you . . ." Barnes turned to Claudia. "What a dullard I am for not seeing that. You were in the old fire station. Embedded in the gang. Airplane's piss and vinegar undercut the op, so you got pulled out and pushed back into uniform, to get close to him."

Claudia said nothing, but looked up at Barnes from under a heavy frown.

Barnes smiled, and then grimaced. "So if you were ensconced in this crew, why the hell don't I know any names besides Handsome and Roland? Deceased Roland, I might add."

"We were getting there," she said. "But these pricks are careful. Why give you a name when they don't need to? They're the ones making the calls. As far as the strategy went, we didn't need to know their real identities, just as long as the bracelets went on them with a decent amount of gear in their hands. Then we'd have all the time in the world."

"So, who? Who's the master puppeteer?" Barnes said, suddenly riled. "Some nameless public-school chinless DAC up in the smoke? Some simpering sycophant with sloping shoulders for whom a local DI is just an occupational hazard?"

Claudia gave him a look that answered his question beautifully. Barnes dropped his hands.

"What? Not even a phone call? Not even a shot across the bows? Not a quiet word in the car park at midnight to say wind your neck in, the grownups are looking at this? They just let me run around in circles with my hair on fire? Waiting for me to get tired?"

He looked back at Reeve.

"And yet, you brought me to you. *Me.* No one else."

"If it helps any, you're the only one I could trust."

Barnes folded his arms. "Well, I just got goosebumps all over. So now what?"

Reeve picked up the plastic can carelessly. A spurt of petrol gushed out of the nozzle onto the carpet.

"Sorry I asked," Barnes said.

"I gave you Roland."

"Served him up like a kipper, more like."

"He'll have had a phone on him. Get to work on that, and you might yet unravel this thing. I've given you the rest of it."

"What about you?"

"I've been in no man's land for the best part of a year. I have no intention of staying. Can't go forwards, can't go back. There isn't any scenario where I'm not dead or in jail. This is the best option."

"Can't let you do that, James."

Barnes heard the slide of the nine-mil ratchet as Claudia appeared beside him, with the sidearm pointed at Reeve.

Reeve smirked, and picked up one of the soaked rags by his feet.

"What's that, a Glock? You're twenty feet away. If that even singes my crown I'll be impressed."

"I need to bring you in."

"No chance."

"It will be better. Hotel, shower, breakfast, new clothes. Armed guard so you can relax a bit. Then new identity, new address. Start over."

"If only that weren't complete bullshit."

"So what? Self-immolation is so much better?"

Reeve sloshed some petrol onto the rag, placed it carefully on the floor by the nearest fruit machine.

"James, I swear to God, stop doing that or I will fire," Claudia said.

Reeve ignored her, then repeated the effort with six, seven, eight more rags until the centre bank of machines was neatly decorated, ready to blow.

"James . . . No more."

She raised the gun a little higher, just as Reeve started to shove the cash into a holdall.

Barnes placed his hand on Claudia's forearm and exerted gentle pressure until she lowered the gun.

"You're just going to let him torch the place and keep half a million in drug money?" she said.

Barnes held her gaze.

"Tell them I died?" Reeve said.

Barnes nodded.

"Tell that nurse I'm sorry too."

Reeve flicked his lighter. The fumes in the air caught before anything else, and leaped towards his sleeve. Reeve just about managed to pat them out and retreat towards the rear doors.

The first detonator caught half a second later.

The heat ripped through the arcade like the end of things, gobbling up the ancient and — as it turned out — extremely flammable velour carpet. Barnes and Claudia shielded their faces from the blinding light of the flames as it illuminated the gloomy arcade, suddenly, like the halls of hell.

38

Claudia shoved the gun into her waistband, grabbed Barnes's arm and yanked him towards the entrance doors. At the vestibule, Barnes chanced a look back through the curtains of smoke and yellow licks of flame. In the murk he saw Reeve, holdall in hand, just about to disappear through the rear doors and to God knew where.

Reeve nodded. Barnes raised a hand. Then a ceiling beam collapsed in a shower of sparks, and Reeve was gone.

There were sirens in the distance. Barnes and Claudia staggered out onto the promenade, trying to scoop up walkers as they went, until they were back on terra firma at the mouth of the pier. They put a makeshift cordon on, using till receipt roll borrowed from the donut shop, and watched as the fire punched its way through the domed glass roof of the arcade and along the dry boardwalk, while a quill of smoke inched its way skywards.

As the crowds gathered, Barnes moved slightly east, giving up a view of the lower promenade — and under the pier. Clinging to the dark seaweed-and-limpet-encrusted stanchions was James Reeve. He did not look in distress; in fact, he moved quite nimbly through the pier's supporting framework — not towards land, but towards the Channel.

A portion of the boardwalk collapsed in a heap of blazing wood. The scorched timber struck the stanchions in a chorused crashing sound, and settled into the water.

Barnes thought he had lost sight of Reeve, but as the dust and sparks dissipated, he saw him at the very end of the pier, moving back and forth like a ski jumper building himself up to a particularly sharp descent.

Then he slung the holdall across his back, pushed himself forward, let go of the pier, and for an instant he was just hanging in space before he crashed down onto the surface of the sea. He disappeared for a moment, and then his head reappeared, and he began to swim out to sea — broad, powerful strokes that went with the tide and took him rapidly east.

Barnes shook his head. He wanted to close the book there and then.

But there was another man under the pier.

Barnes ran forward and gripped the bright blue rail of the promenade, staring helplessly. The man had pulled himself out of the water and was mountaineering between the pier supports like a very wobbly Spider-Man, about ten feet above the surface of the water.

The floating debris from the collapsed floor took a moment to clear, but when it did, Barnes recognised the maroon hooded top and baseball cap.

He opened his mouth to yell.

Claudia saved him the trouble.

"AIRPLANE!"

She had appeared at Barnes's side, but the piercing power of her voice was no match for the rumble of the fire and the crash of the waves, and it was very quickly lost.

"What the hell is he doing?" Barnes said.

"He's going after the murderer you just let escape," Claudia said.

"He must have followed you," Barnes murmured.

Pumps had begun to arrive at the mouth of the pier. Barnes ran over and grabbed the one with "INCIDENT

COMMANDER" on his tabard, and got quickly redirected to the coastguard and RNLI.

"The big hot orange thing up there is our priority, mate," he said, pointing with a grubby finger.

Barnes's fist bunched, but he refocused his energy on calling the control room to deploy the coastguard and life-boat — which, as it turned out, was already tripping across the waves.

He ran back to the promenade. Claudia had gone, and after a quick scan of the area he saw her down on the beach, trying to call to Riaz.

Barnes stumbled over the shingle to the dark underbelly of the burning pier. The stench of acrid smoke was concentrated here, and he suddenly realised that the procession of dog walkers and joggers gawking at the scene were far too close — and were actually inching forward like zombies.

Barnes couldn't understand it. The heat, even down here, was fearsome, and the flames eating the wooden edges of the boardwalk and pier buildings trembled and danced with rhythmic precision, as if they were drawn onto the pages of a sketchbook being flicked back and forth by an idle thumb.

Barnes grabbed Claudia's elbow. She slapped him.

"We have to get these people back," he yelled over the noise. "If this thing comes down it will take out all of them."

She stared at him, then allowed herself to be steered back up to the lower promenade.

They took a side of the pier each, warrant cards aloft, and started yelling at the crowds to move off the promenade.

Barnes chanced a look back at Riaz, who was making slow, crawling progress, clambering through the stanchions towards the sea. He either hadn't realised Reeve was already long gone, or he was just trying to escape the fire, which was still seated mainly in the arcade — the bars and nightclub at the end of the pier were, as yet, largely unaffected.

The smoke was like a second sky, white and black and filling every conceivable element of his field of vision. His eyes started to stream, and he was suddenly beset by a coughing fit that felt like it wouldn't ever end.

He doubled over, just as firefighters with ladders and hoses appeared on the beach, alongside, Barnes was glad to note, a string of yellow-jacketed police officers, who started to funnel people back in a snowplough.

Realising his dulled senses would make him of use to neither man nor beast, Barnes went with them. He looked back at the domed arcade, which seemed to be bowing and sagging alarmingly. He only realised after he was on the upper prom that Claudia was back on the beach.

She was practically in the water, arguing with a firefighter who was trying to get her off the shingle and looking around for a cop to help remove this woman.

She was trying to point Riaz out to the firefighter, but she was becoming increasingly frantic, which was just giving the firefighter tunnel vision and licence to treat her like a maniac.

Which was not entirely unreasonable. When she pulled out the Glock, Barnes forgot his coughing fit and went barrelling back to the beach. The firefighter was backing away, his hands up, as Barnes sprinted as fast as it was humanly possible to do across a pebble beach with a gammy leg, and rugby tackled Claudia roughly.

The Glock flew out of her hand and splashed into the water, and they both ended up in the shallows.

She sat up, sobbing and coughing.

"Why is no one helping him?" she said. "Airplane!"

They both looked over to where he was now clinging to one of the furthermost stanchions. It was impossible to communicate with him, let alone get to him. His feet, precariously positioned on a diagonal cross-support draped with seaweed, were scrabbling for purchase. If he slipped, he'd fall into the water and be submerged in seconds.

"Where the hell is the lifeboat?" Claudia said.

"There," Barnes said, pointing at the orange vessel pitching across the water some quarter of a mile out. "He'll be okay. They'll only be a few minutes."

There was a sudden groaning and creaking from above them. They back-stepped hurriedly across the beach just as another huge portion of the boardwalk collapsed. The timber fragments struck the stanchions as they went, flipping and disintegrating.

The darkness under the pier was enough to erase the daylight. Barnes strained to look, and saw Riaz flailing for a foothold at the very end of the pier, clutching a slime-ridden, limpet-infested metal girder that provided little in the way of sanctuary.

"He's panicking," Barnes said.

"Oh, Jesus," Claudia said. She ran further across the shingle and began waving frantically at the lifeboat.

She was still looking at the lifeboat when Barnes saw Riaz slip.

Whether he caught his foot on a bolt, or caught it in one of the lipped girders, or simply slipped on a stretch of glistening seaweed, Barnes wasn't sure.

He tumbled through the stanchions like a scorched piece of timber. It wasn't a long way to fall, and with water below him a decent swimmer might have fancied their chances.

But the network of closely plotted, diagonally placed cross-supports did not make for a clean fall, and when Riaz struck his head on the way down, it jerked up like he'd been struck by a heavyweight boxer.

His body flipped, dead weight, and hit the churning green water. He disappeared from view almost immediately, and Barnes knew he wasn't coming back up.

Claudia turned back, her face going from dim hope to something else as she took in Barnes's expression and saw that Riaz was no longer visible.

"No."

"Claudia . . ."

"No!"

She looked like she might attempt to wade in, but instead she sat heavily down on the shingle, her shoulders silently hitching, as the bright orange lifeboat rolled up to the end of the pier and began its search.

Barnes looked out at the sea, a hand on Claudia's shoulder. Gulls kept a watchful eye on the shore, while a small number of planes were little more than specks on the blue as they silently paraded in formation back to Shoreham. Barnes squinted, thinking he could make out the shoulders and powerful strokes of James Reeve in the distance, moving through the water to the headland at Beachy Head and beyond — maybe to hunt for a handsome criminal in a long overcoat, maybe to try to forget his life and start again.

EPILOGUE

February, 2007

The day started badly. Despite spending the morning pacing around the kitchen and polishing his shoes for the ninetieth time, Barnes still managed to leave only just about bang on time. A slow-moving tractor and roadworks meant his stomach was in a knot of impotent frustration for most of the journey.

The rain was relentlessly drilling his windscreen by the time he arrived at headquarters, and he thanked his assiduous tendencies for packing his dress uniform rather than wearing it to travel.

Even this turned out to be a dubious economy, however. His instructions were to wait in reception, but the only changing room was in the gym, which meant a five-minute walk back down to reception in the driving rain.

He changed in the gym, taking care with the whistle, adjusting the silver buttons to ensure the crowns were straight and making sure his hat was just so. He studiously avoided eye contact with the only other guy in there, whom he didn't recognise. This overzealous caution was rendered pointless when he exited the changing room — the corridor had been empty when he had entered; now, he found it peo-pled by members of his old section, many of whom he had not clapped eyes on in years. They had assembled, it seemed, to await summoning into the main sports hall to be assessed, one by one, as part of a personal safety training accreditation.

As a result, they were almost as tense as Barnes, and despite coming eye to eye with his former sergeant, John Callaghan, a man to whom he owed his life and more, the pleasantries were stilted and awkward.

Besides, Barnes mused as he hurried through the rain, encountering a colleague in full dress uniform meant a funeral, promotion interview or misconduct panel, and Barnes couldn't blame his former team for not wanting to speculate on his own situation.

He arrived in reception, the damp tunic of his uniform reminiscent of a wet dog, and tried his best to make himself presentable again by removing the rain spots from his hith-erto-immaculate shoes with a piece of paper towel.

The usual business of reception carried on around him — eager new recruits, contractors, visiting dignitaries from sister forces — but he did not have to wait long before some-body arrived to collect him, umbrella in hand, to escort him back up the hill — past the changing rooms, no less — to the main block.

He found himself deposited outside a classroom in the training wing, shuffling from foot to foot until he was summoned.

He took a deep breath and opened the door, realising as he sat down that this was the same classroom he had sat in the day he joined, sitting with twenty other wide-eyed hope-fuls as they were inducted by career cops into the adventures that awaited them — cops who, Barnes realised now, each had their own story for why they had ended up off the streets and in a classroom.

It had been painted and recarpeted since, but Barnes still recognised the Brutalist design, still remembered the metal slatted blinds shredding the sunshine as it filtered down into the valley from the green spread of Malling Down, late into the afternoon as they learned legal definitions, learned about acceptable language, and prepared for the sixteen weeks at residential training school that lay ahead.

There were three of them, sitting in a straight line in the middle of the room, an equal distance apart. The rain had — typically — eased off, and the clouds had hurried away to reveal the late afternoon sun. It was low in the sky, and their faces were half-shrouded in shadow. Each of them held a clipboard and pen.

Barnes sat down in the chair opposite the panel, a jug of water and paper cup to his right. The man in the middle — the chair, Barnes presumed — introduced himself as Detective Chief Superintendent Gary something-or-other, a middle-aged chinless wonder with an expensive-looking suit. He said he was the head of crime, a title Barnes found curious — it seemed to be something a bank robber might aspire to, not a cop.

The woman nearest the window was from HR, while the man nearest the door beamed as he introduced himself as Detective Chief Inspector Marlon Choudhury.

Barnes tilted his head. *Detective Chief Inspector?* he thought. *Since when?*

The chair rattled through some preamble, and told Barnes he could remove his jacket if he wanted to. Barnes thought seriously about this. The moment he left home he had wished he had ordered a shirt with a collar half an inch bigger, but the performance of unravelling the whistle chain and working his way through all those buttons was not appealing. He would just have to make do, and try not to pass out as he was slowly asphyxiated by his own necktie.

The chair cleared his throat, and all three raised their clipboards.

"Mr Barnes, I wonder if you could tell us about a time where you have led a team to overcome challenging barriers in order to deliver outstanding performance?"

* * *

Barnes trudged back across the car park to the gym, aching to rip the damn number ones off and get into some jeans and trainers. The sun was blinding in the puddles, and this time he made no effort to avoid them as he reflected on his performance.

He had drunk the jug dry in minutes in order to purchase thinking time, leaving him with nothing for the remainder of the interview. How could he answer? How could he talk about Sofia's death, about Pete Lamb's betrayal, about Jefferson Riaz's suffering in a way that didn't sound like profiteering?

This dilemma was best reflected by the HR woman, who, while Barnes was mid-answer, had looked at her watch, sighed and looked out of the window. Barnes hadn't really recovered beyond that point. Maybe it was just as well.

"Mister Barnes!"

He turned and frowned. The apparently newly promoted Marlon Choudhury was dragging his huge frame across the car park in an effort to catch up with Barnes, who in turn headed towards him to both spare the big man the effort and head off a possible need to deliver CPR.

Choudhury reached him and rested his hands on his knees.

"Just a moment, please," he said.

"This is pretty unorthodox," Barnes said. "Aren't the panel and the interviewee supposed to be kept apart in stasis until the results are out, or something?"

"This isn't about that," Choudhury said, his breathing slowly recovering.

"And when did they promote you?" Barnes said. "I didn't know. Congratulations."

"Mister Barnes," Choudhury said, finally straightening up. "They did promote me. And they posted me to Intelligence."

"Sounds good. Too many bent cops can make you pretty jaded."

"Mister Barnes, I need to tell you something."

"Shouldn't you—"

"It's about your late wife."

Barnes stopped. His blood turned cold. Just the mention of Eve made him feel like he was being flung backwards through time, like the linear passage of loss was being turned inside out. If she could be brought back to life by some scientific miracle, he would feel like he felt now, only more so. The suddenness of death, he thought, the way *right now* switches to *too late* in a heartbeat was what was really unfair, with no time to process, reflect or make amends.

"What about her?" he whispered.

"It is a mere fragment, I am afraid," Choudhury said, looking as serious as Barnes had ever seen him. "A sliver, possibly inconsequential. You may be frustrated that it doesn't amount to anything. But I cannot in all good conscience keep it from you."

"For Christ's sake, what is it? Tell me!"

"One of our covert sources has been connected to us by a gossamer thread for some time. We have kept him in bread for the best part of three years, but he is unable to keep his side of the bargain — that is, he is unable to keep himself from committing crime, and so, per the terms of our agreement, we have had to dispense with his services as an informant."

"Marlon, goddammit, if you don't get to the point, I swear . . ."

"He has just been imprisoned for supplying drugs. He is keen to make amends with us and repair the relationship in so doing. He has offered information."

"What is it?"

Choudhury took a deep breath.

"He was incarcerated with an individual who felt obliged to share his many stories. This individual made certain disclosures. He claimed, among other things, to have been party to a series of daytime burglaries in the Eastbourne and Wealden area early last year. He claimed to have been in the van that hit your car."

400

Choudhury took another breath.

"He claimed to know who killed your wife."

Barnes turned away from him, stared into the puddles reflecting the afternoon sun, and was temporarily blinded.

THE END

ALSO BY ADAM LYNDON

**DETECTIVE RUTHERFORD BARNES
MYSTERIES**
Book 1: DEVIL'S CHIMNEY
Book 2: BEACHY HEAD

Thank you for reading this book.

If you enjoyed it please leave feedback on Amazon or Goodreads, and if there is anything we missed or you have a question about, then please get in touch. We appreciate you choosing our book.

Founded in 2014 in Shoreditch, London, we at Joffe Books pride ourselves on our history of innovative publishing. We were thrilled to be shortlisted for Independent Publisher of the Year at the British Book Awards.

www.joffebooks.com

We're very grateful to eagle-eyed readers who take the time to contact us. Please send any errors you find to corrections@joffebooks.com. We'll get them fixed ASAP.